PRAISE FOR
THE SHAEDE ASSASSIN NOVELS

BLOOD BEFORE SUNRISE

"Amanda Bonilla's Shaede series takes us down an emotional path while drawing us into an action-packed, suspenseful story line that will leave you cheering and crying at the same time. This is one urban fantasy series that maintains a permanent spot on my bookshelf."

—Heroes and Heartbreakers

"Is it possible for an author who writes a stellar 'knock them out of the ballpark' first book to write an equally good second installment? Yes. Yes, it is. Amanda Bonilla has proven this with *Blood Before Sunrise*."

—Yummy Men Kick Ass Chicks

"It was full of everything I love about urban fantasies: The characters are better than ever, the action is always keeping me on my toes, and of course the romance that turns the heat up. This series has climbed to the top of my list as one of my favorites."

—Seeing Night Book Reviews

"Not a single word or scene is wasted, and the payoff at the end is well worth the journey in this fast-paced, mystery-driven plot. With fascinating characters and awesome world building, *Blood Before Sunrise* is exactly what urban fantasy was meant to be."

—Paperback Dolls

"Apparently, Amanda's imagination and creativity knows no bounds because Da⬛⬛⬛⬛⬛⬛⬛⬛⬛ force and the ride is wilder than ever. A⬛⬛⬛⬛⬛⬛⬛⬛⬛⬛⬛⬛⬛ build-ing, this story is u⬛⬛⬛⬛⬛⬛⬛⬛⬛⬛⬛⬛ and just plain shockin⬛⬛⬛⬛⬛⬛⬛⬛⬛⬛t me started!"

—⬛⬛⬛Reads

⬛⬛⬛ed . . .

"Up-and-comer Bonilla adds another layer to her intriguing world, packed with treachery and hard-edged danger. Hang on. Darian's journey looks like it'll be a very bumpy one!"
—*Romantic Times*

SHAEDES OF GRAY

"An excellent new author and series . . . a tough yet compelling heroine. Full of fascinating characters, high-stakes intrigue, and fast-paced action, it's a truly exhilarating adventure! Do not miss out!"   —*Romantic Times* (top pick, 4½ stars)

"A one-of-a-kind, exciting adventure that kicks off from the first page. . . . Urban fantasy readers will want to buy this book."   —Night Owl Reviews (top pick, 4½ stars)

"Truly transcendental as well as gritty . . . an abundance of awesome action, as well as raw romance, all wrapped up in a fast-paced story that is fresh and unparalleled. *Shaedes of Gray* is going down as one of my favorite new series, and Darian as one of my new favorite heroines."
—Heroes and Heartbreakers

"Thrilling, like an amusement park ride I didn't want to get off of."   —Dark Faeire Tales

"I loved this novel; it was full of great characters and a seriously entertaining plot that I wished never ended. . . . An unforgettable new series and I can't wait for the sequel. I highly recommend this novel."   —Seeing Night Book Reviews

"A brand-new series that absolutely wowed me!"
—The Romance Readers Connection (4½ stars)

"My kind of urban fantasy. I was hooked from page one, and I can't wait for book two."   —Urban Fantasy Investigations

"An excellent urban fantasy."   —Genre Go Round Reviews

"Urban fantasy fans will love this one, and I'll be anxiously awaiting the next book in the series!"

—My Bookish Ways

"A one-of-a-kind series and definitely makes me want to stick around for the ride! . . . You want this book!"

—Wicked Little Pixie

"A great urban fantasy."   —Urban Fantasy Reviews

Also by Amanda Bonilla

Shaedes of Gray
Blood Before Sunrise

CRAVE
THE
DARKNESS

A SHAEDE ASSASSIN NOVEL

AMANDA BONILLA

A SIGNET ECLIPSE BOOK

SIGNET ECLIPSE
Published by the Penguin Group
Penguin Group (USA) Inc., 375 Hudson Street,
New York, New York 10014, USA
Penguin Group (Canada), 90 Eglinton Avenue East, Suite 700, Toronto,
Ontario M4P 2Y3, Canada (a division of Pearson Penguin Canada Inc.)
Penguin Books Ltd., 80 Strand, London WC2R 0RL, England
Penguin Ireland, 25 St. Stephen's Green, Dublin 2,
Ireland (a division of Penguin Books Ltd.)
Penguin Group (Australia), 707 Collins Street, Melbourne, Victoria 3008,
Australia (a division of Pearson Australia Group Pty. Ltd.)
Penguin Books India Pvt. Ltd., 11 Community Centre, Panchsheel Park,
New Delhi–110 017, India
Penguin Group (NZ), 67 Apollo Drive, Rosedale, Auckland 0632,
New Zealand (a division of Pearson New Zealand Ltd.)
Penguin Books (South Africa), Rosebank Office Park, 181 Jan Smuts Avenue,
Parktown North 2193, South Africa
Penguin China, B7 Jiaming Center, 27 East Third Ring Road North,
Chaoyang District, Beijing 100020, China

Penguin Books Ltd., Registered Offices:
80 Strand, London WC2R 0RL, England

First published by Signet Eclipse, an imprint of New American Library,
a division of Penguin Group (USA) Inc.

First Printing, March 2013
10 9 8 7 6 5 4 3 2 1

Copyright © Amanda Bonilla, 2013
Excerpt from *Shaedes of Gray* copyright © Amanda Bonilla, 2011
All rights reserved. No part of this book may be reproduced, scanned, or distributed in
any printed or electronic form without permission. Please do not participate in or encourage piracy of copyrighted materials in violation of the author's rights. Purchase
only authorized editions.

SIGNET ECLIPSE and logo are trademarks of Penguin Group (USA) Inc.

Printed in the United States of America

PUBLISHER'S NOTE
This is a work of fiction. Names, characters, places, and incidents either are the product
of the author's imagination or are used fictitiously, and any resemblance to actual per-
sons, living or dead, business establishments, events, or locales is entirely coincidental.
The publisher does not have any control over and does not assume any responsibility
for author or third-party Web sites or their content.

If you purchased this book without a cover you should be aware that this book is stolen
property. It was reported as "unsold and destroyed" to the publisher and neither the
author nor the publisher has received any payment for this "stripped book."

For the fighters and the survivors

ACKNOWLEDGMENTS

Every time I sit down to write acknowledgments, I go into it thinking I can keep them short and sweet. For the record, my short game sucks.

As always, so much love and thanks to my family for putting up with me. I love you guys!

I also have to give a shout-out to my local support team, Nancy, Niki and Cassidy. Thanks for throwing the best release parties, helping me brainstorm, and listening to all of my crazy ideas.

Windy Aphayrath and Sarah Bromley, thanks for everything you did to make this book shine.

To my current Magic and Mayhem sisters, Nadia, Sandy, and Shawntelle, thanks for your support, advice, and sharing your expertise.

And to my new Magic and Mayhem sister, Amanda Carlson, fairy goatmother to my future baby goats and current fairy goosemother, if I wrote down all of the things I had to thank you for, we'd be here for a year! I would have gone crazy months ago if I hadn't had you around. I love you so hard!

Tracey Garvis-Graves, thanks for being there for me this year and sharing your experiences with me. Being able to talk everything out with you has made such a difference in my attitude and game plan the past few months. I owe you one!

And to my agent, Natanya Wheeler, and my editor, Jhanteigh Kupihea, you guys are amazeballs! You make me feel like I can do anything. In fact, I've ordered you both capes to make your superhero status official.

I owe a huge thanks to the bloggers who have read and reviewed my books over the past year. Without you guys, getting new books into the hands of readers would be much harder. And to the readers, thank you so much for taking a chance on me and Darian. I can't tell you how much you guys mean to me. I want to give you all a big group hug!

I also want to thank all of the wonderful people at Signet Eclipse: my cover artist, Cliff Nielsen, and my cover designer, Katie Anderson. Your hard work is so very appreciated!

I'm pretty sure I've missed someone here, as I usually do. Anyway, if I missed you, you know who you are and what you mean to me. I'd like to think that one of these days I'll remember all of the things, but let's face it, right now, I'm lucky I remember my own name!

Chapter 1

Shadow.

That's how I started out; all I was again. A casting of mottled dark. The real me, the me that knew happiness and light, left with him.

"Darian, pay attention." Raif turned in his seat and nudged me with his elbow. I blinked at the sound of his whispered words and brought my eyes up to meet the faces staring back at me.

"Can you repeat the question?"

The seven members of the Pacific Northwest Territories judicial council exchanged frustrated glances. A murmur spread from one end of the long stone-topped table to the other, and the speaker—a Fae with dark eyes and shining, midnight blue hair—shuffled through her notes before addressing me.

"Let me see if I have this straight. You refuse to answer to the charges brought against you. Which are"—she glanced down at the paper in front of her as if she needed a reminder—"kidnapping of a high-priority PNT prisoner, as well as . . ."

I love you.

Tyler had said those words to me.

". . . aiding and abetting . . . conspiracy . . . a treasonous . . ."

Good-bye, Darian.

Right before he'd walked out the door.

My god, is this how a broken heart felt? What I'd felt when Azriel left me was a drop in the bucket compared to the pain I felt now. I was reduced to a hollow shell. Fragile. I wanted nothing more than to feel whole again.

Raif elbowed me once more, and I snapped to attention, sitting up straight in my seat.

". . . in addition to evading PNT authorities and violating section 15-372.1 of chain of command standard operating procedure. Does that cover it?"

My gaze drifted across the stark white courtroom to the Fae woman, her face coming back into focus. They might as well toss me in jail right here and now. I wouldn't deny my guilt, and I sure as hell wouldn't explain myself. Silence hung heavy in the room, and Raif cleared his throat. Apparently, it was my turn to speak.

"You forgot breaking and entering, conspiracy, and all-around willful disobedience. *That* covers it."

Raif pinched the bridge of his nose between his thumb and finger, closing his eyes as he released a heavy sigh. When he finally had his temper under control enough to look at me, he slowly shook his head and mouthed the word: *Seriously?*

Yeah, well, it wasn't like I was going to throw myself on the floor and beg for the council's mercy. Besides, I'd lost everything in this world I gave a damn about. At this point, I had nothing left to lose. The seven PNT council members leaned toward one another, throwing furtive glances my way while they discussed my fate. This was my third hearing in as many months, and I hadn't given them any more information today than I had at my first arraignment. What had happened after I'd kidnapped Delilah, the Oracle who'd plotted against Raif and the entire Shaede Nation and left the PNT's Washington Headquarters with her partner in crime, Faolán, was no one's business but my own.

"You do realize that by keeping this secret, you may very well face imprisonment. Or worse." The worried tone of Raif's harshly whispered words didn't change my mind. And though I knew he was grateful for my secrecy, he didn't want to see me punished, either.

"Doesn't matter." I couldn't muster an ounce of concern in my own voice. I leaned in to Raif so only he heard me. "They can threaten me all they want. I'm not going to endanger your daughter or the natural order by reminding anyone of things best left forgotten."

I didn't give two shits about the PNT's discipline. Nothing

they could dish out would punish me more than I'd already punished myself. My actions had hurt one of the few people in this world I gave a shit about, and destroyed us both in the process.

Tyler.

God, it hurt just to think his name. I broke his heart by leaving him without a word of where I was going or when I'd be back. I betrayed our trust by wishing for him to stay put in Seattle, unable to leave the city, while I traipsed around on my adventure to find Brakae, Raif's daughter. And in the end, my reward was exactly what I deserved: time away from him and the space I needed to decide what I really wanted.

I didn't need time. I already knew what I wanted.

I wanted Tyler.

But he wasn't here with me, was he? Apparently, he didn't think an appropriate length of time had passed for me to get my shit together. I'd tried wishing for him. I'd wished for him almost every day that first month, but he never showed. Jinn magic is full of rules, regulations, and limitations. One of those being that I could wish only for things I really, truly needed. And somehow, the powers that be had determined my want of Tyler wasn't good enough.

"Will the accused stand?" So polite, as if she was asking if I'd stay for dinner or something. You'd never guess the council was about to bring down the hammer.

I pushed my chair out with the backs of my knees and shoved my bound hands against the table in front of me for leverage. The iron cuffs swirled with silver light, charmed to negate my ability to wreak any havoc, if the whim struck. Whenever an accused stood before the council, they were bound with the cuffs. In my case, they prevented me from leaving my corporeal form and weakened me to the point that I couldn't break the bonds. Lucky for the council, I had no intentions of wreaking havoc of any kind. Not now, or in the future. The fight had pretty much drained right out of me.

"Since you refuse to speak on your own behalf, and considering we have sworn statements from many eye witnesses, this council has no choice but to—"

"If it pleases the council . . ." The double doors of the chamber swung wide, and the Shaede High King swept into the room as if he owned the place. "I beg a moment of your time." Alexander Peck—or to me, just Xander—never turned down an opportunity to show off his dramatic flair, and right now, he claimed center stage.

"With all due respect, Your Highness," the blue-haired Fae said, "the time to testify in front of this council has passed."

Decked out in what had to have been a ten-thousand-dollar suit, Xander looked as regal as he did imposing. Though his stance was relaxed, his molten caramel eyes sparked with a cold light that dared anyone to turn down his request. I could only imagine what he was up to. Maybe he couldn't stand that I was the center of attention. Or worse, maybe he just wanted to prove that he could throw his weight around.

"Do I have to remind you about Edinburgh, Amelia?" Oh yeah, Xander definitely wanted to throw his weight around.

The Fae looked at the questioning faces of her colleagues before she cleared her throat, fidgeting with the cuff of her sleeve. She scooped a glowing, pearlescent ball in her hand and knocked the faerie equivalent of a gavel down on the table twice. "We'll adjourn for fifteen minutes. Alexander, if you'll follow us to our private chambers, we'll hear what you have to say."

Xander flashed me an arrogant smile. He waited patiently as the seven council members stood, and then followed in their wake as they walked, single file, from the room. "Sit tight," he said as he sauntered past Raif and me. "I'll be back shortly."

We sat back down at the same time, and I asked Raif, "What the hell is he up to?"

"Your guess is as good as mine. We are talking about Xander, after all."

Raif leaned back in his seat, staring at the ceiling as if his brother's plans were written there. I, on the other hand, had no interest in wondering what His Royal High and Mightiness had up his sleeve. Instead, my mind drifted to where it always did lately: the clusterfuck that was my life.

You'd think I would have lost track of the days since that night Tyler left me. The emerald pendulum that I wore around my neck silenced the sound of time as it ticked within my soul, but I had invisible tally marks etched on my heart. Eighty-seven days, six hours, fifteen minutes, and twenty-two seconds. Twenty-three . . . twenty-four . . . twenty-five . . .

It's not like I'd been brooding the *entire* time. I had a system, alternating between outings for my hearings with the PNT's judicial council, setting up camp on my bed, answering the door for grocery delivery, and occasionally crashing on the couch while I let the TV lull me to sleep with mind-numbing entertainment. I wasn't proud of the fact that I knew every single cast member of *Jersey Shore* down to their cocktails of choice, but it was better than the alternative: allowing my tortured thoughts to drive me to a state of near insanity.

I leaned forward in my chair and massaged my sternum. The imaginary fist that had been squeezing my heart for the past seven months clenched tight, leaving a dull ache I couldn't get rid of no matter how long I rubbed. I'm not a fool. I realized that the blame for our separation rested solely on me. I ran—and spent four months away—from the one person in this world I should have sprinted *toward*. I shunned his protection, disregarded his strength, and stomped all over the love he offered . . . all in the name of arrogance.

Ty showed me how much he appreciated my treatment of him by returning the favor in classic "eye for an eye" fashion. I'd come back to Seattle after a months-long excursion spent in *O Anel* looking for—then protecting—Brakae.

According to Raif, during my absence Tyler had become temperamental, angry, and resentful, not to mention dirty and disheveled. I arrived at his apartment expecting to find a broken man. What I found broke *me*. Calm, clean, showered and shaved, and packing a suitcase for an extended vacation, Tyler gave me one last kiss and left. And he'd stayed gone. Three months and counting . . .

I took a deep breath, tried to slow the frantic beating of my heart that signaled the onset of another panic attack. Dredging up memories of my many mistakes caused my palms to sweat and my breath to stall in my lungs. The floor seemed to tip beneath me and the room swam in and out of focus in a dizzying blur.

"Darian, stand up." Raif's voice was nothing more than a whisper, but it echoed in my mind as if shouted down the length of a tunnel.

The door to the council's private chambers opened, and I just about fell on my ass as I shot to my feet. Raif reached out to steady me, his face etched with concern. I would have given him a reassuring pat to the shoulder if my hands weren't bound in the damn cuffs. A few deep, steady breaths managed to calm me down enough that I was no longer seeing stars at the periphery of my vision, and my head finally felt like its normal size—not floating above my shoulders like a balloon.

Xander sauntered out of the council's chambers much the same way he'd entered. Only this time, the smugness of his expression spoke of victory, not just the prospect of success. *Great.* If he had any pull with regards to the council's decision about my sentence, I'd never live it down. Just one more thing for his royal pain in the ass to hold over my head.

The Fae with the dark blue hair—Amelia, Xander had called her—cast a cautious glance in the king's direction before turning her focus to me. "The accused is officially absolved of any wrongdoing against the PNT and any charges brought against her are stricken from the official record." She brought the opalescent orb down against the table with a resounding *crack*. With the sound wave, a pulse of energy swept through the room and caressed my face like a kiss of warm breeze. The cuffs around my wrists loosened and dropped to the floor. Amelia's eyes narrowed shrewdly as she addressed me. "You are free to go."

Xander turned to leave, his chest puffed out with pride. "You can thank me later," he said and strode from the room.

As the council members rose once again to leave, I said to Raif, "He really gets off on throwing his weight around, doesn't he?"

Raif's laughter was the only answer I needed.

Chapter 2

"*Let me take you to dinner.*"

"*No.*"

Tyler just couldn't get it through his thick skull that I didn't mix business with pleasure. I'd been working for him for a little over six months, and it seemed we'd begun to make excuses to see one another. Problem was, I was the only one who realized this wasn't a good idea and we needed to put the brakes on whatever was developing between us.

"*Come on, Darian,*" *he teased.* "*I don't bite. What's the big deal? It's just dinner. I mean, you eat dinner on occasion, don't you?*"

A smiled threatened, tugging at my mouth. But I bit back the urge to let Tyler see just how charming I found him. He was my employer, for Christ's sake. To-die-for good looks or not, I didn't allow myself romantic entanglements of any kind. Love was a weakness I couldn't afford, and the more time I spent with Ty, the more I thought he'd be very easy to fall in love with.

"*I eat,*" *I finally replied, looking anywhere but right at him.* "*Just not with you.*"

Tyler took a step closer and I breathed in his scent. Delicious. Like warm cinnamon. Such a comforting smell, it put me instantly at ease. It was actually the first thing I'd noticed when I met him. I don't know what it was about Tyler, but being with him felt safe. Like nothing in the world would ever harm me when he was around. Stupid, I know. Sentimentality was another trait I couldn't afford. Sentiment made you sloppy. And sloppy assassins didn't get paid. "*You're invading my personal space,*" *I said flatly. Another step and he'd be close enough to touch. And oh man, how I wanted to touch.*

"Has anyone ever mentioned how ridiculously stubborn you are?" His voice was warm with a sensual edge that gave me chills. "I think if you spent a little time with me, you might just find that you like me."

Damn, he smelled good. My head was so full of his scent I couldn't think straight. And those eyes—gorgeous. I didn't need time for him to grow on me. Tyler was on my mind more times than not lately, and that was bad.

"Look, Ty, you're a nice guy, and I'm sure you know how to show a girl a good time. But it's not gonna happen. Not tonight, not ever. That's just the way it has to be."

He leaned in close, the playful expression gone from his face.

"Who says?" he murmured.

A pleasant chill raced up my spine and I shuddered. Thank god I was leaning against the wall, because I wasn't entirely sure my legs would hold me up. "I say." My own voice was breathier than I'd intended. Damn it, he could rattle me with nothing more than the intensity of his stare.

"Darian." My name on his lips was enough to make me swoon. No one had ever said it the way he did, with so much emotion and reverence. "You don't need to be afraid," he said, his mouth hovering close to my ear. "I won't hurt you."

The way he spoke . . . it was like he knew everything about me, right down to the nightmare of the human life I'd lived so long ago. But he couldn't know those things. The only other men who'd witnessed that weakness in me were long gone. I was beyond repair, damaged goods. And once Tyler realized that fact, he wouldn't stick around either.

"Here's how it's going to work between us from now on," I said. "You call me when you have a mark you need eliminated. I take out said mark and you pay me. That's it. Nothing more, nothing less." Rejecting his advances was the right thing to do. He just didn't realize it yet. As if on instinct, I caressed the ring on my thumb, the very same one Tyler had given me after I'd completed my first job. I hated to admit it, but the damned thing had quickly become a security blanket, sort of a good luck charm, and I couldn't help but touch it.

*"So you're not even going to give me a chance, huh?"
Tyler said with a sigh, obviously frustrated. "You just get to
decide, right here and now, that there can't ever be anything
between us?"*

*"Pretty much," I said. "Believe me, you'll thank me for
keeping my distance later." I let the shadows take me, becoming nothing more than a gossamer form. "Good night, Tyler."*

Some days, it's just not worth getting out of bed.

As if my current heartache wasn't enough, my dreams
taunted me with past mistakes. I felt the sting of that moment
with Tyler as if it had just happened, and wasn't that just
great? Everyone wants to be wanted. Needed. Desired.
Loved. Ty wanted me and I'd rejected him. Putting distance
between us again and again, wasting precious time we could
have spent together. Happy. I guess there was no denying I
was a Class A fuckup when it came to my love life. Not one
man in my entire existence had managed to want me enough
to stick it out. I supposed Henry didn't truly count, but Azriel
had dropped me without a second thought. And as for Ty,
well, I guess he finally realized I was just too broken to fix.

I ran my tongue around the inside of my mouth, which felt
like it'd sprouted fur overnight. Bourbon always tastes so
good going down. But the hangover I suffered this morning,
coupled with the remnants of my memories, made me rethink
ever touching the stuff again. Wasn't it a sign of a problem
when you started drinking in solitude? Whatever. It's not like
I gave a shit, and the liquor wasn't going to do anything to
my preternatural liver. It did, however, make the pain go
away for a while. A very short while. I guess at this point, I
was willing to take what I could get.

One of the benefits of living in a warehouse-turned-
studio-apartment is that I could see every inch of my space
from the bed. The place was a mess: clothes piled in the
corners, dishes stacked in the sink, unwashed. I couldn't
muster the energy to care anymore. I wondered how much
longer Raif would wait before he staged an intervention.
He'd even resorted to bringing my mail up once a day after
he realized that I'd quit checking it. I had no desire to tell him
that I was scared of what I'd find each time I looked in the

box. My eyes wandered to my kitchen table. Laid out across the high-gloss surface, tossed in with the piles of mail Raif insisted on bringing up, were two postcards. At first I'd thought there'd been only the one, sitting on top of a stack of bills and junk mail. But when I'd dug deeper through the pile, I'd found another one. A beautiful bird's-eye view of Central Park. Aside from my address, the only words scribbled across the card stock read: *Wish you were here*.

I tried to swallow, found my mouth too dry for the simple act. A cold lump of dread congealed in the pit of my stomach, sending out icy shards that speared my composure. Almost a century ago, Azriel had helped an Armenian mob boss's son go into hiding. Lorik sent us a postcard from every city he'd visited, writing only: *Wish you were here*. And now, when the mobster's son should have been long dead, the postcards started showing up again. Whatever mess Azriel had left for me to clean up, I had a feeling it would be an unpleasant one. The tremor stretching out from my palms to the tips of my fingers had nothing to do with a hangover. I was straight-up rattled. Damn Azriel and his secrets. *Shake it off, Darian. Jesus. It's just paper. It's not like those cards are going to self-destruct and blow your ass halfway across Seattle. Get a grip.*

The whine and whir of the elevator coming to life drew my focus from the table. I reached for my pillow, for the throwing knives stashed under it. I may have been wallowing in self-pity and apathy, but I didn't fuck around when it came to unannounced guests. And nothing says "Welcome!" like a knife barreling point-over-hilt in a blur of glinting silver light. Of course, it could be Raif again, but I didn't take any chances.

I sat up, gathered the belt that held the six small knives and waited. I shook off the wave of anxiety threatening to pull me down to the fetal position and jacked my chin up a notch while willing my spine starch-stiff. I don't know what I expected. A ghostly apparition of an Armenian mobster, perhaps? The intoxicating aroma of Shaede reached my nostrils long before the open elevator compartment came into sight, and I drew a knife from the holster. I knew the scent well, and though it wasn't the specter from my past that I'd anticipated, this was one visitor I wasn't about to entertain. Waiting, hand drawn back and ready to throw, I let my breathing slow. You need a certain stillness to throw a knife with accuracy. Stillness and patience. The elevator came to a halt, and the gate slid to one side. Heavy footfalls crossed the elevator's threshold and I inhaled. Held my breath. Then let the knife fly.

The throw went wide and the knife buried itself to the handle in the drywall. So much for stillness and patience. God*damn* it.

"Your aim is shit," Xander said, strolling through the living room like he had every right to be there. The King of Shaedes never let anyone forget who he was. Least of all me.

I took another knife from the holster, and sent it hurtling toward my mark. It glanced off the fireplace in a flash of silver, landing with a dull thud on the carpeting. *Son of a bitch.*

As if he hadn't noticed me trying to scar his beautiful face, Xander stopped at the dining room table, idly shuffling through my mail like it was all addressed to him. My heart skipped a beat as he came across the postcards, which he flipped over, seeming to read with interest. But he discarded them as easily as he had my water bill and turned to face me. "I said you could thank me later for intervening with the PNT." He smiled. "It's later."

Knife number three left my hand before I could even think through what I was doing. It bounced off the polished concrete of the kitchen countertop and came to a skidding halt on my stove.

Xander cocked a sardonic brow. "Not quite the show of appreciation I was expecting."

"Fuck off," I snapped. My comebacks were as bad as my aim.

Xander pivoted on a heel and changed his course for my bed. I instinctively reached for another knife before I noticed the gleam in his eyes. Butterscotch flecks glowed in molten caramel depths. He was hoping I'd throw again. It always made my day to keep Xander from getting what he wanted, and so I sheathed the knife and tucked the belt back under my pillow. I wasn't in the mood to play his games.

"I could have left your fate in Amelia's hands," his tone dripped with reproof, "but you are my employee. Paid on retainer, if I'm not mistaken. And I have a job for you. I couldn't have the PNT detaining you when you have work to do. So, my darling, whether you want to admit it or not, you owe me for convincing the council to drop the charges against you."

"Screw you, *Your Highness*." I lounged back in bed, and pulled the covers up nice and cozy. "You can show yourself out the way you came in, because *frankly*, I'm not interested in doing anything for you, and I'm not moving any time soon."

Xander bent toward me, and I reached for my knives. I drew one of the blades from the holster—which, honestly, wasn't long enough to do any real damage—determined to send him on his way. I may have been out of my mind to threaten a king with a weapon, but hell, I'd thrown three of the knives at him when he arrived. What's one more offense?

I didn't have my usual *oomph* to lend credibility to the act. Instead, I sort of held the knife out in front of me, my elbow drawn in like I had no idea how to use the thing. Fact was, I had no interest in picking a fight with Xander. I just wanted him to leave me alone so I could continue to wallow in self-pity, undisturbed.

"You look like a frightened girl, holding that knife," Xander said. His voice was like expensive velvet: rich and luxurious. It's his most winsome quality in my opinion. I could only imagine how many women had gladly dropped on their backs from nothing more than a few words.

Not this girl, though. "Get out," I said, fighting to keep my voice from quavering.

He smiled. "No."

"Xander." My throat burned with emotion. *Jesus, Darian, get your shit together*. I held the knife up, straightened my arm. "I'm not going to tell you again."

So fast that he caught me off guard, Xander batted the knife out of my hand. It didn't take much effort; I wasn't holding it like I was planning to use it. It rang as it bounced off the hardwood floor and I shrunk back into my pillow. Christ, why couldn't he just leave me alone? I didn't want to talk to him, or anybody else. I wanted to be *alone*.

"You *will* stop this childish behavior. Now. I've allowed you these months to mourn the loss of your Jinn. But that time is over. I have work for you and expect you to snap out of this depression and get to it."

Xander's words had me rankled. If I'd been feeling more like myself I would have shown him how much with my fist. I was *not* mourning the loss of Tyler. That would indicate that he wasn't coming back. Like he'd died or something. Tears stung behind my eyes, and I bit down hard on the inside of my cheek to stem the traitorous flow that would betray my emotions. Tyler wouldn't leave me. Not forever. He was coming back. He had to. If he didn't . . . well, let's just say I didn't want to think about what I'd do if he stayed away for good.

"I want you cleaned up, properly dressed, and at my house in an hour." He turned on a heel and headed for the door.

I didn't take my eyes off his broad back as I tried to keep myself from committing an act of violence. Xander's steps grew silent and he paused, shouting from the elevator, "Don't make me come back here for you, Darian. It'll be more than a cordial visit if I do. *One* hour."

The gate slid closed with a rasping of metal, and the gears once again whirred to life, taking the Shaede King from my apartment. I guessed going back to bed was out of the question.

Chapter 3

I glanced down at my black boots. I'd dressed and armed myself, ready to go, without even realizing I'd done it. I held out my arms, kicked up a leg, taking stock. Ran my fingers through my damp curls. I didn't appear any different. Showered—sure. Clean—yep, April fresh. Clothes—my standard black. But on the inside, I was a different person. I didn't feel like the cold, ruthless killer I used to be. Though I could still do some heavy-duty collateral damage, I felt . . . empty. Alone. One half of a whole. "Come home, Tyler," I whispered, praying that he'd hear me. "Please."

Sunlight melded with my skin as I left my corporeal form, obeying Xander's orders lest he come back for a fresh round of torture. It's not that I was anxious to get out of the apartment. The idea of leaving actually made me break into a cold sweat. But I knew Xander. He'd come back. Again, and again, and again. He'd annoy me to the point that my life would become even more hellish than it already was. Besides, going back to work may actually help distract me from the pain. Because the bourbon sure as hell didn't.

I let myself into Xander's house. Why not barge in? He'd barged in to my place easy enough. The usual sounds of daily hustle and bustle seemed absent as I walked past the foyer and down the long hallway to Xander's office. I was just a little over five minutes late. Not enough to encourage his high-and-mighty reproof, but hopefully just enough to rattle his chain a bit. The king's office door was half-closed and I walked right in, unsurprised to find him sitting as his desk, going through a stack of papers as usual. Being a monarch struck me as incredibly boring, but at least he was safe, holed up in his office. Death by paper cut didn't seem to be a concern.

Xander ignored me, his pen scratching against paper as he put his sweeping signature next to several red X's. He set down the pen and pinched the bridge of his nose, eyes closed. Pushing away from the desk, he leaned back against the headrest of his chair and sighed.

"Your immature behavior had Raif climbing the walls with worry. If you were anyone else," Xander said, "I'd have had Dimitri fetch you. And believe me, you wouldn't have wanted to be on the receiving end of his persuasion tactics."

"Raif came by every day," I said, maybe a little too indignant. "And he escorted me to all of my hearings. It's not like he didn't know where I was or what was going on with me."

"For the past few months, perhaps. Though your presence of mind is up for debate." Xander leaned forward, pinning me with his stare. "But before that, when you . . . disappeared, *no one* knew what happened to you."

A truth I didn't enjoy being reminded of.

"The Jinn wasn't the only one affected by your disappearance. And your behavior of late is an insult to those who have cared for you and care for you still. You have been very selfish."

Seriously? Xander was accusing *me* of being selfish? In my opinion, he wrote the book on that particular subject. "Well, excuse me, Xander, for thinking of myself. But—"

"I worried for you," Xander cut me off. "I worried . . . you wouldn't return. Do not, ever again, run off on your own like that. You have my entire military force at your disposal. In the future, use it."

Huh. A reprimand? Or something more? Xander's tone didn't carry its usual kingly arrogance. Instead, he sounded truly concerned. Afraid, even. Maybe I'd hurt more people than I thought, leaving like I had. I'd assumed that secrecy was key. That accomplishing my goals single-handedly showed my strength. Instead, it only made me look stupid. Heartless. *Thanks, Xander, as if my guilt complex wasn't bad enough already.*

"I appreciate your concern, Xander." I fought for a civil tone because the sarcasm was threatening to bleed through.

"In the future, I'll remember your generous offer. But what I did had to be done without an army. It was *my* responsibility. And it wasn't worth risking anyone else's life."

Xander's palm came down on the desktop with a crack as he shot up out of his chair, startling me. "*Your* life is not worth risking!" Fire sparked in his eyes, and he took a couple of calming breaths before sitting back down. "I would appreciate it if you took precautions the next time your *responsibilities* arise." His tone became soft once again, and then he added, "Raif would appreciate it."

Ugh. We could go on like this for hours, and I was way too tired to go twelve rounds with him. All I needed was my assignment and then I could get the fuck out of here. "I'll be more careful in the future," I said through clenched teeth. "Now, what's the job?"

Xander frowned, a crease digging into his forehead just above the bridge of his nose. "Anya," he said with a sigh, looking past me toward the door as if he was afraid she'd hear him. "She's in need of protection."

My feet twitched, ready to turn me the hell around and take me out of Xander's office. No way. Too much slack for me to pick up. A five-million-dollar retainer wouldn't secure my services in this case. I'd rather eat shards of glass than protect her bony ass, and Xander knew it.

"Before you deny me, Darian, you should know that Anya is pregnant."

My jaw dropped, and I was sure it hit the fucking floor. "Pregnant?" *Good. God.* I couldn't imagine. Women like Anya ate their young. "You've got to be kidding me."

"It's rare," Xander said. "Her child is precious to our people, and I won't risk her or her unborn child's safety."

"I've never seen a Shaede child before." Well, that is, until I'd been to *O Anel* and beheld Raif's daughter as a child as well as an adolescent. Time worked differently there. But in the mortal world, I'd thought Shaede children were nonexistent.

"Our history isn't a pleasant one," Xander said. "Our forefather, Artis, took the brunt of his father's prejudice, and his children suffered. The day he banished Artis's children to the shadows, Kreighton tried to ensure that our numbers would dwindle. He meant for the Shaedes to be sterile, unable to reproduce. But thank the gods, nature survives where even the strongest magic would have us fail. Pregnancies don't happen often, but when they do, it's a sacred thing and the child as well as its mother is revered. It is a slap to Kreighton's face each and every time a child is born and survives. And I am happy for each birth to deliver that blow."

I raised a dubious brow. "You make it sound like you did the deed yourself, Xander."

He met my stare with a half smile. "Would you be jealous if I had?"

"No. But I bet Dimitri would."

Xander laughed. "No doubt there. Dimitri would skin a man alive for so much as a passing glance at his wife. I hate to think what he'd do to the man brave enough to lie with her."

"I've never heard the full story, you know. I only got the CliffsNotes version," I said thoughtfully as I took a seat in front of Xander's desk. I propped my feet up on his desktop because I knew it drove him crazy. "The story of how the Shaedes came to be."

"It's a true fairy tale," Xander said. "Maybe I'll tuck you into bed some night and tell it to you."

Oh joy of joys. Xander couldn't help but lead with his dick. I bet his brain felt neglected sometimes. "In your dreams, Xander."

"Nightly," he said, his voice thick with longing.

Time to get back to business. Xander lived for this kind of back and forth. It was all about the chase for him, and if I kept it up, I'd be giving him exactly what he wanted. "Anya," I said, knocking the toes of my boots together. "Why does she need protecting? Can't you just keep her locked up in the house? I'm sure Dimitri would be more than happy to watch over her."

"Dimitri has duties. And Anya . . ." Xander combed his fingers through the length of his golden hair. "Anya is difficult. She's not going to be happy if we keep her under house arrest."

No shit. "And you think having me around is going to make her happy? Apparently you don't realize how much we *don't* get along."

"I don't trust anyone else," Xander said.

"Raif?"

"Really, Darian?" Xander flashed his trademark sardonic smile. "Raif isn't a bodyguard. He's the commander of my military, the director of security, not to mention a head of state and prince. You're reaching."

Damn straight, I was. I'd rather clean Xander's toilets than agree to what he was suggesting. "She won't go for it," I said.

"She doesn't have a choice."

"I don't like being cooped up."

"You could have fooled me." A shadow crept over Xander's regal face. "You've been shut up in that closet you call an apartment for nearly three months."

Low blow. "That's none of your business."

"Like I said, Darian. *Everything* you do is my business. This isn't up for discussion. I need someone to watch over Anya. You're the most capable candidate and the only person I trust to do the job adequately. Besides, you won't be cooped up. Anya's not a prisoner. I just need someone around to ensure her safety. I've paid you—well, I might add—and you accepted the terms of employment."

"You're forgetting, Xander, in the terms set out for my employment, I said I would only follow direct orders from Raif. You can't tell me what to do."

"I'm not worried. If you refuse to listen to me, Raif will give you the exact same orders. Anya needs protecting. You have been assigned that task. End of discussion."

I knocked my heel against Xander's desk, hoping some dried mud clung to the heavy tread of my boot. I heard the dirt drop onto the polished surface of the king's antique desk and felt a perverse sense of satisfaction. "What makes you think she's in danger? It's not like the baby is going to eat its way out of her stomach." At least, I hoped not. Even for Anya, an *Alien*-style birth wouldn't be appealing.

Xander leaned forward, and his voice dropped to little more than a whisper. "There have been threats made."

Of course there had. "By who?"

Xander shrugged his massive shoulders. "She won't tell me."

"And you don't think that's a little suspicious?"

"I think it's very suspicious. But what do you expect me to do, beat the information out of her?"

I cocked my head to the side. Couldn't hurt.

"You don't give Anya enough credit, Darian."

I wished he'd stop saying my name. The tone carried too much possession. It didn't appeal to my ears the way it did when Ty said it. "I think you give her too much credit, Xander."

"You don't even know her."

"Enough to know I don't like her."

"You don't have to like her; you must only protect her."

Xander regarded me with a wantonness that set my nerves on end. As if he were a starving man and I were a ham sandwich. He made no secret of the fact that he "loved" me, though I suspected he loved the chase more than anything. No one denied Xander, except for me. If I jumped on his bed and spread my legs, he'd lose interest before the sun rose the next morning. But I wasn't about to try out that theory. "Can't you please ask someone else?" I didn't have the energy to fight with him. The warm, solitary comfort of my bed beckoned to me. I wanted to go back to it and sleep until Tyler decided to come home.

"There is no one else," Xander said. The worried expression that overrode his lust told me he knew exactly what I'd been thinking, and it didn't sit well with him. "The job is yours."

"I'm not babysitting her for the entire nine months."

"Twelve."

Twelve? Good lord. Pregnant for a year? That didn't sound like a picnic. "I'm not going to sit and hold her hand for an entire year."

"You don't have to. Only until we find out who's threatening her and why. Once the threat is eliminated, you'll be relieved of duty."

Finally, an aspect of this assignment that fit the job description. "And who will be doing the eliminating?"

Xander grinned like he'd just given me a ten-carat diamond ring. "You, of course."

My lips stretched into a smile, and I thought my face would crack; it had been so long since I'd felt any kind of happiness. Funny, how taking out the bad guy can make you feel all warm and fuzzy inside.

Xander beamed. It was one of the few times I'd seen him truly pleased. "I'm also assigning a small task force to operate under your direction. I won't have you working alone. It's too dangerous."

If my smile got any bigger, my cheeks would explode. A task force meant manpower. Manpower meant I wouldn't have to be secured to Anya at the hip. "I want Raif to pick the team members. And I want this task force kept to a manageable number. I don't need an army. But when it comes down to neutralization of our mystery target, I go alone." Assassins don't work in groups. Kind of negates the stealth factor.

Xander inclined his head, though his expression soured a bit. "Fine. Raif will pick the team. An intimate grouping of specialized soldiers. I don't like the idea of you going out on your own, though, but I am aware that you can take care of yourself far better than most."

Damn straight. A tightness constricted my chest, and I rubbed at my sternum, the invisible fist squeezing my heart reminding me of the havoc my cavalier attitude had wreaked on my life. Dizzy and a little sick to my stomach, all I could think about was Tyler. *Come home. Come home, come home, come home!* The words ran a crazy loop in my mind, screaming a wish that wouldn't come true. My pulse quickened with my anxiety, and I felt the urge to jump up out of my chair and run as fast as I could, leave my corporeal form behind and flee from the pain that threatened to drown me. I swung my legs down off Xander's desk, prepared to do just that when the king reached out and seized me by the wrist, his grip an iron manacle demanding I stay.

"Don't do this, Darian." The command was firm, but his velvet voice was warm, reassuring. "No more running. No hiding. You're better than that. Take this hurt you feel and let it make you better. Don't allow it to master you."

I swallowed down the lump rising in my throat, commanded the tears to retreat before they threatened to flow. Whether I was ready to acknowledge it or not, I knew deep down that Xander was right. I couldn't keep running. I couldn't hide in my apartment and let my ragged emotions take me to an even darker place than I was already.

Xander loosened his grip, but he kept his hand right where it was. His thumb swirled in a circular pattern on my wrist, an intricate weaving of sensation that relaxed me. "Darian, I think you should move in for a while. You should be close to Raif, and you'll need to be here for Anya as well."

"Okay." My traitorous mouth let the word slip lazily from between my lips before my brain could adequately think over an answer. I didn't want to go back to my apartment, to my bed, haunted by memories of Tyler. He promised me he'd come back. But when? He hadn't called or sent so much as a text message to let me know where he was. To assure me that he was okay. *Paybacks are a bitch, aren't they, Darian?*

Xander tightened his grip, once again bringing me back to the present. My mind had been wandering all over the place, and he'd seen me drowning and threw out the life preserver. I pulled my hand away and he didn't fight me, but his touch lingered. Rubbing my wrist, I tried to banish the sensation, the comfort of feeling someone else's skin on mine.

"I'm going to go find Raif," I said, turning on a heel. "We've got details to work out and I'd rather just get straight to work."

"Darian," Xander called out from behind his desk and I stopped midway through the door, not bothering to turn and face him. "I never would have left. Only a fool could walk away from you."

Goddamn it. I was in for a shitload of trouble.

Chapter 4

I found Raif in Xander's solarium, of all places. It struck me as odd to see him so relaxed, bathed in sunlight while he ate lunch. My stomach growled, and I realized that I hadn't eaten a proper meal in some time. I'd been more or less eating only to survive. I would've eaten cardboard and been satisfied with it. But the chicken piccata artfully arranged next to a pile of penne pasta and Caesar salad looked too damn good to my emerging appetite.

"The kitchen is sending up a plate for you," Raif said. "I figured you'd be hungry."

"You're a traitor, you know that?" I asked, taking a seat across from him. "You ratted me out to your brother and sent him to my apartment."

"I did," he agreed. "And I won't apologize for it, either. You were living like some sort of shut-in. Someone needed to intervene, and you wouldn't listen to me."

"But you figured I'd listen to Xander?"

Raif stared me down. "You're here, aren't you?"

Damn. He had me there. "I'm sorry," I said. "For making you worry. Again." Apologizing was about as pleasant as swallowing tacks, but Raif deserved it. No matter how much I hated to admit it, Xander was right. I'd been selfish.

"Well," Raif said, clearly as uncomfortable as I was, "let's just eat and call it good. I take it Xander filled you in on your assignment?"

The aroma of hot food hit my nostrils, and a moment later a plate was brought in and set before me. The plate was still warm and my stomach jumped to attention, the meal taking precedence over any other thought. I had half the chicken and most of the pasta stuffed down my throat by the time I brought my face up from the plate.

"I've seen soldiers in the field eat with less gusto," Raif said, picking at his own food with fastidious precision. "Hungry much?"

"I guess I haven't been taking care of myself," I said, pausing only long enough to take another bite.

"I'd say that's pretty obvious. And just so you know, bourbon is not one of the four food groups."

I grimaced. Clearly my antics had crossed over into the careless idiot category and Raif had seen it firsthand. I was ashamed of my behavior, holed up in my apartment, tangled in my bedsheets for three months straight with just enough food to keep me alive and more than enough booze to kill a horse. Maturity, thy name is Darian.

"She'll never go for this, you know," I said, steering the conversation back to work. "When she finds out what Xander has planned, she'll blow a gasket."

"Anya doesn't have a choice."

"That's what he said."

Raif gave me a strange look, and I really wanted to know what the hell he was thinking. But another wave of gut-cramping hunger hit me and rather than dig into my friend's psyche, I turned my attention to my plate.

"You're moving in?" Raif asked, interrupting the sound of me inhaling the rest of my meal.

I nodded, mouth too full to answer politely.

"For what it's worth, I think it's a good idea."

Again, a nod.

"But not for the reason you think."

I looked up from my plate. *Damn.* Guess I'd have to talk about this. "Why do you think I'm moving in?"

"Xander suggested you stay so you'd be close to Anya and whatever team we form to work under your direction. But he—*we*—thought you needed to be away from your apartment for a while."

Of course, *they* did. But I didn't blame them for suggesting it. It had been my motivation for accepting Xander's invitation so quickly. I needed to be away from anything that reminded me of Tyler until I could get my head on straight.

"Well, you got your wish. Here I am. Now we can be one big, happy family."

Raif rolled a piece of pasta around his plate with his fork. "He's arrogant, I know. And an ass more times than not. He's stubborn, opinionated, and spoiled. Demanding to a fault. Which is why you need to be very careful. He is nothing if not opportunistic."

He being Xander. I *so* did not want to have this conversation. "I don't care what *he* thinks or feels. Tyler's coming home."

"I know he told you that. But what if—"

"I love him. He loves me. He's coming back. End of discussion."

Raif did the smart thing and kept the rest of his opinions to himself. If I was going to stay here—and I was—the subject of Tyler was not open for discussion. He was coming back. He'd promised. And Tyler never disappoints.

Once Raif and Xander managed to get me out of my apartment, they made it their mission to ensure that I *stayed* out. Someone packed up most of my clothes and a few other personal items and had it all unpacked and organized in one of Xander's guest suites before I'd even finished lunch (and a second helping).

"I'm going to have to go back eventually," I remarked as I stuck my head into the doorway of the suite I'd be occupying until Xander was assured of Anya's safety.

"Eventually," Raif said. "Not now."

"My place is wide open. No security. I'll have to check on it every once in a while."

Raif smiled in a very self-satisfied way. "I've already taken care of that. I'm having a security system installed that we can monitor from right here. So you have nothing to worry about."

Jesus, he'd thought of everything, hadn't he. Smug SOB. "You know, Raif, going from self-imposed solitary confinement to house arrest isn't a step up."

Raif shrugged. "Call it what you want. You're here and that's all that matters to me. Besides, you'll hardly be under house arrest. Your hands are going to be more than full."

Right on cue, my new pet project stepped onto the second-story landing from the top of the stairs. Dressed from head to toe in a black leather catsuit, Anya looked about as happy to see me as I was to be protecting her. God, how in the *hell* was she going to rock the leather once her pregnancy began to show? I wondered if she'd have some custom outfits made. I pictured her, waddling down the hall, belly protruding in a basketball shape and wrapped in shiny pink leather.

"You might as well turn yourself around and go back to where you came from," Anya said with a sneer. "I don't have any intention of allowing *you* to be my shadow."

"From what I hear," I said, closing my door behind me, "neither of us has a choice."

We made quite a pair, Anya and me. Standing in Xander's hallway, the wall on one side, the banister on the other, we looked like a couple of gunfighters about to draw. And my trigger finger itched. I couldn't even give her a proper beating due to her condition. From what Xander said, everyone would be treating her like she was made of glass for the next year. And I wouldn't be the exception, either. Oh, no. I was going to have to keep her safe.

I leaned against the banister, one foot slung casually across the other. I crossed my arms in front of my chest and looked her over, silently daring her to open her mouth and deny Xander's orders. Tears glistened in her eyes, and I straightened. Anya's gaze narrowed, and she swallowed hard before clenching her teeth. With balled fists and a quivering jaw, she spun on a heel and headed down the hallway and right back down the stairs without a single smart-ass remark. I had to put in some serious effort to keep my own jaw from falling slack. Whaddaya know, even stone-cold Anya wasn't insusceptible to hormones.

"Making friends wherever you go," Raif said, coming up behind me. "You'd better find out who's threatening her and take care of it—fast. Otherwise, you might not survive each other's company."

"About that"—I kicked at the intricate carving of the banister—"I'm not exactly in fighting form. It's going to take a bit of work to get me back in shape."

"I'm not worried." The gleam in Raif's eye echoed a warrior's lust for battle. "I've been waiting for months for a decent workout. Since you're a little rusty, I plan on taking full advantage of the opportunity to take you down a peg or two."

"Don't get too cocky." My own blood was rising, my body gearing up for the prospect of battle. "I can still kick your ass."

"We'll see about that," Raif said, taking off down the stairs in front of me. "Hope you're ready to get worked over."

"I hope *you're* ready," I said, following after him. I became one with the light and regained my corporeal form at the foot of the stairs, several feet in front of him. "First one to the gym gets dibs on the best weapon." I disappeared again in a shimmer of light, Raif's profanity-laced complaints trailing behind me.

He beat me fair and square. Probably the first of many beatings to come. Just one more reason for me to be ashamed of my shut-in routine.

"Ready to go again?" Raif asked.

Hunched over, hands on my knees, dragging in ragged drafts of breath, I wondered, *Do I look like I'm ready to go again?* Raif appeared barely winded. Toweling his forehead and sipping from a water bottle, he looked like he'd just got home from a leisurely jog.

"I think I'm ready for bed," I muttered, straightening and stretching from side to side. The audible crack in my back and neck did little to ease the various aches. God, I was out of shape. Thankfully, I healed almost instantly. Otherwise, I'd be flat on my back for another three months recovering from the ass-whooping I'd just received. One thing about Raif, he took everything to the next level. Even a simple workout.

"It's still early," he said, tentative. "How about dinner first?"

The concern showed in his tone, the worried expression on his face, the way he closed the space between us like he thought I'd bolt at any second. It was nice, really. "Don't worry, Raif. I'm not going AWOL. I'm just fucking exhausted. Seriously, I don't think I could take another step. This is the most I've done in months. I'm ready to crash."

Raif raised a dubious brow. I didn't blame him for not trusting me. He'd been trying to flush me out for weeks. I was like an addict on rehab watch or a cutter in a room full of razor blades. It wouldn't take much to send me over the edge and into a relapse.

"We've been working out for the past five hours. I'm *tired*."

"You're not leaving the house?" More of a confirmation than a question.

"I already told you. I'm staying here. I just need to rest, okay."

He threw the towel he'd been using into a bin near the door. "I'll walk you to your room, then."

Jesus Christ. This was going to get old. Fast. "If you insist." I headed for the door, none too happy with my overprotective escort. "You going to post guards outside my room all night, too?"

"Don't be ridiculous," Raif scoffed as he held the gym door open for me. "I won't need guards. Xander already volunteered for the job."

I stopped dead in my tracks, and threw a caustic glare at the back of his head. Raif kept walking, his exaggerated laughter echoing down the hall.

Ha. Ha. "You're hilarious, you know that?" I said, running to catch up. "You do realize that I'm going to be sleeping with one eye open from now on."

"You gave me the perfect opening." Raif fought another burst of laughter. "It was just too hard to resist."

For two flights of stairs and a couple of hallways, Raif watched me from the corner of his eye. His little joke about Xander standing guard outside my room apparently got him only so far in the entertainment department. "Tomorrow, I'll select candidates for your task force. You can have final approval, but I'll make the initial nominations."

"I trust you," I said. "I don't need final approval."

Raif's mouth became a hard, thin line. He kept his gaze straight ahead. "I can't trust you to be in charge of your team if you leave the decisions up to me. A leader leads, Darian. You should only delegate menial tasks."

Oh, fine. "I don't know any of them. I'm not sure how I'll choose." I figured he needed fair warning. An informed decision, he wasn't going to get. I opened the door to my room and leaned against the jamb.

"I'll have personnel files sent up in the morning. You'll have all the information you need. Also, I can arrange for an exhibition if you'd like to see the candidates fight. Sometimes seeing a warrior in action helps."

Wonderful. Paperwork *and* a show? Administrative duties, exactly what I signed on for. "We'll see." I wasn't about to commit to a morning of watching Raif's warriors fight unless I was sure I needed to. "I'll read the files first and make a decision afterward."

"I can live with that," Raif said. "But, Darian, I'm serious about being a leader. Don't disappoint me."

That was the last thing I wanted to do. But, damn it, why did he have to heap so much on me? Was Raif trying to keep me occupied so I wouldn't have time to think about the shit pile my life had become? Probably. He was such a noble, pragmatic pain in the ass.

I nodded. For some reason, I was afraid of making any verbal promises or reassurances. Honestly, I had no fucking clue if I was up to this job or not. Raif didn't need to know that. Not yet, anyway. And if I promised him I could take care of business, well, I'd have to follow through. I just didn't know at this point if it was a promise I could keep.

"I'll be close if you need me," Raif offered, albeit awkwardly.

Jesus, how bad was I? Did I look like a flight risk? Or worse? "I know," I said, just as awkward. "I'll be fine." I moved to close the door, but Raif didn't budge, his lean warrior's body taking up most of the space in the frame. "Raif." I repeated a little firmer this time, "I'm. Fine."

He took a step back and inclined his head. "Good evening, then."

"'Night." I closed the door and leaned against it, exhaling the breath I didn't realize I'd been holding. The ache in my chest had returned somewhere between the gym and my room. Time sped by, minutes passing as I tried to regain control of my emotions. I rubbed at my sternum, tears springing to my eyes. The pain wasn't going to go away overnight. It might not ever leave. Only Ty could fix me. Until he came home, I'd remain broken.

The door rattled on its hinges, the demand of a pounding fist. I stretched my neck from side to side, took a couple of deep, cleansing breaths. If I denied anyone entry, it would be like throwing up a red flag. And right now, the last thing I needed was another intervention.

"Raif . . ." I said throwing the door open wide. Not Raif. Fuck me.

"Why aren't you coming to dinner?" Xander asked in a tone that screamed bossy.

I met his stare, gold flecks blazing. He looked agitated. Go figure. "I'm not hungry. Raif kicked my ass in the gym. I want to take a shower and go to bed. Is that all right with you, *Your Highness*?"

Xander barged past me, and I realized if I was staying here, I would have to invest in some heavy-duty locks. Maybe I could get Reaver, the Time Keeper of the mortal realm, to throw down some wards for me. I'd like to see Xander get past Sidhe magic. He wandered around the room, assessing it for livability for all I knew. "Is this room big enough to suit you?" he turned and asked.

First dinner, now the room? Since when did he become my personal concierge? I looked around the suite, half as big as my apartment. All I was missing was a kitchen and I'd never have to leave. *If only.* "It's more than big enough, Xander," I said. "Now get the hell out of here so I can go to bed."

"And your things," Xander continued like I hadn't asked him to leave. "Everything is here?"

"I don't know." I tried to keep from sounding too testy. "No one will give me a moment's peace to see for myself."

The King of Shaedes looked around the room, anywhere but right at me. Usually the epitome of calm, cool, and collected, Xander came across as nervous and unsure. He studied a Monet on the far wall, and I was pretty sure it wasn't a reproduction. "I'm . . ." He paused, cleared his throat. "I'm worried about you."

"I'm fine."

"You're *not* fine. You can tell Raif whatever the hell you'd like, but do not lie to me."

I kicked at the plush Persian rug with my boot. Fuck him. He didn't know shit about me.

In three quick strides, Xander stood before me. He put his hands on my shoulders, gripping me tight. Adrenaline kicked up in my veins as the heat from his touch warmed my flesh through my shirt and his gaze locked with mine. "I wish you could see yourself through my eyes right now, Darian. Your cheeks are sunken. Your skin, sallow. Your eyes no longer sparkle like emeralds, but are instead complemented by these black circles." He brushed the hollows of my eyes with his thumbs, as if sweeping away invisible tears. "Raif says you sleep too much, but do you get an ounce of rest?" He gently traced the skin along my jaw and I shuddered. "Your expression never changes. Your mouth is a hard line. And I remember what you used to look like: fierce and full of passion. You were as the sun. And now, there is nothing but shadow."

Shadow. There was a shadow on my heart.

"No, Darian," Xander said, tipping my chin up so I'd meet his gaze. "I see you retreating within yourself. Don't go there. You deserve more than what he gave to you. Your heart is too good for a Jinn to break."

I'd made so many foolish mistakes and I was haunted by each and every one. I could feel the panic mounting, my pulse picking up, a sweat breaking out all over my body. The need to run away from myself overwhelmed me, and my vision darkened at the periphery. Maybe if I passed out, I'd get the peace and quiet I deserved.

Swaying on my feet, Xander's grip tightened, holding me steady. Damn him. I wanted to hate him. Lived for hating him. I didn't want or need his support. Or the feeling of calm that began to wash over me as his presence anchored me.

"Take a shower." His velvet voice snaked around me, held me enthralled. "Rest. I need you to be strong." Xander's eyes pinned me in place as I stared at his face. "For Anya and her unborn child. I'll expect you at breakfast tomorrow morning. Dinner as well. There will be no more hiding as long as you reside under this roof. This is the last night I'll entertain your desire for solitude."

Of course. Manipulation was Xander's forte. He wielded it like a sword. All he cared about was protecting Anya. And he'd say whatever he had to as long as it ensured I'd be primed and ready for the job. He didn't give a shit about me or what I was going through. He cared only about what I could do for him. Silly, Darian, for thinking otherwise. "No worries, Xander." I pulled away, took a deep, cleansing breath, and threw my shoulders back. "Your girl is as good as safe." I walked past him, through the sitting room, toward the bathroom and faced him only when I was over the threshold and standing on the marble floor. "I'm going to take a shower. Get the fuck out."

I slammed the bathroom door and turned the spray on full blast. I didn't know if I could stand being alone, and I didn't want to hear him leave.

Chapter 5

I wished I couldn't feel the approach of morning.

Rain pounded against the windowpanes with a gust of wind, but my skin tingled as the cloud-shrouded sun crested the horizon. I sensed the changing of the hour even though my room was dark as night. Thank god for heavy blackout drapes. No skylights, no uncovered windows. I might be able to sense the sunlight, but at least in my darkened room, I couldn't actually see it. No bright reminder that another day had gone and come again. Another day without Tyler.

Half asleep, I twisted the silver ring on my left thumb, stopping when I felt the engraving. I caressed the image, knowing the bear's shape though I couldn't see it in the darkness. Only once I'd beheld Tyler in his animal form: a large golden bear, the bestial embodiment of his protection. He'd kept me safe then. Draped his hulking, furry body over mine and kept me warm. And he'd almost died protecting me. I didn't deserve him. I'd never deserved him.

"Darian, are you awake?" Raif's voice penetrated the door as well as the remaining dregs of sleep. I wondered if he or Xander, or both of them, spent the night with their ears pressed against the walls—listening.

I thought about answering, but really, it seemed like too much effort. Besides, I wanted to sneak in another half hour of sleep. The idea of black oblivion appealed to me so much more than greeting another loathsome, lonely day. Maybe if I was very still . . .

"Darian!" Raif shouted this time, laying his fist to the door. The successive pounding reverberated through my chest, like a heavy bass drum. Damn him and his persistent nature.

"Jesus, I'm up!" I shouted back. Cordiality was never one of my strong suits. I left my body behind, and regained my physical form as I threw open the door. "A few rounds from an AK-47 would have been less annoying."

Raif pushed his way into my room—I guess privacy was a concept lost on the royal family—and shoved a stack of thick manila folders into my arms. "Candidate files. Look over them and meet me for breakfast in thirty minutes. We've got a lot of work to do, and you won't get anything accomplished lying in bed all day."

He slammed the door behind him, and I listened as his footsteps grew quiet and, finally, faded.

I nodded an acknowledgment to a couple of Xander's staff as I walked down the stairs, and tried not to complain out loud as I made my way toward the formal dining room. That didn't mean I couldn't bitch up a storm in my mind. I must've been crazy to agree to stay here. There was no way I'd be able to stomach the constant attention if it kept up at this rate. Everyone was so fucking worried I'd go off the deep end; I couldn't even be allowed to sleep in for a measly half hour. I wanted to pick a fight. Bad.

Raif and Xander were already seated and eating when I walked into the dining room. Whatever. It didn't bother me. It's not like I expected them to sit and wait for me before they dug in. The food smelled too delicious for my empty stomach to ignore, but it didn't improve my sour mood. I took a seat in one of the pristine Chippendale chairs across from Raif and as far from Xander as possible. Light from the chandelier above glinted off the crystal goblets and gleaming white and gold china setting. I wondered how long it took Xander's kitchen staff to prepare for the many meals they served their king and whether or not he made them take their own meals in the kitchen. His house wasn't a castle, but the opulence—not to mention abundant staff—was a reminder that I was, in fact, now living in a royal household. Before I could even put a napkin in my lap, a silver platter of food was displayed for my inspection. When I didn't acknowledge her, the poor Shaede looked at her king expectantly and once he gave a nod of approval, began to dish the food onto my plate.

She must've been waiting at the kitchen door, poised and ready for the moment I decided to sit my ass down, which made me feel a little guilty for showing up late.

"Good morning," Raif said, a little too pleasant for me. "Did you sleep well?"

My response was a bitchy sort of grunt from deep in my throat.

"That well?" Raif asked. "I'd say if your glowing attitude is any indicator, today should be an absolute joy."

I didn't react to his needling. Instead, I focused my attention on the French toast, fresh fruit, and bacon. It wasn't exactly a bowl of Honey Nut Cheerios, but it would do. I was so hungry, I was pretty sure I could eat my body weight in bacon. Head down, eyes on my plate, I ate in stoic silence. But in my peripheral vision, I couldn't help but notice Xander. He'd set aside his fork, propped an elbow up on the arm of his chair and rested his chin on his fist. His eyes were hooded by lowered lashes, but I could tell he was watching me, just the same.

"Good gods, I see broody attitudes are contagious this morning," Raif replied over the lip of his coffee cup. "Can't anyone wake up on the right side of the bed?"

His comment went unanswered. I wished Xander would quit staring at me. It made me feel like I had something embarrassing on my face.

"As long as you're going to be uncommunicative"—Raif indicated the stack of folders I'd set on the table next to me—"we might as well discuss the candidates for your team. Out of the nine candidates we've recommended, you need to narrow the selection to four."

"Why four?" I didn't look up to meet his face.

"Four is a lucky number. One team member to represent each of the cardinal directions. That way, you'll always have someone at your back."

"If there's one member for each direction, what does that make me?"

"You are the center of the compass," Xander answered. His voice was smooth, darker than usual with an undertone that gave me delicious chills.

Goddamn him.

"Are you sure you're giving me a task force to help find who's threatening Anya?" I paused to sip my coffee. I needed a caffeine boost. "Or are you having me choose my own babysitters?"

"Do you *need* babysitters?" Xander said in that same infuriating tone.

"No. I don't."

Xander sighed and clamped his jaw shut. I noticed the muscles working in his jaw as he ground his teeth together. He pushed his chair out from the table and threw his delicate linen napkin down before nailing me with an accusing glare. His purposeful stride as he all but stomped out of the dining room let me know that my mood had, in fact, rubbed off on him.

"What was that all about?" I looked from Xander's now empty chair to Raif, who was watching the doorway as if he expected his brother to stomp back into the room.

Raif shrugged, but turned his attention to his own breakfast in a way that made me think he knew exactly what Xander's pouty routine had been about. "I stacked the files in order." He indicated the pile of folders. "Top recommendations first, and so on."

I mopped up the last of the syrup with French toast and popped it in my mouth before pushing the plate away. Damn. I was still hungry. I really did need to take better care of myself. I slid the files in front of me, noting how neat and precise each one had been kept. No doubt to Raif's standards. I wondered what he'd do if I spilled coffee on one of them. And I didn't dare mention that I hadn't bothered to look over any of the files yet. "All trained by you?" I asked as I opened the first file.

"For the most part." The pride was unmistakable in Raif's tone. "Though my brother made a suggestion or two. All are fine warriors."

Of course they were. Raif would never settle for anything less. "By what criteria did you base your picks?"

"Skill in battle, stealth, intelligence. I wouldn't have you working with an unseasoned trainee or upstart who might be tempted to question your authority."

Gee, thanks for your undying faith, Raif. "Afraid your troops won't take kindly to me?"

"Don't be ridiculous." Raif's face became the serious mask of the warrior that frightened so many. It was the expression I admired the most. "They know an order from you is as good as an order from me. But remember, Darian, there was a time when even you didn't think twice about questioning me."

True. I'd been a little full of myself the first time I'd met him. But it hadn't taken long before he put me in my place. No one fucks with Raif. I flipped through the first file, and the second, and then the third. Each new candidate seemed as good as the last. How would I ever make a decision? "Maybe you were right about seeing these guys in action." Not that I liked admitting it. "I'm not getting anywhere reading their stats. I might as well be looking at baseball cards."

"I figured you might say that. They're assembled in the gym."

Always prepared. Raif was a goddamned Boy Scout. No need to sit around reading about his carefully handpicked troupe of Shaedes. Time to see the goods firsthand. "Let's go."

The gym was silent when we pushed open the double doors. The kind of silent when you know everyone was talking about you moments before. They may as well get an eyeful while they had the chance, because five of them were going to get the boot.

Like good little soldiers, Raif's candidates lined up against the far wall, feet braced wide and hands clasped behind their backs. Expressions of inspired awe crossed their faces when he entered the gym, and I couldn't help but smile. Raif was indeed inspiring on many levels. Identical in dress, the candidates would've put a battalion of Army Rangers to shame. Dark blue fatigues, long-sleeve, formfitting black knit shirts, and polished combat boots, Raif's potential task force members showed up battle ready.

I cross-referenced each file's picture with a face as I looked over the assembled warriors. Three women and six men waited for the honor to beat each other to a pulp only to prove they were worthy of Raif's recommendation.

"Let's get to it, then," Raif said, eyeballing each Shaede

individually. "Louella . . . and . . . Julian." Raif jerked his
thumb behind him. "Start us off with a decent sparring."

"Hear that, Loulie?" The one called Julian elbowed a
dark, feisty-looking girl in the ribs. "You get to be the first
ass-whoopin' of the day."

She didn't respond to her opponent, just walked, eyes facing front toward the mats. I liked her. Even before she caught
Julian off guard with a low, sweeping kick to the ankles, I
knew she'd be the first member of my team. Louella was
shorter than me by a good four inches. Her petite build, coupled with wide, brown eyes and bronze skin made her look
more like an innocent girl than a trained killer. But she put
every inch of her body to good use and managed to pin her
much larger male opponent to the mat in under a minute.

Julian lay still, catching his breath. Six feet tall and as fair
and blond as Louella was dark, he watched her walk back to
the wall with a goofy smile plastered on his face. I had a feeling he enjoyed every second of the beating, and his good-
natured attitude definitely earned him a spot at the top of my
list.

Raif gave Julian a hard, appraising stare as he hauled himself upright. "You went a full ten minutes before she bested
you last week."

The cocky smile quickly vanished from Julian's face, and
he bowed his head. When he looked up, Raif jerked his chin
toward the back wall, and Julian retreated like a scalded dog.
Raif never had to say much to get a reaction and no one
wanted to disappoint him. And when you did, well, the disappointment was far worse than any punishment he could ever
dish out.

A tall, lanky redhead stepped forward, and I flipped
through the files until I found the right one. Myles Caffray.
He didn't really look like a Myles. Taller than Julian, his
green eyes glowed against ivory skin. His freckles made him
look unassuming and almost boyish, but something about the
catlike slant to his eyes made me think twice about my first
impression. Without being asked, he stepped onto the mat,
feet braced and standing at ease. Apparently, he wanted to go
next and wouldn't wait around for an invitation from Raif.
Nice.

"Fine," Raif said to no one in particular, but the annoyance seeped through his tone. "You're so eager—you can go up against Liam."

Liam stepped forward, a big, scary son of a bitch. He looked older than the rest, or, at the very least, more battle hardened. Blue tattoos chased a swirling pattern on his bald head, running down his neck and disappearing beneath his shirt. Both of his ears were gauged with large black plugs that only accentuated the aura of brutality that surrounded him. I had a feeling he could break Myles in half if he wanted to. And from the expression on his face—he wanted to.

"Weapons?" Liam asked, his voice like gravel in a cement mixer.

Raif inclined his head. "But remember, this is a training exercise only. Nothing more than an exhibition."

I have to say, Liam looked a little put out. He walked to the back wall of the gym, perusing the weapons like he was a suburbanite window-shopper. If I hadn't had the emerald key to *O Anel* hanging around my neck, the sound of seconds ticking away while he made his selection would have driven me insane. He finally settled on a wooden *bokken,* which he tossed to Myles, and then he simply walked to the mat. Unarmed.

"Really, Liam?" Myles asked, giving the wooden version of a samurai sword a couple of practice swings.

"I figure you can use all the help you can get," Liam answered, cracking each of his knuckles.

"This should be interesting," Raif whispered in my ear. "Liam has an axe to grind with Myles."

"Over what?"

"What else." Raif shrugged. "A woman."

Wasn't it always? If they couldn't put their petty bullshit aside for a couple of minutes, I didn't think I wanted either of them. Liam looked like he wasn't worried about the outcome of the sparring exhibition. In fact, his sheer size and hulking muscle coupled with the bored expression on his face would have sealed the deal for any odds maker.

But my money was on Myles.

In the course of my life, I'd learned it was the unassuming ones you had to watch out for. And those shrewd, calculating cat eyes didn't miss a thing. Myles observed every minute shift of Liam's weight with an intensity that made the hairs stand up on the back of my neck. Myles was deadly. Myles was a killer. And I would know.

Liam circled Myles, his arms like tree trunks swinging with every step. Myles smiled, inviting the challenge, twirling the *bokken* once, and then again. He lunged forward, jabbing with a quick, well-maneuvered extension and Liam jumped back, surprising me with the deftness of motion. Their battle dance continued: lunges, reactions, and still Liam circled his prey. No words passed between them, not the cocky, self-absorbed bragging that accompanies an approaching fight. These guys were dead serious. This wasn't a game to them. It was personal.

Raif shook his head in disgust, apparently rethinking his decision to let them air out their differences on the mats. He took a step forward, and I threw out my arm, stopping him. "You said Liam had an axe to grind. Let him do it."

"Perhaps this isn't the place," Raif said.

"If they don't do it here, they'll go somewhere else to settle the score. And believe me, if they take the fight out of this gym, one of them isn't going to walk away from it."

Raif relaxed, but I knew he wasn't happy. He was all about control and in the blink of an eye, his carefully orchestrated demonstration had turned into a full-on grudge match. At least here, under supervision, we could make sure both parties lived to fight another day. And in my opinion, letting the testosterone run its course was the best and only option.

Myles lunged again, this time with an upward cut, and rather than jump out of the way, Liam parried the thrust with his arm. The *bokken* cracked as it made contact and I couldn't help but wince. Liam's arm had to have hurt like a bitch, but he didn't even flinch. I had to give it to him, the guy was tough.

I stole a glance at the candidates lined up against the wall, watching, like me, with intense interest. The one named Louella leaned in to whisper in the ear of the female standing beside her and she nodded, her eyes wide. It impressed me that none of the Shaedes seemed to take a side. Instead, they kept their expressions mostly neutral. Taking in the goings-on with ambiguity solidified the fact that ultimately they were all on the same team. I admired them for that.

"Why can't I just take all of them?" I asked Raif, my gaze still passing over the candidates. My eyes met feral amber, and I stopped. Stared straight through the kid giving me look for look.

"Four." Raif said. "Numbers aren't open for discussion."

I wanted to argue, but I'd lost my train of thought. By my estimation, the Shaede ignoring the fight to stare straight at me was the youngest man in the room. Probably even younger than my own one hundred and twenty-one years. His eyes were lighter than Xander's by a couple of shades. Translucent and wild. White-blond hair, shining, thick, and wavy reached to about his collar, giving the impression that he ought to have a skateboard tucked under his arm. I couldn't shake the look in his eyes, though. As I took him in, I wondered what had happened in his life to make him look so hard.

"How long has he been with you?" I inclined my head toward the boy.

"Not long. But he's smart. A quick learner, too. And tough as any hardened soldier. One of Xander's recommendations."

I tore my gaze from the boy and turned my attention back to the mats. Liam had managed to wrestle the *bokken* from Myles, and the two were throwing punches and kicks like an action movie fight scene right out of the eighties. Liam was big, not to mention strong. But Myles was quick and managed to keep the upper hand despite his opponent's strength. Bloodied, panting, sweat beading on their foreheads—I realized they could go at it all day. Neither one of them would be willing to drop any time soon.

"That's enough!" I shouted over the din of fighting.

Liam and Myles froze in a tangle of arms and legs. Usually, I'd be thrilled to have thrown my weight around. But today, I wasn't in the mood. I just wanted to get the selections over with and go back to bed.

"We all get it," I said, approaching the edge of the mat. "You're both big, tough motherfuckers and can kick each other's asses raw. Point made. You're done and can get back in line."

The two detangled from one another and shot me a matched set of sullen stares as they made their way to the group.

"One more thing." Liam and Myles froze, though neither turned to look at me. "If I see you two fighting over petty bullshit again, I'll bring a world of hurt down on both of you personally. And I can guarantee you won't be walking out of this gym without help."

Raif didn't chime in. He knew he didn't need to. He'd told me to be a leader, and whether I liked it or not, I'd stepped up to the plate. Guess it was too late to back out now.

The remaining candidates sparred in mixed groups, Louella fought twice, impressing me even more the second time. Asher, the wild towheaded blond, was everything Raif said he'd be. Quick, skilled, precise. That kid was lightning in a bottle. I wondered what would happen when someone finally pulled the cork.

"You're all dismissed until further notice," Raif said once the parade was over. He waited until the gym door closed behind the last candidate, the sound reverberating off the cement walls. "Would you like a couple of days to make a decision?"

"That's not necessary," I said, flipping through the files one last time.

"All right, then. Who would you like?"

"Louella for sure. That girl can fight. And Julian, because I have a feeling he's usually not too far from Louella anyway." I scanned the files again. Julian hadn't been an impressive fighter, which might have been because he was too preoccupied with his apparent crush on Louella to put serious effort into sparring against her. But his file indicated that he was smart. Genius smart. And I needed brains as well as brawn.

"Good choice. Though you'll have to watch out for Julian. You have to use a heavy hand if you want to keep him on task. That leaves two empty seats," Raif said. "Who else?"

"Myles." I flipped through the files once more. I didn't know how I'd handle the both of them, but I never did anything halfway. "And Liam."

"Will it matter to you if I advise against taking them both?

I'd suggest keeping Liam and dismissing Myles." That surprised me. If anything I'd thought he'd want Liam left off the list. He seemed the most hotheaded.

"You said I made the final decision. Liam has the muscle, but Myles is ruthless. I need ruthless as well."

Raif inclined his head, though I could tell he wasn't happy with the concession. "That should do it, then. I'll—"

"And Asher," I said over the top of Raif. "I want him."

"I said four."

"I want him, Raif. I won't take no for an answer."

Raif stalked to the double doors, shaking his head as he walked. "I suppose not, but there's a first time for everything. I don't trust him, Darian. He's Xander's candidate, not mine. Best to leave the boy to other pursuits. Take the four you've got. You've made a decent selection, and they'll work well enough together."

"I'll take the four. For now. I'm not giving up on this, Raif. There's something about Asher. I can't put my finger on it. You'll cave and let me add him. Eventually." Call me overconfident, but I knew that Raif would have no choice but to give me what I wanted.

"Gods, but you're a stubborn woman."

I followed behind him, thinking I deserved a nice, long nap for putting up with this circus. "Would you like me any other way, Raif?"

"No," he said, holding open the door for me. "I would not."

Chapter 6

I left Raif, and my corporeal form, at the gym door and headed for my room. No way was I going to let him follow me around for the rest of the day. I'd been a good girl. Dragged my ass out of bed, ate breakfast, and played nice with the troops. Now, *he* could do me a favor and leave me the hell alone for a couple of hours.

As I fell back onto the bed, my body became a solid thing. The expensive memory foam didn't exactly let me land with a bounce, but it accepted my weight like strong, welcoming arms. *I missed you, Darian. Why don't you lie right here and take a nice, long nap.* I was going to do just that. Screw Anya and her precious offspring. To hell with task forces, and mysteries, and loyalty. Take your brooding attitude and velvet voice and stick it right up your ass, Xander. The dark void called, and I was about to answer.

I drifted—faster than I expected—toward sleep. Drift might be a bit of an understatement. I jumped in a freefall toward unconsciousness. My stomach rumbled with hunger; it was almost noon and I'd only eaten twice in forty-eight hours, but nothing seemed as important as leaving reality behind for a while. I rubbed at my sternum, knowing that it wouldn't be long before the pain would be too great for me to handle. God, I missed him. Wanted him. Needed him to forgive me for how I'd left him and take the pain of my guilt away.

"Tyler . . ." I whispered sleepily against my pillow.

My cell played a muffled tune in my pocket, pulling me from near sleep. I swore under my breath and dug in my pants for the phone. Without checking the caller ID, I answered and held the receiver to my ear. "When I get my hands on whoever this is, I'm going to tear you a new asshole!"

"Jesus, did I interrupt something?"

I sat up, jumped off the bed and switched the light on, shielding my eyes from the sudden burst of light. "Marcus?"

Tyler's sometimes lackey laughed humorlessly on the other end. "Miss me? I sure as hell didn't miss you."

I tried to speak, but my brain was cranking too hard and fast for my mouth to catch up. Why the hell was Marcus calling me? Was Ty okay? Where the hell was he? What the fuck was going on?

"Since you're not answering, I'm gonna guess the feeling's mutual. I told Tyler never to send me on an errand that had to do with your scary ass again. Guess I drew the short fucking straw this time."

"What?" The word dragged out, like I was talking through a mouthful of pudding. Had I heard him right? Tyler had asked him to call me?

"Tyler has a job for you," Marcus said, slowly like I might be having comprehension problems. "Where you wanna do this? I've got the deets—and the confirmation on the wire transfer. The paycheck for this gig is too big for cash."

"My place." Small talk wasn't on my agenda. I wanted more than job information from Marcus and beating it out of him in public wasn't an option.

"No. Fucking. Way."

Coward. He was an insufferable piece of shit. "Fine. The back alley behind The Pit, then."

"I suppose it's better than your place, but not by much. I'll be there in a half hour."

"Marcus," I said, grabbing one of my black dusters from the closet. "If you're not there in fifteen minutes, I'm going to go looking for you."

Marcus cleared his throat. I could practically feel his nervous energy reaching out like twitchy fingers through the phone. "I'll get there as fast as I can. But, Christ, Darian, give me some time to get through traffic. It's the noon rush."

"Fifteen minutes, Marcus. Don't be late."

*   *   *

I'd never met any of Tyler's people in the middle of the day. In fact, in all the years I'd worked for Ty, I couldn't remember a single time an exchange had been made before midnight. All the more reason to be suspicious.

The Pit hadn't opened yet, so I didn't have to worry about prying eyes. Usually, I'd never meet anyone—not even Marcus—in such a conspicuous place to make an exchange. But the fact that Ty had sent one of his employees on this errand without at least calling me first left a bitter chill in the bottom of my stomach. Why?

I removed the emerald pendulum from my neck, just so I could count the passing minutes with perfect accuracy. I wasn't screwing around. If Marcus was one *half* of a second late, I was going after his ass. Pacing from wall to wall in the narrow alley, I waited with what can only be described as forced patience. I fingered the dagger at my thigh, felt for the katana hidden under my duster at my back, and thought of the many ways I was going to use them to pry every little drop of information I could out of Marcus's scrawny hide.

"You're certifiable, you know that?" Marcus said, coming around the corner. Four minutes early, smart boy. Running a shaky hand through his dark, greasy hair, his eyes darted from side to side. Beneath a worn, too small AC/DC T-shirt, every soft bulge of his middle was visible. Still wearing the same torn jeans and secondhand army boots, Marcus's wardrobe obviously hadn't improved since I'd seen him last. Sweat beaded on his upper lip, and he scrubbed a hand across his mouth. He looked nervous as hell, and he should've been.

Without even thinking, I jerked my dagger free of the sheath and grabbed the little shit by the collar. Ramming forward, I slammed him in to the brick wall with all the care of a jackhammer and shoved the dagger's point into the flesh at the hollow of his throat. "Marcus, you slimy piece of shit, I want to know what the hell is going on. Now."

"Jesus!" Marcus whimpered. "Are you off your meds or something? It's just a job, Darian. You don't need to go all paranoid, psycho bitch on me!"

"Who sent you?"

"What do you mean, who sent me?" Marcus had graduated

from whimpering puppy to squealing girl. "Tyler fucking sent me."

"You talked to him?"

Marcus swallowed, his Adam's apple bobbed in his throat, and he nodded his head. "Of course I talked to Tyler. Jesus-fucking-Christ, Darian. Who the hell else would send me?"

The dagger slipped from my grasp, clattering to the pavement at my feet. Tyler sent him. Talked to him. And not me. "You brought something for me?" My voice had lost some of its fire, instead returning to the hollow-sounding representation of myself that had been dragging ass around Xander's house for the past couple of days. My chest ached, my heart constricting to the point that I thought it would crumble. What the hell was going on?

"You wanna take your hands off me?" Marcus must have noticed my systematic breakdown and thought it gave him the right to get cocky. "He's pretty worked up about this job, said it's a top priority. So if I were you, I'd step off the crazy train and get to work." He pulled a folded manila envelope from inside his coat and dangled it in front of me. "Better get busy, don't think you wanna upset the boss man."

I took two steps back and threw the punch before I thought better of it. My fist caught Marcus square on the jaw, and he spun a full circle before his head knocked against the wall and he slumped to the ground. I squatted down, scooped up the envelope and my dagger, and leaned in toward Marcus's ear. "Talk to me like that again, asshole, and you'll have more than a headache when you come to."

Tucking the dagger back in its sheath and the envelope into my pocket, I became one with the light. Ty was back. He had to be. I tried to ignore the churning stomach acid eating away at my gut and the lump that had risen to my throat. My heart thundered in my chest, beating double time to the seconds ticking away within me. No time to put the emerald around my neck. I'd deal with that annoyance later. Right now, I had only one thing on my mind: Tyler.

Like a breath of air, I swept through the city. I was fortunate that I could travel unseen whether it be day, night, or anytime in between. Stealth and speed were what I needed as

I raced toward Tyler's building, and I used every preternatural gift at my disposal.

I managed to make it across town in less than five minutes, but when the moment came for me to go inside, I found that my body refused to move. What if he wasn't there? Or worse, what if he was. If he'd wanted to see me, he would've called. Right? Or maybe he was still upset and used Marcus as a means to reach out to me. In which case, it might not have been a good idea to knock him out.

Fuck it. Either way, I had to know.

I wasn't about to announce myself and run the risk that I'd be turned away. If Tyler was home, I wanted him to look me in the eye and tell me why he hadn't at least called when he got back into town. It's not like I expected him to forgive me overnight. After all, I had left him first. But, Christ, the past few months had been torture.

I forced myself through the entrance, past the front desk, drifting up the stairwell like a wraith. When I reached the penthouse, I regained my physical form only to pace back and forth in front of his door for three minutes and twenty-two seconds. I'd never felt so spineless. Helpless and scared was not how I liked to feel. I'd spent my human life in a constant state of uncertainty and fear; I didn't want to spend my preternatural existence reliving those crippling emotions.

But I already had, though not for the same reasons.

Depressed. Alone. Broken. Unsure. Good god, when had I become the poster child for antidepressants? Marching up to the door, I squared my shoulders and took a deep breath. Tyler was more than likely on the other side of the wall. Just a foot or two of steel, wood, drywall, and insulation separating us. My stomach clenched, and I rubbed at my sternum.

I laid my knuckles to the door, bypassing the polite chime of the doorbell. I gripped the dagger at my thigh, sliding the blade in and out, in and out of the sheath. Thirty-four seconds passed, and I knocked again—louder this time. And still I slid the dagger in and out of its sheath. The sound of steel scraping against leather comforted me somehow. The door swung open, and I gripped the dagger below the guard, squeezing until I felt the sharp blade bite into my skin. The pain, accompanied by the warm, sticky trickle of blood confirmed the worst. I wasn't dreaming. This was real.

Beautiful didn't even begin to describe the woman standing in Tyler's doorway. Long chestnut hair, straight and shining like polished wood, hung to her narrow waist. Golden skin complemented eyes that weren't quite green, or blue, or hazel, but rather, a harmonious blend of all three colors, pale and nearly translucent. Taller than me, with an air of sophistication I could never pull off, I was looking at pure, seductive, feminine perfection.

"Can I help you?"

God, even her *voice* was perfect. Not too high, not too low. Smooth like hot chocolate. A *pit, pat, pit, pat* sound drew my attention and I looked down at my hand, realizing I hadn't let go of the dagger. I'd squeezed it so hard the blade penetrated a quarter inch into my palm and blood was dripping onto the expensive hallway carpet. I released my grip and let the dagger slide back into the sheath before I forced myself to look up again. Over Miss Perfect's shoulder, I saw him walk out of the kitchen.

Tyler.

Shit, what had my life become? Some cliché, melodramatic Lifetime movie?

Air. I needed air. *Where is all of the fucking air?* My lungs stalled in my chest, my surroundings blurred out of focus as my eyes drank in every godlike detail of Tyler's face. I would have wept at the sight of him if I'd had anything left to cry. But everything in me dried up; my blood turned to dust, my tears evaporated, and every soft part of me compressed into stone. Even my lips had gone numb. Was it possible to get hypothermia of the soul?

Tyler stopped dead in his tracks, several feet and one gorgeous supermodel vixen separating us. The mask of emotion on his face was more than my brain could comprehend, because I knew it was a lie. His beautiful hazel eyes burned right through me, his brows drawn in what could only be described as pain. He looked like he wanted to say something, but was at a loss for words. *Yeah, join the club.* At the heart of it all, though, was a tenderness so intense I had to avert my eyes. There was no way he could look at me with that kind of longing while another woman stood between us. He didn't have the right to do that. It just didn't work that way.

I had to get out of there. Now. As involuntary as breathing, my skin melded with the light. Thank god for it too, because it was the only sensation I could feel. Back through the city, I pushed myself as fast as possible, no longer a passing breeze, but a vengeful wind. A tornado. Hurricane Darian. No wonder Tyler sent Marcus instead of coming himself. Guess that explained his lack of phone calls—or any communication, for that matter—too. Why bother? There was nothing left to say, was there? A picture's worth a thousand words, and I'd just hit the visual jackpot. No need to make a bad situation worse with apologies and awkward explanations. I got the message loud and clear: whatever it was we'd had was over.

Chapter 7

I walked through Xander's front door as my solid self. With an assassin's quiet steps, I made my way to my room, knowing if I ran in to any curious Shaedes with nosy questions I might just crack. I eased open my door, worried that even the slightest creak of the hinges would give me away. Just as carefully, I eased the door shut behind me and allowed for a deep breath. My lungs ached from the effort, my body rejecting the comfort of oxygen. I hadn't taken a decent breath since leaving Tyler's penthouse.

"I'm surprised they don't have an ankle bracelet on you. You know, the kind that human prisoners wear."

Holy shit! Anya's voice gave me a full-body shock, effectively sealing off the smooth intake of air I'd been trying to enjoy. Why did everyone in this house have to be so far up my ass? "Anya," I said, fighting for composure. "What in the *hell* are you doing in my room? Don't you have leather booties to craft or something?"

"You look like shit."

At least she wasn't crying anymore. Her observation seemed pretty apathetic, actually. It's not like I expected her to be . . . I don't know . . . concerned for me or anything. After seeing her cry the day before, I guess I thought she'd be a tad more off-kilter. A little less like herself. I had nothing to go by, though. I didn't have much experience with pregnant human women, let alone pregnant Shaedes.

"If I look like shit, it's because I have your ass to worry about," I said, turning away so she wouldn't have a clear view of my face. "What the hell do you want?"

"You missed dinner."

No shit. "Is that why you're sitting in here waiting for me? To let me know I'd missed another *meal*?"

"I have to go out tomorrow," Anya said. "I'm not allowed to leave the estate without an escort."

Escort, meaning me. "Fine." No matter how much I wanted to hole myself up and tell the world to go to hell, I couldn't let Raif down. "Are you going to tell me who's threatening you so we don't have to spend any more quality time with one another than necessary?"

"Honestly," Anya said, "I'd rather have bamboo slivers shoved under my fingernails than spend time with you. But don't think for a second that I'm going to open up. About anything."

"It's your neck," I said with an exasperated sigh.

"That's right," Anya replied, heading for the door. "It is. By the way, I think you've finally pushed your luck too far with Alexander. His Highness was not pleased that you skipped the evening meal."

Anya closed the door behind her and I stripped off my coat, slinging it across the settee in the corner of the room. I kicked off my boots, peeled my socks off, and shed my pants lightning fast. I ran to flip off the light switch, blacking out the room, and jumped into bed. If I pretended to be asleep, maybe I could avoid the royal ass-chewing I was no doubt in store for. I didn't want to see or talk to anyone else for the rest of my life. I just wanted to lie in bed and let the grief eat me alive.

I closed my eyes and tried to appear serene, but the image of that inhumanly beautiful woman was burned in my memory. Maybe I could get rid of it if I washed my brain out with bleach, or scrubbed it clean with steel wool. Lobotomy, anyone? Sleep was my only sanctuary. What would I do if that tiny bit of peace turned on me as well?

Panic overwhelmed me. The thought of returning to my life as it had been—detached, lonely, without compassion or companionship, without love and tenderness—made my head spin. Cold, clammy sweat broke out on my skin. Throat closing up, I felt the need to swallow ten times more than usual, and I launched myself out of the bed and beelined it for the bathroom. Palms slapped down on the expensive marble tile as I dove face-first over the toilet seat. My stomach clenched but I hadn't eaten in so long, all I could manage was a succession of painful dry heaves that made every inch of my body ache.

Warm hands brushed my neck and gently pulled my hair back. Shit, I hadn't even thought of making sure the ends didn't dip into the toilet. *Lovely.*

"You certainly know how to take the wind out of a man's sails," Xander said close to my ear as he kneeled beside me. "I came in here prepared to fight and I find you hanging over the toilet. I feel cheated."

I folded my arms in front of me on the seat and rested my forehead on them. Drawing deep, steady breaths, I tried to calm my stomach from another round of cramping heaves. *Go away, Xander,* I thought, unable to speak. *Leave me alone and let me yak in peace.*

"What happened to you this evening?" His voice was so soft, gentle. *Damn him.* "I have a feeling that rather than improve, you've just taken ten steps back."

Understatement of the century. What the hell did he expect me to say? *Yep, Xander, you hit the nail right on the head. Ty's back in town, and he's shacked up with a woman so breathtaking, if you saw her you'd never look at me again.* I don't think so.

I didn't want to sit there all night face-first in the toilet, but I was afraid to move. What if the anxiety hit me again, and harder? What was the next step up from vomiting? Complete brain hemorrhage? "Not that I don't appreciate you holding my hair and all"—I didn't dare look up—"but I'm fine, Xander. You can go now."

"You're not fine." He was so close, I could feel his breath on my face.

"Yes, I am."

Xander sighed. "Come on," he said, pulling at my arms. "I'll help you back to bed."

Once upright, Xander bent and swept an arm under my knees, gathering me up into his arms. "I'm not a child, Xander, I can walk on my own." But, honestly, I didn't think I had the willpower necessary to put one foot in front of the other.

"No, you're certainly not," Xander chuckled. "Though you choose to act like one on occasion."

The panic drained out of me like an ebbing tide, and my stomach felt not just empty but raw. My throat wasn't faring much better, burning from the acid, the only thing my depleted body had left to give. Utterly exhausted, it wasn't just physical, but emotional and spiritual. I felt paper-thin and spent. I let my eyes drift shut as Xander carried me to the bed, but in my mind's eye, Tyler's face full of unspoken emotion loomed behind a vision of perfection. Would I ever be able to think of him again without having her face in my memory as well?

Xander set me down with care, as far to the center of the bed as he could reach. He sat down beside me, his weight on the mattress somehow reassuring. I didn't look at him, afraid he'd read in my eyes what I wasn't willing to speak: that I might not ever be the same after tonight. He smoothed my hair away from my face, and I let him. A snarky comeback wasn't what he deserved. He'd held my hair while I'd puked my guts out. That was enough to earn him a bye for the night.

"I told you, you weren't allowed to skip dinner again," Xander's voice broke through my thoughts.

"Why do you care about Anya so much?" I didn't want to talk about me and the train wreck I'd become. "What makes her so special?"

Xander eased back onto the pillows and swung his legs up on the bed. "She's younger than you," he said. "By a few decades. Did you know that?"

I didn't know anything about her other than the fact that she had an atrocious leather fetish. Xander shifted, and rather than let my curiosity get the better of me, I turned my back to him and picked a spot on the wall, staring at the pattern on the fancy silk wallpaper until I lost focus altogether. Anything was better than closing my eyes.

"If I've ever known a more infuriating woman than you, it's Anya," Xander continued, his voice lulling me. "Women like you aren't meant for mundane lives, and Anya is no different. Raif caught her trying to break into my house and, curious, I had him bring her to me."

Anya, a criminal. Her loyalty to Xander was so uncompromising; I could never picture her trying to steal from him.

"I suppose I should have let Raif turn her over to the area's governing authority or at least, punish her himself. It probably would've only spurred her on, though. She had her reasons for breaking in, and at the time, she had no idea the house belonged to her king. They were homeless, hungry, desperate. She'd made Dimitri one of us by then, and I was curious. I'd never known anyone else capable of performing the feat."

Raif had told me Xander's wife had once been human and he had changed her, but nothing more had ever been spoken of her. Probably why he'd been curious about Anya. I'm sure Xander, in his royal arrogance, thought only he could be strong enough to make another Shaede. My eyes grew heavy as Xander's rich voice lulled me, and I blinked away the sleep. God, I was tired.

"I know you find her . . . abrasive. And I realize that you'd rather not be here, watching her. I want you to know, however, that I care about her a great deal. You do me an honor by helping to protect her."

"Do you love her?" I don't know why I asked. For some insane reason, I wanted to know.

"She is like a sister to me," Xander said. "Family. But just because I'd hate for you to be jealous, you should know that what I feel for her is nothing compared to what I feel for you."

"You don't love me, you know." My voice was weak, muffled by grief and exhaustion. "You just think you do."

His fingertips brushed my hair, feather light, and I shivered. "Shall I tell you how I love you?"

"No," I said, my throat constricting. "I'm not in the mood for lies."

"Or the truth, apparently."

The first tear slipped from my eye and rolled down my face onto the pillow. I didn't want Xander to bear witness to my heartache and shame. I didn't want him to see me this way—weak and vulnerable. "Do you want to know what I found out tonight, Xander?" I willed my voice to sound strong. "That love is bullshit and there's always someone better out there to take your place."

"You speak like your heart is broken."

"I speak like a realist."

"How so?"

"Love is like finding a shiny bauble on the ground. You think it's the most wonderful, lovely thing you've ever seen, and you polish it, keep it safe, and cherish it. Until you come across something prettier, something more interesting. That's love. You're only perfect until you're not."

"Did I tell you that your Jinn came here after you disappeared?"

I knew. Raif had told me. "I know the story more or less."

Xander snorted. "I doubt that. He barged right through the door. Literally. Blew it right off the hinges. I have to say, I'd never seen a Jinn use the full force of his power before that day. Very impressive, indeed. He threatened to bring the house down around my head if I didn't tell him where you were, and by the way the entire house shook on its foundation, I didn't doubt his words."

I bet in hindsight, Tyler wished he hadn't thrown such a fit. "It was my fault. I left him a note and took off while he was asleep. Don't hold his actions against him; he only behaved that way because I gave him no other choice."

"Everyone has a choice, Darian." Had he edged closer? I was pinned beneath the blankets, Xander on top of them. The bed suddenly seemed altogether too small. "You made a choice when you left to find my niece. Your Jinn made a choice when he knocked down my door and threatened me."

"I never should have left the way I did," I said, barely a whisper. "I hurt him."

"You chose to come back. He chose to leave you."

The tears flowed faster, silent. "I did this. I forced his hand."

"Maybe. Maybe not."

Xander rolled away and I assumed he was getting up to leave. If he didn't have an audience, I knew he wouldn't want to stick around. I flipped over to my back, only to find that he hadn't left, but had moved down onto the pillow beside me. Lying on his side, his head propped up in his hand, he studied me with a quiet interest that made my heart jump against my rib cage.

He reached out, wiped the tears from my cheek. His touch was soft, careful. As if he didn't want to frighten me away. "You are the shiniest of baubles."

I put my arm over my eyes to block him completely out of my vision. "You're wasting your breath, Xander. Sweet talk doesn't work on me."

"I never waste my breath." He traced a finger across the bare skin of my forearm, up and down in a swirling, intricate pattern. "I would have chosen to stay." He closed the distance between us, and I couldn't have been happier for the heavy blankets creating a barrier between our bodies. His hair brushed my shoulder as he leaned in close to my ear. "I would do anything to have you."

Chills chased over my skin, and the panic rose up fresh through my chest, squeezing my heart. "Get out," I said, my own breath speeding up to keep pace with my thundering pulse. If he didn't get the hell off the bed and out of this room, I was going to spontaneously combust. I covered my face with both of my hands, fighting to slow my heart rate. "Go." I choked on the word, a half sob.

Xander went still for a moment before he pushed himself off the bed. I listened to his footsteps, quiet, each one precisely placed. He came around the bed and stopped beside me, placing his lips to my brow. "Good night, Darian."

Only after the door closed behind him did I allow my tears to flow unchecked.

Chapter 8

I gave the bag a nice, hard kick. Followed through with a right hook, then a left. Kick, jab, swing. Elbow up, I rammed the heavy sandbag where my opponent's face would be. It swung back and forth on its chain, and I lunged out of the way, leapt, and rammed my heel at stomach level. Sweat dripped down my neck, trickled under the white Under Armour T-shirt and soaked into the waistband of my yoga pants. I'd rather fight a living, breathing opponent, one who could actually hit back. But this early, I doubted I'd find anyone willing to join me.

Six in the morning, and I'd already been at it for two hours. It's not like I could sleep. In fact, I doubted I'd ever sleep again. *Fantastic.* I'd done a total one-eighty, going from sleeping twenty hours a day to four. Somehow, though, beyond the pain of my broken heart, I felt a strange sense of calm. Not because Ty had found someone else to love—I'd never get over that—but rather, because I had answers. Before Tyler had left me, he'd said nothing was worse than the wondering. The *not* knowing. And he was right. At least I had an explanation for his silence. At least now I knew why he hadn't called me when he'd come home. I rubbed at my sternum, trying to banish the hollow pain in my chest that would probably never leave me, before grabbing a towel and mopping the sweat off my face and neck. I thought I heard the gym doors swing open, but the sound was so faint, I almost hadn't noticed. I closed my eyes, my hand easing to my side to retrieve the dagger I kept strapped to my thigh. Still and barely breathing, I let my unique senses do the work, zoning in on the sound and signature of the stealth-quiet form approaching, inaudible to anyone but me, and even I had to strain my ears and reach out with invisible feelers to both hear and feel the presence.

When the hairs stood up on my arms and at the back of my neck, I knew it was time. Eyes open, I whirled around, grabbing my assailant by the collar—or rather, shirt—and pressing the dagger to his . . . er . . . chest instead of his throat.

"I didn't mean to startle you," Asher said, too soft and calm for his size. I hadn't noticed the first time I'd met him how big he really was. I guess the haunted look in his light amber eyes had distracted me from everything else. "I heard someone working out, thought I'd see what was up."

Interesting. "I didn't think anyone would be awake this early."

Asher shrugged his shoulders. "I don't sleep much."

"Me either." Well, not anymore.

Asher looked down at the dagger I was still holding to his chest. "I can leave—if you want to be alone."

I sheathed the dagger, seeing my salvation in the tall Shaede, probably strong enough to break me in half. He wasn't as big as Liam, but pretty damn close. How did I not notice it before?

I'd decided after Xander left me alone last night, that the only way to rid the image of Ty and that other woman from my mind would be to beat myself into exhaustion. Besides, I owed it to Raif to be in my best fighting form. I couldn't protect dick moping around feeling sorry for myself. And who better to give me a run for my money than Asher? I swept my hand in front of me, an invitation.

"Mind if I stretch, first?"

Whatever floats your boat, buddy. I watched as he lifted an arm over his head, elbow to sky and palm to his back.

"So," he said, switching arms. "Why didn't you pick me for your group of good little soldiers? Afraid I might be too rough for Raif's star pupils?"

The smirk on Asher's face didn't hide the hard glint of his eyes. I'd known tough guys like him. Hell, I was just like him. Acting like he didn't give a shit was just a smoke screen to keep people at a distance. "Are you saying you want babysitting duty?"

"Why not," Asher said, moving on to stretch his hamstrings. "I haven't seen much action lately."

Really? Action? Following Anya around sounded boring as hell to me. "I'm not sure what your idea of action is, Asher, but I doubt any of us are going to see much action tailing after Anya for the next couple of months." Or longer. *Shit*.

"Are you kidding?" He rotated his ankles, eyes sparkling with anticipation. "The last time she went out alone, someone shot the shit out of her ride. Sniper rifle. Fifty cal."

I guess Xander's definition of "threat" and mine were a little different. I'd been thinking harassing phone calls, nasty letters in the mail—my stomach clenched involuntarily—a mysterious postcard or two . . . not exactly execution-style shootings. And a fifty-caliber bullet? The monster rifle capable of shooting that kind of ammo was more of a sniper cannon. Bullets that size would rip through a tree trunk from half a mile away. Someone meant business.

"That's not the best part, though." There was a best part? Asher was bouncing on the balls of his feet, swinging his arms back and forth. "Whoever shot at her left a wicked calling card. The bullets were engraved with some sort of symbol. Nice touch, if you ask me."

He sounded way too adolescent-boy-excited for his tight, muscular build and feral gaze. I couldn't help but crack a grin, and I wondered if my face would crack as well. "What did it look like? Could you draw the symbol for me?"

"I can do one better. I can show you the bullets."

Good. Better than good, actually. Whatever this symbol was, it could be the first step in finding out who'd threatened Anya. "Later. In the meantime, you ready for a workout?"

Asher stretched his neck from side to side and cracked his knuckles. "Ready."

I didn't waste any time showing off. I figured the best way to assert myself as the new alpha in town was to prove right from the get-go that I was more than able to kick some serious ass. Melding with the light, I left my corporeal form, passing back to my solid body right behind Asher. A swift kick to the middle of his back sent him flying face-first to the mat.

"You've got to be quicker than that," I said.

Before I could blink, Asher turned over and kicked himself up to a standing position. The kid was way faster than I thought. He'd been holding back during Raif's exhibition matches, and I had a strange feeling he was holding back, even now. Food for thought.

"That was awesome," he said, adopting a defensive stance. "I heard you could do that, but seeing it firsthand is even better."

Not many Shaedes in Xander's household had seen me merge with the light, though all of them—and most of Seattle's supernatural population—had heard about it. I was used to being a freak show, but the novelty didn't seem to slow Asher down. He didn't stand around and wait for an attack. His defensive posture turned to offense in a single breath. He charged with steps as light as any assassin worth her salt and looked to my right shoulder. I spun left to avoid impact, but the glance had been nothing but a feint. Lunging left, he caught me just below the ribs with an elbow and I went down—hard.

I *so* wanted to stay right there on the mat. I forced myself up, fought through the crippling ghost of pain stabbing through my chest. It wasn't *real*. Not truly physical. A broken heart couldn't kill me. Asher didn't give me time to recover. He spun, kicked his leg out, aiming for my head. I blocked with a forearm, before dissolving into nothing, reappearing at his left side. He favored his right side. Not good. He'd have to learn to use all of his body when he fought, or his opponents would capitalize on his weakness. I went for his knee. He needed to learn his lesson from me before someone else taught him the hard way. I rammed my heel where the joints met, careful not to exert enough pressure to break his kneecap. Asher buckled, and I followed up with a sharp jab to the lower left quadrant of his back. The kid didn't even whimper.

In fact, it seemed to only fuel his determination.

I have to admit, since I didn't have much in the way of formal training, Asher had me beat in the style department. Raif had primarily trained me in swordplay, though he'd thrown in some martial arts and hand-to-hand combat along the way. My own style was more like a sampling of several martial arts styles combined with a heavy dose of street brawl. Asher, on the other hand, possessed an in-depth knowledge of Tae Kwon Do and Kung Fu, and every movement of his body favored his expertise. Flowed like river water.

His confidence impressed me, and his speed amazed me. Asher's focus became unbreakable as he settled into a rhythm, his arms swirling above his head and in front of him, fists jabbing in quick succession. He alternated between knee kicks and straight-legged assaults that had me leaving my corporeal form time and again just to avoid impact. Fast. Lightning in a bottle. My first impressions are never wrong; Asher was definitely dangerous.

My breath came heavy, sweat beading on my forehead and rolling down my back. Every contact made was a pain I welcomed because it made me forget for a moment about the hollow ache in my chest. Shaking off the sorrow, I forced the crippling emotion down into the deepest part of me and stepped up my game. I didn't consider it cheating; I wasn't the only creature in the world that could pass invisible in the daylight hours. A Lyhtan attack would be far worse than anything I could dish out.

So I didn't go easy on Asher. Or myself. I had to work my ass off to keep the upper hand, but I fought like my life depended on it. My reputation sure as hell did. Kick, jab, lunge. Elbow up. Duck and roll. Block once, twice. Over and over. And again. Incorporeal more times than not, I regained the upper hand through speed and stealth, rather than technique. A sweeping kick to his feet sent Asher to the floor, and I pinned him down with my fist to his shoulder. He bucked against me, and I increased the pressure. "Stay down, kid. We're done."

Asher relaxed. In fact, he looked relieved. Thank god. I was beat to shit and tired as fuck. Asserting yourself as the alpha is hard damn work.

"So, when do you head out for babysitting duty?" Asher asked as he toweled his face and neck. The adrenaline-infused sparkle had left his eyes, but the wild glint remained. He seemed much too young to look so haunted. I wanted to ask if I had the same look in my own eyes.

Instead, I pressed my heels into the soft foam mat, anchoring myself in place. "Don't you mean, when do *we* head out?"

Asher didn't even bat a lash at my words. The kid was damn near unflappable. "You sure you want to go head-to-head with Raif? Because the way I heard it, your team doesn't have room for a fifth member."

"You let me worry about Raif. Be ready by noon. I want everyone assembled and prepped before we go anywhere."

Asher gave me a sidelong glance. "Do you want to see those bullets first?"

"Yeah. Let's do that."

I smelled like a locker room. Every inch of me was sticky with sweat and my stomach was bitching up a storm. Food and a shower would have to wait another few minutes, though. I wanted to see our hit man's calling card.

Off the gym in a smaller, separate space was a weapons room. Swords, guns, axes, ammo, body armor . . . everything an army would need and then some. Even custom-made and black market shit from the looks of it. What did Raif, or Xander for that matter, care about legality? The Shaede Nation considered itself a kingdom apart from human laws. They wouldn't bat a lash at procuring some less-than-legal weaponry.

"When Raif recovered the bullets, he hid them in here," Asher said, moving a few boxes away from the far wall. "Put them in this safe."

I leaned against a counter, my fingers tracing the pattern carved into one of the axe handles. "Who else saw him do this?" Didn't sound like Raif to be so secretive and yet not watch his back.

Asher turned his attention to the safe. "Only me."

"How many have the combination?" Again, a little strange.

"Just Raif."

I pushed myself away from the counter, walked toward Asher. "And you have it how . . . ?"

Asher turned around and flashed a wicked, totally unapologetic grin. "I was in here when he hid the bullets, watched him enter the combo."

He punched a series of numbers into a keypad and jerked down on the heavy handle. The safe door swung open, creaking like its uses were few and far between. Raif was the slyest person I knew. No way had Asher been in the room without Raif noticing. "Call me untrusting, but I'm having a hard time swallowing that."

"I'm quiet," Asher said with a shrug. The expression was easy, but his eyes were hard and guarded. "When I want to be, I'm practically invisible." I believed it. When he'd come into the gym this morning, his footfalls had been featherlight. In fact, if not for my own heightened senses, I doubt I would have heard him at all. And, honestly, now that I thought back, I hadn't sensed his actual physical presence until he was right on top of me. It was like he'd materialized out of thin air.

What had been a growing curiosity about Asher was now steering toward suspicion. The young Shaede obviously had his secrets, and secrets could be dangerous. I was more determined than ever to put him on my team. If anything, so I could keep an eye on him. "You're either smart as hell or dumb as a sack of rocks, kid. If Raif finds out you know that combo, you might as well kiss your ass good-bye."

Asher reached into the safe, scooped something up and held his hand out to me. "Are you going to tell him?"

I reached out, and Asher dropped the heavy metal into my palm. "Not unless I have to. Quit spying on people, and don't break into any more safes. Otherwise, Raif won't get the chance to deal with you because I'll take care of it myself. I don't have patience for eavesdroppers or thieves. Got it?"

Asher's gaze dropped to the floor. "Got it."

I wondered how long Raif was planning to keep this little tidbit to himself? If I was supposed to find the asshole responsible, I needed all the information I could get. I picked up one of the bullets; the front had been mashed flat, the tip curling back like shredded ribbon. But the butt of the bullet was intact and completely pristine.

Some calling card. I traced the engraving with my finger. The symbol wasn't anything I recognized, but that didn't mean much. A crescent moon lying like a boat, tips pointing to the sky—"It's called a horned moon," Asher interjected when he noticed me tracing the crescent—was wound from tip to tip by the thick body of a serpent. The artwork was intricate, with every scale of the serpent's body etched in detail. Its eyes stared out at me, the irises speared with a vertical slash of black pupil, and the creature's mouth gaped open to expose twin fangs jutting down from its upper jaw. I couldn't imagine what sort of tool you'd need to engrave something so small with such precision. Quite beautiful, actually.

"Do you know what this symbol means?"

Asher shook his head. "I don't think Raif does, either. He looked at it for a long time before putting it away. Might not mean anything at all."

I doubted that. But until I could figure it out, those bullets needed to stay right where Raif had left them. "Here." I handed them back to Asher. "Put these away and don't *ever* let me catch you pulling anything sneaky again."

Asher nodded, which didn't do much to instill me with confidence. I had a feeling he didn't want to make an outright vow not to stay out of trouble because he wasn't sure he could. Honestly, he reminded me a little of myself, so I could hardly blame him. Trouble had a tendency to follow wherever I went. "Meet me and the rest of the team back here in an hour. And for god's sake, lock that safe, and put everything back the way you found it!"

It was scary how quiet Asher could be. I barely heard a rustle as he moved the boxes back into place.

Chapter 9

I twisted the ring on my left thumb. An unconscious act, one I usually did when something worried me. I'd been so shocked at seeing another woman in Ty's apartment, I failed to give a passing thought to our bond. Was it still intact? And if it was, how would Tyler feel about being bound to me if he no longer loved me? He might even expect me to break our bond. My fingers traced the carved outline of the bear with tender affection and I felt the unwelcome sting of tears at my eyes.

Damn it.

Damn him.

Damn *her*, whoever she was.

And *damn me* for being foolish enough to care.

As I approached the formal dining room, I became one with the light, opting to see the seated diners before they saw me. When I passed through the door, I let out a sigh of relief and regained my corporeal form. Empty. *Hallelujah*.

My absence hadn't gone unnoticed, however. A silver dome covered a plate right at the place I sat for the couple of meals I'd attended. At least I wasn't going to have to spend my morning hungry. Removing the dome, I inhaled the aroma of frittata, fried potatoes, and delicate fruit tarts. Xander sure as hell didn't scrimp on the food budget. And he didn't eat anything that didn't look Food Network perfect. Which suited me just fine. The most elegant breakfast I'd ever made was a bowl of cereal.

"What happened last night?" Raif said from the doorway.

"Don't you have anything better to do than follow me around?" Raif's stalker act was totally unimpressive.

"Shouldn't you be walking through the house glowering at people?"

"I think you have me mistaken for my brother," Raif replied, leaning against the jamb. His cool demeanor raised my hackles. "He's in quite the mood this morning. It appears he's readying himself to defend your honor for some reason. He thinks something very bad must have happened to you. You went out yesterday?"

I didn't bother sitting down, just picked up a fork and started shoveling food into my mouth. "If you know I went out, why are you asking for confirmation?" I wasn't in the mood to discuss what happened yesterday with Raif or anyone else. "Since when am I under house arrest, anyway? It's Anya you have to worry about, not me." Raif quirked a brow and I thought, for a second, about throwing my fork at him. "It's none of your business."

"True." He folded his arms in front of his chest, hunkering down for a standoff.

"So, drop it."

He answered me with silence, but his blue eyes looked straight into my soul. I hated that he knew me well enough to see through me. "What's on the agenda for today? Anya said she has some kind of appointment."

Silence. And that goddamned stare.

I shoved enough frittata into my mouth to choke a horse. I figured Raif wouldn't expect me to talk if it was almost too full to actually chew. I managed to swallow without suffocating, and I met Raif's stare head-on before popping in a few potatoes to join the frittata.

"Quit staring at me!" I didn't quite yell, but I wanted to. I chugged a glass of orange juice and popped an entire tart into my mouth. I bet I looked just *fetching*, stuffing my face like I was. Ignoring my uncouth behavior, Raif only looked at me as if he already knew what had happened and just needed verbal confirmation.

I cleared my throat and tried to lend an apathetic air to my words. "Tyler's back." My gaze dropped to the polished surface of Xander's antique table, and I fought like hell to keep the tears at bay. "He didn't come home alone."

"I'm sure there's a reasonable explanation. . . ." Even Raif didn't sound convinced.

"Like what?" I snorted. "She's his long-lost sister? Cousin? Niece?"

Raif shrugged as if to say, *Could be.*

"A drop-dead gorgeous, supermodel cousin. Yeah, sure. Believe me, Raif, she wasn't family, and she's *way* out of my league."

But not Ty's, obviously. He'd finally met someone better. Beautiful. I'd always thought Tyler deserved a softer woman than me. And he found her. Boy, did he find her. A goddess made of luscious curves, a cherubic mouth, liquid shimmering eyes, and feminine delicacy. For the first time in my life, I found that I was jealous of a woman for being . . . womanly.

"I have a hard time believing he would treat you so carelessly." Raif pushed himself off the jamb and rubbed the back of his neck. "But it does explain Xander's gallant mood this morning."

Please. The last thing I needed was the King of Egocentric Bullshit coming to my rescue. "Yeah, well, he spies on me more than you do."

Raif's brow regained its curious arch, but he could just keep on wondering. The goings-on in my room last night were none of his business and that was one stand-off I would sure as hell win. "He left the food for you," Raif said and jutted his chin toward my now empty plate.

Wasn't that big of him. The only thing anybody gave a shit about around here was whether or not I'd eaten. I felt like a fattened calf being prepared for the slaughter. "Are we through discussing my love life so we can get to work? Or do you want to braid my hair while I tell you the rest?"

"Anya has a meeting with Dylan McBride this afternoon to discuss some business matters pertinent to the Crown." Guess the comment about braiding my hair had done the trick. "Dylan's office has top-notch security, but what I'm concerned about is getting her from point A to point B."

That was a given, considering someone had shot her car to shit the last time she'd gone out. "What are we talking, a full-on motorcade? Or are we keeping this nice and intimate?"

"Low-key. One vehicle, with an unmarked escort following."

"And why would that be?" I left the door open for him to volunteer the information about the bullets.

"Someone opened fire on her Mercedes last week."

At least Raif had come clean to me. Though I knew there shouldn't have been any doubt. Raif would never keep secrets from me that would prevent me from doing my job. "Ballistics?"

"A fifty-caliber bullet with a strange marking etched on the casing. Whoever shot at her knew the car was armored."

"Can I see it?"

"I'll get you detailed photos of the etchings. I have some people looking into it. Could be relevant to nothing at all."

I doubted that. Assassins loved calling cards. In an anonymous business, it was the only thing that made us real. Unlike my brethren, though, I never left a calling card. I liked being invisible too much for notoriety. "I have someone who might be able to identify it." Levi, the part-time bartender at The Pit, was a supernatural encyclopedia. For a few—or rather a few hundred—bucks he could answer almost any question. I didn't want to use him unless it was absolutely necessary, though. And if Raif was stumped, it was necessary.

"I'll let you know if we need to bring someone else in on it." Raif liked to play things close to the hip. "I'd rather not involve outsiders at this point."

Outsiders being anyone who didn't live within Xander's walls. "Fair enough. When should I be ready to leave?"

"No later than one thirty."

Perfect. I'd told Asher to meet me and the rest of the team at noon. That gave me plenty of time to lay out a game plan. "You'll provide the cars?"

"They'll be parked out front."

"One more thing." I wasn't sure how Raif would react to me adding Asher to my team. I hoped to hell he wouldn't blow a gasket. "I told you that I wanted Asher, and I haven't changed my mind. I'm taking him with us."

"So, you think you're able to make that sort of decision, do you?"

The flat, dark edge to Raif's voice told me he sure as hell wasn't happy. "Look, the kid can fight. He's smart, too. And"—I chewed my bottom lip, trying to find the words to convince him—"yeah, I know, he's one of Xander's, not yours, and you think he might be a little untrustworthy, blah, blah, whatever. But I think we need him. Don't ask me why, my gut's just telling me *I* need him with me."

I tossed my fork down onto the plate, for some reason perversely satisfied at the loud clang disrupting the quiet. I pointedly ignored Raif's hawkish gaze, letting the sound of silver on porcelain distract me. Shit. He was going to shut me down. It was written all over his face. So I didn't give him the chance. He couldn't deny me if I wasn't here to listen.

"Where are you going?" Raif asked as I slipped past him and out into the hallway.

"You need to get a new hobby, Raif," I said over my shoulder. "Because if you don't stop breathing down my neck, I'm not going to like you so much anymore. I'm taking Asher."

By his derisive snort, followed by a low chuckle, I knew he was willing to risk it.

After a screaming-hot shower, I changed into my signature black. The shower hadn't done much to revitalize me, but at least I didn't smell anymore. My body wasn't happy with me; I'd thrown it into patterns of sleep and malnutrition and then shocked it back to life with gourmet food and insomnia. If I was going to retain any shred of sanity, I was going to have to find balance. Soon.

I strapped my katana to my back and sheathed the dagger at my thigh. I reached for my duster but reconsidered. Long, flapping tails and loose sleeves weren't conducive to close-range fighting, and I needed to be as unhindered as possible if anything sketchy went down. I cracked each of my knuckles, lifted my arms to the sky, and stretched. Was I ready to take responsibility for someone's safety? I usually took lives; I wasn't in the business of saving them.

My cell phone vibrated on the dresser, an annoying pulse that set my teeth on edge. I grabbed it, checked the caller ID, and my heart took a nosedive right into my gut: TYLER. Fin-

gers twitchy to answer, I held the phone in my palm and
stared at the digital screen. I wanted to answer. I needed to
hear his voice, to know in his tone if he'd truly fallen out of
love with me. But my pride clamped down tight on my emotions and prevented me from doing what I longed to do. Instead of answering, I shoved the phone in my back pocket
and left well enough alone. I didn't need to hear his apologies, his heartfelt well wishes, his lamentations that things
hadn't worked out between us.

I waited for the buzzing to start up again, like it always did
when I didn't answer. The silence that stretched out for what
seemed like forever both frightened and disappointed me. I
should've answered. Just to hear his voice. No matter how
painful it might have been. And honestly, without even a
voice mail, I had no reason to call him back. Damn my stub-
bornness. Now I'd never know why he'd called. What he'd
intended to say.

As I whispered through the hallways, a breath of air toward the gym, I focused on the task at hand. No room for
personal demons and emotions while Anya—and her unborn
child—needed me on high alert. I tucked that excess baggage
deep down inside of me, turned off everything but the hard,
coldhearted bitch Azriel had taught me to be. I guess he'd
been good for something after all. The sound of low voices
coupled with the dull clink of metal on metal greeted me as
I took corporeal form and entered the armory off the gym.
Asher and the rest of the team had assembled, and they were
arming themselves for battle.

"Check it," Julian said, flashing the pair of guns clutched
in his fists. "I modified the clips. Homemade ammo, too. Totally badass. Don't think I'm going to share the secret, either.
You want custom shit, get creative and make it yourself."

"Custom shit," Liam grunted. "Weak shit, more like. Guns
are for pussies."

Though I didn't exactly agree with Liam, he did have a
point. With the ability to heal so quickly, most supernaturals
wouldn't be fazed by a bullet. Effective for slowing down an
opponent, but not killing. Shaedes in particular could easily
avoid a bullet or even a blow from a sword at night. We were
most vulnerable during the day. And even then, a gunshot

wound wasn't deadly. Of course, there were exceptions to every rule. Certain bonds such as marriage and birth gave us dominion over each other's lives no matter the hour, but in the case of Anya's protection, I had a feeling Julian's "custom shit" was more for show than anything.

"You're just jealous," Julian said playfully before he kissed the barrel of each gun, "that you're not fucking brilliant like me."

"Can the shit talk," I said, gripping the dagger hilt at my thigh. "We're rolling out in less than an hour, and I want everyone ready to go."

The chatter died, and an uncomfortable silence took its place the second I walked through the door. Asher stood at the rear of the group, on the outskirts, watching me with a guarded expression. His arms were crossed at his chest, and he looked outfitted and ready to go. I guess I could be thankful someone was on task.

I eyeballed the four other members of the team, taking note with a glance those who hadn't finished getting ready. "Here, Loulie." Julian's tone had lost some of its arrogance. He handed Louella two sheathed daggers. "You need anything else?"

She attached the daggers to her belt, one at each hip, and pulled the hem of her hip-length jacket over the top of them. "I'm good."

Myles and Liam quietly grabbed a sword and dagger each, while Julian added a set of throwing knives to his already overloaded ensemble. Aside from the guns tucked into holsters dangling from each shoulder, he carried a dagger and a short saber. Not the low-key escort I was hoping for.

"You never know what you might need," he said with a smile when he noticed me giving him the once-over.

"Well, if you ladies are done choosing the right accessories for your outfits, let's get out of here. I don't want to keep Anya's admirer waiting." Each member of my team had the good sense to adopt serious expressions. This wasn't a game, this was a job. And I don't fuck around when it comes to work. "There'll be two cars waiting for us out front. I want Asher and Liam with me in the first car with Anya. Louella, Julian, and Myles, you'll follow in the second car. Who's the best driver?"

"Loulie, for sure," Julian smiled. "She's Gran Turismo good."

"Louella, you drive the unmarked, but keep a few car lengths back. If Anya's attacker is watching us, I want him to think she's alone. Got it?" She responded with a curt nod. I liked her more by the second. "If you see anything suspicious, I don't want any of you charging off like overeager idiots, you got that?" The group nodded. But, damn it, how was I supposed to communicate with the second car? My phone? Not very practical if we found ourselves in a quick-reaction scenario.

"Here." Asher handed me a small earpiece as if he'd read my mind. "We all have them."

Gotta love technology. I slid the bud into my ear and guided the clear spiral cord behind my neck. I clipped the tiny battery pack to my collar along with the mic. The setup wasn't bulky or awkward, and it solved my communication problems. Pretty slick, actually. Made me feel all double-oh-seven. "If you notice *anything*, you tell me. I'll deal with it. Anyone who tries to pull heroic bullshit stunts is off the team. Understood?"

"Uh, what's up with the extra wheel?" Myles jerked his head in Asher's direction. "I was under the impression that this was a four-man team."

Louella cleared her throat, and Myles added, "You know what I mean."

"If you want to get technical," I said, "this is *my team*. And if I want to add one or fifty more people to this group, that's my prerogative. Got it?"

Myles held his hands up in surrender. "Got it."

Myles's questioning of Asher's presence on the team made it obvious that no one was interested in angering Raif. Lucky for them it didn't bother me all that much. "Asher is coming, end of story. Anybody else have a problem with that?"

Silence answered me, signaling the end of the discussion. "Well, then, let's get moving."

Spinning on a booted heel, I led the way back through the bowels of Xander's ridiculously large house, up one flight of stairs and out to the foyer. I didn't turn back to see if my team followed, but I heard their footsteps trailing behind. Anya waited by the front door, her violet eyes focused on her husband's face. Dimitri stood in front of her, hands perched atop her shoulders, speaking quietly in Russian. Her expression was soft, her gaze drinking him in. He leaned down and placed a gentle kiss on her lips. The damned hollow ache throbbed in my chest as I watched their tender moment, and I forced the pain away. *Screw love.*

"Ready, princess?" I asked, heading straight for the door. "Let's get this show on the road."

I yanked open the door with unnecessary decorum and swept my arm in front of me, careful to keep my head bowed. Yeah, it was completely bitchy, but misery loves company, and I wanted the whole world to share in mine. Anya took Dimitri's hand and brought his palm to her cheek before turning, her thick, dark braid lashing out like a whip. She stalked right past me, didn't even give me a passing sneer. Her nose was so far up in the air she might as well be a princess. Xander treated her like one, after all.

I waited for my team to file out the door behind Anya. I turned to give Dimitri a wave in parting—he *was* a good guy, after all—but all I got was an eyeful of the king himself. He'd come down the stairs and stood at the third to last step, one hand resting on the banister, the other clenched at his side. His gaze burned right through me, his lips drawn in a tight line.

"You missed breakfast," Xander said, his voice low.

Seriously? Brooding over *another* meal? Give me a break. "No, I didn't. I got the plate you left."

Xander took the last three stairs at a slow and measured pace, probably to amp up the drama factor. "How are you feeling?"

"No offense, Xander, but I'm a little busy. You know, keeping an eye on your girl. How about we save the small talk for later?" Xander opened his mouth to speak but I cut him off. "And seriously, if you mention one more meal, snack, or otherwise, I'm not coming back tonight or ever again. Understood? I'll eat when and where I want. What *is* it with you and food?"

The king clamped his mouth shut, and his expression became hesitant, unreadable. Or was it something else. Hurt?

"Be careful today." He walked right to the door and turned to face me, blocking my way out.

"Don't worry, Xander, I'll take good care of her."

Xander leaned forward, so close I could feel him, though we weren't yet touching. Electricity charged the air between us, almost tangible, crawling over my skin in a way that wasn't entirely unpleasant. The thrill of anticipation. A nervous sizzle exploded in my stomach. "I was talking about *you*, Darian." His eyes clouded with an emotion I couldn't decipher. He lifted my hand from the doorknob and brought my fingers to his lips, soft and warm. His gaze drank me in the way Anya's had Dimitri. Like he was dying of thirst and I was a pool of water. "If I'd known moving you in would ignite your jealousy so easily, I would have done it ages ago. Be safe today."

Damn him and his royal arrogance. I should have listened to Raif. The King of Opportunistic Bullshit would have me climbing the walls in a week. He'd use every chance he got to exhibit his cocksure posturing. He held on to my hand, his grip gentle, not possessive. Just his skin on mine. My breath hitched in my chest, and tiny pinpricks of sensation migrated from my head down the length of my body. "Hurry back," he murmured and stepped to the side of me, out of the doorway.

I didn't answer him. Honestly, I doubted my mouth would work well enough to form coherent words. I just walked right past him, through the door to the cars. I hated the way Xander could play me like a well-tuned instrument. Playing to my need for independence, he hadn't tried to stop me, hadn't insisted on watching over me. He simply stepped out of the way so I could do my job and walk straight toward danger. Xander treated me like he knew I was capable. Trusted me to take care of myself, my team, and Anya.

And the bastard knew I'd like that. I liked it a lot.

Chapter 10

Our driver's name was Robert, and he was armed almost as heavily as Julian. He wasn't too talkative, but that didn't matter to me. My team was already small, and with Louella piloting the second car containing Myles and Julian, I couldn't spare another body being tied up behind the wheel if shit went down. Ever pragmatic, Raif had arranged for our chauffeur and I couldn't have been more grateful for his forward thinking. Anya sat in the backseat; I wanted her out of plain view. She wasn't being used as bait, per se, but I knew from my own experience that when a mark becomes hard to hit, it makes the job that much more enticing. I wanted our assassin to believe Anya's life had been turned upside down—which wasn't too far from the truth—thereby putting her just out of reach. A low-key escort was perfect. It told our assassin, "*We* know about you, we just don't want *anyone else* to know." We rode in one of Xander's tricked-out Range Rovers. Black, of course. With custom everything, right down to the stitching on the leather seats and tinted, bullet-proof windows.

I took the front seat while Asher sat next to Anya, and Liam took the third row. Literally. He was so goddamned big his body almost didn't fit in the bench seat. He didn't look too happy about the seating arrangements either, but he'd just have to stick it out. The drive from Capitol Hill to downtown wouldn't take *too* long.

"How long will your meeting take?"

Anya tilted her head to stare out the tinted window. "An hour. Maybe less."

Dylan McBride's office was conspicuously located in the

heart of downtown in the Columbia Center building—a sky-scraper jutting over the Seattle skyline. The tallest building on the west coast, seventy-six stories, and chock-full of high-end tenants. I guess being the human liaison for the super-natural world made you about as high-end as you could get, and apparently Mr. McBride liked his flash 'n flair.

I'd met him only once, at the PNT Summit with Xander a little over a year ago. Dylan handled business matters perti-nent to many of the Pacific Northwest Territory's heavy hit-ters, so he automatically earned a seat at the grown-ups table. Dylan was the "face" of many a faceless client, something that came in pretty handy when you looked as far from hu-man as possible. Case in point: a seven-foot-tall, praying mantis–looking Lyhtan. Inhuman looks aside, the supernatu-ral population often had issues such as the transference of property and ownership; sticky business at best when you lived for hundreds—if not thousands—of years. That's where Mr. McBride came in.

I had no idea what Anya's business with Dylan was, and I didn't care. That was between her and Xander. My job was to find the asshole trying to kill her and take him out before he did permanent damage to the king's favorite pet and her unborn child. "Julian, you see anything?" I felt a little awk-ward talking into thin air, but the mic worked like a charm.

"Nada. Unless you count a shit-ton of traffic and enough human pedestrians to clog a subway tube. Seriously, how in the hell are we supposed to pinpoint a threat with so much congestion?"

Beat the hell out of me. Singling out a threat in downtown Seattle would be like looking for a needle in a *stack* of nee-dles. It was the perfect place to take down a target unde-tected. Just the right amount of cover. Ingenious, really.

"Keep your eyes open," I said, checking the street at either side. "He's out there; I can feel it."

The rest of the drive passed in silence. I kept my eyes peeled for any sign of trouble, reaching out with invisible feelers to better sense any supernatural creatures in the vicin-ity. It wasn't a Shaede gift; I assumed it had more to do with my position as a Guardian of *O Anel*. Every creature had a unique signature, like a sound wave that rippled across my skin. At the moment, I couldn't feel a damn thing except for the Shaedes a couple of car lengths behind us and the ones sitting next to me.

"Circle the block twice," I told our driver as we approached the Columbia Center. It might confuse a potential attack if we got lost in the shuffle of traffic. Robert gave me a sideways glance but didn't argue as he changed lanes and sped up—at least as much as midday traffic would allow.

"Louella, I want you to drop off Myles at the back side of the building, and Julian, you take the south end. Keep circling the block after you've dropped them off. If we have to get Anya out of here in a hurry, I want you mobile and ready to go."

"Gotcha," Louella answered in my ear. "I'll backtrack, take some alleys if it comes down to it. I won't be tailed."

"Good." I turned to the driver and pointed at the building's front entrance. "No use trying to sneak her in the back. Our guy will be waiting for that. Let's keep this business as usual for now."

Robert nodded as he finished lap number two, changed lanes, and pulled up to the building. I turned back in my seat, made eye contact with both Liam and Asher. "Ready?"

Liam's eyes were glazed over with excitement, but Asher's were serious, dark. And damned deadly. He looked straight at me. "Ready."

"Anya?" I said without looking at her.

"You don't need to be so dramatic, you know. Let's just get this over with."

I nodded to my team, knew Louella was ready to go with Julian and Myles. "All right, then, time to meet Dylan."

I jumped out of my seat and unstrapped the dagger from my thigh, tucking it inconspicuously in my waistband at my back. I pulled my shirt over the hilt—no use drawing unnecessary attention. I left my katana in the car—gave it one last, longing look—and though it killed me to do it, opened Anya's door for her. Asher and Liam followed my lead, leaving everything bulky behind and concealing what could be easily hidden, which still left us well armed. My senses were fine-tuned to everything around me, a sort of sonar that bounced off of every living thing within a hundred-yard radius. The entire transition of ushering Anya out of the Range Rover and into the building was a little too anticlimactic. I suppose I'd been a tad overdramatic—hence the cache of weapons we'd left in the car—but if something went down and I failed to protect her, Raif and Xander would have my ass. Not a position I wanted to be in.

The staccato of Anya's ridiculous heels echoed on the marble lobby floor. Curious stares followed us to the wall of elevators, but none of them carried the energy of the supernatural. I tapped a booted toe as the silver doors slid shut and the elevator jettisoned us to Dylan McBride's office. Anya looked bored. Liam stood, arms crossed, legs braced apart, the blue tattoos on his scalp reflected in the mirrored ceiling. Asher stood eerily still, the rise and fall of his chest as undetectable as it was inaudible as he breathed. Damn, that kid was scary quiet.

I allowed a sigh of relief when the elevator deposited us on Dylan's floor. I'd been particularly worried about an attack on the ride up. It's what I would've done. Sort of like shooting fish in a barrel. I was glad that Anya's hit man and I didn't share the same sense of imagination.

The lobby of Dylan McBride's office was no less impressive than the rest of the building. Glass tables, modern leather chairs, rich woods, and expensive art graced the small space. His receptionist's desk looked like it cost more than the average person's monthly salary. She looked up from her computer screen, her eyes alight with recognition. A pleasant smile curved her lips, and she pressed a button on her headset without uttering a word to Anya. "Mr. McBride, your one o'clock is here."

She nodded her head—as if he could actually see her—and depressed the button on her headset. "He's expecting you, Ms. Chernikova, go right in."

Anya didn't even give me a passing glance, just strode right through the door into Dylan's office. I rocked back on my heels, looked at Asher and Liam, and jerked my chin toward the waiting area. No sense hanging around the receptionist's desk for an hour. I felt like an idiot, and the strange looks I kept getting from her weren't doing much for my mood. I mean, give me a break, at least I wasn't wrapped in head-to-toe leather like Anya. But I might as well have had horns growing out of my head or something. I felt like I was being sized up, and I *hate* that.

As I paced the lobby, I wished for the millionth time that I'd told Xander to shove this job up his royal ass. I thought I might just *die* from the excitement of it all. Following Anya . . . driving her around . . . waiting as she went to this appointment or that.

Though Anya wasn't concerned about her entourage, at least she didn't keep us waiting. Her meeting took just under an hour. In the same manner she'd gone into the meeting, she exited, paying just as much attention to me.

Asher and Liam fell in step behind me: Liam's footfalls were precise, exact, and Asher's—well, I wouldn't have known he was there at all if I hadn't *felt* his presence, and even that seemed barely there. The ride down the elevator was much too slow for my taste, and the quiet that settled in the metal box sucked most of the breathable oxygen right out of the atmosphere. We were all tense for whatever reason, mine being that I felt this whole day thus far had been a monumental waste of my time. Although, what would I be doing if I wasn't shadowing Anya? Sleeping? Guzzling a fifth of bourbon? Drowning in my sorrow?

I gave a heads-up to Robert—the earpiece was a godsend—and he was waiting for us at the front entrance when we emerged from the building. I let Liam move out in front, sandwiching Anya between us. Her heels clicked in rhythm with the sway of the long, dark braid cascading from the top of her head. I wondered how in the hell she could be so comfortable and self-assured dressed like she was. But I guess if you looked as striking as she did in the leather ensemble, self-consciousness was the least of your problems.

Eyes focused on the Range Rover, I sent out a blanket of invisible feelers. Nothing out of the ordinary tripped my senses. Anya's step faltered, and she looked nervously behind her, reaching back to lay her fingers on her left shoulder blade. She shrugged as if trying to shake something away and paused—looked right, and then left—and quickened her pace toward the car.

"Anya."

I heard her name on the wind, like a whisper.

"Anya."

A little louder this time.

"Anya!"

Roared like a battle cry, her name echoed off the walls of the surrounding buildings.

Liam stopped dead in his tracks, and Anya crouched behind him like a rabbit hiding from a predator in tall grass. I saw nothing. Felt nothing. Focused all of my concentration on my surroundings and still: *nothing*.

"Get in the car, Anya," I commanded. "Get in the fucking car, *now*."

Had no one else heard the voice? We all sure as hell had, but the humans passing by seemed totally unfazed.

"Gun!" Asher shouted from behind me. "To your left!"

Liam spun on the balls of his feet, quick and agile despite his size, and seized Anya around the waist. He tucked her against his body and ran toward the car. Robert's door flew open, and he ran to open a door for Liam, flinging it wide before jumping back behind the wheel.

"Don't wait for us," I shouted. "Just get her the hell—"

Before I could finish my sentence, the shots rang out. People screamed and scattered, brakes screeched, and the sound of metal crunching and glass shattering added to the cacophony. I drew my dagger from behind my back and hit the ground, turning as I fell so I could identify the shooter.

Shooters.

Fuck.

Four of them—and each one human. What the hell was going on? "Don't fire back," I warned my team. "Just get Anya out of here."

I rolled to my left and took a chance, merging with the light. No one noticed; the humans on the street were all too busy looking for cover. I watched as Liam threw Anya in the backseat of the Range Rover, climbing in after her. Asher was gone, but I didn't have time to worry about him—he was a big boy, he could take care of himself.

"Darian, where do you want me?" Louella asked in my earpiece with the calmness of a trained soldier.

I paused to take stock of the situation. One shooter was

situated thirty yards away, his torso hanging out of an older model sedan. Another stood across the busy street, standing at the edge of the sidewalk as if ready to run straight through the buzzing traffic for a shot at Anya. The third shooter waited farther down the street, blocking our way out, and the fourth . . . well, the fourth shooter had burst through the doors of the Columbia Center, racing toward the Range Rover in a full-out sprint.

"Robert"—my breath came heavily, keeping pace with my pounding heart—"watch out for the gun at the crosswalk. I don't want any innocents taking a bullet because of us, but get through the intersection—fast. Louella, take Julian and Myles and comb the area—half a mile radius. Our guy's here somewhere, the humans are just a distraction."

I had no doubt about that. I'd seen humans under the influence of magic before. Lyhtans could compel humans, and under the right circumstances, so could the Fae. I'd experienced compulsion firsthand. And these people had no idea what they were doing or why.

My business had always been killing. Innocent lives were saved inadvertently because I took out the bad guy. But I'd never had to play the hero and act with the sole purpose of protecting someone.

Until recently.

I didn't have time to devise a game plan. Guns were firing from all directions. The bullets wouldn't kill us—or Anya—but again, our assassin must have known that. Today's objective: chaos. Rattle Anya as much as possible. I had a feeling it worked. Starting down the street, invisible in the cover of daylight, I headed for the human whose body was half out of his car. He wasn't looking at anything but Xander's Range Rover, a nine-millimeter clutched in his hands. I became corporeal as my elbow swung, catching him in the temple. His head jerked back, his eyes unfocused and blank. It didn't stop him from squeezing off a couple more shots. With a quick jerk, I wrestled the gun out of his hands and delivered another blow to his face, harder than the first, but not hard enough to do too much damage. He slumped out of the car's window.

One down, three to go.

The wail of sirens sounded in the distance. I didn't have much time. If I couldn't neutralize the threat, someone would be killed. "Darian!" Asher's voice came through loud and clear in my earpiece. "I've got the shooter across the street. You've got one behind you, running like hell for the intersection."

I turned, and sure as shit, the woman who'd come out of the Columbia Center hightailed it down the street as fast as her Jimmy Choos would carry her. I took off after her, no longer concerned with being unseen. The Range Rover's tires squealed as Robert dodged through traffic, and the windows of a nearby cab shattered as a spray of bullets pelted its way from trunk to engine.

As I leapt toward the woman—she was shooting as she ran—I said a silent prayer of thanks that I hadn't worn my duster. I crashed into her, ramming my shoulder into the middle of her back and wrapping my arms tight around hers. I rolled to my back, taking the brunt of the unyielding sidewalk, protecting the woman from any unnecessary breakage. The air left her chest in a whoosh and she gasped, fighting to regain control of her lungs. Her gun skidded down the sidewalk, and she flailed against me, her fingernails breaking and biting into the concrete as she scrambled for her weapon. Compulsion is a scary fucking thing.

I knocked her out, just tapped her head against the sidewalk. She'd maybe come out of it with a slight concussion, but it was a hell of a lot better than dead. Across the street, Asher dodged in and out of the terrified crowds of pedestrians, taking out shooter number three in a football tackle similar to mine, though I had no doubt his had been a thousand times more graceful. The kid moved with the fluidity of a hunting cat, and it almost mesmerized me to watch him in action.

One shooter left.

And the son of a bitch was standing in the crosswalk, legs braced apart with a monster .38 pointed at the Range Rover like he was Dirty *fucking* Harry. Just *great*. My boots pounded on the cement, thundering in my ears with each stride. I'd never make it, even with my preternatural speed. Robert couldn't stop; he had orders to get Anya out of here.

He couldn't dodge any more traffic without causing a nasty wreck. He'd have no choice but to plow right over the human.

Shit.

Out of nowhere, Myles leapt into the crosswalk, grabbing the shooter by the shoulder and flinging him to the other side of the street. Not quite as gentle as I would have liked, but it got the job done. Myles straddled the gunman and ripped the .38 from his grip. Using the butt of the gun, he delivered a punch to the guy's face, and then another. He sagged to the pavement, blood running in a steady stream and dripping off his chin. Myles raised his hand high to deliver yet another blow. . . .

"No!" I'm not sure why I shouted, the whole team could hear me just fine in their earpieces. "Myles, I said no casualties."

I continued to run as he raised his hand higher, and I let a string of swear words fly that would've made a construction worker blush. Myles was going to feel that human's pain firsthand if he didn't stand down in three . . . two . . . one . . .

As if he'd sensed the threats inherent in each and every curse I'd muttered, Myles lowered the gun, tucked it into his waistband, and stood.

"Get your ass back to the house," I called, changing course and heading back toward the Columbia Center.

The Range Rover sped down the block, turning the corner in a drift of squealing tires, and disappeared out of sight. I could almost let out a sigh of relief.

Almost.

Supernatural energy snaked across my skin—faint, almost too subtle to identify—and I stopped dead in my tracks. A man stepped out from the shadows of the towering Columbia Center skyscraper, and I reached for the dagger I'd tucked back into my waistband.

Beautiful. Angelically so with golden blond hair and icy blue eyes that backed up his connection to something heavenly. He strode right up to me with a confident swagger that only enhanced his perfection. A soft blush painted his cheeks and his lips spread into a sweet, cajoling smile. Good lord, he was damn near blinding to look at.

"You're trouble, aren't you?"

Not the worst thing I'd ever been called.

"And not a Shaede, either. Not exactly." He reached up with his right hand, palm facing me as if he were feeling the air around me. "Delicious energy. Powerful."

Okaaaay. "You must be the asshole I should be introducing to my dagger right now." I allowed a glance behind me; the sirens were getting too close for my comfort. A slew of human police would converge on the street in a matter of seconds. This was not the time or the place for a supernatural showdown.

The angel's smile didn't fade. "Tell Anya her past has caught up to her. She knows what I want and tell her to watch her back."

Without thinking, I lunged, thrusting the dagger in front of me. I stumbled, stabbing nothing but air. I spun a circle, ready for anything and expecting an ambush. The bastard vanished, leaving nothing but a shimmer in the fabric of reality with his passing.

Don't you just hate it when your day goes to shit?

Chapter 11

"He knew you."

"So, a lot of people know me."

I stepped close enough that I could almost smell Anya's discomfort. "You're not helping me to protect you, Anya. Who is he?"

She averted her gaze. "I don't know."

"Bullshit."

The door to Anya's suite swung wide, and Dimitri rushed to his wife's side, checking her over for even the tiniest scratch. The only parts of her body not covered in leather were her hands and face; you'd think Dimitri would have been put at ease.

"I'm fine," she said, brushing his concerns aside. "I wish everyone would quit treating me like I'm going to break at any second."

That made two of us.

Dimitri turned, and without a word, wrapped me in a bear hug, squeezing me so tight I doubted I'd be able to take a normal breath ever again. "Thank you," he murmured, giving me an extra-tight squeeze.

"No—oof!—problem," I replied through clenched teeth. I actually liked Dimitri. He was a good guy, despite his taste in women, and he'd been there for me as well as for Tyler when he'd been suffering.

"Anya," I said, as I took a deep breath to replenish the air Dimitri had squeezed out of me. "Help me, so I can help you."

"You can go now, Darian." I could tell by her warning tone she didn't want Dimitri to know about her mysterious

admirer. "Thank you"—she almost choked on the words—
"for being there today."

"If you want *real* help, Anya, you know where to find
me." I pinned her with a stare, hoping she'd get that I meant
business. She may not want to come clean now. But she
would. Even if I had to rat her out to her husband to get the
truth out of her.

I closed Anya's door behind me, only to hear the sounds
of angry voices floating up the staircase. I strained toward the
sound, my preternatural hearing homing in on something I
doubted to be real. But the closer I got to the head of the
stairs, the more the truth sank in. My heart hammered against
my rib cage, fighting for a way out. Legs weak from the sudden adrenaline rush, I crept down the stairs one at a time,
listening.

"I will not tolerate your presence in *my* house!" Xander's
voice was a controlled burn.

"I don't give a shit what you'll *tolerate*, Xander. I'm not
leaving until I speak with her."

Oh god. His voice speared me like a dagger. I couldn't
breathe. Just hearing him turned my stomach into a tight knot
of nerves.

"You're a nuisance," Xander said, disgusted. "Don't you
think you've done enough already? You can't just show up
here after months and demand to talk to her. Where were *you*
when the PNT attempted to bring her to justice when her
secrets forbade her from speaking on her own behalf? What
did *you* do to help gain her freedom from the Judicial Council? Do you know what she's been doing for the past three
months?" Xander continued to rail. "How she's been holed
up in her apartment? You've certainly kept her safe and
sound, haven't you, *Jinn*."

I couldn't bear to hear another word. I backed slowly up
the stairs, ashamed to look Tyler in the eye. Terrified that
Xander would continue to lay out for him—in detail—the
train wreck I'd become. Wouldn't that be wonderful? A viv-
idly painted picture of my weakness to reinforce Ty's decision to leave me.

"Xander, I suggest you shut up before I shut you up." Tyler's tone was dead calm. The air temperature dropped about twenty degrees and stirred with energy. Not a good sign.

"And I suggest you leave before I kill you with my own hands."

The backs of my calves hit the top stair, and I tripped backward, falling right on my ass. This moment just couldn't get any better. Silence descended, my graceful maneuver no doubt audible to both Xander and Ty. I held my breath, willed my pulse to slow its frenzied pace. I could stand toe to toe with any badass with a weapon. But put me in a room with those two men, and I tucked tail.

I bit back the tears stinging at my eyes. Jesus Christ, why couldn't I get my shit together? I wished they'd both leave before I lost my grip entirely.

"It's time for you to go," Xander said, sounding suddenly distracted.

"Go. To. Hell."

Sounded like Ty wasn't going to take no for an answer. I doubted my shaky legs would carry me down the stairs. And if they did, then what? Confront Ty and let him know how much he'd managed to hurt me? I didn't think I could handle that. A spark of power lingered, Tyler's magic weaving with the air, drifting up the stairs as a cold draft toward me. I could try to wish him away. He was still my bound genie and had to grant my wishes. But despite everything that had changed between us, one thing stayed the same: I didn't like to exercise that kind of control over him. Which made me the world's biggest hypocrite, because it hadn't seemed to bother me the last few times I'd wished him into uselessness.

"Darian, I know you're up there!" God, the way he said my name. It would've brought me to my knees if I hadn't already been flat on my ass. "I need to talk to you! Please."

I grabbed on to the banister for support, hauled myself to my feet. I could do this. I could face him.

"Get out!" The control was gone, Xander's words infused with pure malice.

Tyler ignored him, his voice carrying up the stairs. "You need to look in the envelope that Marcus gave you—"

"I said, get the hell out of my house!" Xander railed.

I stopped midstep. This was about the *job*? The sounds of Xander and Ty arguing became nothing more than white noise in the back of my mind. Really, what did I expect? That he'd come over to beg me to take him back? Acting on instinct, my body merged with gray twilight, the transformation wrapping me in stifling warmth.

"Oh, no, you don't," a voice said from behind me.

"You know, I'm getting sick of you," I hissed, becoming my solid self as I turned to face Raif.

"I don't doubt it," Raif countered with a smile. "Want me to handle that?" he asked, jerking his head toward the stairs.

I wondered what would happen if he didn't handle it. Ty and Xander had been itching to take shots at each other for almost a year. If left alone, the situation could get messy pretty damn fast.

"I suppose you'd better," I said with a sigh. "I can help, if you want—you know, diffuse the situation."

Raif laughed. "Darian, the last thing your presence would do is *diffuse* the situation. Stay. Put. If you run, you'd better run fast. Because I will come after you."

No escaping Raif, it seemed. He refused to let me chicken out. He brushed past me, descending the stairs with an infuriating calmness. Xander and Ty continued to argue, their voices rising and boiling like a coming thunderstorm.

"Tyler." Raif sounded casual, though not accommodating. "Haven't seen you in a while. How are you? I don't suppose we can talk outside. Just you and me." Raif never asked anyone to do anything. Every word spoken was a gently urged command. "I'd hate to have to replace another door, you know." I heard the latch let loose on the front door, the hinges sighing as it opened. "Darian isn't available at the moment . . ."

The door closed again, shutting out the sound of their voices, now just a dull muffle in my mind. I leaned over the banister but saw nothing. I sunk to the floor and closed my eyes. Darkness followed on the heels of twilight, cool and smooth, like satin flowing over my skin. I felt a presence behind me, but didn't turn around.

"Let me take you away from here for a while." Xander's breath caressed my ear, bringing with it a ripple of chills.

I nodded my head. Anywhere was better than here.

*   *   *

We traveled as shadows. Quick, quiet, sliding through the city like an indiscernible breeze. I let Xander lead the way, and he was much faster than I'd expected. Faster, even, than Raif. I made a game of it, keeping up with him, and I think he knew it because he took me throughout the city: up, down, in, out, over, under, and through. I barely had time to calculate my next move. I needed this, to be out in the open air, unhindered and unburdened. I felt fifty pounds lighter, the tension melting away by slow degrees like icicles in the sun.

Once we'd left the city behind, Xander's pace slowed. When we finally stopped, spring blossomed all around us. I'd been here before, but never this early in the season, and never under the silver glow of the moon.

"I like it here," Xander said. He walked to the handrail of one of the arched wooden bridges of Kubota Garden, looking at the water below. "It's quiet at night. I thought you might need to be somewhere calm. Drama free."

Drama free was good. I closed my eyes, breathed in the scent of fresh, green things and dew. In a few months, the cherry trees would be heavy with blossoms and the sweet smell of encroaching summer would scent the warmer air. The Japanese gardens were an oasis in the middle of a concrete desert. The crisp, early spring air helped to clear the worry from my mind, the self-inflicted anguish I couldn't let go of. "I've lived in this city for almost a century and I've only been here a couple of times." I laughed, my voice sounding unfamiliar and small. "But it's nice."

"When Anya returned without you today, I worried for you—"

I braced myself for the overprotective banter, the warnings that I was in over my head.

"—but then I realized I had nothing to worry about. You handle yourself too well for me to worry for your safety."

I let out a deep breath when I realized that the warnings and admonitions weren't going to come. *Opportunist. Manipulator.* Raif's words echoed in my mind. Xander appeared more than willing to admit I could hold my own when just days ago he'd slammed his palm against his desk proclaim-

ing my life was too precious to risk. What game was he playing? "Thanks," I said, not knowing how else to respond. "I'll
get him, you know. That bastard can only hide for so long.
And when I find him, he's as good as dead."

"I know that," Xander said, still gazing over the bridge at
the water. Silver moonlight danced across its surface, glitter-
ing like diamonds. "I trust you. You're more than capable."

A doubtful snort escaped my lips before I could think better of it. Xander didn't trust anyone, except Raif. And capable? Lofty praise indeed from his high and mightiness. More
games. "Better watch out, Xander, your pretty talk and false
compliments might get you into trouble someday."

He turned to face me, bracing himself against the railing.
He crossed his feet at the ankles and his arms across his wide
chest. His eyes burned as his gaze roamed over my body,
stealing my breath. The shadows played against his features
making the mask of kingly authority, the sarcasm that seemed
as much a part of him as his regal smile, almost dangerous.
And his casual posture contradicted the muscles flexing
across his shoulders as if he were ready to spring into action
at any moment. The gold flecks in his eyes glowed brightly
in sharp contrast to the silver rippling across the water and a
slight breeze teased the golden strands of his hair. Xander
was many things: a liar, a manipulator, an arrogant, royal
pain in the ass. But, damn, he was something to look at.

He took a step toward me, and my brain told my legs to
take a step back. But the damn things wouldn't listen. Like a
rabbit in a snare, I was caught.

"Darian," he whispered, but it was as good as a shout in
the still night air. "The Jinn was a fool. Rather than weep,
you should make him pay."

My throat felt like it was closing up. "Pay?" I managed to
choke out.

"For hurting you. Forsaking you. Betraying you," he murmured.

I looked out over the water. At the trees overhead. The
shadows dancing in the moonlight. Anywhere but at him.

"And do you know what would wound him to the quick?"

I gave a nervous laugh. "A slip with a nail file?" If Xander's lack of laughter was any indicator, he hadn't found my

attempt at turning his words into a cute pun very funny. I cleared my throat and scuffed my boot against the cobbles.

"Look at me."

No way. Butterflies swirled in my stomach, my heart lurched into my throat. Was I actually sweating? My entire body felt clammy. I glanced over my left shoulder as if I'd heard something. But the only sound was my own pulse thrumming in my ears.

Xander reached out, cupped my chin in his hand, and turned my face to meet his. He'd taken another step closer, our bodies almost touching. I took a steadying breath, focused on the gold flecks shining in his gaze. He really did have pretty eyes . . .

"It would *kill* him to see you with someone else."

Damn if he couldn't hold me captive with a stare. "I doubt that very much, Xander." He had no idea that Ty had already one-upped me on the whole rubbing-his-new-arm-candy-in-my-face thing. And I wasn't about to tell him, either.

"He hurt you. Strike back. There's no greater torture than knowing another man is touching the woman you want. Tasting her naked flesh. Taking her in ways you can only imagine. I could help you"—he flashed a wicked smile—"torture him."

Delicious chills raced up my spine, turning my insides liquid.

"You're beautiful," he murmured.

My god, when had the air become so stifling?

"Strong."

His lush, velvety voice seemed to brush against every nerve ending and I shuddered.

"Intelligent and intriguing."

I'd heard these compliments before from Xander, but never with such sincerity behind them. I didn't know what to think. How to feel. Xander reached out to capture a few errant strands of my hair floating on the breeze and smoothed them behind my ear.

"I fall asleep every night wanting you. I wake every morning wanting you. I'm tortured by your nearness, yet if you were to leave, I don't think I could stand it."

I took a deep breath, exhaled sharply. *Snap out of it! This is Xander*, I reminded myself. *Master manipulator and shit talker extraordinaire*. He'd like nothing more than to parade me half-naked in front of Tyler so he could be seven different kinds of smug about stealing me away from him. I wondered what Xander would think if he knew by getting his hands on me, he'd be getting nothing but Ty's castoffs. I couldn't trust anything he said. And still . . . how could I deny the truth reflected in his eyes?

"Xander." My mouth was almost too dry to speak. "You just want what you can't have. Your sense of entitlement is going to get you into trouble someday."

He placed his hands at my waist. The heat from his touch seeped through my clothes, pulsing. Or was that the blood pounding in my veins?

"Oh, it already has." Xander's head bent to mine, his mouth hovering, but not yet touching. "But believe me, it's worth the trouble every time. I *always* get what I want," he whispered before closing the distance between us completely.

His body pressed against mine and his hands moved from my waist, wrapping around me and settling at the small of my back. I didn't pull away, though I knew I should. He held me close, and as if I had no self-control, I leaned into him, letting the moment sweep me away from the crippling pain of the past several months. His mouth slanted against mine, one hand caressing slowly up my back, and I responded by arching against him and letting the moment progress. Xander's tongue slid across my lips, tasting, searching, and greedy for more.

Common sense tugged at the edge of my brain, a microscopic germ of sanity threatening to infect the moment. I pushed it away. Ty had found someone new to love and left me alone and empty. He hadn't even warned me that he'd brought his lover home with him. Instead, he'd let me humiliate myself by coming face-to-face with her right at his front door. But I didn't want to make Tyler pay. If anything, I was the one who'd deserved the payback. This wasn't about hurting him for what had happened between us, but rather, my desire to be wanted. Needed. Loved by someone with all of his heart and soul. An erotic purr escaped his throat as

Xander's fingers threaded through my hair, and I lost myself to the moment. Chills raced over my scalp and across my flesh all at once, cold and then infusing me with a liquid heat that chased a path from my stomach straight to my core.

Xander pulled away, his lips dipping to my throat, up my neck, settling near my ear. He nuzzled against me, burying his face in my hair and breathing in deep. "You smell like spring," he murmured, his words hoarse with desire. "And you taste like oranges and cinnamon." His mouth latched on to the skin below my earlobe, his teeth grazed my flesh and I shuddered. He leaned back to look at me, one regal brow arched sardonically. "Are you cold?"

Are you kidding? My blood was on fire. "No," I said, my voice a little breathy. "Just the opposite."

The smile that dawned on his face was pure victory. His stance widened, and he pulled me so close I had no other choice but to place my palms against his chest. I felt his muscles flex beneath my fingers, and I allowed myself a little liberty, traveling upward and caressing back down to the flat expanse at the outer ridges of his stomach. I thought about going lower, but that damned shred of common sense stayed my hands.

Xander licked his lips, and my eyes locked on to his mouth. I felt the urge to take my finger and trace the soft curves. A low growl reverberated in his chest, rumbling against my skin, and my own lips quirked at the corners. It was nice to feel wanted. Desired. Even if it was in the name of petty jealousy. I was probably setting myself up for a crash and burn later, but right now, I *needed* this.

I leaned up on my tiptoes, wrapping my arms around Xander's neck. His hair brushed my knuckles, and I reached out to tease the silky-soft strands. Xander's breath caressed my face, quick little bursts of air. I knew how he felt; my own chest rose and fell like I'd run a few miles without stopping. His lips brushed my forehead, my temple, high on my cheekbone. My eyes drifted shut as I reveled in the feel of his mouth on my skin. I allowed my head to relax, tip back, and Xander, always the opportunist, seized the moment to taste the flesh at the hollow of my throat.

The ringtone I reserved solely for Raif, Darth Vader's theme music, interrupted the quiet of the night. Xander muttered a curse against my skin. "Ignore it," he said before placing another kiss at my throat.

"It's Raif," I said.

He placed a quick kiss on my lips. "Then definitely ignore it."

I fished my phone out of my pocket, wondering if Raif's call had been shitty timing or divine intervention. I touched the screen and put the receiver to my ear. "I didn't run away," I said, already on the defensive.

"Oh, you ran away." I could only imagine Raif's disgusted expression. "Just not alone. You need to debrief your team. And me."

Xander grabbed my free hand, placing lazy little kisses on my palm. His gaze didn't waver, locked on mine, dancing with mischievous light. I wondered if he could sense the tiny tremors jolting me from my head to my toes. He flipped my hand over, kissed each of my knuckles, pausing as his tongue flicked out at my index finger before he took it into his mouth and sucked . . .

Oh—my—god.

"Raif." I cleared my throat, afraid I might moan right into his ear. "Can we do this in the morning?"

"I expect you in twenty minutes," he said with reproach. "And tell my brother he'd better have been a gentleman tonight."

"Busted," I said, tucking the phone back in my pocket. I knew Xander heard everything Raif had said. A moment of forgetting, of building passion and fire, was now little more than cool awkwardness. *Damn it.* I took a step back, as much to clear my head as anything.

"Stay," Xander said, pulling me back to him. "Stay here with me."

The way his hand warmed mine, the raw desire in his eyes, almost convinced me to do just that. "I have a responsibility to Raif," I said. "I have to go back."

Xander sighed, but he didn't let go. Instead, he pulled me closer and kissed me. Just once. Slow. My toes nearly curled in my boots.

"Let's get you back." He let go of my hand and became

one with the shadows. "Don't want you looking unprofessional. It reflects badly on me."

I smiled. Leave it to Xander to first and foremost be the king. Shedding my corporeal form, I chased after him through the city toward Capitol Hill. But somewhere, buried deep under Xander's offered revenge, a dull, ceaseless pain remained.

Chapter 12

"Let's start with what we know."

I paced back and forth in front of the long table in the king's council room, virtually ignoring whatever it was Raif was saying as I forced the memory of Xander's kisses to the back of my mind. Had I made a huge mistake? How could I have let things go so far? *Shit*. What the hell was wrong with me? I'd played right into Xander's hands, letting him bait me over and over. When was I going to learn?

". . . which is why I didn't stop. My earpiece must have malfunctioned."

I looked up at Myles, drawn back to the conversation by his statement, and pinned him with an accusing glare. He'd heard me call him off that man. He'd just *chosen* to experience temporary hearing loss.

"We'll deal with *that* later." Raif's tone could have cooled lava to stone in a second flat. "Are you sure the humans were under the influence of magic?"

I'd bitten my thumbnail down to the quick. Tyler's ring glinted in the light, taunting me with its presence. "They were being compelled. I know the look. None of them were aware of what they were doing. The blond is our mark. And he knows Anya—personally."

"No one else saw him?" Raif eyeballed each member of my team, his gaze lingering a little longer on Asher.

"I didn't get out of the car." Louella sounded a bit put out. "After Julian and Myles took care of the gunmen, we headed straight back. Darian's orders."

Raif looked to me and I nodded, confirming what she'd said.

"And where were you, Asher?"

The kid sat up a little straighter in his seat, but his face never lost its guarded expression. "I returned on foot."

Raif stared him down, the silence becoming thick and heavy in the air. Julian cleared his throat, drummed his fingers on the polished tabletop. Asher gave Raif look for look. And damn it, I almost admired the kid for it.

"I sent him back." Someone had to break the standoff; might as well be me. "Anya was the priority, not me. Once the humans were no longer a threat, I told the team to make sure Anya was safe."

Raif focused his hawkish gaze on me and I rolled my eyes. *Really, Raif?* He was wasting his time. I wasn't about to rat anyone out. Not even Asher. Besides, I planned on finding out what he was up to myself.

"So, getting back to *business*," I said, taking yet another lap around the room. "What do we know?" Silence answered and I continued, "Obviously our guy has a bead on Anya. He's watching the house, or at least has someone keeping tabs on her comings and goings."

"And there's a possibility he might be Fae," Raif added.

"Maybe." But I doubted it. There was something mysterious about the angelic blond, but his energy wasn't Fae. Familiar—but somehow not. And I didn't have a clue how he'd managed to control the humans. "Whatever he is, he's dangerous. Too fucking calm for my peace of mind." Calm was bad. Calm meant our guy had a plan and wasn't above exercising patience to see that plan brought to fruition. "One thing I know for sure, low-key won't cut it. Neither will game playing. This guy doesn't give a shit about secrecy. Obviously. He's going to get Anya, wherever and whenever he can."

"We can't keep her prisoner," Raif said, his tone suggesting he wished he could do just that. "But I'll see what I can do about limiting her outings. At least until we can identify her attacker."

"She *knows* him." Christ, was I the only one pissed off by this? "And she's not telling anyone who the son of a bitch is."

"Perhaps." Raif's deference was getting on my nerves.

"Perhaps, my ass."

Julian stirred in his seat, his brow furrowed in concentration. "Anya is a prominent figure and well known to be a member of the king's inner circle. Anyone could claim they *knew* her."

"But what would motivate someone to kill her besides a personal grudge?" Liam spoke from the far end of the table. His boots were propped up on the glossy surface, arms folded in front of him. He may as well be watching a movie or playing video games instead of having a tactical meeting and debriefing.

"I agree." I wanted to kill Anya on a good day and didn't even hold any grudges.

"What about political motivations?" Louella ventured. "Any policy changes . . . proposals . . . endorsements someone might not be too thrilled with?"

Raif pondered that for a moment. "Not that I'm aware of. She doesn't exactly function in a political capacity."

"Besides protecting Xander every once in a while, what other capacity does she operate under?" I wondered.

The members of my team exchanged curious glances while Raif pointedly ignored my musings. Interesting.

"So we're back to a personal grudge," I said, trying to keep my tone from sounding too suspicious.

Raif looked away. He knew I was right. His frustrated expression mirrored my own. We hadn't made any ground. Back at square one, we had no idea who wanted Anya dead or why. And she wasn't making our job any easier. "Everyone but Myles may go." Raif sighed. "Darian will keep you updated if anything comes up."

The group exchanged some wary glances as they filed from the room, and Liam chuckled before knocking Myles on the shoulder. "Sucks to be you, man," he said, strutting out the door.

Myles leaned sideways in his chair, flinging a casual arm across the back. The defiant smirk on his face made me want to wipe it off—with my fist. "You want to explain why the hell you went ape-shit on that guy today?" I put my palms down on the table, leaned forward until I was inches from his smart-ass face. "I told you to neutralize him. Not beat the piss out of him."

Myles shrugged, and I pressed my fingertips against the tabletop to keep from grabbing him by the collar. "I told you, my earpiece malfunctioned."

I moved closer, our noses almost touching. "That's a total crock of bullshit and you know it."

Myles's lips compressed into a hard line. "I *don't* know that."

The sound of a throat clearing brought me upright, and Raif and I turned in unison toward the open doorway. "Excuse me." One of Xander's staff stood at the door, a female I'd seen around the house now and again. "There's someone here to see Darian."

Raif and I exchanged a curious look and my heart skipped in my chest. Had Tyler come back for a repeat performance?

"I asked her to wait in the foyer," the Shaede said, as if she'd picked up on our private exchange.

Raif raised a brow in question. "Hell if I know," I answered. I glowered in Myles's direction. I wasn't done with him yet.

"I've got this." Raif and I almost didn't need words to communicate anymore. He'd known what I was thinking. "Go receive your guest."

I trudged up the stairs, not particularly excited to have a visitor. Until now, my luck hadn't been stellar. I doubted the woman waiting in the foyer was here to bring me good news. As I hit the top stair and rounded the corner, I clamped my jaw down tight. I just couldn't catch a break. My night had become progressively worse.

She had her back to me, but the shining length of her honeyed-chestnut hair gave her away. I threw my shoulders back as I walked, made sure my stride was long and sure, my footsteps echoing as I approached. I might have been thrown when she'd opened Tyler's door. But she'd come to me, and I considered this my home turf. I wasn't going to run from her this time.

"Can I help you?" I couldn't hide the sneer in my voice as I echoed her earlier words. I doubted my voice was as beautiful, but I knew it carried a hard edge and that's what I wanted.

She turned to face me, a Miss America smile plastered on

her face. I gave her a head-to-toe appraisal, from the top of
her frizz-free hair, down the length of her sleek silk dress,
and stopping at her designer heels. I looked down at my own
black boots, thick-soled and scuffed from wear and tear.
Delicate, I wasn't. But strength could be beautiful, too.

Ty's new girlfriend didn't seem to mind my roaming gaze.
In fact, she seemed to revel in it. I let my fingers linger on the
hilt of my dagger. Intimidation was something I was good at.
And I needed the upper hand in whatever this was.

"I didn't realize who you were the other day." Her voice
held a soft, buttery quality that fit her perfectly.

I stuffed my left hand in my pocket and Ty's silver ring
caught on the hem. It felt heavy on my finger, cold against
my skin. I kept my mouth soft, my expression blank. Emotional pain wasn't a weakness I could afford right now. "And
now you know who I am?" I wondered how my voice
sounded to her.

"I do. And I thought it was only fair you know exactly
who *I* am."

"Well, then, exactly who are you?"

"I am Adira."

Of course. Awesome. I balled my fist in my pocket, resisting the urge to rub the stabbing pain from my sternum. Adira
smiled when she saw the recognition in my eyes. It must
have been a nice ego boost for her that I knew the story of
how Tyler had come to exist and that Adira had found him in
the desert and taken him in. A moment of self-realization was
all it took. Jinn are born from magic. They have no mothers,
no fathers. No family. But they're drawn to the magic in one
another, and Adira had found Tyler roaming the deserts of
Sudan. He'd spent a few hundred years or so with her before
they'd parted ways. But apparently they'd kept in touch over
the millennia. Who else would rescue Ty from hurt and heartache but Adira?

God, I needed a drink.

"I have no intention of asking you to break your bond
with him." She flipped her long hair over her shoulder as she
spoke. "He has, after all, pledged his protection to you."

I wanted to laugh. She knew damn good and well there
was nothing she could do about Ty's bond with me. It was

one of the rules. Jinn are forbidden from interfering with the bonds of others. I'm sure she hoped to come off as gracious, but really, I knew the truth. If it had been within her scope of power, our bond would be as good as broken. "That's big of you," I said. I kept my right hand wrapped around the hilt of my dagger for effect. "Is that all you came here for? To tell me Ty's bond with me is good and intact?"

Adira smiled. Lovely, really. "He's happy," she said. "I know him better than anyone, and I'm what he needs right now. *That* is what I came here to tell you."

"Well." I hadn't meant for the word to come out as a single thought. But I couldn't wrap my head around anything more coherent to say. It was like getting a kick to the ribs while you were down. She'd already slapped me in the face with her presence in Tyler's life. Was she expecting me to turn the other cheek? "You don't have to worry your pretty little head about me. I can take a hint."

"I'm not worried about you, Darian," Adira said as if I were totally inconsequential. "I just thought you needed to know where everything stood."

"Gee, thanks."

Adira gave me one last, blinding smile. The air shimmered around her, and she faded from sight.

Something about her energy signature struck me as familiar. As if I'd felt it somewhere before. Probably from Ty. They were both Jinn, after all. Thoughts slogged through my brain like slush in a wintery creek, too congested to search through memory for confirmation, though. I relaxed my fist and pulled my hand from my pocket as I backed against the wall. Slumping to the floor, I took a few deep breaths in a desperate attempt to squelch the anxiety rising up from the pit of my stomach. The need to flee was strong, overpowering any determination I might have had to stay put. I twisted the ring on my thumb and paused. It was the only thing I had that connected me to Tyler. With a tug, the ring slid up to my knuckle, but I didn't have the willpower to remove it completely. What a coward I was.

I needed some air. And the walls of Xander's house felt like they were closing in on me. As if I hadn't already seen with my own eyes the evidence that Tyler and I were through, now I had to hear it as well. A stellar end to a shit-tastic day. Pushing myself up to stand, I reached out to the shadows, entreating them to join with my flesh. No need to bring undue attention to myself. What I needed was a bit of peace and quiet. If anyone knew I was leaving, I could expect a babysitter. That was the last thing I wanted. And so, as my shadow self, I made a stealthy escape and left the protection of Xander's house behind.

Chapter 13

I hadn't been back to my apartment since the morning Xander had ordered me to his house and back to work. Just as he'd promised, Raif had installed a state-of-the-art security system, complete with camera. I stared up at the tiny, inconspicuous glass bubble, confident the high-tech lens couldn't see me in my shadow form. I didn't even know the security code to disarm the system. But again, shadows worry little over such things.

My mailbox was stuffed to capacity, and I retrieved the pile before going up to my studio. Most of it was junk mail, but it couldn't hurt to weed through the stack and make sure I hadn't ignored something pressing. Besides, I needed the distraction, otherwise I'd be forced to think about my visit with Adira. And at this point, I'd rather be dunked in a pot of boiling oil than revisit that conversation.

I dropped the pile of mail on the table, and it scattered in a disorganized mess. I looked around my apartment, my heart sinking into my heels at what I saw. It hadn't been so long ago I'd been holed up here, depressed and on the verge of something rash. What a fucking mess. My bed was unmade, the sheets twisted, blankets balled up and tossed to the floor. Dirty dishes sat in neglected piles on the countertops and empty cereal boxes mingled with empty bottles. Bourbon, mostly. The place smelled stale, reminded me a little of The Pit. Thankfully someone had the presence of mind to take out the trash, though that person hadn't been me. Discarded clothes made minimountains near the bathroom, and a thin layer of dust covered almost everything.

Jesus. Miss Havisham, anyone?

Eventually, I'd have to address the mess. But not tonight. I sifted through the ocean of mail, most of it a waste of perfectly good trees. Almost all of my bills were set up for autopay, so really, the paper bills were more of a formality. A flash of color caught my eye, and I fished through the expired sale ads and catalogs. My fingers shook when I picked up the postcard, a lovely picturesque view of Battery Park. *Charleston, South Carolina* was scrolled across the top.

I flipped it over to find, *Wish you were here!* written in black ink. Not that I was surprised. This made three postcards in just over six months. What the fuck was going on?

"Who are they from?" Raif asked from behind me. I should have felt his presence, but my concentration had been elsewhere. The air pressure changed, a shifting of matter as Raif passed from shadow to his solid form. He stepped to the wall where a keypad had been installed, and a series of beeps was followed by a long, drawn-out tone—at least someone knew the security code.

"A dead man," I answered, becoming corporeal myself. "Still following me, huh?"

"Someone's got to keep an eye on you. Who is he, Darian?"

I turned to face him and leaned my hip against the table. "His name was Lorik. He was the son of Vasili Egorov, an Armenian mob boss who'd been a pretty big deal on the west coast in the thirties. Vasili asked Azriel to hide Lorik after he'd gotten in deep with one of the old man's rivals. I don't know the hows and whys of it, but Az helped Lorik lay low— pretty much all over the country. I think he figured Lorik would be tougher to pin down if he was always moving. He sent postcards from every city he settled in. But . . ." My voice trailed off, lost in memories.

"But what, Darian?"

"He's human, Raif. By all rights, Lorik Egorov should be dead."

Raif stood, contemplating. His right hand contracted into a fist and relaxed.

"I never should have killed him, Raif."

He lifted his eyes to me in question.

"Azriel. I never should have killed him."

"You're afraid." Raif's voice was just louder than a whisper in my quiet apartment.

"Yes. I mean, Lorik was nothing more than an overindulged playboy. He never took anything seriously as far as I know. I have no reason whatsoever to fear him. And yet . . . how can I not be scared? No one knew about the postcards but Lorik, Azriel, and me. No one. What does this mean? How many secrets did Azriel keep from me and how many of those are going to rear their ugly heads? I'll never know. Azriel is dead and took his secrets to the grave."

Raif averted his gaze. I knew he refused to look at me because he agreed with me one hundred percent. Thanks to Azriel and his deceptive bullshit, I'd be looking over my shoulder for the next few hundred years. Maybe longer. Who knows what waited to jump out at me. Raif took a seat at my bar, trying not to look disgusted by my utterly neglected studio.

"I was bad, wasn't I?" My voice sounded hollow, emotionless.

"Bad is an understatement," Raif scoffed. "Look at this place."

I was ashamed of how I'd let myself go. Usually tidy, only an act of god could have reduced my living space to such a disastrous mess. I supposed a broken heart could produce a storm to make nature cower in its wake. But I'd lived through it, right? Or was I simply waiting in the calm eye of the tempest, catching my breath before I rushed through to the other side?

"The woman who came to the house tonight . . ."

"Adira," I said, interrupting Raif's thought. "She's the one I saw in Ty's apartment. She stopped by to clear the air, I guess."

"And is it?" Raif asked. "Clear."

I chewed on that question, for some reason unwilling to answer. Adira made it crystal clear that she and Tyler were happy. I couldn't shake the image of Tyler's face that day as I stared past her in the doorway, though. The look of affection and—maybe—regret on his face was so deep, so honest. Could it be that some part of him held on to what we'd shared? Even when he'd left me all those months ago, he said he loved me. Our love had made stone flesh; it almost merged the realms of time. How could something that strong be so easily cast aside?

"Darian?"

"It's as clear as it's going to get," I answered at last. "I don't have time to worry about it. Any word on how the police are reacting to today's shootout?"

"According to the news, the humans are under the assumption it's gang related, though if the human shooters have no recollection of their actions, it's going to complicate matters for the human law enforcement." Raif sighed. "I've contacted a friend at the PNT to notify them of the situation and he's assured me that he'll deal with both the shooters and the human authorities. We don't want to draw any undue attention or arouse the suspicions of any ambitious detectives."

For the most part, humans lived in ignorant bliss of the supernatural community. But the circumstances surrounding the shootings today were bound to pique someone's curiosity. I could only hope that Raif's friend at the PNT would nip any investigations in the bud. "What about Anya's Mercedes? Are you going to tell me about those bullets you recovered?" Raif had yet to delve into the evidence left by Anya's mystery assailant. Now that we were alone, it was time to get down to business.

Always prepared, Raif produced one of the bullets from his pocket and held it out, placing it in my hand. "I figured the actual evidence would be better than a picture. I've cross-referenced the symbol with everything I know. Nothing."

I turned the bullet over in my hand, running my thumb over the etching. My gaze wandered to Tyler's ring and the bear carved into the silver. "It's not meaningless. Anya knows what it is." I returned the bullet to Raif, who stuffed it back in his pocket.

"For what it's worth," he said, "I'm inclined to agree with you. For the time being, though, I'd like to keep that between you and me. If the rest of your team grows suspicious of Anya, their loyalty might falter. They'll get sloppy."

Agreed. "So, what made you come around?"

"It's too neat and tidy. Political motives *would* bring this to Xander's door, but then, Anya wouldn't be the target, would she?"

"No. I'm sure Xander's pissed off enough people to raise an army against him, but this isn't about him. It doesn't explain why she won't tell us anything, though."

"Your guess is as good as mine. Everyone has secrets, I suppose."

Wasn't that the truth. I was beginning to hate secrets. "Raif, Xander said that when you first met Anya, you'd caught her breaking into his house."

"Mmm, yes," Raif said, remembering. "At Xander's estates outside of London. Sixty or so years ago. She was just a child. Nineteen or twenty. Dirty, waifish, packing an atomic bomb's worth of attitude. I think she was looking for something of value she could pawn. She had no idea whose house she'd broken into. I wanted to teach her a lesson. But my brother found her . . . amusing."

Xander and his pets. I brushed my fingertips across my lips, wondering, had I become one of them? "Sounds like she was running from something."

Raif's hawkish gaze met mine. "Or someone."

We sat in silence for a moment, each of us lost in thought.

"What are you going to do about *your* problem?" Raif gestured to the postcard on my table.

"Nothing. Yet." Really, there was nothing I *could* do. Not until Lorik, or whoever this was, decided to come out of his hole. "I'll cross that bridge when I come to it."

Raif stood. "If you need me . . ."

I smiled, glad I could count him as my friend. "I know."

His footsteps echoed off the floor and then faded to silence as he passed into shadow. "Don't worry about Anya. I'll keep her close to home for a while. Maybe she'll decide to tell us something. The alarm code is thirty-six, ninety-three," he said. "Be sure to activate it when you leave."

A rustling near my bed drew my attention and I wandered to the far corner of my apartment, but found nothing out of the ordinary. Could have been my imagination. My once comfortable home now had a haunted quality that sent a shiver down my spine. I stuck around my studio for only a few minutes after Raif. I couldn't bear to look at the mess I'd made of my life, to see the physical proof of how I'd let myself go. Perhaps my and Tyler's love had been like an act of nature. A source of power . . . beauty. And at the same time, a force of great destruction. I had a sinking suspicion that it wasn't done with us, either.

Before heading back to Xander's I decided to stop at The Pit. Raif had hit a brick wall searching for the symbol engraved on the bullets retrieved from Anya's car. But that didn't mean he was the be-all and end-all of arcane knowledge.

As I fiddled with the pen, careful not to tear a hole in the napkin I was drawing on, I wished I'd had the presence of mind to keep the damn bullet. I'm no artist, and I was having a hard time giving Levi a basic sketch to go from. He looked at my drawing and raised a dubious brow.

"What? It's the best I can do."

"I think I'll have better luck if you can get me the actual bullet." Levi gave my sketch a last appraising glance, and with a grimace stuffed the napkin in his pocket. "When you're dealing with symbols of any kind, an abstract isn't going to do much good."

I brought the soda I'd been sipping to my lips. I still had an aversion to alcohol after my months-long bender. Just smelling it made my stomach turn. "I'll see what I can do. In the meantime, is this enough to get something started?"

Levi gave me one of his pearly-white smiles and shrugged his shoulders. It made him look much younger. "Honestly, I don't know. But I'll see what I can do. I have a friend who studies symbology and an ex-girlfriend who's high up in one of the local covens. I can ask her what she thinks."

Coven? I paused midsip. "You used to date an actual witch?"

He grinned again, this time looking more like an imp of Satan than innocent kid. "She was wild in bed."

I hid my smile behind the rim of my glass. A question scratched at the back of my mind. Something I'd wondered about for a while but hadn't ever pressed Levi about. I jabbed an ice cube with a cocktail straw before swirling it around my glass. I didn't meet Levi's gaze.

"You wanna ask me something, Darian?"

I took a deep breath. Held it. Exhaled.

Levi bent down, forcing me to look at him. "It's on the house."

"Levi . . ." God, this was hard. "Let's say someone wanted to break their bond with a Jinn. How would they go about doing it?"

He rocked back on his heels, whistled low before leaning back toward me. "Why would you want to do something stupid like that? Ty's a good guy."

Jesus. Did *everyone* know about our bond? "Do you know how to do it?"

"Ty's crazy about you, Darian. You go and do something like break your bond . . . it's not gonna sit well with him."

Guess Levi didn't get the memo about our breakup. "I doubt he'd mind."

"A binding like that—well, let's just say it's not a superficial thing. It's *soul* deep. And if Tyler bound himself to you, it wasn't because of a passing fancy. If you don't know how to break it, I'm not going to be the one to tell you. I think for the time being you'd better stay away from rash decisions. If you break your bond with Tyler, it can't ever be remade. It would do more damage than good at this point, and you'd be sorry."

I stabbed the straw to the bottom of my glass. "What makes you think you're so goddamned smart?"

He tilted his head to the side, a gesture that said, *Come on.*

"Seems a little unfair to me. That's all. Why should Ty know how to make the bond, but I'm not allowed to know how to break it? Since I'm the only one who can do it, you'd think that might be information I should be armed with."

Levi chuckled and moved to refresh my drink, but I stopped him. I wasn't staying much longer. "Believe me, Darian. If you *truly* wanted to break your bond with Tyler, you'd know how to do it. You don't need me to supply the information."

Cryptic. Figures. It seemed that people with knowledge of the supernatural got off on keeping the ignorant chasing their tails.

I set my glass on the bar and shot Levi a withering, albeit affectionate, look. "Let me know if you find anything out about my symbol. In the meantime, I'll try to get you at least a better sketch."

"See you around," Levi said as I left. I cast a backward glance in his direction, unnerved by the wisdom in his young eyes. If only he was right about Ty. But our bond, no matter how soul deep it had once been, was now no deeper than a puddle.

"Goin' home, Darian?" The bouncer, Tiny, asked me the same question every time I left. Maybe he couldn't think of anything better to say. It beat talking about the weather, at any rate.

"Yep. I've had enough excitement for one night. See ya."

"Don't be a stranger!" he called after me. "I miss seeing you around here!"

"You got it." I gave him my most earnest smile before I rounded the corner and became one with the dark night.

A week ago, I would've never admitted to feeling safe in Xander's too-big house. But now, walking to my room in the quiet hours of night—or early morning, depending on your outlook—I felt protected. Secure.

I closed the door to my suite, glad to see that it was clean, dusted, well kept. This room didn't hold unpleasant memories. It was a fresh start. Just what I needed. I rolled my shoulders, for the first time aware of the tension that had settled in the middle of my back. I was ready for a good eight hours of sleep. And damn it, I deserved it. Anya was staying put for a couple of days, I had Levi working on the mysterious etchings. Adira—well, I was exhausted.

Kicking off my boots, I pulled my shirt up over my head, extending my arms high to the ceiling before I tossed it to the floor. I stretched, bending sideways at the waist, turned my neck from one side to the other until it cracked. My eyelids drooped, heavy and ready to rest. I looked longingly at the bed . . .

"Darian." Xander barged through the door and froze. His eyes widened as he took in my almost naked upper half, pausing at my delicate red satin bra before bringing his gaze to my face.

"Jesus," I said, too shocked to do anything but stare back at him. "Don't you ever knock?"

Xander flashed a mischievous grin and backed out of the doorway, but not before glancing over every inch of my exposed flesh one last time before he shut the door. I struggled with my shirt, stuffing my head through the neck when he knocked.

"My lady," Xander said through the door. "I know the hour is late, but may I enter your private chamber?"

Ugh. I couldn't help but smile at his mock gallantry. "Might as well," I called toward the door. "It's not like you're going to take no for an answer."

"That," he said, closing the door behind him, "is true."

He crossed the room toward me, his eyes hungry, his gait graceful and sure. My stomach tightened as I watched him, a stirring as I remembered the way his lips felt on mine. *Tyler is happy*, I told myself. His girlfriend even came over in person just to drive that point home. And, damn it, didn't I deserve a little happiness, too?

"Your shirt's on backward." Xander's voice was husky as he tugged at the dangling tag. "And inside out."

"*Someone* barged in on me. I had to put it back on in a hurry."

"My timing was off," Xander said, brushing his thumb along my cheek. "I showed up a little too soon."

I felt a blush creep to my face. "How so?"

He leaned down, put his lips near my ear. "A moment later, and I would've seen you with nothing on at all."

A riot of butterflies took flight from the pit of my stomach, rising toward my throat. I didn't want to become another of Xander's kept things, but, *god*, I wanted someone to want me.

"Where did you go tonight?" he asked as he combed his fingers through my hair. His eyes delved into mine, so intense I had to look away.

"To my apartment. Just wanted to check in."

"I missed you," Xander breathed as he rested his mouth at my temple. The sensation of his hot breath sent pleasant shivers dancing across my skin.

"I wasn't gone *that* long," I tried to laugh, but it came out stilted, nervous.

"Long enough."

Xander pressed his forehead against mine and closed his eyes. He sighed heavily, and we stood there for a moment in silence, my hands resting in his. "I came to wish you good night," he said. "But now that I'm here, I find that I don't want to leave."

Manipulator. Opportunist. I had to keep reminding myself of who the Shaede King really was. "Xander." I didn't know what I wanted to say. I only knew that I wasn't ready for whatever was about to happen between us.

He brushed his lips against mine, a whisper of a kiss. "Sleep well," he said and kissed me one more time, just as soft. "Good night."

His hands lingered on mine as he pulled away. The door closed behind him, and I let out the breath I hadn't realized I'd been holding. I rubbed at my chest, *hard*, willing that hollow ache to leave me once and for all.

"Damn you, Tyler," I whispered. "Damn you for making me love you."

Chapter 14

Just like he promised, Raif kept Anya on a short leash for a couple of weeks. It ensured her safety, but damn, I was bored. I spent most of my free time sparring in the gym with members of my team. I've never been much of a people person, but I found myself enjoying their company. Nothing brings a group together like comparing bruises and cuts.

I kept my distance from Xander. It wasn't too hard. He had kingly business—whatever that was—to keep him busy, and since I'd decided that the king's strange obsession with making sure I ate regularly had to come to an end, I'd begun to eat more of my meals in the kitchen or my room. It's not that I was avoiding him per se, I just wasn't sure I wanted to fall victim to his persuasion tactics again. He knew which of my buttons to push—and not just the physical ones—and I'd succumbed to his manipulation too easily to think that it wouldn't happen again. I thought about Tyler every day, despite the pain it caused me. How could I possibly move forward with my life when the memory of Ty kept pulling me back?

"I have a doctor's appointment this afternoon."

I looked up from the book I'd been reading—a retelling of the Arthurian legend—to find Anya staring down at me. "Can't the doctor come to you?"

"No." The sound of her leather-booted toe tapping on the hardwood made my eye twitch. "They're doing an ultrasound today, and frankly, if I have to sit in this house for one more second, I'm going to kill someone."

"Then tell me who's got it out for you and you can go your merry way any time you want."

"Go to hell, Darian."

"Keep jerking me around, Anya, and you'll beat me there."

Anya clamped her jaw down tight and rested her hands on her hips. Her fawn-brown leather ensemble hugged every curve of her body; the pregnancy hadn't even begun to show. How much longer was she going to dress like this? I mean, shouldn't she be wearing some trendy maternity outfit? Violet eyes glowed with defiance, staring out at me from beneath her long, black lashes. I didn't know why we rubbed each other the wrong way, but we did. No amount of quality time was going to change that, either.

"An ultrasound, huh?" Why not change the subject? Anya had no intention of telling me who was after her. It would be a waste of energy to keep trying. "What does that entail?"

Anya's hands instinctively moved low on her stomach. "I have no idea. I suppose they'll be checking to make sure everything's all right with the baby."

I was annoyed with Anya because she was being difficult. I'd failed to acknowledge the fact that she might be worried or even . . . scared about her current situation. According to Xander, Shaede pregnancies were rare. That alone put Anya in the spotlight. Add to that the fact that she couldn't leave the house without armed guards . . . Well, maybe her plate was a little too full.

"What time's your appointment?" I sighed. At least I'd be getting out of the house. I *was* bored, after all.

"Three o'clock."

I brought the book up to my face, effectively blocking her out. "We'll be ready."

"'Bout time they let her off her leash," Julian said, rubbing his hands together. "I hope we see some action. I'm ready to crack some skulls."

I'd have been worried if Myles said it, but since Julian never took anything too seriously, I knew it was just flashy talk. Julian, Anya, Asher, and I rode in the first car while Dimitri, Liam, Louella, and Myles rode in the second car. I'd abandoned my low-key approach, making sure the identical bulletproof SUVs rode together down the street. I instructed our driver to take back streets, though. I might've been brazen, but I wasn't stupid.

Anya seemed to ignore Julian's comment, instead looking back to the car behind us every few seconds, making sure they still trailed close. She seemed more nervous having Dimitri out in the world than she was being out herself. *Interesting*.

The clinic was located in Pioneer Square, a private facility catering specifically to the supernatural community. Xander's private doctor had an office there, and though security was tight, there were far too many people for me to feel comfortable.

Nestled between Julian and Asher, Anya fidgeted in her seat. Just watching her made me nervous, and I sure as hell didn't need the added stress. We arrived at the clinic without incident, but I didn't expect an attack while we drove. If Anya's attacker had a personal grudge, he'd want to see the whites of her eyes when he killed her. He could have easily immobilized her with the sniper rifle the first time she'd been attacked, allowing for a quick, easy end to her life. His intention hadn't been to kill her. He'd sent her a message.

"Darian, wait," Anya said as Julian and Myles filed out of the car. I sat with my door half open and turned to face her. "If anything should happen, make sure Dimitri is safe first."

"Xander isn't paying me to protect Dimitri." I found it curious that she assumed her husband was in danger. "I doubt he would want me putting his safety before yours, either."

"I don't care what Xander or Dimitri want," Anya snapped. "*I* want you to keep him safe. If anything happens to him, I'm laying the blame at *your* feet."

I didn't answer her. We would only have continued to argue. If I failed to keep her safe, I wouldn't just have Xander to worry about. I was doing double duty, not only keeping an eye on Anya, but also her child. *Dimitri's* child. If anything happened to either of them, I doubted I'd want to face him.

The nice thing about the clinic was that we didn't have to play covert ops. Staffed with supernatural beings, there was no need to hide our weapons, what we were, or our purpose for being there. My team was efficient, scanning the entire clinic for weaknesses, places where someone could sneak in undetected. I posted Myles at the entrance, Julian at the rear, and Liam covered the perimeter of the building, watching for anything suspicious. Asher and Louella had been delegated the task of sweeping the clinic, and while they secured the unoccupied exam rooms, I escorted Anya and Dimitri to the ultrasound room.

I wondered at the normality of it all. A nurse walked in, her scrubs as standard as any human nurse's. She had a clipboard and a medical chart, blood-pressure cuff, electronic thermometer, all the standard medical equipment. I don't know what I expected . . . supernatural accoutrements for a supernatural patient? Shaedes weren't much different from humans, really. I guess it stood to reason she'd be treated just like any other person, medically speaking.

When the nurse asked Anya to get undressed, I took it as my cue to leave. I did not want to see her wrestle with peeling all that leather off her body. Thank god Dimitri was there to help her with the zipper at her back. With loving care, he moved her long braid aside, draping it over her shoulder, and kissed her neck as he pulled down the zipper. I averted my gaze, embarrassed to witness their moment of intimacy. When I heard her pulling the leather top from her shoulders I looked up—and froze.

On her left shoulder, just to the side of her shoulder blade, was a tattoo. Smaller than my fist, but not by much, the ink looked like henna mixed with some kind of shimmery substance, like a fine mist of glitter, or moonlight. The symbol was unmistakably the same one etched into the fifty-caliber bullets Raif had pulled from Anya's car: a crescent moon sitting on its back with a serpent coiled around it. The tattoo was every bit as intricate as the engraving on the bullets. It almost pulsed with life, like it fed off Anya's energy, seeming more like a part of her skin than a simple tattoo.

I took a step forward, prepared to shake some information out of her if I had to, when a timid knock came at the door and the ultrasound tech entered the room. *Damn it.* I stepped out of his way, deciding this wasn't the time or the place for an interrogation and left them to their private moment. I'd have my opportunity to question her, and she wasn't going to put me off again.

I paced the hallway, trying to shake the sensation that the walls were closing in on me. Something prickled my senses, a subconscious stirring that caused me to feel like my skin was shrinking, hell-bent on suffocating me. I headed for the reception area for a little space and a lot more oxygen when the explosion nearly knocked me off my feet. One by one, the windows shattered, the sound rippling in a palpable wave. *Jesus Christ*. First day out of the house, and Anya attracted attention before we could even settle her in. As if I didn't have enough to process, my earpiece rang with the chatter of my team members talking over one another, each trying to figure out what the hell had just happened.

"Julian, get the cars ready to roll, we'll be out in five!" I had to get Anya the hell out of here. *Now*.

The clinic wasn't huge, but I felt exposed with only five other bodies to provide cover. The hallway leading to the exam rooms was too fucking narrow, leaving only one way in—or out. If we stayed here, she'd be easily cornered and there was no way in hell I'd allow Anya to be caught.

As I headed for the ultrasound room, I picked up snatches of my team's conversation. Liam had taken up Julian's post at the rear of the building, and Louella was helping to get the clinic's employees and other patients to safety. *Good girl*. "Julian, we're coming out the back, meet us in the alley."

"I'm on it!"

"Liam, you see anything?"

"Not a fucking thing," he said. "It's too damn calm, Darian. No attack, no rush on the building. What gives? This guy's just going to break some windows and run off? Doesn't make sense."

I slowed down, took stock of everything I'd seen and heard. "Julian, hold up. Wait for us out back, engine running. But I'm not rushing anyone out. Not yet." Liam had a point. After breaking every window in the goddamned building, the next step would have been to rush in, take advantage of the confusion, and strike while we were weak.

"Myles, you see anything out front?"

"Nothing. And I mean that literally. Something's goin' down, I think there's a glamour over the building. The street is crawling with humans, and none of them noticed the explosion. They're totally oblivious. No sirens, no cops either."

Fuck. I was afraid of that. "Don't leave your post. Tell me if you see *anything* out of the ordinary."

"Easier said than done."

I ignored Myles's last comment and drew my katana from the sheath at my back. I missed my duster in moments like this. Crazy, I know. I hadn't worn it out of fear it would hinder me in a fight, and being without it made me feel like I was heading out to battle without a shield. "Asher, where are you?" Silence answered me. "Asher?" Again, nothing. Goddamn it, where was that kid? "Ash! Answer me."

Damn it, I didn't have time to play babysitter. I tore the earpiece from my ear; I couldn't concentrate with all of my team members talking at once. The shattered windows had been meant to drive us from the protection of the building, and I'd almost fallen for it. When I barged into the exam room, Anya was pulling on her boots. Tears welled in her violet eyes, but I couldn't tell if they were tears of anger or fear. "We're leaving?"

"Not yet," I told her. "How secure are we in here?" I asked the tech. "Is there a glamour on the building?"

The technician nodded, and his complexion looked a little pallid. "There are protection spells, too. I—I don't know how the windows could have—what the hell is going on?"

I gripped his shoulder, made sure he looked me in the eyes. "Take these two to the back exit, but don't let them leave the building."

"Darian," Dimitri said. "I can help."

I glanced at Anya, and the look of fear on her face was almost jarring. She was terrified for her husband's safety. "No. Go with Anya, keep an eye on her. I'll send Louella back, and when I give the word, she'll take you out to the car. I think someone's trying to get us to leave the building. For whatever reason, he can't come in. Don't go outside. Not until I give the okay."

I waited until the tech led Dimitri and Anya down the hall. She cast a last furtive glance in my direction, and I gave her a pointed stare right back. Maybe this would be what she needed to finally come clean and tell me who we were dealing with. "Asher?" I lifted the earpiece to my ear as I tucked the katana back in its sheath and headed in the opposite direction, toward the front of the building. Again, he didn't answer. "Myles, I'm heading out front. I want you to bring the second car around, park it by the entrance and wait."

"Want me to wait for you before I leave my post?"

I doubted it would matter. Our guy wanted Anya; he didn't give two shits about the rest of us. "No. Just go."

My boots crunched on pebbles of broken glass as I walked, and the potted plants in the lobby swayed in the breeze. Jesus, the place was trashed. I stepped through the gaping hole in the front door and looked around in wonder. The face of the clinic had been virtually obliterated, but the people driving by and walking on the street were none the wiser. Despite all the crazy shit I'd seen in the last year, the magic of the preternatural world still infused me with a sense of awe.

I stood on the sidewalk, a moment of indecision giving me pause. I had no fucking clue what I was looking for. A not-so-chance meeting with Anya's admirer was all I had to go by. A nameless face, an assassin without motive. Did the bastard have backup? And what the hell was he? Fae? Not likely. A familiar energy rippled through the air, something I'd felt before, and at the same time—not. What the hell was this guy?

A presence brushed at my back, and I whipped around only to see a flash of light too fast to identify blaze past the building and around the corner. Another tap, this time at my shoulder, and I spun again. Alone. *What the—*

"Darian, look out!" Asher shouted from down the street just in time for me to notice the glint of metal from the corner of my eye. I ducked, and a short throwing knife zinged past me, burying itself in the building's facade. "Get down!" Asher barreled toward me at full speed, shoving me out of the way just before another knife cut through the air. It glanced off his shoulder, slicing through the fabric of his shirt, and blood welled from a shallow cut.

"Where the hell have you been?" I growled, rounding on him. "I've been calling for you since—"

Out of nowhere, white-hot pain exploded in my head. I

reeled back, slumping against the building while I maintained a death grip on my consciousness. Stars twinkled in my peripheral vision, and the street slanted at an angle. I felt the warm trickle of blood down my temple and the pull of tissue as my split skin began to close. The cars on the street blurred—and then disappeared altogether as my line of sight was filled with shining blond hair and angelic features.

"Trouble," the angel said by way of a greeting, studying me like I was some sort of science experiment. "Nice to see you again."

I shook my head—it hurt like a bitch—to clear the cottony haze that bogged down my brain. The son of a bitch had come out of nowhere and pegged me with what felt like an iron-clad fist. Palms resting behind me, I pushed off the building, propelling myself into the angel's chest. It didn't knock him down, but I threw him off balance enough to give me the space I needed to gain my bearings. I reached for my katana, the blade singing as it ripped free of the scabbard, and without flare or preamble, I swung it at the angel's head.

"Whoa!" he almost laughed, lunging away from the blade in a movement too fast for my preternatural eyes to track. "You're faster than I thought. It just gets better every time I see you."

The look of exultation on his face was enough to inspire a chorus of hymns. His blue eyes were wide with excitement, his mouth upturned in an innocent yet seductive smile. I lunged forward, stabbing and cutting down, but the bastard was fast. Faster than anything I'd ever seen. It was like he could pop in and out of space in the blink of an eye, and my blade made purchase on nothing but air.

I caught another flash of color to the side of me, this one darker and slower than the angel but still too quick for me to focus. Asher grabbed the angel around the throat in a choke hold, but it didn't do a damn bit of good. The angel dropped to his knees—slid right out of Asher's grip—and managed a solid punch just under his ribs. Asher gasped, I heard the rib crack, and he doubled over.

"See you around, Trouble." The angel graced me with another of his heavenly smiles before darting out into traffic and across the street.

"Asher, let me—"

Damn kid didn't even let me finish. He ducked to my left, so fast he looked like a smear of dark color against the sidewalk, and took off at a full run toward the building across the street. He chased after the fleeing angel, down an alley, until the shadows swallowed him up as his heavy footfalls echoed into silence.

"Asher!" I called into my mic. Of course, he didn't answer.

"Julian." I tried to catch my breath, my lungs burning from excess adrenaline. "I think we're clear. Take Louella and get Anya and Dimitri back to the house."

"What about you?" Myles interrupted in my earpiece.

"I'll ride back with you. I want to do a little investigating and check out the area. We have to wait for Asher, anyway." Had Myles and Asher swapped brains? Asher had seemed like the one I could depend on while Myles was the hothead. Now I was beginning to think my first impression had been wrong.

"We're clear of the building . . ." Julian cut in, giving me the play-by-play. "In the car and headed back. See you soon?"

"Yeah," I said, staring into the dark alley. "Right behind you."

I yanked the earpiece out of my ear once again and turned and kicked a garbage can. I wanted a piece of this guy; I did *not* want him scared off. Asher giving chase was the last thing I'd expected, and now I might not get another chance to take this guy down. And where the hell had he been, anyway? It was like he popped out of fucking nowhere. *God. Damn. It.*

"I wish someone would tell me who the *hell* this guy is." The words escaped my mouth before I could think better of it. Shit. Too late now, I guessed. I was usually so careful. *Shit!*

"Your wish is my command."

I turned, my gaze cast down at the sidewalk. *Damn.* I looked up, almost afraid to meet him eye to eye. The brightness of the day had nothing on the brilliance of his face. It was more than the sun, more than light. Seeing him sucked the air out of my lungs, nearly blinded me with emotion. Mostly pain.

"Hey, Tyler."

Chapter 15

"**A**re you all right? You're not hurt, are you?"

I bit back the sob that rose up my throat, and choked it back down. I'd almost forgotten how much I loved the sound of concern in his voice. I even forgave him the cheesy genie spiel. Of course, my wish was his command. He didn't have a choice in the matter. I stood there like an idiot. Not talking. Barely moving. I wanted to stare at him forever, memorize every detail of his face and tuck it away for a rainy day when I'd need it.

"You okay, Darian?"

With Ty's dramatic entrance, I'd forgotten all about Myles. He'd gotten out of the car and stood on the side rail, staring out at me over the hood. "I'm good. See if you can find Asher, check out the entire block for anything unusual, and then we'll head back to the house and fill Raif in." Déjà vu much? Hadn't we done this dance once already?

"I'm chasing my tail, Ty." I watched Myles duck back in the SUV and pull across the street into the alley. Anything was better than looking into those gorgeous hazel eyes. The familiar ache settled into my chest. I fought the urge to rub it away.

"Darian."

His voice cut me as sure as any sword stroke. So much tenderness. A guilty conscience, no doubt. "He's playing with us. Cat and mouse. This isn't about killing Anya. Not yet, anyway. He's trying to drive her crazy, I think." My voice sounded foreign in my ears. Tired. Small. Distracted. God, he smelled good. "He doesn't want this to end right away. He's going to drag it out, really enjoy himself."

"Darian."

I couldn't acknowledge him. If I did, the tears would pour down my face in a torrent. "And the kicker—she *knows* him. She won't tell me, either. Not a fucking word. She's protecting something. Or someone. No one's pressuring her to come clean, either. I mean, would it *kill* Xander to make her fess up? Or Raif?" My voice escalated; people passing by on the sidewalk were beginning to stare. "I mean, Jesus Christ! Isn't anyone concerned about the fact that it's going to be damn near impossible for me to track this son of a bitch?" The panic had begun to mount. The more I rambled on, the more I attempted to keep my mind off the fact that Tyler was close enough to touch. Knowing that sent me a little closer to the edge. A sudden need to flee spurred my legs to twitch. Adrenaline pulsed through my body, and I trembled. My stomach tensed, a tight knot that refused to uncoil. I took a deep breath, but it wasn't enough. I might suffocate right here on the goddamned street.

"Darian!" Tyler gripped my shoulders, gave me one quick, gentle shake. "Come back to me."

My brain slowed its spinning. Did he say what I thought he'd said?

"You're a million miles away right now. I need you to focus."

No. Apparently, he hadn't. What I'd heard was, *Come back to me, I'm lost without you.* But what he'd really said was, *Snap out of it and get your damn head in the game!*

"I'm sorry," I said, looking at his face, but not really *seeing* him. The pain was just too much to take him in. "I didn't mean to wish for anything. I was thinking out loud and it just sort of slipped out."

"Jesus Christ." Tyler sighed and ran his fingers through his copper-streaked hair. "It's about damn time you wished for something useful." He looked up and down the street and grabbed my hand, pulling me as he walked. "Come on, we need to talk."

Tyler ducked into a coffee shop at the end of the block, and I paused at the door. I still had my sword slung across my back. "Don't worry," Tyler said, noticing my discomfort. "No one's going to pay any attention to us."

He was right. My skin tingled with power, the energy signature that I recognized as Ty's. The temperature dropped a couple of degrees, and I knew it had to do with Jinn magic. Even as he pulled me through the entrance, the naturally curious turns of heads as someone walks through the door was absent from the people sitting around the coffee shop. It was like we weren't even there. "Want anything?" Ty asked, heading for the counter.

Yeah, a bottle of bourbon. "No. I'm good."

I stood patiently, staring at Tyler's back while he ordered a cappuccino. How could he be so casual about this? My insides were tied in knots, and I wanted to throw up. But he was as laid-back as ever, chatting with the girl at the counter while she spooned foam into his cup. His T-shirt rose up as he fished some money out of his pocket, giving me a brief glance of exposed skin. I wanted to reach out and touch, and I balled my hands into fists as if they'd act on their own and betray me. I let my gaze wander, tracing the defined muscles of his back, glad it was warming up enough today to go without a coat. It would have been a shame for him to be covered up, and his shirt was just tight enough to show off his physique.

He dropped his change into a tip jar by the register and headed toward the back of the shop to a booth tucked away in a corner. I thought for a moment about becoming one with the light and making a run for it, but I had a feeling that would make things even more awkward between us. Besides, I'd made a wish. Tyler was obligated to grant it.

I slid the katana off my back and shoved it into the booth, taking a seat opposite Ty. He stared into his cup as if the mysteries of the universe were written in the foam. I guess I wasn't the only one dealing with discomfort issues.

"How long have you been living at Xander's?" I wondered at his tone, sharpened by an edge of possessiveness.

"Not long. A month or so. How long have you been back?" I didn't mean to sound so defensive, but I hated feeling weak, and right now I felt absolutely fragile.

"About the same." He took the paper cup and rolled it between his palms. "Darian, I—"

"Don't worry about it, Tyler." I wasn't about to let him

apologize for leaving me. My heart was breaking all over again and it was all I could do to keep from falling apart. I thought of my trashed apartment, the disrepair I'd let my life fall into, and I willed my spine to straighten. I would *not* let my heartache break me. "I know what's what. You're happy. And I'm glad for that. I didn't treat you the way you deserved to be treated. Like I told you before, I don't know how to do love. Not the right way, anyway."

The expression on his face was something I couldn't identify. Regret? Confusion? Pain? Probably just guilt. Tyler was the most caring person I knew. I could imagine it tore him up to think of me being hurt. The last thing I wanted was for him to worry about me. I just had to convince him I was fine. Trouble was, I couldn't even convince myself of that.

"If you'd only let me explain," Tyler's bemused expression made my stomach do a backflip. His eyes were guileless, searching, as if he could look right into my soul.

"There's nothing to explain," I said, sweeping my hand in front of me. Besides, Adira had already laid it out for me pretty plainly. "I get it. And I don't want either one of us to be tortured with long, drawn-out commentary about what went wrong and why. We know already. No need to unearth it again."

Ty brought the cup to his lips and stared out the window, focusing on some unknown point. I breathed in deep, took his scent into my lungs, and held it there for a moment before letting it go in a sigh. If only I could go back and change how I'd handled things with him. . . .

"I can't interfere," Tyler said, still not looking at me. "Not directly anyway. If you're wishing for answers, you obviously haven't looked in the envelope Marcus gave you."

Holy shit. The envelope. I'd totally forgotten about it after my run-in with Adira at his apartment. It was stuffed in the pocket of my coat, which I hadn't worn in weeks.

"This job." I focused on my thumb and the bear carved into my silver ring. "Who's the client?" Not my usual question. The identity of the mark was more times than not the important part. But not this time. Silence answered me and I looked up to find Tyler still staring out the window. "Who's the client, Ty?"

He turned to face me, his eyes sad and full of regret. "Me."

My brain fogged with confusion. What the hell was going on? "And the hit—it's connected to Anya in some way?"

He nodded once. Slowly.

Lovely. "I don't like getting the runaround, Tyler." I couldn't believe the way shit was piling up. "Just spill it. What the fuck is this about?"

Tyler gave me a very pointed look. "I already told you. I can't interfere. Not directly. I'm pressing my luck as it is. What you need is in that envelope."

Why? I just didn't get it. Tyler was my genie. If I needed something, it was his job to deliver it to me. Why was he beating around the bush? How was interference violating the rules? Unless—no. *Fuck my life.* "Does this have anything to do with Adira?"

He perked up at the mention of her name, though his expression didn't betray his emotions. He kept his face perfectly blank. Only his eyes showed the slightest glimmer of interest. "How . . . ?"

"Doesn't matter." Of course, he wanted to know how I'd figured out the woman at his door had been his long-lost genie soul mate. But he didn't need to know she'd come to see me. Needs versus wants wasn't a one-way street. It didn't matter. She'd told me what he couldn't bring himself to say: that he'd moved on. "This is about her, am I right?"

He nodded again, and his expression became less guarded and more tired. I hadn't noticed before. He looked more like the man I'd come home to seven months ago: a little thinner than he should have been, his hair messier than usual, dark circles under his eyes. But that didn't mean I was interested in helping his new girlfriend out. What could Adira and Anya possibly have in common? Besides the fact that neither were on my favorite people list and their names both started with "A," I couldn't think of anything. So by taking care of Anya's stalker and thereby securing the safety of her unborn child, I'd be doing Ty a solid and taking care of his honey's problems, too. Fan-fucking-tastic.

I had no idea what to say to him. The ache in my chest had become almost unbearable, the emptiness threatening to swallow me whole. All I could think of was how we'd left things. I'd hurt him. He'd hurt me back. We'd left each other. Hadn't either one of us been willing to fight to stay together? I instinctively reached for my chest—the impulse was too strong to ignore—and massaged my sternum. God, I wanted the ache to go away.

Tyler pushed his cup away and reached for my other hand. I flinched, pulling it back before he could touch me. Tears stung at my eyes, and I swallowed down the lump in my throat. If his skin made contact with mine, I'd lose it for sure. And I couldn't let him see that weakness in me.

"Darian." I looked at Tyler, lost in those gorgeous hazel eyes. He hadn't said my name, but someone had. I ignored it, lost sight of everything but Ty. How could he just throw everything we'd had away?

"Darian."

Ty's brow furrowed, and he cocked his head as if he'd heard it too.

"Darian! Can you hear me or what?"

I came back to the present, the spell broken. I tore my gaze from Tyler's, reached up, and shoved the earpiece deeper into my ear. "I'm here."

"I've got Asher," Myles said. "I'm circling back around the block to pick you up."

"You're going to leave?" Tyler asked as I slid out of the booth and slung my katana over my back. "Just like that?"

"Yeah." I felt the lump rising back up my throat. "I am. Like I said, you don't owe me any explanations, Ty. I hurt you. You moved on. End of story."

The screech of tires outside signaled my ride was here. And not a moment too soon. My composure was torn to shreds and if I didn't get the hell away from Tyler, I wouldn't be able to stop the flow of tears.

"Darian," Tyler called out, and I turned. God, he was beautiful. Another piece of my heart splintered off as I watched him shift in his seat and turn to face me. "Gods, you're stubborn. Quit making assumptions and"—he paused, as if looking for the right words—"we need to have a *proper* conversation." I looked around, expecting to have an audience, but the café's patrons were still oblivious to our presence. Ty gave an exasperated sigh and raked his fingers through his hair. "Look, would you *please* just answer your phone the next time I call?"

He didn't say "if." He said "the next time." A tiny ray of hope eased the pain in my chest, and my lips turned up slightly in a wan smile. "Yeah," I said. "I will."

I headed for the door, and the bell above it chimed as I pushed it open and stepped out into the cooling, late afternoon air. I took a deep cleansing breath. And then another. I shook out my arms and dangled my fingers loose from my hands, letting all of the tension drain out. "Let's go," I said to Myles after the car pulled up and I settled into the passenger seat. I didn't look at Asher. He sat in the back, quiet as a fucking church mouse. "You and I are going to have a nice, long talk, Ash. So don't even try to sneak off on me."

"Yes, ma'am." He almost sounded amused.

He wouldn't be for long.

Chapter 16

Seeing Tyler had me riled. Dealing with Asher's bullshit had me flat-out pissed. I knew he would be a handful when I'd insisted he be a member of my team. Hell, I was a handful myself. But damn it, I was in charge, and he needed to realize that now or go back to doing whatever it was he'd done before Raif had organized this task force. I shouldn't have to deal with him. Not when I had an envelope full of information waiting in my room.

"You want to tell me what the hell that was all about?" I massaged my temples. Nothing short of an entire bottle of Excedrin was going to get rid of this tension headache.

"I'm not sure I know what you mean." The feral gleam had returned to Asher's eyes, the calculating gaze of a predator. "You're upset I was doing my job?"

"That's the thing." I pulled out a chair at Xander's council table, drummed my fingers on the polished surface. "I don't think you *were* doing your job."

Asher snorted.

"This is the second time you've disappeared in the thick of bullshit only to show up right in the middle of where you don't belong. You might think that stealth act of yours is cute, but I don't."

"Really?" Asher leaned back in his chair, looking a little too at ease. "I'd think someone like you would find it pretty damn impressive."

"I don't have time for this shit. You want to be a part of this team or not?"

Asher studied my face, the amusement gone from his. When he wanted to, the kid could look downright fierce.

"I've got your back," he said, his tone as serious as his expression. "In fact, I've had it. Twice. Are you saying you don't find that useful?"

"You're not supposed to have *my* back," I snapped. "You're supposed to have Anya's. I can take care of myself."

"I never said you couldn't. I thought we were a team. Team members watch out for each other. They step in when one of their own is about to get his ass handed to them."

"Let's get one thing straight right now." I stabbed my finger down on the table for emphasis. "No one was about to hand me anything."

A corner of his mouth twitched. "Understood. There won't be any more problems."

Somehow that didn't do much to assuage my concerns. Asher was careful with his words, not denying or admitting anything. He didn't offer up any information either, such as where he'd been today when I was looking for him. He didn't seem to mind keeping secrets.

"Where were you? You weren't at your post. You didn't answer me when I tried to check in. Were you ignoring me?"

"I was securing the premises." His response was too offhand for me. "We had no way of knowing if there was anyone already inside the building. He could have had a partner—hell, he could have had a handful of guys inside. I checked every exam room, personally. Who knows, maybe something interfered with our communications? I didn't hear you."

I quirked a brow.

"Come on, Darian. I'm not making excuses like Myles. I'm not saying my earpiece malfunctioned or any shit like that. I'm just saying there might be a logical explanation for why I didn't hear you. It's not like I was hiding out or anything. I was doing my job."

"Your *job* is to follow my orders."

Asher looked me dead in the eye. "Which I did."

I had a tendency to keep my fair share of secrets, but I hated it when someone kept secrets from me. I never said I wasn't a hypocrite. Asher was hiding something. I just didn't know what. Yet.

"How far did you chase the bastard?"

Asher leaned forward, resting his elbows on the table. "Not far. You're right about one thing, though. He isn't Fae."

I relaxed in my chair, my previous anger nearly forgotten, anxious to hear what Asher had to say. "Why do you say that?"

"Well, for starters, he squeezed right through an iron gate when I was chasing him. Fae and iron don't mix. And he disappeared into thin air. He could have gone invisible, but I doubt it. If he were a Sylph or any sort of air creature, I'd have been able to feel, you know, wind or at the very least a breeze. He just vanished. One second he was there, and the next—gone."

"I agree with you there." The first time I'd met the angel his energy had shimmered in the air like heat rising off of desert sand and then—nothing. He'd simply vanished. As for the iron, well, Ty was allergic to iron as well. So it wasn't just the Fae who were susceptible. Although where Ty could tolerate iron to a certain point, direct contact would have debilitated any Fae right on the spot. I'd have known if he were a Sylph. I knew what a Sylph's energy felt like. The angel's was familiar, and yet not.

Asher looked uneasy for a moment, but he hid the emotion behind a mask of passivity. "There's something else."

No shit. Wasn't there always? "What?"

"I don't think he was running away, exactly. More like, he was drawing me away."

"Yeah, that's what I think, too." I wanted to hold on to my anger at Asher, mainly because it kept my mind off of Tyler. But the more he talked, the more I realized I didn't want to be mad at him. I wanted Asher to be for me what Raif was to Xander—a second in command, I guess. A right-hand man I could count on and a ready ear when I needed to talk my way through something. Like right now. "He could have made a run on the clinic. I mean, he'd blown the goddamned windows out. What was keeping him from walking right in?"

"Could have been the protective spells," Asher ventured.

"Maybe. I don't know much about faerie magic, do you?"

Asher shook his head. "Not enough to be useful."

"I know a Sidhe I could ask."

"No shit?" Asher's tone teetered between astonished and impressed. A little too put on. I dismissed it; I had bigger things to worry about than flattery.

"What else did you notice? Was he alone? Or did it feel like he was coordinating with someone."

"I think he's alone. At least, I didn't see anyone else, and it didn't seem like he was looking for anyone. I told you, I searched every room of the clinic and didn't find a thing."

Of course, if he was fleeing, he wouldn't exactly be looking for his cronies. My guess was it was all part of his game—whatever the hell that was. "Alone or not, he's dangerous. If you hadn't taken off after him like you did, we might have had a chance to catch him."

Asher slumped in his seat. "So we're back to this again?"

"Yeah, I guess we are. Damn it, I thought I'd made it clear on day one. This guy is *mine*. Your job is protecting Anya."

Behind the youth of Asher's face was a wisdom that unsettled me. His expression wasn't outright mocking, but his eyes had an "aren't you a cute little thing, thinking you're a tough girl" quality. Let me just say, I didn't really care for it.

"Like I said," Asher shrugged, "there won't be any more problems."

Again, I got the feeling he wasn't being completely forthright, or more to the point, that he was simply placating me. "Did you get a good look at him?" I wanted to get this over with. I had an envelope full of goodies to peruse.

"Good enough to know he's different."

That was an understatement. Rays of sunshine might as well have filtered through the clouds to bathe him in heavenly light. Anya's stalker was too inhumanly beautiful to be anything other than an angel, though his devilish intent belied his ethereal good looks.

"Way different," I agreed. "Scary different. I need you to get your shit together, Ash. You're the best backup I've got, and Anya needs someone like you watching out for her."

"What?" Asher's face once again took on the guise of youthful innocence. "You don't want Myles as your wingman?"

I laughed and the air seemed lighter. "He's something, isn't he?"

"He's a brawler for sure. You want someone to pick a fight for no good reason, call Myles. He's your boy."

"Noted." Not that I'd need him to push anyone around like that. But there was something to be said for muscle. And Myles filled an enforcer's boots to a T. I could think of more than a few high rollers in the organized crime circuit who'd pay through the nose for someone like Myles. If he got to be too much of a problem, maybe I'd lend him out to Ty for a while, have him show Marcus how a lackey was supposed to behave. "Are we good?" Despite his rash behavior, I knew Asher was a good kid. He didn't need any more of an ass-chewing than he already got.

"We're good."

"Get out of here." I pushed my chair away from the table, anxious to get to my room. "I'll talk to you later." I turned my back to him—it couldn't have been more than a second—and when I spun around to face him, he was already gone. "Creepy," I murmured to myself as I headed for the door. "Fucking creepy."

I traveled as a shimmer of sunlight through Xander's house as I made the trek back to my room. Not that I'm ever particularly social, but I just didn't have the patience to sit and talk with anyone on the way. My conversation with Ty ran a loop in my head, and it wasn't just the wish-granting that had my wheels spinning. How in the hell was I supposed to work for him when all I wanted was to avoid him?

Gliding through the sturdy planks of the door, I reclaimed my solid self only after I was safely inside my suite. I dug through the closet, yanked the sleeve of my duster and broke the hanger in the process. *Great.* I rifled through the pockets until I found the large manila envelope Marcus had given me. I couldn't believe I'd forgotten all about it. Stuffing the duster back in the closet—I didn't feel like expending the effort to hang it back up—I carried my precious cargo to the desk. I turned on the banker's lamp in the far right-hand corner and spilled the envelope's contents out onto the desktop. Unfortunately, I didn't find quite what I was looking for.

Ty was usually pretty meticulous if a job required reconnaissance. Name, aliases, address, places of business (or preferred street corner, depending), known associates . . . hell, one time he even supplied me with a mark's favorite flavor of ice cream and restaurants he frequented. Setting aside the paper with the wire transfer information for my fee, I stared down at the photographs—black and whites mostly, all different snapshots of the same angelic face. I spread them out across the surface of the desk, looking for a clue, anything that would tell me who the bastard was. How could Ty have possibly thought this stuff was going to help me? I mean, I got the rules issue. Jinn were bound to follow a strict set of rules just like they were bound to their wish-makers. But, Jesus, this shit couldn't have been any more useless. No address, no business info, not even a list of places the guy frequented. Hell, he didn't even tell me if the SOB lived in the city. What was I supposed to do with a stack of glossies that looked better than most actors' headshots?

I picked one of the photos up, held it under the light. In the close-up shot, my mystery guy was climbing out of a car, back turned to the camera. I suppressed my astonishment, traded it for outrage. "Son of a bitch," I snarled, tossing the picture on top of all the others. A name was scrawled in black marker across the glossy surface: Kade. I took one last long look at the image, particularly the tattoo on the angel's neck before scooping up the pile and storming out of my room.

"Anya!" I shouted as soon as I was out the door. "Get your ass front and center!"

I knew she'd heard me. In fact, every Shaede in the house had probably heard me. I stood my ground and waited for Anya to come to me. I'd be damned if I was going to traipse all over Xander's mansion looking for her.

It wasn't long before I heard the muted footfalls of stiletto heels on expensive carpet. I leaned against the railing and glanced down at the open foyer as if I hadn't a care in the world.

"What the hell do you want?" Anya didn't try to hide her annoyance. "Haven't I been through enough today without having to deal with your pathetic needling?"

"Who is Kade?" I kept my voice level, calm.

Anya bristled. "I don't know what you're talking about.

Jesus, Darian, do you always have to be so damn dramatic? I mean, did no one pay attention to you when you were a child? You're just not satisfied unless you're the center of attention."

She was nervous; the slightest hint of her native Russian accented her voice. "You know damn good and well who he is." I ignored her baiting words. I was through playing games. "And you're going to tell me."

"Go to hell." Anya nearly spat the sentiment. "You're nothing. Less than nothing."

Not the first time she'd said that to me. But goddamn it, it sure as hell was going to be the last. I pushed myself away from the railing and tossed the pictures at her. They fell all around Anya's feet, Kade's face staring up at her. I rushed forward, put the toe of my boot on the photo showing the tattoo and pushed it toward her.

Anya looked down at the photos. She didn't even flinch. "I don't have to tell you anything. I'm not afraid of you."

"I saw your back today, Anya. If you want to get yourself—not to mention your child—killed, I suppose that's your business, but I *will not* allow you to put my team members at risk. You *are* going to tell me every last detail, or I'll make sure you don't leave your goddamned room for the next year. You think hanging around the house is boring? Try solitary confinement." I hadn't realized how my voice escalated until I heard frantic footfalls coming up the stairs.

"Darian." Dimitri's voice was a rumbling growl. "What has gotten into you? You're supposed to be protecting her, not threatening her!"

Anya stared me down, her violet eyes ablaze. "Go, Dimitri. Darian and I need to have a talk."

"About what?" He sounded suspicious and had every right to be. The wifey had been keeping secrets. "Is this about the attack at the clinic today? Does she know who's responsible? I have a right to know."

Anya stepped forward, putting the photographs behind her. Ah, married life. "This is between Darian and me."

"Milaya"—Dimitri softened his tone for his wife—"what is going on?"

"Girl talk," Anya said. "Go, now. I'll be fine."

She gave him a kiss to send him on his way, and if I'd been in a better mood, I might have found her actions endearing. "Pick those up," Anya hissed, jerking her head at the photos, "and come with me."

Chapter 17

I gathered up the pictures and flipped through them one last time. I wondered if Ty had snapped the shots himself as I noted the Kremlin in the background of one. Where in the hell had he been for the past three months? Anya didn't look back or pay me an ounce of attention as she made her way to the suite of rooms she shared with her husband, and why should she? She'd made it pretty clear she'd just as soon gnaw her own arm off than talk to me about anything.

Xander favored Anya, everyone knew it, but it was apparent when you walked into her suite. Located at the rear of the house and positioned over one of two four-car garages, it was an apartment unto itself.

"Do you know what the most annoying thing about you is, Darian?" Anya said with contempt as I closed the door behind me. "It's that you don't care. About anyone or anything. You have no respect."

She did *not* just say that to me. She had no idea what I cared about. Or who. And as far as respect went . . . I didn't give it freely. Respect was earned. Baby on board or not. "I don't have to justify myself to you—or anyone—Anya."

"Take Xander for instance." She strolled through the apartment, heading for the kitchen. "Hell if I know why, but he's in love with you. In all the years I've known him, I've never seen him so infatuated. And you'll ruin him for it."

I stared with my mouth just a little slack. Since when had this become about me? Anya grabbed a wicked-looking knife from a butcher block on the counter, brought it down with a swift slice, and halved an apple. "First of all, my love life is none of your fucking business."

"He's a king, Darian. Do you have any idea what that means? How important he is to his people? Ever since you crawled out of the woodwork, you're all he can think about. His kingdom doesn't matter, his people. Only you. We should have left Seattle months ago, and yet he stays. He will jeopardize his crown for you."

"Bullshit. That's not true." Damn it, how could I have let her take charge of the conversation? This was my interrogation, not hers. "Xander's a big boy, Anya. He doesn't need you looking out for him."

"Well, you're sure as hell not interested in what's best for him. I think someone should have his interests at heart."

"You have no idea what's going on between Xander and me."

"I see the way he looks at you. The way he tracks your every move. That tells me more than enough. And you're using him for whatever reason. If you're looking for someone on the rebound, go hunt down some unsuspecting human and give him a good toss. Don't use Xander to get over your breakup."

As Anya chomped on her apple like a stabled horse, I tried not to let her words sink in. There was no "us" when it came to me and Xander. She thought her king was some lovesick victim, but I knew the truth: the King of Deception had no romantic notions about me. Sure, he wanted to get me into bed. That was the only thing he'd been forthright about since we'd met. He was itching to get under Tyler's skin, and he was trying to get me on board to do it. Xander had to win. Always. Love had nothing to do with it. He wanted to put Ty in checkmate, plain and simple. No matter what Anya saw in his eyes, love wasn't a part of Xander's agenda.

"You're just trying to take my mind off your little secret," I said. "And that's not going to happen. Mind your own business. I can handle my personal life without any help from you."

"Whatever you say. How about you mind *your* own business?" She discarded the seeds from the first half of the apple and dove into the second half with vigor. "You'll destroy Xander just like you did your Jinn. You're like poison. It's probably better you killed Azriel when you did. No doubt his torch still burned for you despite the length of time he'd been without you."

"Shut up, Anya." My self-control slipped another notch. I'd be throwing punches in a matter of seconds if not for Anya's delicate state.

"You should have seen Tyler when he showed up here. Did you even consider what it would do to him when you ran off? He didn't even figure into your plans, did he? No, you're too busy worrying about yourself to consider anyone else. He was wrecked. Angry. The rage was palpable. He almost killed Raif and then turned his fury on Xander because he thought my king knew where you'd gone. We could barely control him. The rest of the household cowered at his display of power. Are you proud of yourself for that? Does it make you feel formidable to destroy men the way you do?"

"Shut up!" When I found Kade, I'd turn Anya over to him myself. "You are not allowed to talk about Tyler. Not. Ever."

"What?" Anya kept a safe distance behind her kitchen counter. "Does the truth hurt? Do Xander a favor, Darian. End whatever it is between the two of you now, before you decide to cast him aside. I don't want to see him broken and left to pick up the pieces of his shattered life like your other lovers."

"You have no right to stick your high-and-mighty nose where it doesn't belong. You don't know the first thing about me." Then I added for good measure, "And your fashion sense sucks ass." Anya pissed me off to no end, but her words rang with truth. I was poison. Every relationship I'd ever had ended in disaster. I was selfish. But knowing it and hearing someone else say it made it hurt so much more.

"I'm going to ignore your juvenile attempt to make me cry," Anya said. She moved from the kitchen to the small living area and flopped down on the couch. "Because there's nothing wrong with my fashion sense. At least I don't look like I'm trying to win the Teen Goth Cutter of the Week Award. It stings to have someone rub salt in old wounds, doesn't it, Darian? You don't like it a damn bit. So why not stop rubbing salt in mine? Leave well enough alone and quit asking questions I'm not ready to answer."

So she thought she could school me by giving me a healthy dose of my own medicine. Wasn't going to work.

"You can't keep your secrets any longer, Anya. Dimitri's going to figure it out. And since you've been so kind as to shove my own bad decisions back in my face, let me tell you from experience, keeping secrets from the man you love isn't conducive to a healthy relationship."

Anya scoffed, "Don't think for a second you can teach *me* anything about love. I've done more in the name of love than your whiny, selfish ass ever has or ever will."

Rather than sit too close, I took a stool at the counter. I was afraid I'd be tempted to throttle her if I got within touching distance. "Again, Anya, you don't know the first thing about me or the things I've done. But you said it yourself—I'm a first-rate relationship destroyer. Maybe you ought to take my *expert* advice this one time."

"Fine. You want to know about Kade?" Her throat was thick with encroaching emotion. "I'll tell you. But let's get this straight: he's not after me."

Yeah, sure. "Then who's he after?"

"Dimitri."

My first thought was, what in the hell did Dimitri have to do with Adira? Or Tyler? It made sense, though. Anya had been nervous as hell to have her husband out of the house today. I put my anger on the back burner. "Do you know who Adira is?"

"No," she said. "Should I?"

"I guess not." My curiosity devoured most of the residual anger clinging to Anya's slights against my character. "So, tell me about Kade."

Anya stared at nothing for a while, lost, perhaps, in her memories. "Kade isn't what you think he is. He's a chameleon. The perfect predator. If he decides to kill you, it won't be quick and painless. He'll make you suffer. He'll drain you until you're nothing more than a husk, and he'll enjoy every minute of it."

Charming. "What is he?"

Anya raised her gaze to mine. She'd never looked so troubled. "He's *chërnyi*. A demon."

Ironic, considering I'd thought of him as an angel, albeit with a devil's disposition. "He doesn't really look the part."

Anya smiled. "That's the point. Kade is a Cambion. The

offspring of an Incubus and a human. He's technically only half demon, but no less powerful than his father. Kade can charm the panties off a nun in five seconds flat."

I held her gaze for a moment. "Did he charm your panties off?"

She flashed a rueful smile. "What Kade wants, Kade gets. There was a time when I was what he wanted."

Fair enough. I had to admit, Kade looked good enough to eat. It probably didn't take much coaxing on his part to get even the most reluctant lady into bed. But if Kade got whatever he wanted, no wonder Anya was twitchy and secretive. "Why does he want Dimitri? Jealous lover syndrome?"

Anya snorted. "Hardly. Kade and I didn't last long as lovers. He was more interested in what I could do for him."

Apparently that meant besides give a good blow job. "And what was that?"

"You probably have no idea what it's like to be poor, do you, Darian? I imagine your life was always pretty easy."

Just showed how much she didn't know about me. Sure, my father had been well off, but all the money in the world couldn't compensate for the emotional detachment. And my well-to-do married life hadn't been a walk in the park. Unless you considered regular beatings marital bliss. "You don't know shit about my life, Anya."

"Maybe not." She shrugged. "And I rather you knew nothing of mine. But I told you I'd tell you about Kade, so I guess I don't have a choice.

"I was born in Russia during the second World War. I'm not going to bore you with the details. When I was ten, my parents were killed, and I was sent to an orphanage. Being a Shaede child in a world of humans isn't something I'd wish on my worst enemy." She gave me a pointed look. "And that's saying a lot. I ran away when I was sixteen, and I learned pretty quickly that my Shaede nature made me the perfect thief. I could sneak in and out of anywhere without being detected. I was good at what I did and made a lot of money doing it."

"There weren't any Shaedes who could take you in?" I couldn't help but wonder why Anya would have to live among humans when she'd grown up with her own kind.

"They were few and scattered in my region."

As I continued to listen to Anya's story, I realized that she didn't sound too different from me, really. I'd been set adrift in the world, and with no other options had relied on my Shaede gifts to keep me afloat in a less than legal—or moral, for that matter—way. Survival has no morality. You do what has to be done. Period. "So Kade's a thief?"

"Kade is whatever he wants to be. He gets bored easily. When I met him, he had grandiose plans to run the granddaddy of all crime rings. For a while, we did pretty well. We stole, blackmailed, kidnapped. We found the leverage we needed and used it for whatever reason. He's ruthless. Not above or below anything.

"He really got off on blackmailing powerful figures. Having control over someone because he knew their dirtiest secret made him feel like a god or something. He used to say that guilt was the sweetest and most powerful human life essence. And nothing brought out that guilt like waggling dirty deeds in front of someone's face."

I thought back to the first day I'd met Kade, outside the Columbia Center. *Delicious energy. Powerful.* I didn't know anything about Incubi. Or Succubi. I'd never heard of a Cambion before today, I didn't even know demon/human hybrids existed. "Kade can sense someone's energy, can't he?"

Anya gave a bitter laugh. "Not just that. He feeds off of it."

I thought of the Lyhtans, how they could inject their prey with a venom that would melt the internal organs, making them easy for consumption. Perhaps that's what Kade did as well, but on a more spiritual level. "Sounds lovely."

"Believe me, it's not pleasant, though at the time you'll think you've died and gone to heaven. Kade can subdue his prey with a toxin he secretes through his pores and saliva. It's like a drug and instantly addictive. Taking the life essence from a human will kill them almost immediately. When he takes from a supernatural being, though, it's different. It won't kill you, but it will weaken you to the point where you wish you were dead. Or at the very least in a coma. Once he drinks your energy, though, he can temporarily absorb whatever ability you might have."

Jesus. We'd definitely crossed over into comic book territory.

"So if he . . . drank from a Shaede's life energy, he could become a shadow at sundown?"

"Yes." Anya's voice was barely a whisper. "I've seen him do that firsthand."

I suppressed a shudder. Essentially, having something taken from you without your permission . . . what Kade did to his victims was the equivalent of spiritual rape. "What's with the tattoo?" I had to know everything about Anya's past relationship with Kade if I was going to track the motherfucker down. Know thy enemy and all that.

"The tattoo is a brand." Anya reached over her shoulder and brushed the spot on her back where I'd seen the tattoo. "Kade's mark. It acts like a homing beacon. Once he's branded you, you become his property. He can find you—no matter how hard you try to hide."

"You've been hiding for a while, haven't you?"

Anya said, pensive, "Forty-five years. Maybe longer. I knew I wouldn't be safe forever. But I hoped . . ."

Her voice cracked, and I looked away, giving her a moment to compose herself. It sort of pissed me off to think that we had anything in common, but Xander had been right: Anya and I were very much alike. *Damn it.* Realizing that made protecting her more personal. Besides, I liked Dimitri, and I owed him. He needed protection just as much as Anya. This wasn't just a job anymore. Not really. "You knew when Kade showed up in the city, didn't you?"

"Yes." She sniffed a little and cleared her throat. "It was a month ago. At first he didn't do anything. He knew I'd feel his presence, and I think that was enough for him. But he grew restless. I watched my back and watched Dimitri's even closer. I didn't tell anyone, not even my king. It wasn't until he decided to use my car for target practice that anyone knew I was being threatened. I told Dimitri it was probably someone after Xander, using me to deliver a message to the king. He's believed me. So far."

"Don't you think he has a right to know he's in danger, too?"

Anya fixed me with a hawkish stare, her violet eyes glowing. "What have you done to protect the ones you love, Darian?"

What indeed? Lied. Deceived. Withheld important information. Exercised control I swore I would never use. I looked away. Buried painful emotions I couldn't afford to unearth right now. "How does Dimitri factor into this if Kade's motivations aren't jealousy?"

"Cambion are just as attractive as their Succubi or Incubi parents. Humans are drawn to them. Kade was like the Pied Piper, gathering followers wherever he went. Dimitri was one of them." Her smile grew wistful, her expression full of love. "He had nowhere else to go. But Kade never kept anyone around unless they could do something for him. Dimitri was dangerous, even for a human. Deadly. Skilled with a gun and blade alike. I'd never seen a better fighter. Kade used him as security, and he was expendable. But not to me. He was different with me. Loving. Gentle, even. He wanted to take me away, protect me. Dimitri didn't know that Kade had branded me. Not that it would have mattered. No man had ever loved me like that before—with all of his heart and soul. I protected *him*. From Kade, from the reality we both wanted to escape.

"Kade decided he was tired of meddling in the affairs of humans. He was after bigger prey, namely, his father. Kade loves secrets, and his father kept one in particular that he was hot and heavy for."

I'd come to accept that keeping secrets was standard practice in the supernatural world. "What secret?" It must have been a good one for a father to keep it from his own son. Azriel had kept my true purpose from his own father, Xander, for almost a century. Secrets are a precious commodity.

"Kade's father possessed a codex. Filled with spells, esoteric rituals. More or less it's a demonic bible; more specifically, it's a sort of Incubus manual. A how-to for the demon world. Being half human, Kade was forbidden from knowing anything about his kind. I think it was the only thing he truly hungered for."

"I take it you stole it for him?"

"Yes. But I ran into a snag. Dimitri had insisted on coming along. He was caught by Kade's father. I tried to trade the codex for Dimitri, but Kade's father didn't want that. He wanted his son."

"And you gave him what he wanted, didn't you?"

Anya sighed. "What would you have done in my situation?"

I didn't have to answer her. She already knew.

"Kade's father was ruthless, his reputation for cruelty well known. I don't know what he did to him or where he kept him. I only know that once his father took him, I no longer felt the connection between us. Unfortunately, I felt him the moment he escaped from his father's imprisonment."

She still hadn't gotten to the point. "Seems to me his beef would still be with you. And not Dimitri."

"Kade had a woman," Anya whispered. "At the time of his capture. She was pregnant. She died in childbirth, as did Kade's son."

Fuck me. "An eye for an eye, am I right?"

A single tear trickled down Anya's cheek, and then another. "I made Dimitri a Shaede. I changed him to protect him. To make him strong. I can't protect him from a demon's wrath. Not even the shadows will keep Dimitri safe."

"How can I find him?"

"I don't know." Anya's tears had begun to fall in a steady stream. "The brand only works one way. Kade knows I won't be able to stay shut up in this house forever. More so, he knows Dimitri won't let me keep going out without him. He's using me as bait, to draw Dimitri out. Kade won't just kill him, Darian. He'll make him suffer first."

I stood up from the stool. I'd had enough of love and the lengths people would go to protect it. My experience had taught me that no matter how hard you try, you always suffer in the end. It was unavoidable. "Kade won't get the chance, Anya." I walked to the door and left her to worry and sorrow. "Because I'm going to kill him before he can lay a hand on either of you."

Chapter 18

I walked down the hall toward my room, armed with a little more information than I'd started out with. Maybe Levi could help. I hadn't asked Anya if she knew how to kill Kade; maybe it took something special to get the job done. Hell if I knew, anyway. At least I had a better idea of what I was up against now, and that had to count for something. Right?

My back pocket vibrated, and my stomach jumped up into my throat. Ty said he'd be calling me, and I promised to answer when he did. I probably shouldn't have agreed so readily. Still pretty raw from our earlier encounter, I didn't think I had it in me to talk to him right now. I pulled the phone out of my pocket and checked the caller ID: UNKNOWN. Only one person called me from an unlisted number. It surprised me, how quick I was to smile. "Hello?"

"You've been avoiding me," Xander's velvet voice said through the receiver. "Where are you right now?"

"I haven't been avoiding you," I said as I continued walking. "I've been busy. And where the hell do you think I am?"

"I have no idea," he said in mock innocence.

"I'm in *your* house."

"I'd rather you were in my bed."

I felt the heat rush to my cheeks, and I stumbled on the rug. I didn't know what to say or how to respond. Usually, I just told him to go to hell or go fuck himself instead. But I'll be damned if Xander's tactics didn't have me a little off my game.

"Darian?" Xander laughed and my skin rippled with chills.

"I'm here."

"Meet me in the foyer. I'm taking you to dinner."

I looked down at my black outfit, more suited to fighting than a night on the town. "I'm not really dressed for going out."

"Don't worry," Xander said. "You look fine."

I neared the end of the hallway and stopped at the top of the stairs. "How do you know how I look?"

"Because I can see you."

Xander stood at the foot of the stairs, his eyes fixed on me. The memory of his kisses was still fresh in my mind even though it happened weeks ago. I thought for a moment about Anya's warning. But I doubted I could ever destroy Xander. He was too cocky to be destroyed by any woman. It was all about the chase for him, no aspirations of love, no matter what Anya thought to the contrary. This was safe. I could feel a little less lonely with him around. I forgot about Anya, about Adira, and Dimitri, and Kade. Xander's eyes roamed over my body, glowing with warmth. I told myself it wasn't affection in his expression. Admiration, maybe. Desire, definitely. I put thoughts of my broken heart to the back of my mind and whether or not Xander really cared about me. How could I think about anything else when he looked at me that way?

I tucked my phone in my pocket and took the stairs in a steady descent. Ty was happy. He'd found someone else. He hadn't meant to hurt me when he'd shown up with Adira, but he had just the same. Those words were my mantra, the justification I needed to seek my own joy. And joy was waiting for me at the bottom of the stairs. Xander smiled, the expression tinted with his trademark arrogance. "You look beautiful." He held out his hand. "I hope you're hungry."

"I do not look beautiful." I took his hand and the warmth was delicious. "Pretty words don't work on me, remember? And yes, I'm starving."

Xander wasn't exactly decked out for a fancy night on the town. He still looked pretty damn good, though. The navy blue striped dress shirt probably cost more than my entire wardrobe. Armani, if I had to guess. It brought out the amber flecks in his eyes and made his hair look honey blond. Tonight he'd traded his slacks for jeans and dressed up his look with leather loafers. If the rest of his wardrobe was any indicator, the shoes could buy groceries for a family of four for a month.

"You're better dressed than I am," I said, making sure my tone was rueful.

Xander opened the door and ushered me through. "Hardly. Come on, let's get you fed."

"Good lord, Xander, can't you do anything low-key?" I asked when I got a look at his car. The black Aston Martin Vantage fit him to a T, of course. "I mean, can you say ostentatious?"

"This *is* low-key for me. Would you rather we took a limo? Or had a driver take us in one of the Range Rovers?"

I gave an exaggerated sigh. "I suppose if I have no other choice. . . ."

"You don't." Xander opened my door and waited for me to crawl inside. He made his way around to the driver's seat and settled behind the wheel. "It's so rare I get to drive it. In fact, it's rare I get to drive at all. You're just going to have to humor me."

I leaned back into the plush leather seat. I wondered if this was how Anya felt all the time in her leather outfits. "I can suffer through it."

"That's what I thought." Xander flashed a mischievous grin before revving the engine. The tires squealed as he punched the accelerator, barely missing the gate as it swung open to let us out.

He drove us to a little diner in the Queen Anne district called Dick's and pulled up to the drive-through window. "Best burgers in the city." Xander turned to look at me. "Too fancy for you?"

I laughed. The meals prepared in Xander's kitchen were five-star gourmet. Burgers? At a drive-through? The laughter continued to bubble up and wouldn't stop. It felt so good. Cleansed the pain that had spread like a cancer through my chest the past several months.

"What?" Xander asked, amusement accenting his features.

"Nothing." I stemmed the flow of laughter, though I didn't want to stop. "This is perfect."

*   *   *

Paper bags in hand, we settled onto a bench in Kerry Park on Queen Anne Hill. The view of the city took my breath away, the lights twinkling against a dusky sky and the Space Needle standing watch over it all. On a clear day, you could see Mount Rainier, but its snow-capped peak was shrouded by a bank of low clouds on the move toward the city.

"I don't know what's better," I said, popping a fry in my mouth, "the food or the view."

"The company has them both trumped," Xander said.

I didn't know what to say, so I stuffed my face with the delicious cheeseburger instead.

"I heard about what happened today at the clinic," Xander said. "I'm glad you're all right."

I washed down the burger with some Coke. "Yeah, well. It's no big deal."

"I expect in a life as exciting as yours, tussles like that really aren't a big deal."

The sarcastic edge in his tone made me laugh. "I guess not. Xander," I said, tentative. "Can I ask you a question?"

"Anything."

Of course. He never denied me anything. Yet. "Why don't you ever talk about your wife? Is she dead?"

He gave a bitter laugh. "She's certainly not dead. Evil like that never dies."

"So—you're divorced? How does that work with the whole monarchy thing?"

"It works just like it does in any other race or social structure. Padma lives comfortably and as far away from me as I can manage. The farther away, the better."

I stared out across the city, not sure why I wanted to know, or even why I cared. I guess my curiosity had been piqued because he'd never really spoken of her. She'd been human, just like Dimitri, and Xander had chosen to make her a Shaede. "You obviously loved her once. Enough to change her."

"Hmm . . ." Xander took a bite of his cheeseburger, chewed thoughtfully. "Perhaps."

"Do you miss him?" Good lord, what was wrong with me? This was supposed to be a light evening, and I couldn't help but bring up painful topics. "Azriel?"

Xander looked at me. His eyes glowed with a soft, sad, light. "Azriel was always more Padma's son than mine. He had her fire—and was quick to anger just like his mother. Azriel always felt entitled to more than he was given. He was insufferably hard to please."

"And you don't think this is even a little strange?" I fiddled with my straw. "You and me? Whatever this is between us." I mean, Azriel *had* been my lover, after all.

Xander cupped my cheek, brushed his thumb across my skin. "Should I?"

Fuck, I didn't know. It's not like my life was defined in black and white. The gray was my comfort zone. This development between us should have been right up my moral alley. "I don't know."

"I took his mother," Xander said matter-of-factly. "I wanted her and took her right from under the nose of her male. She was already pregnant when I changed her."

My brain skidded to a halt and did an about-face. I'm sure my shocked expression was of the what-the-fuck variety. "Are you saying what I think you're saying?"

"He was not my child. But I claimed him as my own, and no one was the wiser."

Surely Raif would have told me something so important. Xander had to be bullshitting me to sway my judgment. "Raif never said—"

"He doesn't know," Xander interrupted. "I told no one."

"No way." I didn't buy it. It was just too damn convenient. "You're just telling me this to avoid some sort of moral stigma."

"Believe what you want. And for the record, I don't give a damn about your insufferably *human* moral stigmas. Azriel was not my son by blood or birth. Padma was the lover of a Raksasha prince named Mahaveer. I'd thought her a slave when I first met her and reveled at the prospect of stealing her from the bastard. It wasn't until much later that I discovered she'd gone to the Raksasha willingly. He'd promised to make her immortal, and in return, she'd agreed to lure innocent victims to him that he sacrificed in order to strengthen his magic."

"What's a Raksasha?" I interrupted. I thought I was pretty

familiar with most supernatural creatures by now, but this one was new to me.

"They claim to be demigods, but they're nothing more than an evil, malevolent race of ghouls. They absorb power by eating the flesh of the dying and drinking their blood. The worse the victim's suffering, the greater the power they ingest."

Lovely. Just the sort of creature I wouldn't mind taking out. This Mahaveer sounded like a real piece of work. And apparently Padma was no better. *Way to pick a winner, Xander.*

"No one suspected the child wasn't mine," Xander continued. "I sought only to protect Azriel. He was in his mother's womb when I changed her, and he inherited the Shaede gifts I'd given her. It didn't change his nature, however. Azriel was always a cold, calculating child. Whether I wanted to admit it or not, nothing I'd done to change him on the outside could affect his parentage. His Raksasha nature was much too dominant."

"Jesus." My mind struggled to wrap itself around this revelation. "Did Azriel know?"

"I never told him," Xander said softly. "And he never had reason to question his lineage. He may have had a ghoul's blood and parentage, but physically, he was simply a Shaede. I cannot speak for his mother, though. Once I learned the truth of her involvement with the Raksasha, I sent her away. I kept Azriel close, though. I hoped"—he sighed—"I hoped if he stayed close to Raif, some of my brother's honor would rub off on him. I was wrong."

If only . . . I fiddled with the straw in my cup, utterly speechless. Even for Xander, the story was just too wild to be fabricated. Azriel, the son of a ghoul. It almost made perfect sense.

"You're certainly introspective tonight, Darian. Does this have anything to do with seeing your Jinn today?"

I snapped to attention at Xander's change of subject. "How did you know I saw Tyler today?"

Xander smirked. "I'm the king, my love. I know *everything.*" He leaned over, bumped his shoulder against mine in an almost playful way. "Eat your food. You need to keep that question machine you call a mouth occupied for a while."

We finished eating in comfortable silence as I tried to process everything that Xander had told me. Not even Raif knew the truth of Azriel's parentage and I wondered what, besides Xander's usual ploys, had prompted him to confide in me. Darkness swallowed twilight, and the city lights stood out in stark relief against the navy blue backdrop. This had been a day full of revelations. I'd have to start looking for Kade tomorrow. I'd probably have to call Tyler too; not exactly something I was excited to do. And I'd be picking Levi's brain for sure. If anyone would hear the rumblings of a demon in town, it'd be him.

I wadded up our trash and put everything in one of the nearest trash cans. Xander leaned back, bracing himself on his arms and stared out at the cityscape.

"I'd sit here all night like this with you if you'd let me." His voice was soft in the quiet night. "Why have you been avoiding me?"

"I told you, I haven't. I've just been busy."

"Liar."

"Xander." I tried to sit, but he grabbed my hand and pulled me toward him until I stood between his knees. I couldn't relax, so I took a deep breath. "I just don't know what I'm doing right now. I don't want to give you any mixed signals or make you think that what's going on here is something more or less than it is." *Lovely.* How could I explain how I felt when *I* couldn't even make sense of it? "The other night was a mistake. I needed a distraction. Something to take my mind off just how much I hurt. You touched a nerve when you suggested that proving I'd moved on would make Tyler jealous. And is that okay with you, Xander? I mean, Jesus. Are you seriously okay with me using you for some kind of emotional manipulation just because I've been hurt?"

"Darian . . ." It wasn't pity in his voice—exactly. More like he was amused that I was looking out for him. "Maybe you should quit overthinking everything and just let things progress naturally. You might enjoy living a little more if you released the choke hold you have on your life."

Something in my brain snapped at his words. The *choke hold* as he called it was what had destroyed my relationship with Tyler. And now it was all I fucking had. It's all I'd *ever* had in an existence that was completely *out* of my control. Fine. If Xander wanted to see me release the choke hold, I'd do just that. He'd all but dared me with his arrogant expression and mocking words. I lifted my gaze, and this time it wasn't Xander closing the distance between us. I held on to him like a lifeline, gathering his shirt into my fists. When our mouths met, it wasn't shy or tentative. It was fierce. Hungry. Demanding. His lips crushed mine, his tongue thrusting into my mouth. I returned his ardor, pushing against him so that my breasts rubbed against his chest. My nipples hardened, and an electric blast of excitement crashed over me in a wave of sensation. All I could think of was his hands on me. I wanted to feel his skin against mine, lose myself in his touch.

I pulled away to catch my breath, but I wanted more. More of his mouth, his body . . . My pulse thrummed in my ears and I felt a need deep in my core, an emptiness that I longed to fill. "Xander," I said, my voice thick. "Let's go."

Even with Xander driving like a maniac, he couldn't get us back to the house fast enough. My hands wandered, tracing his fingers, his arm, venturing to his thigh. I could see his profile in the glow of the dash, his jaw clenched and his chest rising and falling with his heavy breath. "Darian," he warned. "This car isn't very accommodating, and if you don't stop what you're doing, I'm going to be forced to pull over and utilize the space as best I can." My throaty laugh didn't do anything to calm either one of us down. "Gods," Xander breathed. "I've never wanted *anything* more than I want you."

When we stopped in front of the house, Xander killed the engine and turned to look at me. The hunger in his gaze renewed my own lustful feelings and rather than bother with the door, he faded into shadow and glided toward me in a rush of fragrant air that reminded me of roses in full bloom. I followed suit, and we drifted through the car door, our bodies nothing more than the essence of darkness, entwined as a single shape.

"Darian," he said against my ear, his body becoming solid against mine. I caressed him, still shrouded in shadow, winding and twisting myself around him like a curl of ribbon. Xander moaned, the sound muffled by my lips as I became corporeal. Without another word, Xander's mouth moved on mine as if he were starved for me. Passion ignited deep within me as I wrapped my arms around his neck and kissed him back with everything I had. His mouth slanted against mine, our tongues meeting again and again while he walked backward, leading me into the house.

The door slammed behind us without regard to anyone we might've woken, and we climbed the stairs, never breaking the kiss. I fumbled with the buttons on his shirt, desperate to feel his chest bare beneath my searching fingers. He tripped, and I laughed as we fell, sprawled out on the stairs. "We'll never make it at this rate," I said, nipping at his neck.

"To hell with it." Xander pushed me away enough that he could unfasten my pants. "I don't care if we're caught."

The idea of having sex on Xander's staircase struck me as incredibly hot, but the thought of having an audience did not. "I don't know about you," I said. "But I'm not much of an exhibitionist."

Xander kissed me, just a flutter of his lips on mine. "No, I don't think I'd like to share the sight of your naked body with anyone." He wriggled out from underneath me and stood. Grabbing me by the hand, he pulled me along and took the stairs two at a time.

At the top of the stairs, he pulled me against him. His hand slid inside my pants to cup my ass. I moaned into his mouth and it only seemed to excite us more. We bounced off the walls, the banister, any obstacle in our path, the rest of the way to Xander's room, too wrapped up in one another to give a damn about watching where we were going or who might be watching us.

Hands groping, greedy for bare flesh, we tore at each other's clothes once we were safely shut inside Xander's suite. He peeled my shirt over my head, throwing it behind him. I don't know where the discarded clothing landed, but it was followed by the sound of breaking glass. I kicked off my boots, and one flew onto the coffee table in the sitting room, sending a stack of coasters flying; the other may have skidded into the bathroom. Xander claimed my mouth in another ravenous kiss as I undid the last few buttons on his shirt and pushed it down over his shoulders.

His skin exuded a fiery warmth, and I was glad for the difference. Xander was the heat to Tyler's cold, and I wanted nothing in this moment to remind me of past pain and heartache. Being with Xander was a cleansing. Like a phoenix, I'd be reborn from Xander's flame. I rubbed my palms against his chest, his nipples hardening at my touch. My stomach clenched, spreading lower still, as I ventured down over the ridges of his abs to the waistband of his jeans. I ran my fingers inside, and Xander drew his breath in sharply. It was all the encouragement I needed. With a quick tug, I had the button loose and with slow, achingly slow precision, I pulled the zipper down, tooth by tooth.

I raised my gaze to his, and a grin spread across his regal face. "Going commando tonight, Your Highness?" I teased. "Nice touch." Without waiting for a response, I reached down, taking the hard, velvet smooth length of him in my hand. My eyes were locked on Xander's lips as they parted, deliciously tempting, and I slowly dragged my gaze up until our eyes met.

I worked my hand up and down his shaft, enjoying the feel of him, the power of giving someone pleasure. Xander cupped my hips in his hands, using my body to steady himself. His fingers flexed and worked my flesh, his eyes burned into mine, and his breathing grew heavy and ragged. "What did I tell you," Xander murmured. "It feels good to let go, doesn't it?" My god, he was big, heavy in my palm, and I used my free hand to work his jeans down off his hips and around his ankles.

"Be quiet," I said, my voice a little too thick with passion. I didn't need Xander reminding me what this was really about. All I wanted was to forget, to enjoy this moment without any crippling emotional connection. I traced my way back up the inside of his thigh and cupped his tender flesh, working every inch of him with languid strokes. He shuddered and grabbed my wrists to stop me. "No need to rush, we have all night."

I backed away from him and took off my pants. Left in nothing but a black lace bra and satin underwear, I moved toward his large, comfy-looking couch. I walked backward, leading him along with the sway of my hips like a snake charmer playing her flute over a basket of cobras. The cushion hit the backs of my thighs, and I stopped. "We do have all night"—my voice was little more than a whisper— "and all day too."

Xander took my face in his hands and brought his mouth to mine, crushing, bruising, in its intensity. He took my bottom lip between his teeth before caressing it with his tongue. His hands were busy fiddling with the clasp on my bra. As slowly as I'd lowered his zipper, he slid the straps down over my shoulders. He waited a split second and held his breath in his lungs before pulling the sheer, lacy fabric from my breasts. When I was bare to his gaze, he exhaled in a rush of breath, eagerly cupping my breasts as his thumbs grazed my nipples. They hardened, and I moaned as my head rolled back on my shoulders.

"Gods, you're exquisite," Xander said before blazing a trail of kisses across my collarbone. He laid his lips to the swell of my breast, nipping with his teeth. I trembled from the delicious near-pain as he continued toward the center of my breast. I wrapped my arms around his neck, and he took my nipple in his mouth, sucking deeply before using his teeth to tease the flesh to an even stiffer peak. Dizzy with desire, I held on to him for dear life, my breath hitching as he ringed my nipple with his tongue before nibbling lightly. I cried out, unable to restrain myself, and he repeated the process on my other breast, driving me to a state of maddening desire that throbbed hot and wet between my thighs.

Xander urged me down onto the couch, positioning me on the center cushion. He knelt before me and spread my legs with his hands, running his palms up my thighs. I arched my back, and he reached up to cup my breast before leaning down and bestowing tiny kisses on the inside of my thigh. Xander looked up, making sure I was watching him, and pressed his mouth to my sex. I could feel the heat of his mouth through the satiny fabric of my underwear, and I nearly came right then and there. Pulling away, he inhaled deeply before continuing upward, his mouth a brand against my hip, stomach, breasts, neck and finally back at my mouth.

He continued to kiss me, deep and urgent, sucking, teasing, tasting. I trembled as his hand inched back down my stomach, fiddling at the elastic of my underwear. He paused for the briefest moment before plunging his hand past the waistband, and when his fingers brushed against my slick heat, he groaned.

"Gods," he murmured against my mouth. "You feel so good." He circled the sensitive knot of nerves at my core, and I gripped his muscled shoulders, throwing my head back with a cry. "So wet. For me."

My body trembled with need, pleasure sweeping over me in waves. Xander's pace slowed nearly to a stop, and I rolled my hips, pressing against his hand, desperate for him to continue. "Tell me you're wet for me, Darian."

"Yes," I whispered. I thrust my hips against his hand once more.

He brushed his finger across my clit once and I shuddered. "Say it."

"Xander . . ." For some reason, I didn't want to say it. Couldn't admit that he could evoke this feeling in me.

Another languid stroke. Just enough to drive me crazy. "Say it," he commanded.

"I—I'm wet . . . for you." I wasn't exactly a world-class sexy talker, but the words shouldn't have been so hard for me to say.

He leaned over me and kissed me deeply. "Say it again."

"I'm wet for you, Xander."

As his fingers stroked, I arched my back, thrusting my hips against him. Xander kissed me, his tongue penetrating my mouth while his fingers brought me to a state of ecstasy. I wanted more. Needed to be swept away from reality. I maneuvered my body to the edge of the cushion, close enough now that I could reach out and stroke Xander's shaft. His breath hitched in his chest, and he pulled away so he could stare straight into my eyes. "I want you," I whispered.

Xander's breath became heavy and his nostrils flared. As fast as a lion pouncing, he laid me out on the couch, his body covering me. His mouth seized mine, his kisses now bordering on desperate. He rubbed his erection against me with deliberate intent, through the fabric of my underwear, bringing me close to the brink. I opened myself up to him, wrapping my legs around his hips and digging my heels into the backs of his thighs. Xander moaned into my mouth, refusing to break our kiss, as I pressed my hips against him. The pressure built up in me with each stroke, every nerve ending in my body alive and sparking with electricity. Pleasure crested over me and I cried out, swept up in the pulsing orgasm that rocked me from the center of my body, outward to my limbs.

As the waves of pleasure began to ebb, an emptiness opened up inside of me, a need to be filled, to be connected on the deepest level with another soul. I brought my hips off the couch and ground them into Xander's loins. "I need you, Xander," I pleaded. "I want you inside of me. Now."

With a groan that was guttural and echoed my need, Xander reached down, too impatient to properly undress me, and jerked my underwear aside. I felt the soft probe as he pressed against me and then a shock of heat as his broad head found my opening. I waited. Longing for him to make that final move and join us once and for all. . . .

"Xander, we have a serious damned problem! I need Darian and I can't find her any—" Raif's voice died in his throat as he came into Xander's suite. He froze for a moment, his jaw slack and eyes wide, before abruptly turning his back to us.

"Doesn't *anyone* knock in this godsforsaken house?" Xander railed. Grabbing a blanket from the foot of his bed, Xander draped it carefully over my body. He didn't seem to have an issue with his own nakedness as he rounded on Raif, his eyes blazing with anger. "You'd better have a good fucking reason for barging in here, brother." I'd never heard such a dangerous edge to Xander's voice. "Because if you don't—"

"Anya is in a bad way, *my liege*," Raif said with a sneer. "She needs to be taken to a hospital immediately."

Chapter 19

"**J**esus Christ, I don't know how she does this every day," I grunted as I worked the zipper up my back as far as I could reach. Granted, I had a little more in the hip and breast department than Anya, but I felt like I was stuffing my body into a sausage casing.

"I don't agree with this," Xander said, zipping me up the rest of the way. "It's too dangerous."

"Do you have a better idea?" I studied my reflection in the mirror, gathered my hair into a high ponytail and began to braid it.

"Your hair isn't long enough or even close to the same color. Your body isn't the same. Anyone with eyes in their head will know the difference."

True. But I didn't plan to let anyone get a close enough look—that is until it was too late to realize the mistake. "Xander, we don't have any other options, and we're running out of time. She's got to get to a doctor. Right fucking now." Even with my nonexistent medical expertise, I knew that bleeding in a pregnant woman was cause for alarm. "I know it's not going to fool Kade. Not really. But if he's out there and decides to take a shot, I'd rather he took it at me."

Xander gave a derisive snort and began pacing back and forth. "Cavalier, aren't you?" His arms were folded, chin resting between one thumb and forefinger. "There's got to be another way to get her the care she needs without risking your safety."

I rolled my eyes. We didn't have time to hash this out. I finished braiding my hair; the long plait hung just to my shoulder blades. Shorter than Anya's by about a foot, but it was the best I could do at such short notice. Besides, like I'd told Xander, I knew I wouldn't be able to completely fool Kade. Not with Anya being his branded property. All I needed was an optical illusion. Something to draw his attention from the real Anya we'd be ushering into the private hospital. I'd wait for him to jump me and then I'd kill his sorry ass once and for all. I just had to hope there weren't any magical rules and regulations regarding demon slayings. Besides, if I managed to take his head from his shoulders during a fight, I doubted there was enough magic in the world to keep him alive.

"Are we ready?" I asked Louella through my earpiece. She was in Anya's suite, getting her changed into a nice black ensemble. My clothes. I'd instructed Louella to put Anya's longer locks in a ponytail and tuck it under in a fashion that would suggest she had shorter hair. Not exactly what I wanted to be doing under emergency circumstances. But at this point, we had no other choice.

"We're ready," Louella answered, "headed for the front of the house right now."

"Good. I'll meet you down there."

"At least let me come with you," Xander said, still pacing like a caged animal.

"Too suspicious. Besides, I need you to stay here with Dimitri and keep him calm."

"Gods, Darian, are you trying to kill me?" Xander raked his hands through his hair, stuffed his hands in his pockets, and pulled them back out again. Lord, but he was jumpy. It was making me twitch. "I'm the king, for Christ's sake, not some helpless child. Stop ordering me around."

Even in an emergency, Xander just had to remind everyone who he was. "Look, Xander, don't worry your pretty little head off. I'll be fine." Hadn't he told me recently that he knew I was more than capable of taking care of myself? What the hell? "Raif will be with me. My team, too. We're protected."

"I just don't think—"

"I don't care what you think." I cringed at the volume and tone of my words. I hadn't meant to be so snappy, but I didn't have time for his unnecessary concern. I crossed the room to him, and he leveled his gaze to mine. "I'll be fine. Promise."

Xander groaned and took my face in his hands. "You'd better be. Go." Releasing his hold, he guided me toward the door. "Take care of her and yourself."

I gave him what I hoped was a reassuring smile. "Take care of Dimitri. *Do not* let him out of this house. I'll be back soon."

With a final glance at my reflection, I ran out of the room, the heels of my—Anya's—boots tapping a frantic rhythm as I rushed to the front door to meet Anya, Raif, and the rest of my team.

As Raif drove like a madman, weaving through and around the late-night traffic, I focused my attention on the cadence of Anya's measured but harsh breaths. She hadn't spoken a word, merely followed directions and dressed in my clothes. I could tell she was in pain. She doubled over and hugged her abdomen, but she never so much as grunted. I had to give it to her, Anya was about as tough and brave as they came.

Raif gave a furtive glance in the rearview mirror, looking quickly away when my eyes met his. I could feel the flush of embarrassment creep to my cheeks. Of all the people to see me undressed and in a compromising situation . . . why, oh *why* did it have to be him?

I couldn't even blame the king's seduction tactics this time. Xander had opened up to me, told me things he hadn't even told his own brother, and in return, he'd simply asked that I try to let go. *Live* my life instead of dictate the course of it. I wanted nothing more than to show him that no matter what he thought to the contrary, I could loosen the reins of my control. I'd wanted to prove to myself that I could move on with my life just as easily as Tyler had. In the aftermath, I was nothing more than a tangled mess of uncertainty and mixed emotions. *Way to go, dipshit. You haven't proven anything but the fact that you're an emotional train wreck.*

I couldn't help but feel that what I'd done tonight with Xander was somehow a betrayal. I doubted Tyler bothered with such torturous thoughts when he was naked and entwined with his perfect Jinn girlfriend. I mean, why waste time thinking of me when his hands were full of perfection that would put a Greek myth to shame?

Christ, I was *losing* it. Anya was right, I was poison. Sure, Xander had egged me on, playing with my emotions to maneuver me right where he wanted me. Namely, underneath him. But what I'd done was worse. I'd let him play me so I'd have an excuse for my behavior. So that in a moment—like right now—when I felt guilty about what I'd done, I'd have someone to blame. This was Xander's fault. He'd practically *dared* me.

Yeah, like that flimsy excuse would help me sleep better at night.

"The cramping's getting worse," Anya said through gritted teeth. "Are we almost there?"

Nice. *Selfish much, Darian?* I gave myself a mental slap across the face. Good god, this was *not* the time for worrying about my twisted love life. What the hell was wrong with me? I stretched my legs—they felt as sturdy as Jell-O—and my brain wasn't much better. I was in no condition to fight, yet here I was, looking for one. It was the only way to take Kade's attention away from Anya long enough for her to receive the care she needed. And one thing I knew for certain: Kade was watching.

"You good to go?" I asked Anya as Raif pulled the car up to the curb. Despite the fact that she was in a lot of pain, she'd have to be ready to put up a good show.

"Ready," she said and took a deep breath.

Raif opened the door, and Anya took one last cleansing breath. Gritting her teeth against the pain, she ushered me out in front of her, glancing around as if checking for potential threats, which, of course, she was. I, on the other hand, ducked my head and clutched my abdomen, doing my best impersonation of pained pregnant female. Anya stayed glued to my side, and when we ducked into the building it was my turn to breathe a deep sigh of relief. I sent Louella and the rest of my team with Anya and the handful of medical professionals who'd been called ahead to meet us.

"Go with Anya, Raif," I said as I pulled a nurse aside. "I need you to stay with her."

Raif nodded in response, taking up the rear of the procession without a question asked. If there was one single person on this planet I knew I could always count on, it was Raif. "If you need me . . ." he turned and said.

"I know." I smiled, momentarily forgetting the awkwardness between us. "How do I get to the roof?" I asked the nurse who'd begun to pull away so she could follow Anya.

"There's a fire escape ladder at the back of the building," she said, pointing down a dark hallway. "Take the exit at the end of that hall. The door should be unlocked."

I left the nurse to her business and took off at a slow jog. How Anya did anything in four-inch stilettos was beyond me. As it was, I felt like I was running on a pair of stilts. But I had to keep the illusion intact for however long I could. I didn't want Kade going after Anya while she was weak. And as for Dimitri, Kade hadn't stepped foot near Xander's property so far. I had to assume he'd continue to stay away.

If running down the hallway had seemed like a feat, then climbing the fire escape was nothing short of a miracle. The slick soles of Anya's boots kept slipping on the rungs of the ladder, and I tripped myself up on the damn heels more than once. What an utter annoyance. By the time I made it to the roof, I was ready to pitch the goddamned shoes right over the edge. I began to sweat, as much from nerves as exertion, and coupled with the too tight leather jumpsuit I sported, made for one cranky bitch. No *wonder* Anya was so sour all the time.

I found a vantage point from the northeast side of the building that let me see the streets that bordered the medical facility as well as the back alley. So far so good. Nothing appeared out of the ordinary. Maybe Kade needed a night off from stalking Anya. God knows I needed a night off from guarding her.

As I monitored the flow of traffic—and pedestrians—on the street below, my mind drifted to my evening with Xander. Even now I felt the heat rush to my cheeks as I thought about the things we'd done and the things we'd been about to do. Six months ago I would have laughed hysterically at the thought of *being* with the Shaede King. And I'd managed to convince myself that what had once been completely unacceptable was the best course of action to make me feel better . . . about what? The fact that the only person I'd ever truly loved didn't love me in return?

No matter what Anya thought, love had nothing to do with what was developing between Xander and me. More like a relationship of convenience. I trailed my fingers down between my breasts, toward my stomach, pausing at all of the places Xander's mouth had branded me. Could there be any truth in Anya's words, though? Was I being cruel, leading Xander on for my own selfish reasons? Or rather, was he an active participant, in it for nothing more than the conquest?

"You're like a walking storm of pure sexual energy," a voice said from behind me.

Ah, shit. Looked like I wasn't getting a night off after all. Kade stepped out of the shadows, his confident swagger lending to, rather than detracting from, his otherworldly beauty.

"The air around you is heavy with desire," he said, making a show of smelling the space in front of him. "Charged with it." He licked his lips in a very sensual way. "Delicious."

My knowledge of Incubi was limited, but I did know they fed from their victim's life force during sex. I had to assume that my erotic thoughts had set off some sort of pheromone beacon. It was one way to hook a Cambion, I supposed.

"Did you really think you could fool me, playing dress-up?" he asked with a laugh. "Come now, Trouble, you *had* to know it wouldn't work."

"Well, I gave it the ol' college try," I said. "Look, Kade"— I took a tentative step toward my target, my fingers caressing the hilt of my dagger—"you're a good-looking guy, charming and all that. Who knows, maybe you've got brains to boot. Leave the city tonight, and if you promise to never show your pretty face here again, I'll promise not to ruin your good looks with the edge of my blade. Deal?"

"How I *love* complicated women," Kade said with a sigh. Instead of retreating like he should have, he took a step closer to me. And then another. "And I'll bet you're very, very complicated, aren't you?"

Damn, he was a sexy SOB. "Nah," I said, slowly drawing my dagger from the sheath and holding it close to my side. "I'm not complicated at all. I'm a pretty simple girl, really.

So, what's it gonna be, Kade? Are you going to leave my city, or am I going to give you a free face-lift?"

"Give me a kiss, and I'll think about it."

Kade closed the distance between us in the blink of an eye. I swung my arm up, the point of the dagger nicking the flesh at his jugular. He stopped dead in his tracks, his clear blue eyes narrowed shrewdly. "Sorry, Kade," I purred. "I don't kiss on the first date."

"Well, then, lucky for me, Trouble," he said in an equally seductive voice, "this is technically our third date."

Kade's movements were a blur in my vision as he knocked my arm aside. The dagger flew out of my hand, landing somewhere in the shadows. I went for my katana, but didn't get a chance to pull it free from the scabbard. He wrapped his hand around my neck, his fingers constricting any intake of air. Slowly, he backed me to the edge of the building until my heels teetered precariously on the edge.

"You're not a tease, are you?" he asked, his fingers biting into my flesh. "Because I'd find that disappointing."

I wanted to grace him with my best snarky comment, but unfortunately, Kade's death grip on my throat wouldn't allow any air in—or words out. He gave me a good, rough shake, and my right heel slipped completely off the ledge. *Do it, dipshit,* I thought. *Give me a proper shove.* Shadows don't worry about things like gravity. In fact . . . I was tired of dicking around.

I joined with the shadows and left my corporeal form behind in a dusting of black mist. Before Kade could process what had happened, I drew the katana from my back. I wasn't about to waste any more time with his jackassed posturing. This was business and it was time to go to work. Right leg behind my left, I drew back my sword arm, ready to strike. Cambion or not, Kade wasn't going anywhere without his head.

He spun around to face me, dodging out of the way before I could properly decapitate him. Damn, he was fast. Faster than any supernatural creature I'd ever gone up against. I repositioned my aim, swung the blade in an upward cut, and Kade jumped backward. Strands of his shining blond hair drifted on the breeze from where the katana's blade had brushed his long bangs. "That was a little too close for comfort," he mused, his fist swinging around and catching me right in the jaw.

The katana flew from my grip as I stumbled backward, unable to achieve any kind of sure footing in the ill-fitting stiletto boots. Goddamn Anya and her shitty fashion sense. Before I could right myself, Kade jumped me, grabbing me by the collar of the leather jumpsuit and pulling me close. "You owe me a kiss," he said, laying his mouth to mine.

The moment our lips met, I felt a strange pull from the center of my being, like I'd let out a great gust of breath followed by a delicious rush that chased through my veins like fire. My legs felt suddenly weak, and my head spun. The sensation of being pelted with tiny beads of hail made my skin tingle, both hot and cold as whatever it was that Kade pulled from me left my body and entered his.

"Whoo!" Kade whooped to the sky as he pulled away. "Damn, what a rush!" He grabbed on to the long rope of my braided hair, forcing my face to his until our noses were almost touching. "I knew you weren't an ordinary Shaede. What are you?"

I struggled for the energy to form even simple words. I felt light-headed and giddy as if I'd just downed a couple of drinks and was beginning to feel the buzz. Forget sex, Kade had managed to feed off my energy from a simple kiss. Granted, the kiss he'd laid on me was hardcore, but still . . . "Try that again, Kade"—my words slurred as I wobbled on my feet—"and I'll introduce your nuts to the pointy end of my dagger. You get me?"

Kade flashed an angelic smile, his expression rapt. "A man could become addicted to what you've got to offer," he said, moving in for another kiss. "I could get used to having you around, Trouble."

I fumbled with my belt, desperate to defend myself before Kade could further weaken me. My fingertips brushed the hilt of one of my throwing knifes, just the weapon I needed for Kade's too close quarters. I jabbed the sharp point just below Kade's ribs, plunging the blade into his flesh. He sucked his breath in sharply and shoved me to the ground as he surveyed the damage I'd done.

"I warned you, Kade," I said, pushing myself up to stand. "I bite." No time to go after my sword, I took off at a run, or rather a quick trot, prepared to take him down in a tackle. I still wasn't one hundred percent after Kade's energy suck. If I had to kill him with the tiny throwing knife, then so be it.

"I wish for my enemy to be immobilized," Kade whispered, his voice carried to me by the wind.

Before I could jab him again with the knife, the air rippled with energy and out of nowhere a force threw me to my back, sending me sailing ten feet from where Kade stood watching the spectacle with perverse interest. A shimmer of light disrupted the surrounding darkness taking the shape of feminine perfection. I fought to stand, but Adira's Jinn magic kept me down. What the *fuck* was she doing here?

"Everyone should have a Jinn, don't you think?" Kade asked as he came to stand behind Adira. He ran his palm down the length of her shining hair, and I could have sworn I saw her cringe away from the contact. "I find having one extremely handy."

Adira didn't meet Kade's eyes, but instead looked down on me, her face a mask of passivity. "The trick is knowing how to manipulate the rules," Kade continued matter-of-factly. "Once you learn to make yourself truly need everything you ask for, it's easy to blur the lines. Isn't that right, Adira?"

Adira inclined her head in Kade's direction, but her eyes never left mine. She was careful not to show her emotions. Son of a bitch, if I hadn't been so worried about my current predicament, I would have been furious. Tyler. He'd used me. He knew damn good and well that both of us were forbidden from using Jinn magic to interfere with the bond between Kade and Adira. But that hadn't stopped Ty from taking a chance and hiring me to kill the bastard. If I was successful, there'd be no bond to fuck with, and Tyler knew it. And I wondered how the hell he thought I'd be able to circumvent the rules—not to mention Adira's protection—to get it done. Damn him.

"Darian?"

"Darian, where are you?"

Two sets of voices shouted from the street below. Raif and Asher.

"Did you find her?" Julian's voice echoed in the distance to join the other two.

Didn't anyone *ever* listen to me? I'd told them to stay with Anya. *An-ya*. Not me. I swore under my breath. If I wanted a job done right, I guess I'd have to do it myself.

"She asked the nurse how to get to the roof," Raif said, his voice louder. *Shit*. The air became dense as several sets of shadows converged at the top of the fire escape. My would-be rescuers who'd abandoned their posts in search of me. *Idiots*.

"I'm going to expect more than a kiss on our next date, Trouble," Kade said before turning to Adira. "I wish I was somewhere far from here, somewhere safe," he told her.

Without uttering a word, the air around Kade and Adira shimmered with magic and in the blink of an eye, they were gone.

"Was that him?" Raif asked, stepping from the shroud of shadows and standing corporeal at my side.

"That was Kade," I said, taking Raif's hand as he offered to help me stand. I limped in Anya's insufferable stilettos as I retrieved my dagger and katana from where I'd dropped them. Goddamn it, I needed a stiff drink. Problem was, Kade's kiss had made me feel like I'd already had a few too many.

"Who was the woman?" Raif asked.

Where to begin . . . "The woman"—I swallowed down the almost drunken laughter that threatened to escape my lips. I sheathed my sword and drew a deep breath to steady myself—"is Adira. Kade's Jinn."

"Holy shit," Raif said.

Exactly.

Chapter 20

"When are you coming home?" Xander asked. His tone, normally so reserved, conveyed his need to command even through the phone.

"Not for a while," I said. "I'm not leaving until Anya is discharged."

I didn't need the medical details; my job was protecting Anya and her precious cargo. Neither she, nor the baby, was in any imminent danger, but she was being held for observation. There was no way I was going to leave her vulnerable. Kade could pop back in at any time. And now that I knew he had a genie in his corner, the situation had become a hell of a lot more dangerous.

Silence answered me, and if Xander hadn't sighed heavily, I would have thought he'd disconnected the call. Several awkward moments passed as we sat in silence, and I wondered what the hell Xander was doing on the other end of the line.

"I have several appointments during the day," Xander finally said. "I probably won't see you until well after dark."

"Well, then, it'll give you something to look forward to," I said.

Another stretch of silence passed between us before Xander said, "Tonight, then. Good-bye, Darian."

Xander hung up before I could say anything in response. I wondered at his strange behavior, not exactly his usual cocky self. More melancholy. Broody. *Great.* Tucking my cell into my back pocket, I headed up to the roof. In my own clothes. Anya had been sporting a hospital gown since they'd admitted her, and I wasn't about to walk around in her leather and heels for another second.

A cool spring breeze caressed my face as I settled myself back on the roof of the hospital. Dawn was still a couple of hours off, and I welcomed the silky darkness that flowed over my skin like satin. I marveled at the way the city never settled down. No matter the hour, the weather, the day . . . What did people do in the calm moments of their lives? I'd probably never know. My life was more like a churning sea.

"I wish Tyler was here right now."

I didn't have to turn around to know he was standing behind me. His energy pulsed against my back, steady, rhythmic, and not altogether unpleasant. For months I'd wished for him to come home to me and those wishes had all been denied. *Need.* Kade had said that the trick was making yourself truly need everything you wished for. Had I merely wanted Tyler to come home? To assuage my guilt and tell me all was forgiven? Had I not *needed* him enough? The rules of our binding made my head spin. Who decided what was a want and what was a need? Because it sure as hell wasn't me.

My eyes drifted shut for the briefest moment as I tried to absorb the calm, to feel that unattainable peace his presence brought. "How could you use me like that?" My voice was barely a whisper as I fought against the lump rising in my throat. "You knew Adira was bound to Kade. She has to protect him no matter what. And still you sent me after him?"

Sure, more or less, Xander had done the same thing. But he hadn't a clue who was threatening Anya or what kind of mystical protection backed him up. But Tyler. The last person I would have ever expected to throw me in the path of danger . . . he'd known all along. And he hadn't even hesitated.

"I told you." Tyler stood so close, I could feel his breath on my neck. "I couldn't directly interfere. I wasn't *able* to give you a heads-up."

What a crock. I whipped around to face him, the rage a mounting inferno in the pit of my stomach. "That's a total load of bullshit, and you know it, Tyler!" The time for closed-up throats and meek whisperings was over. "What happened, did your girlfriend get in a little over her head and she asked you to bail her out?" I rose up onto my toes so I could shout right into Ty's face. "And of course, who better to do your dirty work for you? I've killed a Shaede crown prince and one of the *original* Guardians of *O Anel*. Guess you thought taking out a demon would be small potatoes for someone like me. But you forgot something there, *champ*." I poked my finger at his chest, hard. "Kade's *Jinn* won't allow him to be killed. Not by me or anyone!"

Tyler took a tentative step back and scrubbed his hands over his face. He avoided my pointed gaze, instead looking up toward the stars barely visible in the glare of the street-lights. "You're right," he said, low. "I did think if anyone could kill Kade, it would be you. My actions were com-pletely selfish. I'll own that."

Well, wasn't that big of him.

"But don't think for a second that my decision didn't tear me up." He looked away from the sky and lowered his gaze to mine. His hazel eyes burned with a familiar intensity, swallowing everything around me until there was only the two of us. "You're forgetting, Darian, you have a Jinn as well. I'd never let him hurt you. I'd never let *anything* hurt you."

"Oh, yeah," I scoffed. "Then where the hell were you to-night when that bastard had me half hanging off this roof? Or when he put his Cambion skills to work and tried to suck me dry with a kiss?"

"He put his mouth on you?" Tyler's hands balled into tight fists, and his words rumbled in his chest, an angry growl.

I made sure to keep my tone as level as possible. "He's one hell of a kisser."

The air temperature around me dropped about twenty de-grees and I shivered, suddenly cold. Tyler's anger settled in the air like a winter frost. I took a step back this time. The energy he exuded was so intense, it stole my breath. Why should he care who kissed me? I wasn't his to worry about anymore.

"I want that bastard dead so bad I can taste it," Tyler ex-claimed through gritted teeth. "Gods, I feel so fucking help-less!"

His frustration was palpable, and damned if I didn't feel just a little sorry for him. No one likes to feel helpless, espe-cially when someone you love is in danger. Out of habit, I rubbed at my sternum, the hollow ache of Tyler leaving me as fresh as it was the day he'd packed his bags. He'd cared about me like that, once. And now, his concern was reserved for another woman.

"Darian." The faraway look in his gorgeous eyes faded as if he were snapping back to reality. "I'm sorry, I didn't—"

"Don't, Ty." I could tell from his tone that if I allowed him to give voice to his thoughts, it would break me. Permanently.

"He'll kill her." He avoided my gaze, once more looking at the sky. "Kade is using her for his sick, twisted revenge. And when he's done with her, there'll be nothing left."

"He claims he's found a way around the rules," I said. I figured Ty needed to know everything I knew and vice versa. Otherwise, Kade would have the upper hand. "He mentioned something about making himself truly need everything he asked for. Could Kade have figured out a way to cheat the system?"

I lost Tyler to his thoughts as he mulled over what I'd told him. Wish-granting wasn't a free-for-all; it came with a strict set of rules. You couldn't just want for something; wishes were granted only when you asked for something you absolutely needed. And along those lines, you couldn't make wishes that pertained to death, life, love, or the bonds of others. But if Kade had found a way around all of those Jinn rules and regulations, surely he would have wished Dimitri, Anya, and their unborn child dead months ago.

"Kade is a sociopath," Tyler finally said. "He's blinded by the need for power and revenge. And I don't think he's too bothered about who he uses or kills to get what he wants. He's got nothing to lose, Darian. And someone like that is dangerous."

Wasn't that the fucking truth? I'd known my share of desperate men with nothing to lose. And I'd killed all of them. "Let's say for the sake of argument that I find a way to get the upper hand on Kade," I said. "Adira will try to protect him. Her life is tied to his now. Will you be willing to risk her safety? If I kill him . . . won't she die as well?" Xander had once told me that when a Jinn binds himself to someone, their lives become entwined. Ty had never confirmed it to me, but I suspected Xander's assumption was correct. Jinn were the most complicated and secretive of any supernatural creature I'd ever encountered. Even Tyler was reluctant to share information about his bond with me. Jesus, you'd think spilling the beans would cause a global meltdown or something.

Tyler turned his back to me. It was for the best, I suppose. It's not like I was anxious to see the expression of worry, or even love for Adira, on his face. He bowed his head, ran his hands through his hair. "I was always jealous of Azriel," he said, surprising me with the sudden change of subject. Was he avoiding my question? "Or more to the point, I was jealous of the past you shared with him."

My heart dropped into my stomach at Tyler's words. The pain in his voice cut through me like a well-honed blade. Why couldn't we just stop hurting one another? Was there to be no end to the damage?

"I wanted to be first," he continued. "I wanted it to have been me that saved you from that hell of your human life. Not him. I wanted to be everything to you."

Tears stung at my eyes and I quickly brushed them away. "You were." He was *still* everything to me. But I'd never tell him that. I wouldn't give him the satisfaction of having that power over me. "And for what it's worth, you did save me. I'm the one who let you down. Not the other way around."

"Darian . . ."

God, the sound of my name on his lips, it was breaking my heart all over again. "Go home, Tyler. You'd better check on her, make sure she's okay."

He turned to face me, his expression tearing my composure to shreds.

"I wish you were with Adira," I said, unable to contain the sob that rose in my throat, "where you belong."

"Are you all right?" Raif asked.

The sun crested over the tallest buildings, breaking through a patch of dark gray storm clouds. A perfect representation of my life, really, bits and pieces of light occasionally piercing the darkness. "I'm fine," I said, knowing Raif wouldn't buy it. "Just tired."

"I think that, perhaps I've been selfish," Raif said as he moved to stand beside me.

"How so?"

"Maybe I didn't give you enough time. I should have let you come around in your own way, at your own pace. Instead, I threw the idea of moving you into the house of my brother—and before you decide to go on about my gallantry, you should know that I was fully aware that he'd take the opportunity to distract you from your grief."

If Raif only realized the truth. I was much worse than his brother. "Raif," I said through a deep sigh, "before you go on about my innocence, you should know that I'm not the one being played. Fear for your brother's virtue, not mine."

Raif cleared his throat and I could've sworn as I looked at him from the corner of my eye that he was trying to hide a smile. "Have we bitten off more than we can chew with Kade?" he asked. "We may have to send Anya and Dimitri away for a while."

If only a solution were that easy. "There's nowhere on this planet you could stash them where they'd be safe from him." The brand on Anya's shoulder guaranteed that.

"What about *O Anel*?" Raif asked.

The door to *O Anel*, the Faery Realm, had been locked long ago. The only person with access in or out was a Guardian. And I just so happened to be the girl with the key. Sending Anya and Dimitri to that place was out of the question. My job as Guardian was to protect the doorway and the secret of the Time Keeper, Raif's daughter. No way would I risk her safety by possibly alerting Kade to the existence of this other realm. Time and maintaining the natural order was too important to risk.

"I think you know the answer to that question," I told Raif. "No one is running or hiding from this. As far as Kade's concerned, I never leave a job unfinished."

Raif nodded in agreement. "We need to regroup, form a better plan of attack."

He was right. But then, when it came to strategy, Raif knew his business. "We've been on the defensive for too long," I said. "It's time to bring this fight to Kade's doorstep, and to do that, we've got to level the playing field."

Raif cocked a brow in question. "How do you propose we do that?"

"With Adira protecting him, he's virtually unstoppable. Without her, we've got the upper hand. The only way to defeat Kade is to eliminate Adira."

"Are you planning to kill her, too?" Raif asked, only half kidding.

If only. That plan did have its merits . . . I doubted it would do much for Tyler's and my relationship, though. "I'm not planning to kill her." I couldn't suppress a chuckle. "What I'm planning is a hell of a lot more dangerous than threatening her life."

"What *are* you planning, Darian?" Raif asked.

"I'm going to break her bond with Kade."

"Darian," Raif said with concern. "Are you sure you're up for this?"

I flashed him what I hoped was a reassuring smile. Was I up for this? I guess we'd see soon enough.

Chapter 21

"**D**arian, wake up. They're sending Anya home."

Raif nudged my shoulder for a second time, and I cracked one eye and then the other. The clock in the waiting room read eleven twenty-five a.m. Some bodyguard I was, I hadn't even realized I'd fallen asleep.

"How long have I been sleeping?" I asked as I shot up out of my chair. "Where is everyone?"

"Relax," Raif said, patting me on the back. "I *let* you sleep. By gods, you needed some rest, though I doubt a couple of hours are going to do you much good. Louella and Myles are posted outside of Anya's room. The rest of your team is watching outside and bringing the car around."

Why the hell Raif had thought it a good idea to put me in charge of his soldiers, I'd never know. I couldn't manage to get my own shit together, let alone supervise an entire team of personnel. "Is Anya ready to go?"

"Five minutes, give or take," Raif said as he checked the clock.

"How is she?" Our little clearing of the air had changed our relationship, albeit just a little. I knew Anya and I weren't going to have matching BFF lockets around our necks or anything, but we'd reached an understanding of sorts. I'm not going to lie; it felt good to soften that adversarial edge between us.

"She's fine. The baby as well."

I rubbed my palm against the back of my neck trying to work out the stiffness that had settled into my muscles from sleeping in the chair. Pins and needles stung one leg that had fallen asleep and I shook it out, certain I wouldn't be able to stand on it until some of the sensation returned.

"She's on bed rest for a couple of days," Raif continued. "Which is good for us."

True. But then again, Kade had a Jinn on his side. I doubted keeping her shut up in Xander's house was going to keep Kade at bay for long. After all, this was a game to him. Simply killing Dimitri and stressing Anya to the point of miscarriage wouldn't be enough. He had every intention of making Anya suffer. When he was through playing games, I suspected we'd be shit out of luck. That is, unless I could find a way to break his bond with Adira before he decided to quit with the cat and mouse routine.

"We'll keep Anya glued to her bed for a couple days," I said as if she wasn't already under strict orders. "In the meantime, I'll work on a way to break Kade's bond with Adira."

"Sounds like a decent plan," Raif said. "But I won't have you working alone."

Ugh. Why the hell not? I wasn't the one in danger here; Anya was the lady with the target on her back. "I don't need any help."

Raif stared right through me. I hated that look. The you're-not-putting-one-over-on-me look. "I know what I saw on that roof last night. Kade could be a threat to you as well."

Oh, lovely. "Just what do you think you saw, Raif?"

"I saw hunger in the demon's eyes. I don't think it's a good idea for you to be out and about without an escort."

Hunger. I suppose that was the perfect word. After getting a taste of my energy, Kade *had* seemed overeager. And I didn't think I'd be a very willing participant in whatever he had planned for our *next date.* "Fine," I said. "I'll take someone with me. But I'm not traipsing around with an entire gang. Got it?"

"Gang?" Raif laughed. "All I'm asking is that when you go out, you go with backup. Be it a single man or a handful, I don't care. But go nowhere alone."

Easy enough. "Okay, Raif. Deal."

Dimitri was climbing the walls by the time we got Anya back to the house. And I was beginning to feel another attack of hypocrisy coming on. I didn't think it was fair to keep him in the dark. He was as much a part of this as anyone. In fact, he shared Anya's past. He knew all about the bastard Kade was. He may not know all of the details, but I felt like Anya at least owed him an explanation.

"I'm not telling you what to do," I murmured close to Anya's ear. "But I think he deserves to know the truth."

"You'd be better off minding your own business," she hissed.

"I'm just saying," I said as I pretended to guide her up the stairs. Dimitri had run up ahead to their suite to get a cozy spot ready for her. "He's got to be getting a little suspicious. I mean, we made him stay here while you went to the hospital, for Christ's sake. If he knows the truth, we won't have to keep him under lock and key, and he might be more cautious."

"Or he might fly into a rage and take off after Kade, himself. Darian, he may appear good-natured and easygoing. But you don't know Dimitri. Not really."

She had a point. Both Raif and Xander regarded Anya's husband with a certain level of respect. And I doubted he'd earned it from being the class clown. "In that case, my advice would be to act like the neediest, whiniest pregnant woman on the face of the earth for a while. Give him no other choice but to be stuck to you like glue. Because if I can't find a way to take Kade down in the next few days, you're going to have no choice but to come clean."

Anya sighed. "You think so, huh."

"I know so. I can't keep Kade at bay for an entire year. And I can't imagine that running from him is going to be good for your pregnancy if last night's field trip is any indicator. I don't know if Raif told you or not, but Kade's got a Jinn of his very own now, which makes him infinitely more dangerous than he was."

Anya stopped, one foot on the stair ahead of us. "Shit."

"Yeah," I said, moving her along. "It's a real shit-tastic situation. That's why I don't plan on letting this go on for much longer." Well, that and the fact that I wasn't interested in any future "dates" with the Cambion. I stopped just short of the door to Anya's suite. "Can I ask you a question?"

"Yes," she said suspiciously.

"Exactly how much . . . contact does Kade need to drink a victim's energy?"

Anya's violet eyes narrowed. "Why do you ask?"

"Just humor me."

"As little as close physical contact," Anya said. "An embrace, a kiss. He can intoxicate you with little more than his touch. But that won't get him much. A sip or two of someone's life force. He'd have to get quite a bit closer to draw anything substantial from a victim."

Good to know. I had no intention of letting him get *that* close. The door swung open, putting an abrupt halt to our conversation. Dimitri swept me aside, gently wrapping his arms around his wife and ushering her into their suite. "I know you don't like this bed rest, *Milaya*," he cooed in her ear. "But I'll stay here with you and keep you company."

Anya cast a last furtive glance over her shoulder at me. A couple of days. It wasn't much time to get anything done. But I'd take what I could get. Dimitri didn't bother with me as he used his foot to shut the door behind them. I couldn't blame him. His top priority was his wife. It must be nice to be as cherished as Anya was.

"M-Ms. Charles?"

Ms. Charles? I spun around to find one of Xander's household staff standing directly behind me. I'd kept my married name over the years because, really, I needed it for legal reasons. It's not like I could open a bank account or own property with one name like *Cher* or *Madonna*. But good lord, even when I'd been human, the sound of being addressed as "Ms." or "Mrs." anything made me cringe. "Darian," I said. "Just, Darian."

The girl made as if to curtsy and I fixed her with a stern eye. If she dared as much as a head bob, I was going to wretch. "I'm supposed to escort you back to your suite, Darian. His Majesty has left instructions that you're to have a dress selection made before he returns this evening."

Hold the phone. Dress selection? What. The. Fuck. I don't know what sort of expression had crept onto my face, but the Shaede staring at me took a cautious step back. And then another. "What's your name?" I asked her.

"C-Caitlin," she stammered.

"Do I look like the sort of girl who wears dresses, Caitlin?"

Her deep brown eyes widened, and she looked as if she wondered whether or not I wanted an honest answer. "Ah, no," she said.

"So, since I obviously don't need a dress, I don't need to make a dress selection. Wouldn't you agree?"

"But, Darian," Caitlin stammered. "Th-the king . . ."

I rolled my eyes at nervous little Caitlin and stomped off in the direction of my room. A quick jerk loosened my cell from my back pocket, and I dialed Xander's private number. If he thought for one royal second I'd be going anywhere in a dress, he had another think coming.

"Are you finally home?" Xander asked by way of a greeting.

"If you mean back at my studio, then no." I hoped Xander could tell by my answer I wasn't exactly happy with him right now. "But if you're asking if I'm back at *your* house, then yes. I'm here."

"You're cranky this afternoon," Xander drawled. "Bad night?"

"You have no idea," I said. "And to make an already bad *day* worse, someone just ordered me to my room to partake in a dress selection. I don't suppose you know anything about that?"

Xander chuckled, and if he'd been standing in front of me, I might have been tempted to kick him in the shin. "Are you adverse to wearing dresses, my love?"

I was not in the mood for his cutesy attitude. "I didn't like to wear dresses eighty or so years ago, when I *had* to. Would you care to tell me what the hell this is all about?"

"Wouldn't you rather be surprised?" he asked.

In a word . . . "No."

Xander sighed. How he loved playing his games. "There's a diplomatic event in a couple of days," he said. "And you're my date."

Oh good lord. "Can't you take someone else?"

"I don't want to take anyone else. I want to take *you*."

"You could go solo. . . ."

"Darian." Xander's tone adopted that chiding, kingly

flare. "I won't allow you to argue with me on this. I want you there, and at my side. Can't you humor me and let me show you off at least once?"

Xander's *event* was going to seriously cut into my efforts to break Kade and Adira's bond. Damn it. As if he could sense my discomfort, Xander said, "Even you need a night off every once in a while."

"Anya still needs a babysitter," I countered.

"If she's feeling well enough to attend, Anya will be there," he said.

"And Dimitri?"

"I suspect he'll accompany his wife, don't you?"

Damn. Damn, damn, damn. "Xander . . ."

"Darian . . ."

"They shouldn't be out in public right now. Kade's still out there and—"

"They'll be safe, Darian," Xander interrupted me. "The PNT takes security very seriously. The entire building will be warded and the magic is impenetrable. Anya needs a night of revelry. As do you. You're going. Period."

Did I have a choice at this point? Anya would be off bed rest by the time this function rolled around, and if Dimitri was going with her, they'd need someone to watch their backs. Protective wards or not. "Fine," I said with the heaviest sigh I could muster. "I'll go. But can't I just wear my street clothes? I'll be watching over Anya, after all."

"I won't negotiate that point," Xander said. "So, I'll put this to you in a way that you'll understand. You're just going to have to *suck it up* and wear the dress, my dear."

Smug bastard. "I'll look at them." Did anyone ever win an argument with Xander? He was the most stubborn man I'd ever met. "I'm not guaranteeing anything, though."

"Your Highness," a voice said in the background, "they're ready for you."

"I've got to go," Xander said. "I can't wait to see which dress you pick out."

Before I could respond with my usual snarky comeback, Xander hung up. I stared at the phone for a couple of seconds, glaring daggers into the receiver as if he could see me.

"Well, Caitlin," I said, opening my door, "show me what you've got."

Okay, so the first two dresses weren't completely hideous. That's not to say I didn't feel like an utter idiot in them. I hadn't worn anything but stretchy pants and tight shirts in literally decades. I might as well have been trying on Halloween costumes.

"The Vera Wang is gorgeous on you," Caitlin said. Sometime between dress three and five she'd come out of her shell. She'd gone from stammering and shy to evil fashion dictator in nothing flat. "And it would go great with these black Manolo heels."

The shoes weren't bad. But they made Anya's stilettos look like flats. "You might as well scrap those shoes right now," I said. "If I can't run in them, I'm not wearing them."

"And you think you'll be running in any of these dresses?" Caitlin asked.

I quirked a brow and stared her down. I think I liked meek Caitlin better. She tucked a dark strand of her chin-length hair behind her ear and put the treacherous black shoes back in their box.

Caitlin had a point, though. I wouldn't be doing much of anything in the elegant gowns Xander had chosen for me.

"His Majesty has excellent taste," Caitlin said, running her hands down the flowing fabric of an emerald green dress. I really didn't want to admit that it had caught my eye. "You're a lucky and envied woman."

Envied, huh? "Oh, yeah?"

"Oh, yes," Caitlin said with a sigh. "The king is very handsome. And charming."

Well, she had a point there. Xander was sexy in a very toe-curling sort of way, and the man could charm the skin off a snake. He'd managed me time and again. I mean, I *was* standing in the middle of my room, surrounded by dresses and frilly things that hadn't touched my skin in decades. One thing was for certain, the King of Shaedes always got his way.

He'd wanted me, after all.

And he'd almost gotten me.

I gave Caitlin a sheepish smile and reached for the green dress. "I think this is the one," I said.

Caitlin clapped her hands together. "I was hoping you'd like this one. It was the king's favorite."

The dress was absolutely gorgeous. Vintage. Deep emerald satin overlaid with a billowing layer of lighter green chiffon. The bodice was covered in lace and woven with tiny mother-of-pearl fanning out just above the breast. The dress reminded me of one my mother had worn to a masquerade ball when I was a girl. It was just the right combination of modest and sexy. Despite my tough-girl persona, I liked it.

Smug Caitlin helped me step out of the dress, put it on its hanger, and zip it up in a plastic garment bag. We also managed to agree on a pair of matching green heels that wouldn't kill me if I moved at any pace faster than a crawl.

I stifled a yawn and looked at the clock on my desk. It was only three o'clock in the afternoon, but I'd been up most of the previous night. "So, are we done here?" I asked.

"I think so," Caitlin answered as if making a mental note. "The ball isn't for a couple of days; we'll address issues like hair and makeup the day of if that's all right with you?"

"Ball . . ." I said. "As in . . ."

"It's a PNT soirée," Caitlin said. "Their annual dignitary's ball. Didn't His Majesty tell you?"

No, His *Majesty* did not. Well, Xander had said we'd be going to an *event*. I should have known it wasn't simply going to be an intimate cocktail party. "He didn't exactly mention what it was we'd be attending," I said.

Caitlin looked like she was about to throw up. "Did I ruin a surprise?" she asked.

"No," I said, offhand. "Your king just gets off on being vague."

Eyes focused on the floor, I got the impression Caitlin wasn't sure if she should laugh at my comment or not. I just couldn't get used to all of the royal pomp and circumstance. "I'll notify the king that everything's been taken care of. If you don't need anything else, Darian, I'll leave you to your day."

Thank god. I was so ready to fall face-first on the bed and pass out. "Sounds great," I said, already heading toward the comfort of the memory foam mattress. If I ever moved back into my apartment, that mattress was moving with me. "See you around, Caitlin."

"Good day, Darian," she said, closing the door behind her.

Hello, bed, I thought as I dove onto the pillows. *I've missed you.* I hadn't realized how much Kade's little smooch had drained me. Sluggish, not to mention teetering on the edge of loopy, I knew I wasn't just sleep deprived. The Cambion had stolen something from me with his impassioned kiss. And I had no idea how long it would take to recoup my depleted energy. Or was it life essence? I had no fucking clue. As I drifted toward sleep, I thought about what Ty had said to me. *I was always jealous of Azriel. Or more to the point, I was jealous of the past you shared with him.* What had he been trying to tell me? I tried to find my way through the fog of exhaustion to coherent thought, but Raif's words mingled with Tyler's, confusing me even more. *I saw hunger in the demon's eyes.*

I'd seen that hunger, felt Kade's rapt attention as my energy nourished him. And experienced the resulting momentary euphoria from his touch.

Damn, I thought as sleep finally overtook me. *I'm so fucked.*

Chapter 22

"*Ah*, to be an aristocrat's wife."

Juliana Brighton all but sighed as she ran her fingers down the silk draperies Henry had just purchased for our great room. In fact, I'd never seen anyone look at drapery the way she did. Her eyes practically rolled back in her head, and I could have sworn I'd heard a moan escape her lips. I wondered, as I looked on, what could possibly be so appealing about curtains.

"You're certainly lucky, Darian. Henry lavishes you with such fine things. Bernard has put an end to my spending, for a while at least. He says he'll have to build a larger house to accommodate all of the new furniture if I continue to purchase new pieces!" She laughed as if frivolity was somehow amusing. If the local gossip had any merit to it, Bernard Brighton had lost half of his fortune in a bad investment. If Juliana wasn't careful, he'd be selling off her expensive acquisitions one piece at a time.

"More tea?" It was the only response I could think of. Though truthfully, I hoped she'd decline and go home. I'd been entertaining the local socialite for an hour and she'd already overstayed her welcome by a good fifty-five minutes. I was obligated to be an accommodating hostess, though. And if I managed to offend Juliana Brighton in any way, Henry would not be pleased. I absentmindedly massaged my upper arm, the bruises still tender from my husband's abuse the night before. The last thing I wanted was for my husband to not be pleased.

"I really must be going," Juliana answered. "I only stopped by to formally invite you to our Christmas Eve cel-

ebration. Only the most important people will be there, of course."

"Of course," I murmured.

"I can't wait to see your gown," Juliana sighed. "No doubt Henry will dress you up in something fine and impossibly expensive. He wouldn't dare have you out in public in anything less."

I smiled, resisting the urge to tell Juliana exactly what I thought about their lavish get-togethers. I hated them. Even now, the thought of being paraded around on Henry's arm, nothing more than a pretty ornament, another thing used to proclaim his status, made my stomach knot tight with nerves. I wanted to live a quiet life, a peaceful life where I was loved and cherished for the woman I was on the inside, not a superficial symbol of a match well made. I wanted free of this existence, but for me, there was no escape.

"Well, I must be off," Juliana exclaimed as if the world waited with bated breath to do her bidding. "I hired new kitchen staff last week and want to make sure they're doing their jobs properly. Bernard wasn't happy with our last cook. We do have to please our husbands, don't we?"

"Yes," I whispered. "We certainly do."

If Xander's house were cut down the middle, one half pressed up against a large pane of glass, I'd bet it would resemble an ant colony in many ways. Everyone rushed to do his bidding, to make his house picture-perfect every day. Cooks who spent their entire day preparing lavish meals, staff who kept his already immaculate home clean, secretaries, assistants, and whatnot. It reminded me of a life I'd been desperate to escape in my human existence. And I'd traded my humanity for that escape.

I didn't like the idle time. I despised being fawned over by Xander's staff. They treated me like the lady of the house, asking for my opinion, my . . . permission. A familiar anxiety took root in the pit of my stomach. I didn't know how much more I could take.

Raif had duties that took him away from the house, and Xander was so busy ruling his kingdom, I hadn't seen him once since our hot night of almost-sex. That's not to say he didn't call me between this meeting or that, and with his house full of eager staff, I never wanted for anything.

I was lonely, though.

"I'm not getting a damn thing accomplished," Xander said when I answered the phone. "You're all I can think about. I need to feel your bare skin, and make love to you for at least a full twenty-four hours before I'll be sated. And maybe not even then."

"Lofty goals, Your Highness," I said. The High King of Manly Prowess, among other things. "But with the way things are going, I doubt you have twenty-four minutes free, let alone a full day's worth of hours."

"I should be home in an hour or two. We can have a late dinner together. And afterward." He sighed. "Ah, my love . . . the wicked things I'm going to do to you. . . ."

"Umm . . ."

"Darian," Xander's velvet voice carried an edge of frustration. "Do not tell me you're not going to have dinner with me."

I rolled my eyes. Xander and his damn meals. I swore his entire day revolved around eating and making sure that *I* ate. I wondered if all males possessed some primal urge to feed their females. As if their genetic makeup demanded that they provide sustenance. I didn't think having my meals prepared by a staff of professional chefs counted in Xander's favor, however.

The sun had been past the horizon for an hour already, and tonight was Anya's last night of bed rest. Tomorrow night I'd be trussed up in green satin and heels for the PNT soirée. Levi had finally managed to track down a lead on breaking Kade's bond. I was running out of time, and I had to use this opportunity to go after the pain-in-the-ass Cambion before he got his hands on Dimitri, Anya, or both. *Oh, right, dinner.* I'd almost forgotten. "Fine, I won't tell you that. Just don't expect to see me in your dining room tonight."

"You're not going to be home when I get there, are you?"

For some reason, when Xander referred to his house as *home* it made me break out into a cold sweat. The term was so damn . . . *domestic.* And he used it with such casual ease.

Like, *Honey, I'm home!* or some shit. Donna Reed, I wasn't. Xander had to know that.

"I'm working tonight," I said. "Anya's still confined to her suite, and I need to try and track Kade down before he manages to cause any more trouble."

"Send your team after the demon," Xander said. "You don't utilize them enough. That's what I gave them to you for."

Oh, I was going to utilize them, all right. Raif refused to let me set foot out the front door without them. "I'm using my team," I said. I checked the edge of my dagger before slipping it into the sheath at my thigh. "But I'll be damned if I just sit here, useless, barking orders."

"You infuriate me," Xander said. I could almost picture him folding his arms across his chest as he pouted. "I command an entire kingdom, and I can't get one slip of a woman to do as I ask."

"Wow, Xander," I said, making sure a sufficient amount of snark leaked through in my tone. "That's a real progressive attitude you're sporting. Where'd you pick that up, anyway? I'm thinking sometime around 1412 . . ."

"You're not funny." Xander snorted.

"I'm hilarious."

Xander sighed again, and this time it had nothing do with wistful fantasies. "I'll wait up for you."

"You don't have to." I strapped my katana on my back. Time to go.

"I'm afraid I do. Be careful tonight."

"Always," I said, before disconnecting the call.

Too impatient for even my preternatural speed, I blew down the stairs as nothing more than a wisp of shadow. Incorporeality had its benefits, but it didn't do shit for tension headaches. There wasn't enough Excedrin on the planet for the sharp pain that had begun to pulse between my temples. Xander stressed me the fuck out. I had enough on my plate dealing with Anya and Kade. Couldn't he see that this was not the time to go all neglected lover on me? And what gave him the right to even try? True, we'd been about to seal the deal the other night, but after my earlier encounter with Tyler, I knew I wasn't even close to being over him yet. What was brewing between Xander and me was more like—

"Let's rock this bitch!" Julian said with his usual gusto, materializing before me in the foyer.

One by one each member of my team recovered their corporeal forms, standing in a semicircle near Xander's front door. Julian's enthusiasm was admirable. I wished I felt the same. But for what I was about to do, I'd need more than a goddamned pep talk.

"I need everyone on task tonight," I said, my gaze roaming over both Asher and Myles. "Anyone not prepared to follow my orders to the T, better just stay right here for the night. I'm not putting up with any bullshit. Got it?"

Myles nodded solemnly, but Asher just grinned. I suppressed the groan that threatened to rise up my throat but I couldn't do anything about my eyes rolling. That kid was going to be the death of me. "If I set out a task for you, you do it. No questions asked. Kade's got an ace in the hole, his very own Jinn. And whereas that wouldn't normally bother me too much, he's learned how to make the most of his wishing experience. He's beyond dangerous."

"Shit," Julian scoffed. "I'm not worried. Bastard's goin' down tonight."

"Gods, Julian," Liam joked from my left side. "Does your mouth ever quit running?"

"Hater!" Julian coughed into his fist.

"Fuck you," Liam said with a grin.

"Both of you shut up." I didn't have the patience for any frat-boy antics. But at least I knew Liam would be on task. Maybe I should have left the rest of the team home and taken the hulking, tattooed Shaede as my backup. God knew he'd be able to hold his own in a fight. "Let's go," I said, jerking my chin toward the door. "We haven't got all night, and I want to wrap this up."

"Ladies first," Julian said, sweeping his arm in front of the group to open a path for Louella. She snorted and brushed past him, jabbing her elbow into his ribs as she swung open the door.

Julian's gallantry ended at the petite, dark-haired beauty, though. He stumbled after her like a puppy, leaving the rest of us to trail behind. I'd have to separate those two before someone—namely Julian—got distracted. And killed in the process.

Since we didn't have anyone to cart around security-procession-style, we traveled as our shadow-selves. Not having to worry about a vehicle or who was going to drive it made for one less logistical issue. In fact, if for some reason I had to continue carting Anya around for the next few months or so, I was going to insist we travel only at night. When we were stronger. Why had I not thought of this before?

When we arrived at Tyler's building, my stress levels ratcheted up to an almost incomprehensible level. You'd think I wouldn't feel like most of my internal organs were on the verge of bursting into flames at this point. But every time I laid my eyes on him, my wounded soul was torn asunder to reveal fresh, raw damage.

"Julian," I murmured as I tipped my head back to gaze at the penthouse floor. "I want you to go with me to The Pit."

He cocked his head curiously. "Are you talking that bar over in Belltown?"

"That's the one. There's a bartender there—Levi. He's got something I want and we're going to go get it."

"And exactly what is it we'll be picking up?"

I tore my gaze from Ty's building to look at Julian. "Information. You're the genius, right? Well, Levi's pretty damn smart, too. Between the three of us, we can figure out a way to put Kade down once and for all. I want to learn *everything* about him, right down to the bastard's favorite breakfast cereal."

Julian cast a wary glance at Louella and nodded.

"Cambions, too," I said as an afterthought. "I want details. If they're rare, how they relate with their Succubus and Incubus families . . . all of it. And after that, Levi is going to tell us how to break a Jinn bond."

"And after that?" Julian asked as though I'd told him we were going to bring peace to the Middle East and end global hunger in one fell swoop.

"After that," I said, "we're going to break a few rules."

I knew Julian wasn't listening. His eyes had strayed to

Louella again. It didn't take much to realize he was nervous. Anxious about leaving her. If I hadn't been such a broken-hearted cynic, I might have felt bad. Maybe. "Julian," I barked, grabbing him by his collar. "On. Task."

"Right," he said, giving his head a little shake.

"Can she fight?" I asked, looking him dead in the eye.

"Yes."

"Is she capable of taking care of herself?"

"Oh, yeah."

"Could she kick your ass?"

A smile broke out on Julian's face. "And then some."

"Then don't worry about her. The team's got her back."

From the corner of my eye, I noticed Asher inching his way toward us. He'd been listening to our conversation, the little sneak. I'd show him how I felt about that. "Ash, I want you to stay here with the rest of the team. Keep an eye on the building and watch for any sign of Kade."

His light amber eyes seemed to glow brighter than usual against the backdrop of night, and his jaw took on a stubborn set. He gave an almost imperceptible shake of his head. "I'm going with you."

I'd known our talk the other day hadn't completely sunk in. That didn't mean I thought his punk-ass would disobey a direct order right here in front of the entire team, however. "I'm taking Myles as additional backup," I said, my voice sharp enough to cut glass.

"You need *me*," he said.

Either the other members of my team were too distracted to pay us much attention, or they were really good at pretending not to listen. I had too much on my plate right now for the added stress. Asher wasn't a threat to me or the team. On the contrary, I had a feeling he'd put his body in the path of a bullet for me. But why the cocky lone wolf routine? And why did he feel the need to supersede my commands?

"What the hell's with you, anyway?" I finally said through gritted teeth. "This isn't up for debate. You're staying here."

In two long strides, Asher was standing nose to nose with me. He moved his head to the side and leaned in so close that I could feel his breath in my ear. "Darian," he said. "Leave

Myles with the team. You need *me* to come with you. Trust me."

Trust him? I wanted to punch him in the face. "You have done *nothing* to convince me that I should trust you."

"You need me," was all Asher said in answer.

When had I so totally lost control of him? For that matter, had I ever had control? "What I need is for you to do as I say. Dealing with your constant disobedience is a time suck we can't afford right now. Every minute wasted is a minute tipped to Kade's advantage." I sighed. "I could just send you back to Raif . . ."

"You could," Asher murmured. "But I wouldn't advise it."

"Maybe you didn't get the memo, Ash. I'm in charge here, not you. So you don't advise me of anything. Got it?" I didn't have time for this shit. And whereas I knew the best course of action right now was to send Asher right the fuck back to Xander's house, something in my gut told me I'd be better off bringing him along. *Damn it.* Until I could unravel Asher's secrets, I had a feeling it would be best to keep him close. "Myles." My voice was a controlled burn, scalding its way up my throat. "Stay here with the rest of the team. Watch out for anything unusual." Wouldn't you know, Myles didn't even bat a lash. "And one more thing . . ."

Myles gave me a questioning look, and I held my breath for the barest second, wondering, did I really want to know? "If you see any sign of Tyler, I want you to tail him. I need to know everywhere he goes and *everyone* he meets with. Got it?"

Myles's expression turned dark, and he shared a knowing glance with Julian. Let them think what they wanted. I turned my back on the redhead and headed in the opposite direction from Tyler's building. I didn't have to worry about Myles or the rest of my team; they'd do what I'd told them to do. As for Asher, well, at the moment, I couldn't give two shits what he did as long as he stayed out of my goddamned hair. I probably should have taken Raif's advice and cut Asher loose. Damn, I hated when he was right.

"What exactly are we doing here, Darian?" Louella asked, trotting up beside me.

I stopped. Turned to face her. "Spying on a Jinn," I said. "Yours?"

The one word hung in the air, and Louella cringed as if she wished she could suck it right back into her mouth. It was no secret that Tyler was bound to me. I suspected the whole of Xander's kingdom and most of the supernatural community were aware of the fact. That word—*yours*—it just rubbed me the wrong way. Tyler was bound to me, sure. But he wasn't *mine* anymore.

"Kade's Jinn is in the penthouse." At least, I hoped she was. Pausing at the crosswalk, I waited for Julian and Asher to catch up. "I'm not taking any chances. Kade might show up. Adira might leave to meet him." I swallowed down the bitter taste of betrayal that rose up in my throat. "And Tyler might be more involved than I think. We can't take anything for granted at this point. We have to have every angle covered. This city is too goddamned big, and Kade could be hiding right under our noses. I want his ass put down once and for all. If you see anything suspicious, call me. If Adira leaves, follow her. If Tyler—"

"Okay," Louella said, holding up her hands. "I get it. What if we get hit with option D?"

I raised my brows in question.

Louella leveled her gaze to mine. "All of the above."

"Then split up." It wasn't the best option. But I wasn't sending my team out to fight, just to observe. "Don't engage anyone on your own. That goes for Liam and Myles, too. Get your asses back to Xander's if you're made. You keep an eye out and report back to me. Nothing more, nothing less."

"You think there's a chance of things going south?" Liam asked. He rolled his massive shoulders and stretched his neck from side to side until it cracked. I looked him up and down from his tattooed bald head and gauged ears right down to his size thirteen boots. Damn, he was scary.

"Kade's dangerous enough," I remarked. "But with a Jinn at his beck and call"—I shrugged— "anything's possible."

Without another word, I melted into shadow. The remaining members of my team followed suit as we crossed the street and headed for Belltown. I still wasn't thrilled about having Asher tag along. My patience had been shot to hell hours ago, and if he decided to get cocky with me, I doubted I'd be able to restrain myself. At this point, the only thing that was going to make me feel better was a good old-fashioned ass-kicking. And if the night went according to plan, Kade was going to be on the receiving end.

Chapter 23

With as much as I'd paid Levi over the past year, I wondered why he even bartended at all. Then I noticed a
cute twenty-something in a leather micromini and scarlet
bustier whisper something in his ear before she slid a folded
piece of paper into his shirt pocket. He looked past her,
though, returning the flirty smile of a guy who looked like
he'd just gotten off work at some swanky downtown office.
Jesus. That preppy bastard got a *shit ton* of play from every
angle. No wonder he kept his part-time gig.

The Pit was slow, even for a Thursday night. Tiny sat on
a stool near the cash register, nursing a beer. His face lit up
with recognition, and he waved.

"Hey, Darian," Levi called from the end of the bar. He
retrieved the slip of paper from his shirt pocket, read the
digits/note/shameless solicitation Miniskirt had passed him.
A wicked grin spread across his Abercrombie poster boy
face. "I'll be with you guys in just a second."

Julian looked around the bar; it seemed he enjoyed
people-watching as much as I did. Asher, on the other hand,
kept his gaze locked on me as we made our way to my favorite table in the back of the bar. His expression was severe,
and tension seemed to cling to him like beads of sweat.

"What's your problem?" I settled myself into a chair.
"You're making me nervous."

Asher sat down beside me, leaning in toward my face.
"You're taking the long way when we have a shortcut solution."

"Oh, yeah?" I remarked.

Asher's gaze shifted to Julian, who'd taken a seat across

from me. "We should kill the female. Without his Jinn, Kade will be easy to take down."

Julian shrugged as if to say, *Why not?* But I couldn't do that to Tyler. Killing Adira would destroy him. I had to try to find a way around the rules—no matter how much it would hurt me. "No," I said, looking Asher dead in the eye. "No shortcuts. We're doing this my way."

"Even if your way sucks?" Asher mumbled.

"I'm sick of your shit!" I shoved my chair away from the table and stood so that I loomed over Asher's face. "Get out of my fucking face and get your ass back to Xander's." I lowered myself so our noses were almost touching. "Now."

Asher stood, slowly rising out of his seat until he towered over me. Stupid little shit. If he thought being bigger and taller intimidated me, I'd show him how I felt about that. With my fist.

"Whoa, am I interrupting something?" Levi put his hands between us and eased me back by the shoulders. "Let's just calm down and take a little breather."

I broke my gaze from Asher's and took a deep breath. My hands shook with rage, and I stuffed them into my pockets, more to keep from popping Ash in the nose than anything. I wouldn't pick a fight inside the bar, but that didn't mean I wouldn't put him in his place later. That blond-haired pain in the ass was more trouble than he was worth.

"Take a seat," I said to Asher, just barely loud enough for him to hear. "And keep your mouth shut. You make so much as a fucking peep and I'm going to lay you out."

His expression softened, and his brow furrowed. I could see stress—worry—etched in every line. I needed to get to the bottom of what had Asher acting like an idiot. Too bad I didn't have a free second to deal with my own problems, let alone his.

Julian hadn't moved a muscle since Asher and I squared off. He lounged in his chair, looking completely at ease. Only the hard line of his mouth and the wary concern in his blue eyes suggested that he was just as worried as I was. Levi settled in, and all eyes shifted to him. Music pulsed around us, the heavy bass coming alive with its own heartbeat. A few humans danced, drank, and laughed, all but oblivious. But I swear to god, the anticipation in our small circle was so intense, you could have heard a pin drop.

"First of all," Levi drawled, "I'm going on record here by saying that this doesn't sit well with me. Which is why I'm giving you this information for free. And if this comes back to me, I'm going to deny that we ever had this conversation. Feel me?"

I nodded slowly, wondering what sort of rules Levi might be breaking by revealing this information. From my own experience with their bonds and magic, I knew all too well that the Jinn coveted their secrets like an invaluable treasure. I could only imagine what would happen if they found out that Levi was handing out little golden nuggets of knowledge. "What conversation?" I asked innocently.

Levi smiled and settled back in his seat. "When a Jinn is compelled to bind himself to a Charge, he secures a part of his essence to the Charge's soul. This can be done with or without the Charge's knowledge."

Yeah, no shit. Ty had bound himself to me and I'd been none the wiser. Levi gave me a strange look, as if my thoughts were written all over my face. I cleared my throat and looked away.

"By 'giving' a part of himself to the Charge," Levi continued, "it creates the connection that allows a Jinn to sense when their Charges are in danger and helps them to locate that person, even when they're separated by hundreds—even thousands—of miles. That soul connection also links the Jinn's magic to the Charge's wishes, thereby granting with absolute certainty only the wishes that are needs and not simply selfish wants. That same binding is what makes them vulnerable."

Levi looked uncomfortable as hell, like revealing this information would cause him to self-destruct or some shit. "So if you kill whoever the Jinn is bound to, the Jinn will actually die?" I'd been told, more or less, but having it confirmed sent a pulse of adrenaline through my bloodstream. I'd thought of the times I'd been knocking on death's door. Instances where I'd put my own safety second to someone else's. I'd risked Tyler's life right alongside mine.

"Not exactly," Levi said with a shrug. "A Jinn can choose the level to which he wants to bind himself to a Charge. The need to protect is sort of like instinct, so the Jinn is compelled to answer the call of the Charge's soul. But a certain level of compatibility is necessary for a binding to be successful. A Jinn is larger than life or death or physical embodiment. Whether or not a Jinn's existence ends with the death of their Charge relates directly to the level of the binding."

Level of the binding? What the hell was that supposed to mean? "This is news to me," I said. "Are you telling me a Jinn can choose how he's bound to a Charge? Sort of like gold- or platinum-level protection?"

Levi laughed. "That's a good way to look at it. I'll have to remember that one."

"So let's just say for the sake of argument, a Charge gets the basic package. A silver-level binding. If the Charge dies . . . ?"

"The Jinn would probably be fine," Levi finished for me. "I can't say for sure, though, Darian. I know a lot, but I don't know it all. Their magic is supersecret, which is why I'm going to forget about this conversation the second you walk out the door. A Jinn anchors his essence to the Charge in a sense. A Jinn doesn't just see a Charge as a person or creature. A Jinn can see the Charge's soul—bared for what it is. Good, bad, or in between; therefore, the compatibility comes down to the nature and essence of the Jinn, be it good, bad, or indifferent."

I could hope that Adira did the smart thing and bound herself to Kade at the economy level. But aside from outright asking, I couldn't be sure. Which was why my best option at this point was to try to break Adira's bond with Kade. "So how is it that a Jinn's magic and existence doesn't fade when the Charge breaks the bond?"

Levi fidgeted with a cocktail napkin, tearing off little shreds. "When the bond is made, the Jinn is essentially imposing his will on the charge." He shook his head as if trying to find the right words. "That's not really right. It's more like a donation. Protection . . . wish-granting . . . all of it. It's a gift of magic—a part of his soul—given of the Jinn's free will. When the bond is broken, I guess it works just the opposite. The Charge is giving back the gift, essentially rejecting it, of her own free will."

It wasn't lost on me that Levi had been referring to his generic Jinn as *he* and the generic Charge as *she*. He'd dissected the construct of Tyler's bond and laid it out for me in tiny, understandable pieces. The bond that Ty had made with me—that gift of magic—was nothing less than a piece of his very essence. His soul. My heart ached at the knowledge that, at one time, Tyler had thought me worthy of that gift. Once, he'd wanted to give *himself* to me.

"How do you break it?" I asked, my voice thicker than I liked. I forced my ragged emotions to the back burner. I couldn't afford the luxury of regret right now.

"Basically," Levi said with a sigh, "you just . . . will it away. Because a Jinn binds himself to a Charge on a soul-deep level, the bond has to be broken in pretty much the same way. Just as a binding is made from an instinctual urge, the bond is broken from an instinctual rejection. The Charge may even break the bond without consciously realizing it. The thing about a Jinn bond is this: it's as easy to break as it is hard. So much of the binding is made on a subconscious or spiritual level. Just as Jinn can sense an inherent need in a Charge's soul when granting wishes, the Jinn can sense when a charge no longer needs their wishes granted or protection offered. A bond is automatically broken the moment a Charge no longer needs the Jinn. And due to the soul-deep change that would have to take place in order for the Charge to reject the Jinn, once broken, the bond can never be remade."

Ugh. Levi had told me, after all. He'd said that if I wanted the bond broken, I'd know how to do it. Breaking my bond with Tyler could never be as simple as a set of spoken words or giving back his ring. I had to truly want it. No, I had to *need* it. Deep down in the pit of my being. And in the process, I'd be rejecting Tyler—everything he was—proving that he meant nothing to me.

"Then we're back at square one," I said, massaging my temples with the tips of my fingers. "Because, how in the hell can I possibly manipulate Kade into believing that he should break his bond with Adira?"

Levi rapped his knuckles against the tabletop in a nervous rhythm. "That's where Pamela comes in."

I quirked a brow. "Pamela?"

"My ex. You know, the witch. She's agreed to help, but, Darian, it's going to cost you."

A cold lump of dread coiled in my stomach. "How much?"

Levi's eyes met mine. "Maybe more than you're willing to pay."

From the corner of my eye, I noticed Asher shift in his seat. His jaw was set, and the muscle in his cheek ticked. "You don't want to go down that road, Darian," he said. "Dabbling in witchcraft isn't going to get you anything but a shitload of trouble."

Julian nodded in agreement. "I gotta say, Darian, this doesn't sound like a good idea."

I didn't know the first thing about witchcraft. But I didn't like the worry in Julian's or Asher's expressions. "Have either of you got a better one?"

Julian shrugged. "Kill the Jinn, like Asher said. Once Kade is unprotected, he'll be weakened and easy to take down."

I ignored Julian, and my better judgment. "What's the price?" I asked Levi again.

"That's the thing about a witch's magick," he said. "It depends on the person, and everyone's price is different."

I slumped in my seat, the bitter taste of defeat rising in my throat. "I take it we're not talking money."

Levi shook his head. "It's never just about the money. Sorry, Darian. I wish this could be an easy fix for you."

It never is, I thought ruefully. "Can I see Pamela tonight?"

Asher shot up in his chair straight as a soldier, his eyes practically burning a hole through Levi as he waited for a response. "Not tonight," Levi answered. "I'll get ahold of her, and she'll arrange a meeting. Might not be for a couple of days. She'll have to prepare for whatever you decide you want her to do."

Well, damn. That took a crap on my plan of wrapping this up tonight. Anya would be off bed rest by tomorrow morning. And then my evening would be occupied with Xander's damned dignitary ball. This was not the turn of events I was expecting. "Why a couple of days? Does she have to stock up on eye of newt or something?"

Levi gave me a wan smile. "If only."

Man, this situation got more depressing by the second. I was going to need a boatload of medication to get through it. "Okay, now that that's settled, let's talk Cambions. What do you know?"

"What do you want to know?"

"How to kill the fuckers, for starters," Julian said.

"They die easy enough." Levi motioned for a cocktail waitress. "You guys want anything?"

"I'll take a rum and Coke," Julian said, like we were just a bunch of college buddies shooting the breeze.

"Water," Asher grunted. Guess he wasn't as chummy as the rest of us.

"Water for me, too," I said in answer to Levi's questioning glance.

"Hey, Jill," Levi called to the cocktail waitress. "Would you bring us a rum and Coke, a Stella, and two waters?"

Jill gave him what must have been her fuck-me smile and started off toward the bar. *Give me a break.* Was there anyone here who *didn't* want to climb into bed with Levi? "Can we get back to business, please?"

Levi flashed a mischievous grin. "You're no fun lately."

"I'm no fun *ever*," I stressed. "Cambions . . . ?"

"Right. Cambions can be killed just like a human. They don't heal particularly fast, no physical gifts that I know of. I'm pretty sure you could take one down with a well-aimed gunshot. Probably even a bash to the head. They feed off of sexual energy. It sustains them, adds years—sometimes centuries—to their lives."

"Our Cambion has a special diet," I told Levi. "He's feeding from supernatural creatures."

"Shit." Levi let the word drag out nice and long. Jill showed up with our drinks, and Levi waited for her to leave before he spoke again. "That definitely complicates things."

"Why's that?" Julian asked before bringing his glass to his lips.

I beat Levi to the punch. "When a Cambion drinks energy from a supernatural being, he absorbs that being's abilities and can use them for a short time." He gave me a surprised look. "What?" I said. "I know things."

Before Levi could give me the kudos I assuredly deserved, a familiar energy crawled across my skin, writhing and twisting like a nest of snakes. *Damn.* I'd never felt it quite as strong as I did right at this moment and I swallowed down the lump of fear that had risen in my throat. I held my hand up to halt any further conversation, scanning the crowd for any sign of danger. Pretty hard to pinpoint, too, when the most dangerous person in the room is also the most angelic looking. It's not like he stuck out as the evil, murdering sort.

Kade walked through the entrance and into the bar like he owned the place. His full mouth spread into a smug, sexy smile as all eyes—well, mostly the *female* eyes—turned to him. And despite my loathing, even I couldn't help but admire his angelic features and lean, muscular form as he made a beeline for our table. He moved with reptilian grace, like a boa constrictor weaving its way through the tall grass, something that caused my internal danger sensors to go on high alert. My gaze darted to the faces seated around me: Levi looked nervous, as if he was already assessing the potential property damage from our impending supernatural showdown. Julian sat up straight, no longer laid-back. His brows came together, and I could almost hear the gears spinning as he attempted to think a way out of our predicament.

While Julian looked hyperaware, Asher had never looked so relaxed. A complete oxymoron, Ash couldn't help but do the opposite of what I expected of him. He smiled, as if at a private joke, and no one else at the table paid him an ounce of attention. He'd all but melted into the scenery.

"Trouble," Kade said affectionately. "I see you saved me a seat, but I was hoping for something a little less girls-night-out and a little more intimate."

No one but me seemed to be nonplussed by the way Kade indicated Asher's seat as if he weren't even sitting there. Ash chuckled to himself, and I resisted the urge to kick him under the table. He winked at me and put a finger to his lips before pointing at Kade, reminding me that was where my attention should be focused. I clenched my jaw until I felt the enamel grind, and forced my gaze back to Kade.

"Julian," I said without looking away, "I think you'd better—"

"I'm on it," he answered without even waiting for me to finish. I knew I could count on him to know what I needed. And right now, I had to make sure that the rest of my team was safe. If Kade had followed us here, he could have known that the others had Tyler's penthouse staked out. Julian's expression as he stood and headed for the exit echoed my concern. He'd want to check on Louella, and I couldn't blame him.

"Would you give us a minute?" I said to the table at large. Levi nodded and cast a wary glance in Kade's direction before heading back to the bar. Asher, however, didn't move a muscle. Instead, he folded his arms across his chest and winked again. It made me want to poke his eye out.

"Ah, alone at last," Kade sighed.

I cast a sidelong glance at Asher, wondering what the hell was going on. Neither Julian nor Levi had paid Ash any attention from the moment Kade approached our table. And now, Kade appeared to not even see him at all. What the hell was going on?

"What do you want, Kade?" I tried to relax, to look as if my brain wasn't a buzzing, jumbled beehive of confusion. My hand wandered to the dagger sheathed at my thigh. I swore I'd stab the bastard the first chance I got, Adira's safety be damned.

He settled in the seat Levi had just vacated and moved it so close to mine that his knee rubbed against my thigh. I raised a sarcastic brow and pointedly shifted my chair a couple of inches away. "Maybe I missed you," he purred, every word dripping with sensual promise.

"I doubt that," I said. "Where's your bodyguard?"

"Adira?" Kade said with a smile. "I expect she's with—what's his name—Tyler?" Kade studied my reaction as he answered, and I did my best to keep my face a mask of passivity.

"What do you want, Kade?" I said again, enunciating every syllable. "Because if you don't have something to say, then I think we'd better just take this outside so I don't get my favorite bar all messy with your blood." Christ, I'd never, in all my years as an assassin, seen a mark parade himself before his would-be murderer. I think Kade got off on it. And since Adira made him practically unkillable, why not dangle that fact right in front of my face. As long as that was *all* he was dangling in front of me.

Kade laughed and motioned for a cocktail waitress. "Bars are the best places to hunt," he said after he ordered a whiskey, straight up. "So many women sexually charged and ready to fuck a perfect stranger."

Didn't hurt that he had the looks and charisma to convince a saint to commit sin, either. The waitress returned with damned-near superhuman speed. Along with Kade's drink, she slid him a cocktail napkin with a string of digits scrawled in red pen. He moved as if to stuff the napkin in his pocket and I reached across the table, snatching it out of his grasp. "Don't get any ideas, Kade." Every word out of my mouth was saturated with menace. "If you think I'm going to let you pluck a helpless victim—"

"Trouble, Trouble," he drawled, interrupting me. "I don't need a human woman to nourish me. I've got all the power I need and then some." He drained his drink in a single swallow and stood to leave. "Though I enjoy the effort you're putting into your attempt to exterminate me, I didn't come here tonight to test your mettle. I want you to relay a message to Anya for me." Leaning in, as if sharing a secret, Kade's breath in my ear sent a shudder through my body. "Tell her Dimitri is just the icing on the cake. She knows what I want, and she has exactly twenty-four hours to give it to me."

In a blur of motion, I kicked my chair out from underneath me, swinging my dagger toward Kade's throat, hoping I'd be too fast for him to wish for any help from Adira. But in the time it took for me to draw my weapon—less than a half second—Kade had vanished. "Son of a bitch," I murmured under my breath. "What else are you hiding from me, Anya?"

Chapter 24

"How do you do it?" I rounded on Asher, wanting to take out my frustration on the closest thing to me.

"Do what?" He all but batted his lashes in feigned innocence.

"You're a cheeky little shit, you know that?" I rolled my shoulders, the feelings of frustration and helplessness pulling my muscles taut. "You're not a run-of-the-mill Shaede."

Asher cocked his head to the side. "Um, hello, *pot.*"

Yeah, yeah. I was the last person who should be pointing out someone else's uniqueness. "I want to know how you do it, Ash." I doubted commanding him to come clean would garner the results I wanted, but I didn't have the people skills to coax it out of him. "Julian and Levi acted as if they didn't realize you were even sitting at the table. Kade too. But it's not like you were invisible . . ." My voice trailed off as I contemplated just *what* it was that Asher could do. "Just . . ."

"Unnoticeable." Asher supplied with a grin.

"Yeah," I said, curt. "Unnoticeable."

"Hey, Darian." Julian sidestepped a few bar patrons as he hurried toward our table. "Loulie says Tyler left his apartment about fifteen minutes ago. They couldn't track him. He pulled the Jinn card and sort of just . . . poof"—he made an explosive motion with his hands—"vanished. Guess we should have figured it would be next to impossible to follow him."

Yeah. No shit. I wanted to bang my head on the table, but stopped short as a thought struck me. Kade had *poofed!* into thin air as well . . . not to mention the fact that while his energy signature was unique, it had always reminded me of something—or rather, some*one*—I'd felt before. Which meant the Cambion was likely getting more than wish-granting out of his Jinn. *Spectacular*.

Darth Vader's theme song burst from my cell, the sound muffled in my pocket and barely audible over the noise of the bar. "What's up?" I answered, knowing that Raif wasn't just calling to see if I was enjoying my evening.

"The security system at your apartment is showing a break-in. So far, the cameras aren't picking up anything un-usual, though. I'm getting ready to send a detachment to check it out. I just wanted you to know."

"Don't bother." I didn't need Raif expending unnecessary energy or manpower on my behalf. "I'm only a couple of blocks away; I'll run over and see what's up."

"That's not a good idea," Raif proclaimed in that insuffer-able, regal way that reminded me so much of his brother. "The Cambion is unaccounted for, not to mention your post-card-sending admirer."

"I'm not worried about Kade," I said. "I've already ac-counted for him tonight and he's not a threat." *Yet*. "And as far as Lorik is concerned"—I gave a heavy sigh—"honestly, Raif, I don't know what to think about that situation, but I don't think he'll be showing up any time soon, either. It's probably just a false alarm. I'll go check it out and give you a call."

"What do you mean the Cambion is accounted for?" Raif asked. "Did you kill him?"

If only. "No. But I know he won't be bothering me to-night. I'll update you later."

"If you don't check in within a half hour, I'm sending reinforcements."

I couldn't help but smile. Raif would always have my back, no matter what. "Deal." I disconnected the call and turned to Julian. "We're done for the night. Gather up the troops, and we'll regroup in the morning."

Julian nodded and headed for the door, and Asher fell in step right behind him. *Figures*. When I wanted him close he always seemed to slip away, and the second I sent him away, the infuriating shit was stuck to me like glue. I'd get him alone sooner or later, and he'd have no choice but to come clean. Until then, I had a potential break-in to investigate.

The last person I expected to find sitting in my living room was the only person in the world who could tie my emotions into tight, unyielding knots. My fingers trembled as I reset the alarm system and focused on leveling out my erratic pulse. I sent a quick text message to Raif assuring him that the break-in was a false alarm and that I wasn't in any danger. The next thing I was sure to do was disable the video feeds. No way in hell did I want Raif, or the king himself, spying on me. Not when I could break down at any moment.

"We sure know how to trash an apartment," Tyler mused quietly from where he'd made himself at home on my couch. I hadn't been back to clean up the mess I'd made in my self-destructive depression. *Super.* Just what I wanted Ty to see. His last bout of self-destructive behavior hadn't been much better, though. When I'd left him in Seattle on my quest to find Raif's daughter, he'd apparently flown into a bit of a rage. I walked through his front door to find a mess a veteran rock star would be proud of. "You've upgraded your security since I was here last."

"Raif's idea." I shrugged, walking into the center of the studio apartment.

Ty gave a derisive snort. "I'm surprised you let him do it. What with your I-can-take-care-of-myself attitude."

Ouch. His words cut deep. I didn't need the reminder that I'd ruined things between us with my arrogant, closed-off attitude. I'd been beating myself up over it every day for months. "Did you come here to twist the knife in my chest, Tyler?" My usual cocky bravado was gone. All that reflected in my voice was the hollow ache I couldn't escape.

"Maybe," he said, sending me back a step. "I don't know. Fuck." He sounded as torn up as I felt. Were we gluttons for punishment, or what? "Would you rather I swing by Xander's when I need to talk to you?" He cocked his head as if anticipating my reaction.

No. Certainly not based on his last couple of visits, anyway. There was no telling what might happen if he let his temper get the best of him. "Is it true you almost killed

Raif?" I asked instead of answering his question. "You know, when I . . . left."

"Yeah," he replied reluctantly. Pushing himself off the couch, Tyler stalked toward me so fast that my heart jumped up into my throat. I backed up until the kitchen island stayed my progress, and still Ty came at me in a steady advance. "I hate the fucking rules." His voice burned with each word, the rage barely contained. He leaned in close and I shivered at the sudden chill in the air that accompanied Ty's anger. "Kade is killing her, and there's not a damned thing I can do about it." He placed his hands on either side of the countertop, caging me between his arms. I took a deep breath, filling my lungs with his homey, honeyed spice scent, and yet I trembled with fear. His agitation was a physical thing, charging the air between us. I'd never seen Tyler so close to losing control and it scared the shit out of me.

"I'll get him," I assured him. The muscle in his jaw flexed and I swore I could hear the enamel of his teeth grind. I took another deep breath, willing myself to be strong. "I'm close. *So* close. Give me a couple of days and the job will be done." I swallowed hard, my next words stuck somewhere in my throat. "I'll keep her safe for you."

He answered me with a harsh, forced bark of laughter. "Gods, Darian. That's almost the worst part of it. I know you will. I *know* you won't stop until the bastard is dead. And I'm throwing you right in the path of the bullet. I'm one helluva protector, huh?"

"Tyler, I can try—" I clamped down tight on my emotions, forbidding the flow of tears that threatened to spill down my cheeks. "I can try to sever our bond for you. If you want me to . . . to free you. I'm not sure if I can do it or not. I'm still not real clear *how* to do it. But I'll give it a shot."

Ty grabbed me by the shoulders and looked deep into my eyes. Something sparked in the hazel depths as his gaze roamed my face as if he were trying to crawl into my head and read my thoughts. His brows came sharply together, and his mouth formed a grim line. "Don't even think about it," he ground out. "Don't you dare."

I let out a shuddering breath as my chest swelled with suppressed emotion. I didn't want to lose him. Couldn't *bear* to think of my life without him. And his insistence that I keep our bond intact filled me with hope. Keeping our bond intact meant that on some level, Tyler still wanted me. God, how I needed that assurance. As if he could sense my distress, Tyler's expression softened. His hands trailed from my shoulders, down to my elbows before he backed away and raked his fingers through the tousled curls of his bronze-streaked hair. He let out a ragged breath and reached behind him, producing a dagger from where it had been concealed. "When you get close enough to Kade, use this." He handed me the dagger handle first. "It's silver and laced with iron. Should circumvent any extraordinary healing ability he might've come by. Run it through the bastard's heart."

Well, I guess that answered my question about what weapon would be most effective against a demon that could siphon supernatural abilities. "Thanks," I said, tucking the dagger behind me. "I'll get it done, Tyler." I meant it, too. There wasn't anything I wouldn't do for him.

"I know," he whispered. He turned away from me slowly, as if it pained him to do so, and rather than poof away as he'd so often done lately, he stalked quietly to the elevator and left.

An annoying, wet warmth trickled down my cheek, and I quickly swept it away with my hand. Another drop followed that one and another, until there was nothing I could do to stem the flow of tears cascading from my eyes. My breath hitched in my chest, holding in the sobs that wanted out, but I wouldn't allow it. In just under a year, Ty had managed to unlock every single emotion that I'd spent almost a century repressing. And now that the floodgates had been opened, there wasn't a goddamned thing I could do about it.

"Darian, what's wrong?" Raif said when he answered his phone. Obviously the fact that I wasn't composed enough to speak was an indicator that I shouldn't have called him. "I'm coming over."

"No," I managed to choke out. I'd gone from believing that I didn't need to depend on anyone to truly *needing* someone in these moments when I felt like I had nowhere to turn. Thank god for Raif. "I'm fine, really."

"You don't sound fine." Raif's pronouncement wasn't

meant to call me out. It was more his way of letting me know he was there for me.

"Okay, so I'm not exactly *fine*, fine," I sniffed. "I'm not going back to Xander's house tonight. I just didn't want you to worry about me when I didn't show up."

"Darian," Raif said. "Much as I know you won't appreciate me saying this, you can't give Tyler so much control over you."

"What's that supposed to mean?"

Raif sighed. "Leave it to you to automatically go on the defensive. I'm not a fool, so don't treat me like one. I saw the video feed before you so conveniently shut it off. I know who was in your apartment tonight. And I likewise know that you've been hurt. Deeply."

My chest tightened, and my eyes burned from the tears I'd shed. I was a fucking mess. How could Raif have let Xander put Anya's safety in my hands? Jesus, I couldn't even take care of myself.

"Darian?"

"I'm here."

"You allow him to wound you. Every time you see him, you relive the moments between you that neither of you can undo. Do not give Tyler—or anyone—that power over you."

Sometimes I wondered if Raif was meant to be my sibling and not Xander's. He had the wiser big-brother routine down pat. But he was right. I'd once vowed to never again let someone use love as a weapon against me, and here I was wielding it against myself. "Are you speaking from experience, Raif?"

A pause. "I would never preach to you otherwise."

I smiled at the sarcastic edge in his voice. It was true, though. One thing Raif could never be accused of was being a hypocrite. "I'm a mess, aren't I?"

"You've had better moments," he replied wryly. "I think a night away from here is a good idea. Get your head on straight so you don't make any more rash decisions like throwing yourself at my brother."

I laughed. That would have to wait until after tomorrow night's ball. "Can you tell him I won't be back tonight?"

"I suppose I can take the brunt of Xander's rage for you."

"Rage?" I asked, dubious.

"Oh, yes," Raif said. "He'll be positively furious. I can't wait."

I had to smile at Raif's mischievous tone. "One more thing," I added as I remembered Kade's earlier words. "I need you to give a message to Anya. Tell her if she's in possession of anything that Kade might possibly want, I'm going to need it by the time I show up there tomorrow."

"All right," Raif responded slowly. "What's this about?"

"I'm not sure." Yet. I planned on finding out, though. "Just tell her."

"I'll deliver your message," Raif said.

"Thanks. I owe you one."

"Don't worry. I'm keeping a tally," he said and hung up.

I turned off my phone—just in case Xander took it upon himself to call—tossed it onto the couch and surveyed what looked like a residence hastily abandoned in a zombie apocalypse. Grabbing a trash bag and my recycling bin from the cupboard under the kitchen sink, I started by tossing an empty Cheerios box into the bin. Followed by an empty milk carton. Then, I tossed a wad of discarded paper towels and some overripe oranges into the trash bag. I filled the sink with hot water and began to soak the dirty dishes that had been sitting for a couple of weeks. Dirty clothes made their way to the washer, and I stripped the bed, ready for fresh linens.

It wasn't much, but it was an improvement.

And with these small steps toward moving forward—and totally in my control—I felt the burden of my sorrow finally begin to lift.

Chapter 25

By the time I left my apartment the next day, it somewhat resembled the standard of order and cleanliness I was used to. I'd stayed up most of the night cleaning, straightening up, washing months of discarded clothes, dishes, and linens. I waited until well after lunch to return to Xander's house. Anya was under the watchful eye of my team, and I knew with the PNT ball later that night she wouldn't be leaving the house until Xander's entourage left for the event.

I'd been dragging my feet, not wanting to give the Shaede King any opportunity to pull me aside for a little "one-on-one" time. Just because Tyler had asserted that he wanted our bond left intact and I'd cleaned my apartment didn't mean I was completely healed emotionally, and I worried that Xander would use whispered words of passion to spur me into action. Honestly, I didn't think Xander cared how he got me into bed, whether it be through love and affection or a need to show Tyler that I'd moved on. He just wanted me in his bed.

As I headed toward Capitol Hill, I thought of Xander's confession that Azriel was not, in fact, his son. In the end, his own selfish desires had been his undoing and he'd kept the truth of Azriel's paternity from everyone, his own brother included. Even after his death, Xander wasn't going to reveal the truth, and I couldn't help but wonder why. And why he'd chosen me to finally confide in. Perhaps he kept the memory of Azriel as an innocent child close to his heart. The child he hoped to raise with honor and compassion, so unlike his demon father and black-hearted mother. When I asked Xander if he'd loved Azriel's mother, he hadn't given me a direct answer. I wondered: had he *ever* been in love? He claimed to love me, but I wasn't such a fool as to believe him. He didn't even know me. Not truly. He loved the idea of me, the prospect of claiming me. Like Azriel's mother, he wanted me just to prove that he could have me. And the fact that I was an oddity among our kind made me even more desirable. We were a fine pair: me using him to help forget about my heartache, and him using my heartache to maneuver me right into his bed. Maybe we deserved each other.

When I finally made it to the front door, it swung open before I could even get my hand on the latch. I expected Xander to be waiting for me, exasperated and annoyed that he couldn't keep me under his thumb. But instead, I was met with the frazzled countenance of one pissed-off fashion dictator.

"How's it hangin', Caitlin?" I asked, the epitome of innocence.

I thought her eyes were going to bulge right out of her head. She exhaled in what appeared to be great relief—or maybe frustration—and dragged me through the doorway by the arm. Damn, that skinny little thing was stronger than you'd think. She hauled me through the foyer and right up the stairs to my room. "Where have you *been*?" she huffed, slamming the door behind me. "I've been waiting for you for hours! As it is, I'll be surprised if we can manage a decent hairstyle by the time you have to leave."

"Keep your pants on, Caitlin," I said, flouncing down on the bed. God, I loved memory foam. I hadn't slept much the previous night, and a nap sounded pretty good right about now. "It's still early. We'll have plenty of time to get me ready."

Caitlin seemed to go into some kind of shock, her mouth working but no words issuing forth. "We have less than seven hours!" she finally exclaimed. "Get up! Get in the shower! Get *moving*!"

"You look so lovely," Mary said with a sigh, smoothing one last curl into place. "All eyes will be on you, ma'am."

I hoped not. Eyes watching meant tongues wagging. I did not want or need the shrewd eyes of the local gossips on me.

I knew my place this evening. I'd been schooled by Henry early on in our marriage. We attended social events for one reason and one reason only: to be seen. To keep up appearances. To provide the local socialites—not to mention the friends of our aristocratic families—the perfect picture of marital bliss.

Mary draped a lace shawl around my shoulders and I took the stairs as slowly as I dared toward the foyer. My steps were those of the condemned, my feet reluctantly leading me to my doom. Henry waited for me by the front door, impatient as always. He checked his pocket watch and let out an exasperated sigh. "My, don't you look lovely tonight," he said with absolute disinterest before opening the door for me. "After you," he urged, waving his hand before him in invitation.

We walked. After all, the party was only three houses down the street, and Henry kept a respectable distance from me—that being, far enough away you wouldn't even know that we were acquainted, let alone husband and wife—until we reached the Brightons' haughty mansion. Once we stepped foot on the long walkway that led to the front door, he tucked my hand in the crook of his arm and bestowed upon me his most charming smile. God forbid someone would happen to notice us from the window and see anything less than a doting husband and adoring wife.

Once inside, he spun me around to show off my dress to every woman who crossed our path, and to his gentlemen friends he simply bragged that his life couldn't be any better: his practice was thriving and he had the most desirable woman in all of San Francisco on his arm. The more he boasted, the more I hurt from his deceptive words. After we'd made the rounds, greeting our "friends" and placing a gift under the fifteen-foot-tall Christmas tree adorning the Brightons' grand ballroom, he left me to mingle with the other wives while he retired to the library with the men for cigars and scotch.

"Behave, my dear," he murmured in my ear as if whispering secret, heated words. "Be the dutiful, gracious, humble wife the community expects you to be."

I wanted to tear my arm from his grip and shove him away

from me. His close proximity made me nervous, the way his fingers bit into my skin as he held me to him made my heart race with fear. I'd be the wife he'd trained me to be and no one would be the wiser to the truth for the rest of our lives. I smiled as I took my leave and approached a small group of women sipping champagne by the tree. Polite laughter bubbled up from my chest as the ladies made light of something . . . I hadn't really been paying attention. I cast Henry a sidelong glance as he strolled from the room, confident I'd do what he'd trained me to. I knew what awaited me if I didn't. And besides, I could be very, very convincing when properly motivated. . . .

"Gods, you're . . . stunning," Xander breathed as I met him at the bottom of the stairs. He gave me a mischievous grin, grabbed me by the hand, and spun me around. Then, for good measure, he took me in his arms and kissed me. Once. But that brief contact spoke volumes about how he hoped the evening would progress. I took a step back, needing a moment of personal space, but as far as Xander was concerned my actions had more to do with assessing his own appearance than anything.

"How do I look?" he asked, spreading his arms wide.

No doubt his black tux had been tailored specifically for him. No way in hell would the Shaede King wear anything off the rack. But I had to admit, he wasn't exactly hard to look at. His caramel eyes seemed lighter in contrast with his dark clothes, the amber flecks almost citrine. The golden hair he usually wore pulled back hung loose, almost brushing his shoulders, giving his formal attire an edgy elegance. He could have stepped off the runway of an Armani fashion show. And the smile on his face told me that his confidence had kicked into overdrive.

"You know you look good," I teased. "Why do you always need to have everyone around you confirm it?"

"I don't need *everyone* to confirm it," he said. "Just you."

I smiled at the sensual tone in his voice. If I wasn't careful, he'd easily break through my resolve to keep him at arm's length. "Oh, Xander." I sighed in mock exasperation. "Always after a good ego stroking."

"Oh, Darian," he answered, his voice as warm and soft as velvet, "by the end of the night, you'll be stroking more than just my ego."

He reached out for me, but the sound of someone clearing his voice made Xander pause. Raif stood at the top of the staircase, looking just as dashing and royal as his brother in a similar tux. It always made me laugh to see him dressed in modern clothes, since he favored a more antiquated getup when he wasn't out among humans. "Check you out." I spoke a little on the loud side, just to be sure anyone within earshot would hear me. "Damn, Raif, you clean up good."

He rolled his eyes and continued down the stairs as if he just didn't have the patience for my juvenile behavior. "I could say the same for you." When he got to the bottom of the stairs he took my hand, bowing as he bestowed a polite kiss upon it.

I laughed, finding Raif's gallantry utterly hilarious—and charming. "Yeah, well, don't get used to this." I indicated my dress. "This'll be the first and last time you see me dressed up."

"Not much room for toting weapons in that dress, is there?" Raif asked.

No, there certainly wasn't. I couldn't carry an arsenal on my body, but that didn't mean I was going anywhere unarmed. I'd strapped the silver dagger Ty had given me to the back of the dress, artfully hiding it in the folds of satin fabric. A quick tug was all it would take to free it from the sheath. Caitlin had been appalled at the notion of securing the dagger to the delicate gown, but I told her if she didn't hush with the protests, I wouldn't let her do my hair. Shut her up instantly.

Xander looked a little put out as Raif and I exchanged witty banter about what and where we'd stashed weapons in our fancy outfits. While Raif and I chatted, Xander moved behind me, wrapping his arms around my waist as he listened to us talk. A moment of surprise flashed in Raif's eyes, which I'm sure echoed my own expression exactly. It was such a . . . normal, almost . . . domestic thing to do, and it momentarily caught me off guard.

I relaxed into Xander's arms as he joined the conversation, pointing out how hundreds of years ago a warrior gave up his weapons once he entered a king's hall. I leaned in closer. I couldn't help it. I wanted the reassurance, the *comfort* of having someone hold me close. This wasn't about jealousy or proving anything to anyone. This was about me, needing to feel connected to someone. He pressed his lips to my temple, breathing deeply. "You smell good," he whispered close to my ear.

"Caitlin's idea," I said. "Bergamot."

"Mmm." He took another deep breath. "It's perfect."

A motion from the hallway leading to the sitting room caught my eye and I turned to see Anya striding toward us. My jaw just about came unhinged as I took her in. She was absolutely stunning. I'd heard of "pregnancy glow" but I'd never seen it before. Anya had it and then some. Life seemed to radiate from her in a bright aura that softened her usually hard edge. She'd abandoned her typical leather outfit for a strapless chiffon evening gown that drifted around her like a delicate cloud. The deep marigold color complemented her violet eyes and dark lashes. Her long hair had been braided and curled and wound in such an intricate pattern it boggled my mind at the skill it must have taken to create.

I disengaged from Xander's embrace and walked toward her, noting that I no longer felt animosity toward her. It's not like we'd formed some kind of unbreakable bond and she'd make me her baby's godmother or anything, but it was easier between us. Nice. "How are you feeling?" I asked.

"Much better," she answered. "Don't we make a fine pair, impersonating delicate ladies?"

"Yeah," I scoffed. "We're the very definition of feminine grace and charm. Look," I said, pulling her aside, deeper into the sitting room, "I know this isn't a great time to bring this up, but I ran into Kade last night."

"Ran into him?" Anya asked with suspicion.

"Well, I think more to the point, he tracked me down. Anyway, Raif gave you my message, right? Kade thinks you have something he wants. If he keeps to his timeline, I'm thinking you'll have to pony whatever it is up by the end of the night."

Something flashed in Anya's eyes, an emotion too fleeting for me to identify. "I have nothing to give him," she said.

"Kade's messing with you. He probably did it to arouse your mistrust. I told you, he likes to play games. He'll use any means at his disposal to torment me."

I wouldn't put it past the son of a bitch. The first time I'd met Kade, he asked me to deliver a message to Anya. Last night's episode didn't seem to be much different. I think, like all egomaniacal shitheads, Kade just liked the sound of his own voice and got off on terrorizing Anya. He didn't want to run in and bust a cap in anyone's ass right off the bat.

"Okay," I said, leading her back out of the room. "But you'd tell me the truth, right? If you had something else he wanted . . . you'd tell me?"

"Relax, Darian," Anya said. "You shouldn't be on edge tonight. This is supposed to be a nice evening."

A nice evening. Yeah. Right. I couldn't help but be a little twitchy. Tonight was Anya's first night out after being attacked and then sent to bed rest after a near miscarriage. Despite Xander's assurance that they'd be well protected by the PNT's wards, I felt like a *nice* evening would be her and Dimitri shut up in their rooms with a hundred or so guards watching over them. Taking them out for a night on the town was anything but *nice*. Speak of the devil, Anya's husband had arrived in the foyer, and he, Xander, and Raif were just chatting up a storm. Again, the normalcy of it all struck me as odd. Odd, and somehow comforting. But all the "normal" in the world wasn't going to take the edge off. I'd been so busy getting my extreme Caitlin makeover that I hadn't had time to meet with my team. They were escorting Xander's entourage as additional security tonight, but it didn't sit well with me that I hadn't been able to snag them before they'd left. *Damn it.* I hated feeling unprepared.

"What's wrong?" Raif asked as we filed out the door. Xander's limo waited a few feet away, the driver holding the door for us. I sighed. How I hated the pomp and circumstance.

"I wanted to talk to the team before they left," I said. "They need to really pay attention to—"

"Darian," Raif interrupted. "Relax. I spoke with your team, and they know their duties tonight. Now, get in the car before Xander ruptures a blood vessel."

I looked into the car and Raif was right. Xander did look like he was about to pop something. Jeez. Anxious much? It wasn't exactly easy getting into the car: the long hem of my gown kept catching on my heels, but I eventually managed to sidle in next to the king. "What?" I asked at his exasperated expression. "Afraid we're going to be late or something?"

"Nonsense," Xander said, sounding very much like the king he was. "I'm always fashionably late. But we do have to arrive before they close the wards over the building or we'll never get in."

At least I could be thankful for the PNT's military precision and preparedness. Maybe tonight wouldn't be a complete waste of time after all.

Chapter 26

Once you've seen one ball, you've seen 'em all.

Of course, this was the first supernatural soirée I'd ever been to. Most of the ball-goers had let their glamours slip, allowing them to appear as the less-than-human creatures they were. And the dresses and suits were as diverse as the attendees—some resembling medieval garb and others in more current styles. We arrived *fashionably late* just like Xander wanted, with minutes to spare before the wards were placed on the building. The PNT didn't dick around when it came to security, and as soon as the moment came to lock the place down, several Fae stepped forward to cast the magical wards that would not only protect the preternatural partiers from harm, but nullify every supernatural ability of those enclosed within the binding magic.

Tricky.

And super-fucking smart.

Xander handed me what looked like a glass of champagne, but after I took a sip I realized that the pale pink liquid in the glass was some sort of faerie wine. The flavor was like nothing I'd ever tasted before, sweet, but not overly so, and smooth without any bite. The carbonated bubbles seemed to burst in my mouth as I drank, sort of like biting into a fresh piece of fruit. A curious sensation, but not unpleasant. I found myself smiling as I took sip after sip, enjoying this new experience.

"I'm easily amused," I said, shrugging when I caught Xander watching me.

"As am I," he murmured in a husky voice that brought chills to the surface of my skin. "I could watch you all night."

I cleared my throat nervously, looking around the crowded ballroom to distract myself from Xander's heated gaze. I noticed Dylan McBride; with him was a young woman, mid- to late twenties, maybe, with curling mahogany hair that brushed her shoulders and eyes the color of the ocean at night. Not quite gray, not quite blue. Pretty. I wasn't the only one who'd noticed, either.

"Who's the woman with Dylan McBride?" I asked Xander.

He looked at the girl and shrugged one shoulder dismissively. "His niece, I believe. She's an anthropology professor at Washington State University, or something. Her name is Mickie, or . . ."

"Niki," Raif said, not bothering to look at us. His eyes were glued to Dylan's niece. "Niki McBride."

I gave Xander a knowing smile, but dropped the subject of the girl's name. I'd let Raif admire her from afar. God knows he needed something other than Xander's ridiculous monarchy in his life.

Xander led me away from where Raif was content to sit and stare at Dylan's niece, and we began to make the rounds that I'd hoped we wouldn't have to make. The Shaede King wasted no time in showing me off to the crème de la crème of the supernatural society. Anxiety twisted my stomach into knots as he paraded me from one group to another, giving grand introductions and encouraging his peers to compliment me on my dress, hair, or any other silly thing that meant absolutely nothing to me. When Azriel had taken me from San Francisco to Seattle, I'd shunned the wealthy lifestyle he'd offered, instead opting for a low-key existence. But tonight I played the part of quiet, charming escort and made small talk with all of Xander's friends and acquaintances. It wasn't too bad. I had a drink in my hand, Anya and Dimitri couldn't be safer inside of the warded building, and for the first time in months, I felt truly at ease.

Nature eventually called—what with the drinks I'd been guzzling since I arrived—so I excused myself from Xander to search for a ladies' room. The ball was being held at one of many facilities the PNT owned in the downtown area, and I wandered from the ladies' room out into a marbled foyer that made the one in Xander's house look like a coat closet. Leaning against the cool stone wall, I closed my eyes, releasing a long, drawn-out sigh. I needed a break from the crowds, the curious eyes, and whispering voices. I enjoyed the quiet, still moment, and wondered how long I could hide here before Xander came looking for me. . . .

"I think I can safely say this is the first time I've ever seen you wear an actual *color*," a cool voice drawled beside me. "That's some dress."

Well, fuck. Guess I shouldn't be surprised that Tyler would be here tonight. After all, he was a PNT delegate and presumably high up on their food chain. Time to hike up my big-girl panties and face the ex, yet again. "Hey, Tyler," I said, not bothering to push myself away from the wall. The cool marble just felt too good against my heated skin. "You look nice."

Nice. *Whatever.* He looked fucking *amazing*.

He dismissed my futile attempt to make small talk and leaned in close, bracing one hand on the wall behind me. "I bet Xander's getting off on having you by his side tonight." His breath smelled of expensive bourbon. Hmmm, not his usual drink. Bourbon was sort of my thing. I'd never seen Tyler drunk before. I think he was more of a control freak than I was. But he was definitely tipsy enough to let his inhibitions—and that control—slip a little. Ice crystals formed on the marble behind me, causing me to shiver. How in the hell could he use his magic with the wards in place? Not a good sign. "Was it easy for you, Darian?" He leaned in closer, so close that our lips were almost touching. His eyes delved into mine and the beautiful hazel depths swallowed me whole. My breath fogged in the cold, and my teeth threatened to chatter as he continued to stare. "Tell me. Was it easy to just walk away from what we had in exchange for being Xander's kept woman? Do you like being his trophy? Playing the part of consort?"

His words touched a nerve. The wrong nerve. I'd hated being an ornamental wife to my human husband. No freaking *way* was I going to play that role again no matter what Tyler might think. And *consort*? Not a chance. "I suppose it was as easy as your decision to come home with another woman," I countered, infusing venom into every word. "I waited for you, Tyler. *You* walked away from what we had. Not me."

I tried to push myself away from the wall, but Tyler wrapped his hand around the back of my neck, keeping me right where I was. He pressed his body against mine and swept his thumb across my cheek. My skin prickled, the weight of his stare brushing against my senses. The marble behind me continued to grow colder, and I was forced to push myself away from it, tighter against Tyler's chest. A sound like the crack of a whip echoed around us as a fissure opened in the frozen marble and traveled from where Tyler's palm rested against the wall, all the way to the ceiling.

Shit.

"I want you to wish for something." Ty's voice rumbled in his chest.

"Wh-what?" I stammered.

"Wish. For. Something." Tyler's eyes were hard, unyielding, and his stare bore into me with such intensity that I couldn't look away. His hand, still wrapped around the back of my neck, held my face close to his, and the cold that emanated from him chilled me to the bone. "Do you know how fucking frustrating it is for me that you never wish for *anything*? Well," he scoffed. "I guess you make the occasional wish. But only when you want me out of your hair."

"I wished for *you*," I said, my voice thick with emotion. "Almost every day. And no matter how much I wanted you with me, you stayed away."

"Wants versus needs," Tyler scoffed. "Your wishes are dictated by magic, Darian. You might have wanted me for whatever reason but you didn't *need* me. I'm at your disposal . . . night, day, whenever. And still, you only make selfish wishes. Wishes to keep me home and out of your hair. Wishes to bring me to your side to relieve your guilt. Do you know how useless that makes me feel?"

"Tyler . . . I . . ." What the hell could I say? He was right. I refused to make wishes, even though his very nature demanded that he grant them. I hadn't wanted to use him, to treat him like a slave.

"Is it easier to be with *him*?" Tyler asked. "Does he give you space? Freedom? Does he let you be in charge, because

I have a hard time believing that he'd let you. Does he even care what happens to you as long as you're front and center when he wants you to be?" His eyes left mine and his heated gaze swept my body, sending a liquid fire through my bloodstream. "Do you tremble when he touches you?" He swept his forefinger along my collarbone and over the swell of one breast. "Can he make your breath quicken like I can?"

Little puffs of steam burst from my parted lips. "Stop it, Tyler," I said, too breathily. I tried to infuse my voice with strength and resolution, but fell short. "You don't want me anymore. You have Adira. Why are you doing this to me?"

"Make a wish," he commanded.

My gaze darted from his eyes to his parted mouth. I could almost feel his lips on mine: soft, yet demanding. "I wish . . ." *you'd kiss me.*

As if he'd read my mind, Tyler's mouth claimed mine. He pulled me tight against his chest, his free arm wrapping around my waist. I melted against him, flames of desire licking at me with torturous heat. This would ruin me, I knew it, but as his tongue met mine in a slow, tantalizing dance, I didn't care. Nothing mattered but this moment. I wanted to touch him, to tuck my hands inside his tuxedo jacket and run my palms along the hard planes of his chest. I wanted to hold him so close to me that there'd be no chance of him pulling away. Instead, I balled my hands into fists at my side, denying myself the pleasure of touching him. I couldn't open myself up to more heartache. When he sobered up a little, he'd realize what a mistake he'd made.

"Darian," he whispered against my mouth as he pulled away. "I—"

"My king is looking for you, Darian." Anya's voice was like a blade sinking into my chest. "Should I tell him you've found something more interesting to occupy your time?"

I wondered if this was how a teenage girl felt when her parents caught her making out with a boy. Tyler stepped a good three feet away from me, and the frost that had formed on the walls and floor beneath our feet began to recede. My gaze settled on Tyler, the expression on his face unreadable. Nothing like alcohol to encourage bad decisions, I guess. I wanted to say something . . . but what? I was at a loss for words. I wanted to know what he'd been about to say to me before Anya interrupted. I could tell by the look on his face, though, that I'd never know.

Without a word, I turned away from him. It was like spinning out of orbit, prying a chunk of metal from a high-powered magnet, and my feet felt heavy as if they'd disobey the command of my brain. I followed Anya back toward the ballroom, resisting the urge to look back. "What the hell was that?" she hissed, her pace almost too quick for me to keep up with and still look elegant tottering on my too-high heels. "You come on the arm of *my king,* and I find you wrapped around your former lover."

"Shut it, Anya."

"How could you dishonor him?" she continued incredulously.

"Anya, I said be quiet. I wasn't trying to dishonor Xander. I don't know what the hell happened back there. It just . . ." *Why* was I trying to explain myself to her? It wasn't any of her damn business. "Just forget it, okay. It was a mistake." *Yeah, a mistake Ty will probably regret in the morning.* "I'm here with Xander, period."

She scowled, her violet eyes glowing with suspicion, but she let the subject drop. Xander smiled as we approached, his face lighting up and his eyes smoldering as he took me in. But something behind me caught his attention and the smile seemed to melt, turning down at the corners as his eyes narrowed. I stole a glance behind me to see Tyler coming through the door behind us. *Perfect.* Just fucking *perfect.*

"Where have you been?" I'm pretty sure Xander was going for a teasing tone, but he failed miserably. He reached out and took my hand in his, pulling me close. Caught in a ballroom full of onlookers, I couldn't simply reject Xander's attention. I didn't want to hurt Ty, but I'd been truthful with Anya, I had no intention of dishonoring her king. Leaning down, he put his lips to mine, though his gaze had locked on something behind us. As he pulled away, his mouth curled into a triumphant smile, mocking and superior. Obviously meant for Tyler.

Wow. Can you say, awkward? The evening took a nosedive, crashed and burned, and left no survivors. The air crackled with energy, and the ballroom, despite the press of bodies, grew cold. So cold that many of the attendees complained that something must have malfunctioned in the heating system. But I knew better. What I didn't know was why his magic hadn't been nullified by the wards. I knew that many in the supernatural community held a deep reverence toward the Jinn race. I was also aware that their magic was the most powerful. Could it be that the wards simply couldn't negate a magic as strong as Tyler's? If so, I'd been a fool to think that any of us were safe within these walls.

Tyler's gaze had been locked on me since the moment I'd come back into the grand ballroom. I tried to ignore it, but the weight of his stare was almost a physical thing, pressing against me like his body had earlier in the foyer. With each cocky, victorious smile Xander flashed his way, Tyler's anger seemed to grow tenfold. And if that wasn't fucked up enough, I noticed about halfway through Ty's deep-freeze routine that he hadn't come dateless, either. Adira wound her arm through his, looking as devastatingly gorgeous as ever.

She whispered in his ear, soothing words I'm sure. And though it made my insides burn to see her touch him with such intimacy—her hand caressing his upper arm, fingers teasing his hair, her mouth so close to his face that their lips would touch if he turned just a fraction of an inch toward her—she seemed to calm him. The temperature in the room began to regulate once again, and my breath no longer clouded the air. What was with him, anyway? Tyler was here *with another woman.* Why would he care who I'd come with?

I so wanted this night to end already. I was tired of the games, the social graces, the *aristocracy.* I wanted to change into a nice pair of stretchy black pants and my boots. I wanted to check in with my team to see if they'd seen any sign of Kade. And after that, I wanted to deliver Anya and Dimitri safely back to Xander's house and go to bed.

A waiter passed by with a tray full of drinks, and I scooped one into my hand. Something a little stronger was in order, but I'd have to take what I could get. This was the first and last function I was going to attend, political or otherwise. How I let myself get talked into coming was beyond me.

"I can't wait to get you home," Xander murmured in my ear. He'd come up behind me and wound his arms around my waist, pulling me against his chest. Chills chased across my skin as he placed light kisses up my neck. He stopped at my ear, taking the lobe between his teeth. "I'm going to undress you slowly," he whispered. "And I plan on taking my time with you. Nothing is going to get in the way of my having you. Not my brother." He kissed my neck. "Anya." His tongue darted out to taste my skin as he kissed my shoulder. "Or anyone else. Tonight, you're *mine*."

He swayed to the orchestra's waltz, pulling me along with him. My eyes drifted shut, if only to block out the faces and curious stares of those around us. I'm sure the supernatural community's elite would have plenty to gossip about tomorrow. Just what I wanted: to be the goddamned center of attention. *Lucky me*.

My eyes flew open as I was jostled to the side, none too graciously, I might add. It took me a second to gain my bearings as Tyler slammed into Xander, sending him against the wall. He held the king by the throat, his chest heaving with his labored breath. Fuck. *Oh, fuck*. I didn't think you could assault a king at a dignitary function and just walk away. But, then again, I doubted that Ty actually gave a shit.

"If you don't want to die, Jinn," Xander's voice strained as Ty squeezed his throat, "you'd best take your hands off me."

The music stopped. The chatter died. Every eye turned to our corner of the ballroom. You could have heard a cotton ball drop it was so fucking quiet. And I just stood there like an idiot, watching. *Nice*. Of course, the wards on the building kept Xander confined to his corporeal form and nice and cozy in Ty's chokehold. Delicate tendrils of frost formed on Xander's skin as Tyler wielded his power, despite the wards.

"What did you say to her?" Tyler's voice dripped with menace. "What lies did you tell her to turn her against me?"

"Lies?" Xander sort of laughed/choked. "You broke her heart, *Jinn*. What did you think, that she'd pine for you forever?"

Tyler shoved Xander hard against the wall, and his kingly head bounced off the marble. "Tyler, stop it!" I shouted, finally coming to my senses. Frantic footsteps echoed in the silence and yeah, the shit was about to hit the fan. I put myself right in the thick of the action, prying Tyler's hand from Xander's throat before Raif could intervene. "Tyler, please." Jesus, he was strong. I could barely budge his hand. "Everyone's watching." Anxiety pooled in my stomach, turning to adrenaline. "Why are you doing this?" I tried to make him hear me, to appeal to his better judgment. "Think of Adira." This can't have looked good to his date, fighting with another man over his ex. "Raif, I've got this," I said, feeling him at my back.

"You dare lay your hands on my king?" Raif brushed past me as if I wasn't even there. "I warned you, Tyler, your outbursts would not be tolerated again. Darian's protector or not."

"Stay out of this, Raif," Tyler spat. "Why don't you let your brother fight his own battles for once?"

"I don't need anyone's help to fight you, Jinn." Xander always used the term, Jinn, as if it were a dirty word. "You've already proven you're not a worthy enough male to hold on to what was yours."

Oh, boy. That did it. Tyler released his hold on Xander's throat. And he wiped the superior, gloating smile from the Shaede King's face—with his fist. The punch landed squarely on Xander's chin and he reeled backward. It took only a moment for him to recover, though, and he charged Tyler, taking him out in a tackle that would make a linebacker proud. Fists flew as Raif and other members of the in-house security staff attempted to pull them apart. The party had come to a standstill as all eyes were focused on the epic knock-down, dragout, tuxedo-clad fight.

Until a heart-stopping shriek rent the air.

Chapter 27

The crowd parted like the Red fucking Sea, turning their backs on Xander and Tyler to take in this new drama. It took a moment for my brain to register just exactly what I was seeing, but when everything finally clicked, the leftover adrenaline from Xander and Ty's scuffle kicked back up—and went into overdrive.

Kade had crashed the party, and he used the ballroom as center stage. In front of him, Dimitri was on his knees, his head pulled back by the grip Kade had on his hair, and a long, shining dagger pressed to his throat. My heart stopped beating for what felt like several minutes and then crashed against my rib cage in a frantic rhythm. I had no way to communicate with my team, and thanks to the wards on the building, any advantage I might have against Kade was null and void.

"It's been twenty-four hours, Anya," Kade said in a pleasant, almost conversational tone. "Time to settle up."

"Kade." Tears distorted Anya's voice as she pleaded. "Please, I'll get what you want. Just . . . spare him."

"Oh, Anya," Kade said with irritation. "You should know me better than that by now. I don't do mercy."

Panic swept Anya's features as she met her husband's gaze. A moment passed between them. Apparently, Kade didn't bluff. The once-hardened expression set into Dimitri's face melted away, and his light brown eyes drank her in as if for the last time. *Bullshit.* No fucking way was I going to let this be the last time Dimitri would look upon his pregnant wife. I reached behind my back and slowly slid the silver dagger from the sheath I'd sewn into the seam.

I'd forgotten all about Tyler and Xander as I kicked off my

shoes and wound my way through the crowd toward Kade. He seemed to be enjoying his moment in the spotlight and drew it out to heighten the drama. I wondered if any evil mastermind considered the possibility that they'd have more luck without the big production. But right now, I was glad that Kade happened to be a drama queen. I needed the extra time for a sneak attack. A charge into battle wasn't going to help anyone.

What I wouldn't give to have my headset right about now. I needed to talk to my team. To coordinate with Raif. *Goddamn it.* But I didn't have time to contemplate what I needed. This was going to have to be a solo mission. No wishing, no backup. One on one. Me and Kade. Nothing I wasn't used to. I tuned everything out as I crept closer: Anya's pleading, Kade's snarky comebacks, and the apparent mobilization of security as they focused their efforts from one bad situation to another. I could use the distraction, though. Kade would be expecting an assault from the PNT troops. And while he was busy with them, I'd run my dagger through the bastard's heart. *Perfect.*

Right on cue, a team of six PNT soldiers converged on Kade. I recognized their leader, a Fae named Adare, calm and cool as ever with weapons drawn and a look of grim determination on his face. I didn't think Kade would go down without a fight, but the bastard just stood there, all smug and self-satisfied. Carefully, Adare's group surrounded Kade; he still had a dagger pressed to Dimitri's throat after all. Adare squared his shoulders and approached the demon with careful steps.

"I don't know who you are, or what your business is, but if you try to settle it here, you're as good as dead." His moss-green eyes narrowed as he assessed the situation. "You're surrounded, and the building is warded."

Kade flashed Adare an amused smile. "Warded?" His incredulous tone bordered on melodramatic. "Fuck your Fae magic. This man's wife owes me a debt. And I don't give a shit about your *wards.*"

Adare looked ready to throttle Kade. I didn't think anyone openly defied him. And tonight, Kade was all about putting on a show. I wanted to kick myself. I should have known he'd want an audience. He'd harried Anya at every turn, but when it came to the big showdown, he wanted as many people as possible to see what he was capable of. *Asshole*.

While Kade and Adare squared off, I used the opportunity to make my move. I'd catch him unaware, tackle Dimitri, and get him out of the reach of Kade's blade. Then, I'd bring the hurt. At least, that was my plan. My ball gown had become a royal pain in the ass, and I'd be lucky to accomplish the maneuver without flashing my boobs to the entire supernatural community. Fucking strapless piece of shit. I ducked behind a group of Fae females who watched the scene unfolding before them with an almost perverse interest that I found a little on the sadistic side. Dimitri's life hung in the balance and they looked on as if they were watching some kind of reality TV show. So I took a certain amount of grim satisfaction when I burst through their group, sending them careening in different directions.

Using the marble floor for as much traction as my bare feet would allow, I charged Kade while he continued to bait Adare into action. I sprinted toward them, dodging through and around the spectators who apparently couldn't be bothered to intervene and help Dimitri. I broke through the barrier of onlookers, prepared to dive for Anya's husband. A powerful energy washed over me, thick and snaking through the air like a chill breeze, causing the tiny hairs on my arms to stand on end. I'd felt it before. I recognized it. *Shit*.

My shoulder slammed into the invisible barrier protecting Kade and Dimitri, and if I were to guess, it enclosed them in a sort of magical bubble. Tyler had cast a similar barrier of protection over me once. Now I knew with certainty why Kade's energy had felt so familiar. It was Jinn magic that clung to him. *He's killing her*, Ty had said to me a few nights ago in my apartment. I'd suspected, but this new development confirmed it: Kade had obviously been siphoning Adira's power. *Ho-ly shit*. This was much worse than Kade simply using Adira for wishes and protection. *Much worse*.

"Hey, Trouble," Kade said with amusement. He looked me up and down before his gaze settled on the dagger clenched in my hand. "Nice dress."

I pulled my arm back and slammed my fist into the barrier. Pain radiated from my wrist up to my shoulder, and I almost dropped the dagger as my limb went practically numb. "Darian!" Adare barked, his gaze sparking with animosity. "This is a PNT matter. Stand down."

"Wrong, Adare." I didn't take my eyes off of Kade, who seemed to be getting off on the whole scene. "This is *my* business. Not yours. Now lift the goddamned wards so I can kill this motherfucker."

I honestly had no idea if lifting the wards would help. Jinn magic was stronger than anything in the supernatural world, but there had to be someone here who could at least weaken the barrier. Tyler could, for sure, but thanks to those lovely Jinn rules, he was forbidden from interfering with the bonds of others. Adare gave me a look, not exactly trustworthy, but like he hadn't really thought about having the wards lifted. He whispered an order to a Fae colleague beside him who took off like a shot through the crowd of onlookers.

"Your wife threw your life away, Dimitri," Kade mused. He choked up on the dagger's hilt, pressing the sharp blade into Dimitri's skin. Blood dripped from the cut, running in a rivulet down his neck. I expected something defiant, a struggle, or threats and curses at least, but Dimitri remained silent. Proud. There was more defiance in his silence than words could express. My heart leapt into my throat as I realized what he already knew: his time had run out.

"Kade!" Anya's voice broke from her chest in a shrill near-scream. She cried in earnest, tears streaming down her face. Her words came frantic, a stream of sound that I couldn't understand as she abandoned English for her native Russian. But her tone could not be mistaken. She was frantic, begging for her husband's life, and if I had to guess, she was trying to strike a bargain. Hell, I bet she promised him the world and then some.

I looked around, my pulse rushing in my ears, for any sign of Adare's soldiers. How the fuck long did it take to lift the goddamned wards, anyway? Kade graced Anya with a cold, evil smile and she dropped to her knees, sobbing. *Oh my god. Ohmygodohmygodohmygod. No!*

Kade's eyes locked on hers, his face a mask of serenity as he slit Dimitri's throat. Anya screamed, the sound so devastating that it tore my heart to shreds. I slammed my body into the invisible barrier, stabbed at it with the silver dagger again and again. Bodies joined mine: Xander and Raif, fighting like hell to break through the magic that kept us out. Dimitri stared at his wife as he bled out, his brows drawn as he took her in one last time. "No!" I screamed, joining Anya's mournful wails. "Goddamn you, Kade! Dimitri, hold on! We're coming! *Hold on!*"

Dimitri struggled to speak, and what issued from his mouth was a sickening gurgle deep in his throat, followed by a quick string of Russian. As the life slowly drained out of him, he kept his eyes locked on Anya, his expression so full of love and emotion that it stole my breath. I ached for Anya, shared in her sorrow as Dimitri's expression went blank. His soft brown eyes became empty, void of life, and as Kade released him, he toppled face-first to the floor.

"I'm feeling generous, so I'll give you forty-eight hours this time, Anya," Kade warned. His angelic expression melted away, revealing nothing but calculating menace. "If you don't give me what I want in two days' time, you'll join your husband. And I guarantee your journey to the afterlife won't be nearly as pleasant as his. You aren't safe *anywhere* and you know it. I'll come for you. Don't disappoint me again."

Anya screamed at Kade, a string of profanities and curses that should have killed him right on the spot. He looked my way and flashed a superior smirk before his form shimmered and disappeared. With his disappearance, the barrier that protected him vanished. Anya scrambled to her husband's side, gathering him up in her arms. With the wards in place, Dimitri had become easy prey for Kade. No amount of supernatural healing could save him now. Blood pooled on the polished marble floor and soaked through Anya's gown. She held Dimitri close to her, rocking back and forth as sobs wracked her body.

Xander rushed to Anya, going to his knees. Raif joined them, shifting Dimitri's body away from Anya, and she threw herself into Xander's embrace. He shushed her as he rocked her in his arms, passing his hand along her hairline and whispering words of comfort in her ear. He looked back at me, the sorrowful expression on his regal face tearing at my own composure. *I failed.* I let Kade get to Dimitri. All she'd asked of me was that I keep him safe, and I failed her.

Another startled gasp and the murmur of excited voices made its way to me from the back of the ballroom. Not wasting any time, I pushed my way through the throngs of useless onlookers to the source of the commotion. In the center of the group, Adira lay on the floor, unconscious. Tyler was there as well, scooping her up into his arms. His eyes met mine, his face hard and his mouth a grim line. "She's alive," he said, "but barely. Kade's draining everything from her. If he takes from her again, she'll die."

Jesus Christ. Could this get any worse? On second thought, I didn't think I actually wanted that question answered. I *knew* it could be a whole hell of a lot worse. I stormed for the exit, bare feet slapping on the marble floor. The members of my team rushed through the entrance, crossing the foyer to the ballroom. They stopped when they saw me, their faces grim.

"I don't know how he got in," Louella said, as if apologizing. "We had every entrance covered, and—"

"I know." There was no point in hashing out what happened. It happened. Dimitri was dead, Adira was dying, and no amount of replay would change those facts. "He got past us. It's no one's fault. Right now, Louella, I want you, Julian, and Myles to escort the king, Raif, and Anya back to his house. I don't want you guys more than a few feet away from her at all times." I paused, thinking of Anya's grief and despair, and amended my order. "Louella, Anya's going to need a certain amount of . . . space. Don't crowd her. Watch her, but don't be obvious about it. Understand?"

She gave a solemn nod, and I swear, tears glistened in the young Shaede's eyes. "We've got her covered."

"Ash, you and Liam go with Tyler. I know he'll try to send you away, but don't you dare leave." I eyed Asher as I spoke. "Be as invisible as you can." Which I knew was pretty *damn* invisible. "If you see, hear, or even *feel* any hint of Kade lurking around, call me ASAP."

"Where are you going?" Asher asked with suspicion.

"I'm going to make sure Levi has this meeting set up with

his ex. We've got forty-eight hours to put Kade down. Keep an eye on Tyler," I told them as I headed for the exit. "I'll send someone to relieve you by noon."

I could tell that Asher wanted to ask me something else, but I didn't give him the chance. Silky shadows flowed over my skin, and I joined their company as I burst through the heavy glass doors and out into the night. Kade had put an expiration date on Anya's—and her unborn child's—life. No way in hell was I going to fail her a second time.

Chapter 28

I refused to leave The Pit until Levi confirmed my appointment with his ex, Pamela. But now we had a plan in place.
Levi instructed me to come alone, thirty hours from now, to
where her coven met in Pioneer Square, an old abandoned
retail space that the coven had had reclassified as a religious
sanctuary. I tried to argue that my time frame didn't allow for
thirty hours of waiting, but Levi countered that Pamela would
need the moon to be in a certain phase, at the perfect position
to draw on etheric energy—whatever *that* was—and so forth.
He instructed me to get as much detailed information from
Anya as I could about Kade, his pregnant female who'd died,
and anything else she thought might be pertinent. This would
be no time for secrets, and though I knew that Anya deserved
to be left alone so she could grieve for her husband, her life
was on the line and I had to act. Now.

By the time I trudged through Xander's front door, the sun
was about to rise. Stifling—much too warm—the gray hour
of dawn brushed against my senses like someone was trying
to roll me up in a wool blanket. I wanted to shut myself up in
my room and pray that when I woke, all of this would just be
a nightmare. The soft sound of Anya's sobs filtered down
from the second story of Xander's mansion, echoing into
eerie silence like the wails of a haunting spirit. As I took the
stairs, my bare feet weighed me down as if made of lead. I
could barely boast the people skills of a Rottweiler, so I
wasn't quite sure how to act or what to say when I finally got
to her apartment suite.

Louella, Julian, and Myles stood watch outside of Anya's
door, just like I'd asked. I breathed a sigh of relief, glad that

I could count on them to follow orders. I tried not to think about Asher and the fact that he defied me every opportunity he got. I could only hope that he'd done as I asked and escorted Tyler and Adira back to his apartment. Right now, they needed protection just as much as Anya did. "How is she?" I asked in a hushed tone as I approached the group.

"The king is with her now," Louella said quietly. "She's been inconsolable, and he seems to be the only one who can calm her."

Xander said that he loved Anya like a sister. Aside from Dimitri, I'd never seen Anya being social with any other members of Xander's staff. In fact, I'd never really seen her be social with *anyone*. Just one more personality trait that we shared. What I was about to do wasn't going to be fun. "Stay out here," I said. "Julian, check in with Liam and get an update on the situation at Tyler's for me."

"Can do," he said as I pushed open Anya's door.

The room was completely dark. Despite the fact that the sun was just about to crest the horizon, the heavy drapes had been drawn to prevent any light from seeping in. Anya sat on the couch, curled into a ball, resting her head on Xander's chest. He absently passed his hand down the length of her unbound hair as he murmured in her ear. His rich voice accented the cadence of the words he spoke to her in Russian. And though I couldn't understand a word of it, I got the gist of his comforting tone all the same.

My heart lurched in my chest at Xander's compassion. He seemed so much more real to me in this moment. Not just the king: haughty, entitled, gorgeous to a fault and arrogant enough to brag about it. Now he seemed so selfless, softer somehow. His voice infused me with calm and I wondered if it had the same effect on Anya. "Anya . . ." My own voice broke, the total opposite of calm. Palms slick with sweat, I wiped them on the ball gown and twisted the ring on my thumb nervously. A chill raced up my arm as if the ring were somehow angry with me. Did it perhaps echo Tyler's emotions?

"All I asked is that you protect him." Her sorrowful words were muffled by Xander's shirt. "While you played my king and that bastard Jinn against one another, Kade slipped in without notice! You killed him, Darian! *You* let Dimitri die!" She choked on the words that were followed by more of the wracking sobs that made my gut knot up.

Xander's gaze met mine, glowing like warm embers in the dark room. He didn't have to use words to express what he was trying to say; I could read it on his face: *She doesn't mean that. She's consumed with grief. She's lashing out. Forgive her.* "You're right, Anya. This *is* my fault."

Xander's eyes widened a fraction of an inch, but otherwise he didn't react to my statement. Of course, he'd tell me later not to blame myself, that none of this was my fault, blah, blah, blah. But I'd never stop feeling guilty, or considering myself responsible for what had happened tonight. "Xander, do you think Anya and I could have a few minutes alone?" I asked, knowing that I had a snowball's chance in hell of getting her to open up to me. "I need to talk to her privately."

He gave me a look like he really, *really* didn't think that was a good idea. Anya pulled away, assessing me with a slightly less contemptuous look than I expected. "I have nothing to say to you."

"Anya . . ." Jesus, how to proceed? "You heard Kade. Forty-eight hours. It's time to end this. Let me help you." I paused, glanced down at her bloodstained dress. "Let me help your child. Dimitri's child. Please."

"Five minutes." She sniffed. "And no more."

"Are you sure you want to do this?" Xander looked at Anya, but I knew the question was directed at me. "You're overwrought . . ."

"I want to talk to her," she said. "But"—she reached out and grabbed on to Xander's shirtsleeve—"will you come back when she leaves?"

Xander brought Anya's hand to his lips and gently kissed her knuckles. "Of course. I'll be right outside the door if you need me."

As he walked past me, Xander reached out and took my hand in his. He didn't stop, just let my fingers brush through his palm as he walked. I turned my head, watching from the corner of my eye as he left the room. The High King was many things, but heartless, he wasn't.

"The death rites will be performed tomorrow at midnight," Anya said through another round of tears. She sniffed and cleared her throat as if steeling herself against emotion in my presence. When she spoke again, she was the stone-cold bitch from our first meeting. "I won't be able to participate," she said, flatly. "Because of my pregnancy, I am prevented from sending my husband's soul to the afterlife."

I'd never been to a Shaede funeral, and I couldn't help but wonder what had been done with Azriel's body and *soul* after I'd killed him. "Why?" I probably shouldn't have pushed her, but I wanted to know. "What's going to prevent you?"

"My pregnancy prevents me from joining with the shadows." Anya gave a sad laugh. "I must remain corporeal until the child is born."

I put two and two together, deducing that the death rites revolved around leaving the physical body behind. Probably metaphorical for something. It made me hate myself even more for failing to keep Dimitri alive. "I failed him," I said, coming to stand beside her. "I let you down, and I'll never forgive myself for what happened tonight. Nothing I can do will make amends, I know. But I'm going to protect you no matter what. I just—I need your help."

"What? Too weak and foolish to do the job on your own, Darian?" Tears glistened in Anya's violet eyes but didn't spill over her lashes. "I always knew that bringing you into our fold would be our undoing. If only my king had listened to me."

If only. "Anya," I pleaded, "*help* me. I know you'd just as soon kick me as give me a hand, but if I'm going to have any chance of beating Kade, I need you."

Anya snorted. "Xander puts too much faith in you. But not me. I *knew* you'd let me down. You're worthless."

"That's enough, Anya." Xander strode through the door and slammed it behind him. One of the drawbacks to superhuman hearing is the fact that conversations are rarely private. "You are grieving, so I will forgive your thoughtless words. But know that future disparages against Darian will not be tolerated."

"She let him die!" she shouted through a fresh round of tears.

"She did nothing of the sort," Xander said with a sad shake of his head. "Did you not see how she fought to get to Dimitri?"

Anya bit down on her bottom lip to still its quaking. "She promised me she'd keep him safe."

"And she did everything in her power."

I really hated being talked about right in front of my face. Xander's rationalizing wasn't getting me any of the information I needed and it certainly wasn't doing anything to assuage Anya's grief. She'd lost her husband just hours ago. She deserved every bit of the rage she felt. And if she wanted to take it out on me, I was more than happy to be her punching bag. "Xander, I don't need you to stand up for me." He gave me an incredulous look so I added, "Not that I don't appreciate it. Look, I'll meet you in your room when I'm done here, okay?" I looked to Anya for concurrence. "Would that be all right with you?"

She gave a solemn nod of her head and I turned back to Xander. "Please. Leave us."

It wasn't a question so much as a request. Xander's interference was making an already bad situation worse. I walked—okay, *pushed*—Xander to the door and ushered him out. "I can take care of myself," I whispered. "Go away." I shut the door in his face without another word. "Can you say, *high-handed*?" I asked in an attempt at levity as I walked back to the couch.

"He's the king," Anya said, her voice monotone. "It's his right."

"If you say so." Damn, this was hard for me. I wanted to offer my condolences, tell Anya how sorry I was for her loss. I wish I hadn't been so closed off from the world for so long. Because now more than ever, I didn't want to come across as an insensitive bitch. "I really liked Dimitri."

One corner of Anya's mouth turned up. "He liked you, too."

"I have a plan. I know how to take Kade down. But I can't get to him without your help."

"What do you want to know?" Anya asked, scooting over to offer me a place on the couch.

"Let's start with this demon bible," I said as I sat down, "and go from there."

As I walked down the hall to Xander's room, I processed everything Anya told me. What Kade had really been after was the book. I'd had a sneaking suspicion. A coldhearted bastard like Kade wouldn't have gone after Anya simply over a broken heart. That was just his excuse. Anya had kept the demon bible—a sort of esoteric insider's guide to the Incubus world—after she'd stolen it from Kade's father. Trouble was, it was thousands of miles away, in the keeping of someone she trusted. Plus, according to Anya, she'd never been able to open the damn thing. It had some sort of magical lock that prevented anyone except for maybe Kade's father from getting a look inside. We'd negotiate with Kade if we had to. Give him the location of the book. But she and Dimitri had agreed long ago that if the contents of the codex were so well protected that no one could get past the locks, it probably contained information that would be dangerous in the hands of someone like Kade. In fact, as he lay bleeding on the ballroom floor, Dimitri made his wife promise that she'd never give Kade the book, no matter what. So out of respect for her husband's wishes, I promised Anya we'd give up its location only as a last resort.

Not an option I was particularly excited about.

Demon bibles aside, Anya had given me all the ammo I needed against Kade and then some. I had his dead female's name and stats down to a T. And I hit the jackpot when she'd managed to find me a picture to give to Levi's ex. I felt confident that I'd have more than enough to offer Pamela when I met with her tomorrow. I was going to stop that Cambion bastard. No one else was going to die at his hands.

It was already nine in the morning, and most of Xander's household staff had been up and working for hours. I entered the king's suite wanting nothing more than a few moments of peace so I could get my thoughts in order and maybe get a few hours' sleep before preparations for Dimitri's funeral began.

"How is she?" Xander's quiet voice seemed to encircle me.

"Sleeping," I said. "But you should check in on her soon."

"I'll let her rest for a while," he said. "How are *you*?"

I didn't even know how to answer. Exhausted . . . frustrated . . . confused . . . angry as hell . . . disappointed in myself . . . the list went on and on. "I let everyone down," I said. "Anya's right, Xander. You shouldn't have put your faith in me."

"Darian . . ." The Shaede King's arms wrapped around my waist, and he brought me against his chest. He smelled like the forest after a hard rain. "You aren't some superhero. You must accept that there will be disappointments in life. Good men die, and sometimes the villain wins. It has nothing to do with you letting anyone down. It's simply the nature of this life. You have to learn to take the good with the bad."

He put his hands on my shoulders to put me at arms' distance. He bent down, his face close to mine and stared into my eyes. "Breathe, Darian. Clear your mind of worry."

"I can't." Jesus, I couldn't breathe. My lungs refused to work. "Oh, god, Xander. How could I have let him just stroll in like that and slit Dimitri's throat?" As I drew in tight little breaths, I wondered if I'd pass out. For weeks—no for months—my world had felt like it was spinning out of control. And after years of holding on so tightly and exercising complete control over my life, I felt more lost than ever. Losing Dimitri and witnessing the destruction of Anya's happy life was my breaking point. The pain—the outright injustice of it all—was just too damn much.

Xander's hands wandered from my shoulders to my back as he pulled me close to him. The warmth of his body did nothing except remind me that Anya would never know that comfort from her husband ever again. He cupped the back of my neck and cradled me against him. He laid his lips to my temple and moved lower, next to my ear and then down my neck. I pulled away, unwilling to let the moment progress and Xander whispered in my ear, "You need to forget for a moment and be free of these damned thoughts that torture you so. Let me comfort you."

"No, Xander," I replied, choking on the words. "Please."

He held me tighter. "I love you."

"No." Panic rose in me. This wasn't what I wanted. I couldn't bear for him to say those words to me.

"Darian," Xander's distressed tone served to further tear my composure to shreds. "Don't push me away."

"I just can't . . ." The words died on my tongue. So many words could finish that sentence.

"What?" Xander demanded. "You can't bear to hear me tell you how I feel about you? You can't acknowledge the fact that you belong here, with *me*, with your own kind?"

I didn't belong anywhere. Even among Shaedes I was an anomaly. Why couldn't Xander see that?

"I want you." Xander stressed the words as if trying to pound them into my head. "Not just for the night or the moment. I want to be there for you. To comfort you, to protect you, to cherish you. Why is that so hard for you to comprehend?"

"I think we both know I'm not the one who needs comfort right now." I pulled away from Xander's embrace, though he kept my wrist firmly in his grip. "Anya needs you. *She* needs your protection and support. She's going to need you for weeks to come, too."

"You're deflecting," Xander said, his tone becoming more agitated. "This isn't about Anya. This is about you and me."

"There is no you and me," I murmured. "There can't be."

"Why? Tell me, Darian. I'd like to hear your list of excuses, your denial that you feel anything for me."

Of course I felt something for Xander. How could I not after the weeks we'd spent together? He'd grounded me. Gave me permission to let go and release the choke hold I had on my life. He'd brought me back from the precipice of self-destruction and helped me to move forward when I thought my heart would permanently break. But I didn't love him. And I knew that deep down, he didn't love me either.

A timid knock came at the king's door, saving me from any further conversation, and Xander's body slumped as he released his grip on my wrist and took a step back.

"Your Highness," a voice said from the other side of the door. "Anya is asking for you."

"You should go check on her," I said. "You promised her you'd come back after I left."

"I've called in my physician to see her," Xander said with a heavy sigh. "With her recent distress, I want to be sure she and the baby are all right. He should be here in a few minutes if he's not waiting for me in my office already. I suppose I should go." Before he turned to leave, he added, "There never seems to be enough hours for us, Darian. How can I possibly prove myself to you when we have so little time? I hope that changes. Soon." He pulled open the door and said, "You should sleep. You need to rest your mind and clear your thoughts."

My heart sank into my chest at Xander's dark tone. I didn't know how much more heartache any of us could take. "You should apologize to her," I said. "For bursting in and reprimanding her earlier. I could have handled Anya's temper on my own."

"To insult you is an insult to me," Xander replied. "I will not abide any of my subjects' mistreatment of you. No matter how beloved."

I was too exhausted to reply. Besides, it would only encourage him to stay and argue the point. I watched as he pulled the door closed behind him. Xander's words weighed me down with anxiety that made my stomach twist and my chest burn with suppressed emotions. Xander was supposed to be safe. Too arrogant and frivolous to form emotional attachments to anyone or anything. I couldn't let this go on. Not while I still loved Tyler with all of my heart and soul. I refused to be responsible for any more sorrow and Xander didn't deserve to be played.

I was tired of playing games.

My thoughts became muddled as sleep tugged at my mind. Xander was right about one thing: I needed rest. Both physically and emotionally. I couldn't afford to worry about my own problems or insecurities right now. Dimitri's funeral would take place at midnight, and I didn't want to be too tired or distracted to stand guard.

Nothing more than a breath of shadow, I left Xander's suite. By the time I made it to my room, my eyes had begun to drift shut of their own volition. I flopped down on the bed, and as I raced toward the oblivion of sleep, I tried to block out the sound of Anya's sorrow as she began to cry once again. There were times when supernatural hearing definitely had its drawbacks. I hugged a pillow over my ears and prayed for the strength to bring Kade to justice. Because right now, I felt so, *so* weak. "I wish . . ." My voice was nothing more than a whisper as the words dreamily crept to my lips. What? What did I want? "I wish life wasn't so damned hard and complicated." A familiar energy tingled across my skin, so faint I thought I'd imagined it as I sloughed the last of my consciousness and found a deep and dreamless sleep.

Chapter 29

"What will happen?" I asked Raif as I laced up my boots. I wanted to know what to expect so I didn't disrespect Anya by coming across as a clueless idiot at her husband's funeral.

"We will send Dimitri's soul into the shadows of the afterlife," Raif replied. "It is an ancient ceremony dating back to the beginnings of the Shaede lineage. The tradition has not changed for thousands of years."

"I take it this won't be a small-scale production?" Raif cocked his brow, and I wished I could suck the words back into my mouth. "You know what I mean."

"Xander owns a large amount of acreage near Snoqualmie where the ceremony will be performed. As you're there to protect Anya, you won't be expected to participate."

I threw on my duster, feeling suddenly awkward about my street clothes. Like the rest of the Shaedes attending tonight's ritual, Raif was decked out in an ancient-looking, jet black ensemble: loose-fitting pants and a strange robelike tunic that was held in place with a wide black leather belt. Everyone would be wearing black from head to toe, more for the symbolism of our shadow-selves than for the somberness of the color.

Anya passed the doorway to my suite just as Raif and I were leaving. For the second time since I'd met her, she'd abandoned her usual leather outfit. If I'd thought she was stunning in her evening gown, it was nothing compared to the tragic beauty of the flowing black robes that swirled around her body as if they were made of nothing but weightless shadow. She looked thinner, more vulnerable as the fabric appeared to swallow her lithe frame. Her violet eyes stood out in stark contrast to her dark hair and robes—puffy and bloodshot from hours of crying—haunting in their beauty. She passed me without so much as a sideways glance. Understandable since she was still grieving, and emotionally raw, and blaming me for the fact that there had to be a funeral at all. I tucked the nearly invisible ear bud into my ear and clipped the mic unit to my collar. In my right ear, I could hear the chatter of my team members as they prepared to load the various members of Xander's court into the many SUVs parked in the circular driveway.

"Asher. Meet me in the foyer."

The talk died down instantly as Asher answered, "Gotcha."

"Problem?" Raif asked as we descended the stairs.

"With Ash?" I scoffed. "Probably." A couple of nights ago, I'd wanted nothing more than to wash my hands of the cocky Shaede. But Asher was valuable. Though I still didn't know how he could make himself virtually unnoticeable, I needed that stealth factor in case shit went down. Not even Kade, with all of his stolen power, would see Asher coming. "I just want to check in and see how things went at Tyler's last night." I hadn't been able to get an update the night before because I'd gone straight to Xander's suite.

Asher was waiting for me in the foyer, and I almost couldn't believe the kid had actually followed orders for a change. Raif excused himself to find Xander since they'd be riding with Anya. I fixed a stern eye on the young Shaede as he leaned against the archway that led from the foyer into the sitting room. I couldn't help but wonder if he'd adopt such a comfortable position if Xander happened to walk by. "What happened last night?" I asked.

"Well, you were right about Tyler not wanting a babysitter. He didn't like having Liam and me hanging around. But I told him that my orders came directly from you and I didn't feel like pissing you off."

Whatever. He *loved* to piss me off. "What did Tyler say?"

A lazy grin spread across Asher's face and he shrugged. "He said something about how you always had to have your way and then he slammed the door in my face."

That, I believed. "Any idea how Adira is doing?"

"The female? I think she was all right. I could hear them talking, anyway."

"Any idea what they were talking about?"

"Well, since they knew Liam and I were outside, they didn't let much slip," he replied.

Of course. When your unwelcome guards have superhuman hearing, it was always best to keep your mouth shut. "Great. I was hoping Adira would have said *something* about Kade."

"It was all sort of sobby apologies on her part and Tyler doing the typical sappy bullshit." Asher lowered his voice as he imitated Ty. *"Everything will be okay, baby. I promise."*

I could do without the sappy bullshit.

"No sign of Kade, then?" I opened the front door and waited for Asher to follow.

"Nope. The dude is like a motherfucking ghost."

"Sort of like you," I remarked as a reminder to Asher that I hadn't forgotten about his own little *quirks*.

"No," he said solemnly. "Nothing like me."

The drive to Xander's property took about an hour. The surrounding landscape was nothing but dense forest. Eleven thirty, and the cloudy sky made the night seem impenetrably dark. No stars or moonlight would grace Dimitri's funeral. It was fitting, somehow. As if the very sky mourned his death.

We pulled off the main road and took a trail that was little more than a couple of tire tracks where the vegetation had been mashed down. Brush and tree limbs scraped across the doors of our vehicle as we drove deeper into the forest. We came to what looked like a man-made—or, I guess, Shaede-made—clearing. It was obvious that the copse of trees had been cut back and the area manicured to shape the clearing into a perfect circle. I couldn't help but wonder what it was about the supernatural community that they loved to hold ceremonies in meadows, clearings, or any open spaces out in the middle of nowhere. It must have had something to do with their long lives and ties to their pasts and traditions. All Fae creatures—and the Shaedes perched on a branch of that family tree—seemed to have an affinity for all things nature-related. Made sense. After all, most of them had been alive before the dawn of Christianity, worshipping ancient gods in sacred forests, where civilizations were few and far between.

Hundreds of lit torches lined the outer perimeter of the circle, and in the center was a tall wooden structure that looked suspiciously like a . . . "Raif, is that a pyre?" I asked, in disbelief.

"It is," he said in that infuriating way that let me know he found my questions exhausting.

"This is standard when a death occurs?" Shaedes didn't die often, but Jesus Christ, it was easy for someone as wealthy as Xander to procure a site for a funeral pyre, but how in the hell would an average Shaede family take care of a funeral? Burn the body in their backyard?

"Not always," Raif said. "But I told you, this is an old tradition, and Dimitri was held in high esteem. It is an honor to send his soul to the shadows in this way."

More vehicles arrived to join Xander's own extensive motorcade, and the mourners milled about the clearing, taking their places at the edge of the circle by the burning torches. Dimitri's body had already been placed on the top of the pyre and had been swathed in more of the same black fabric that Anya's robes were made from. I coordinated with my team, setting them a few feet from the clearing, out in the trees surrounding the area. I wanted to see, but not be seen. No need to further distress Anya by reminding her just what had brought about her husband's death.

I stood at the opposite side of the circle from Anya and watched as the sacred ceremony began. A priestess of some sort, garbed in the same flowing robes as Anya, stood before the pyre and spoke words in a language probably older than anything spoken in the world today. I couldn't take my eyes off of Anya and watched as tears slid silently down her face. She looked upon her husband's body with her chin held high, so proud and beautiful and devastated all at once. Xander stood to one side of her and Raif at the other. At one point, the priestess paused, and Anya spoke through her tears, repeating the words in the same haunting cadence. Then, the funeral attendees took their turn, reciting the same words, their many voices echoing into the dark night.

One by one, they each took up a torch. Anya, Raif, and two Shaedes—a male and female that I didn't recognize—joined the priestess at the pyre. Anya stood at her husband's feet with the priestess while the remaining three surrounded the pyre in a sort of triangle. Anya was the first to set her torch to the straw at the base of the structure, and then Raif and the others. Once they stepped back, the other Shaedes moved in, each touching their torch to the structure to add to the building flames. Once the pyre burned bright, illuminating the entire clearing, they retreated, but only enough to give Raif and the other three Shaedes surrounding the pyre a little room.

I held my breath as I watched Raif's eyes drift shut. He bowed his head and exhaled a deep breath. The priestess began chanting again and the other two Shaedes bowed their heads with Raif and exhaled their breath. Glistening tendrils of shadows—known as soul shadows—crept from their mouths like mists of delicate ribbon. The soul shadows searched and twined like graceful serpents, winding and crawling up the pyre as it burned. As the shadows merged with the flames, they darkened from bright orange to red, and then from crimson to black. I gasped in surprise as the black flames flickered, their tips lightening to gray.

Lightning streaked a path across the sky, followed by a peal of thunder. Moments later, the patter of raindrops echoed in the clearing but did nothing to tame the black flames raging from Dimitri's pyre. Above the din of the rainfall, the priestess chanted, and the Shaedes left their corporeal forms. They swirled and circled the pyre as it burned, climbing high in the sky with the smoke and ash that rose above the flames.

"It's beautiful, isn't it?"

Tyler came up beside me, no doubt appearing out of thin air. He could always find me, no matter where in this world I happened to be. We were bound by magic, blood, and at one time, love. Nothing could compare to the bond made by love. Did any of that love remain? My gaze fell on Anya. She stood by her husband's funeral pyre, her shoulders shaking as she wept. She alone couldn't leave her body behind to help elevate Dimitri's body and soul to the heavens, and my heart broke for her. "It's very beautiful," I answered through my own grief. "What are you doing here? I would think you'd be with Adira right now."

Tyler tipped his head toward the clearing. "I came to pay my respects. And also to tell you that I don't want you to go after Kade. He's become far too dangerous."

"Doesn't matter." I refused to look at him. "I'm going to kill him."

Tyler turned me to face him. "What if I begged you to let this go?"

"First, you pay me to kill Kade. Now you're begging me not to?"

"I can't protect you, Darian. I thought I could, but this is just too far out of hand now. If something happened to you . . ."

"Like what happened to Dimitri?" My anger mounted, the sight of Anya standing alone among the swirling shadows as she cried weighing heavy on my conscience. "Maybe I *will* die taking Kade out. But it'll be worth it. I owe Anya, anyway. She'd be safe, Adira would be safe. It's a win-win."

"I can't let you risk your life, Darian. I *won't* let you."

I looked away, focusing my attention once again on Dimitri's death rites. The fire burned hot and fast, unnaturally so, and the pyre collapsed, the black flames dying down. But the shadows of the many Shaedes still swirled high in the sky, continuing to lift smoke, ash, and the soul of Anya's husband to the heavens. "Why are you saying this now, Tyler?" Lord, I wanted off this emotional roller coaster. "Do you know what the past few months have been like for me? I'm barely keeping my head above water. And just when I feel like I can start to think about getting on with my life, you show up here and beg me not to risk it. Why, in the midst of all this sadness, after I just told you that I needed to separate my personal life from this job, are you saying this?"

"Because I still love you."

His words cut straight through me, twisting my heart into a tight, unyielding knot. "You left me for another woman."

"Darian." Tyler took a deep breath and held it for a moment before exhaling in a sigh. "I left because I was hurt. I needed to take a step back as much as I needed to give you space. Our relationship was slowly suffocating, and I couldn't bear to see us self-destruct. Damn it, I regretted leaving you the moment I walked out the door. I never meant to be gone as long as I was. Adira needed help. She needed me. And you didn't. As for my relationship with Adira, it's not what you think. It's . . . complicated."

As the pyre folded in on itself, Anya went to her knees. I took a step forward and Tyler grabbed me by the arm, hauling me back. "I can't deal with this right now, Tyler." I tried to jerk away, but he held me tight.

"Are you in love with him?"

My shoulders slumped. "This is not the time or the place to talk about us. Go back to Adira, Tyler. Protect *her*. You said it yourself. She needs you. She needs your protection more than me right now."

"Darian—"

"Go, Tyler. Before I wish you out of here."

I stalked out of the trees toward Anya. I refused to turn back to look at Tyler, but I felt a familiar ripple of energy in the air signaling—I hoped—his departure.

Chapter 30

"How's it look, guys?" I said into my mic. "See anything?"

One member at a time, my team checked in, none of them noticing anything out of the ordinary in the woods surrounding the circle. It figured that Kade would keep to his word in all things. He'd given Anya forty-eight hours, and she was going to get it. I leaned against a tall evergreen, the bark biting into my shoulder. Dimitri's funeral pyre was nothing more than smoldering ashes now, the magical black flames dying to glowing gray embers sizzling in the rain. The shadow forms of the many Shaedes descended from the sky, swirling in a graceful formation. As they came to earth, corporeal forms were regained, and the mourners took their turns in expressing their condolences to Anya.

I felt the prickle of tears at my eyes. No amount of "I'm sorry for your loss" could bring Dimitri back. Even well intentioned, those condolences were nothing more than hollow words. "Goddamn you, Kade."

"I suppose your Jinn came here tonight to try to make amends?" Xander's velvet voice was warm in my ear, though his tone held an edge, as if Tyler had killed Dimitri himself. He did nothing to hide the outrage and utter contempt in his tone. "His presence here tonight was yet another insult to my kingdom. Insults I'll no longer tolerate. He'll rot in a PNT prison for assaulting a high king. I'm bringing the charge before Adare in the morning."

"No." I turned so I could look at him. "Promise me that you'll let this go, Xander."

"I can't," he said simply. "He assaulted a king. In public.

At a dignitary function. If I let this go, others will perceive it as a weakness in me. I will become vulnerable in my detractors' eyes, and my strength to rule will come into question."

The thought of seeing Tyler thrown into some PNT jail caused my heart to beat much too fast. I'd seen what PNT jailers could do to a prisoner. I couldn't bear to think of Tyler suffering the same fate, sitting in one of their dingy cells for god-knew-how-long. "Xander." I tried to keep the tremor of fear from my voice. "I'm still bound to him. He's compelled to protect me. If the PNT throws him in one of their jails . . . I don't know everything about our bond. It could be dangerous for me if he was locked away."

"You would rather I look weak to my people?" His eyes grew cold like frozen amber, and his voice, hard.

"No." *Think, Darian. Defuse. Deflect.* "What about . . . in-house justice?"

Xander quirked a brow. "Such as?"

"I wouldn't want you to lose face in front of anyone." Even *I* knew the importance of maintaining one's reputation. Sometimes it was all that stood between you and an ass-kicking. "But promise me you won't bring the PNT into it. Let Raif take him into custody. You can mete out your own punishment." That I would work like hell to reduce to nothing more than a slap on the wrist. "No one would doubt your power if you let it be known that you don't run to the PNT for protection. The Shaede Nation can take care of its own problems."

A corner of Xander's mouth quirked in a half smile, and I knew that I'd won a battle, if not the war. "Clever girl. Very well," he said as if making a benevolent proclamation. "I won't involve the PNT. But the Jinn *will* be held accountable for the insult done to me."

I let out a shaky sigh of relief. "Thank you, Xander."

He looked into my eyes as if trying to coax some hidden truth from my mind. I stared back, careful to betray nothing. Xander leaned in as if to kiss me and I put my palm against his chest to stay his progress. No more games. A gust of icy wind blasted my back, and I pulled away, rubbing the prickling hairs on the back of my neck as I looked around. I thought he'd left, but the odd shimmer, like a ripple in the fabric of reality not far from where I stood, made me wonder just how much of our conversation Tyler might have heard.

I still love you.

Ty's words seared my mind like a brand. I thought about the feelings his touch, his kiss evoked in me. No one would ever make me feel the way Tyler did. *Ever.* "Go to Anya, Xander. She needs you."

Xander's expression became hard, almost sullen, and he turned to leave without saying a word. I watched as he walked away, thinking that for the second time tonight, I'd sent a man I cared about into another woman's arms.

"If I have to tell you no again, Ash, I'm going to gut you."

"You can't make me stay here," Asher snorted, folding his arms in front of his chest. "I could follow you and you wouldn't even know I was there."

"You're a pain in the ass, you know that? Fine. You tell me how you do that little I'm-here-but-not-here trick of yours, and inform me as to why in the name of all that is holy I should trust you for *any* reason, and I'll let you ride shotgun. Otherwise, I could just *wish* for you to stay put and you won't be following me anywhere."

Silence answered me. *Figures.* "See ya later."

I strode toward the front door and pulled it open only to have Asher reach in front of me and slam it closed. "Does anyone know where you're going or what you're about to do?"

Raif had been busy arranging for extra guards to watch over Xander's house for the next eighteen hours, and I'd urged Xander to stay with Anya in her apartment after the funeral rites had been concluded. For all I knew, he was asleep on her couch. "*I* know where I'm going and what I'm doing. That's enough."

The only way this was going to work was if no one close to me knew my plan. And when I'd agreed to watch over Anya to begin with, it had been under the condition that when it came to killing whoever was threatening her, I worked alone. Levi knew what I was up to; he was the one who'd set up the meeting and helped me come up with a plan of attack, and of course his ex, Pamela, was in on it as well.

Since I didn't think Kade would know that Levi had hooked me up with the witch, I was relatively safe.

Asher stared me dead in the eye. "You're going to meet with the witch, aren't you?" It was my turn to clam up but he continued to press. "Darian, you don't want to mess with human magick. It's not natural. They try to control forces they don't know shit about. It's trouble."

"Oh, yeah? You know that firsthand, Ash?" Again, that insufferable silence. He must have been taking lessons from Raif on how to get under my skin. "Stay here. Guard Anya. That's an *order*. If I find out that you've left the house or gone after me, it'll be treason. I doubt Raif's punishment would be light."

Asher's jaw took on a stubborn set. No way would he risk Raif's anger. "It's your funeral, Darian."

Little shit. I eyed his palm, still lying flat against the door and then slowly dragged my gaze up to his face. He pulled back and gestured in front of him with a sweep of his hand. "Better get going. Wouldn't want to be late for your appointment."

As I stepped through the door, sunlight peered through the fluffy white clouds, remnants of last night's storm. My skin tingled, and I allowed the light to permeate my skin as I left my physical body behind and joined with the day. The door slammed behind me, and I would have felt smug over getting the upper hand on Asher. But as I left Capitol Hill behind, I couldn't help the sense of foreboding that settled in my stomach like a heavy stone. I hoped that by going out without him, I wasn't digging my own grave.

When I arrived at Pamela's retail-space-turned-place-of-worship, she was already there, set up and ready to go. She was alone, which seemed to intensify my anxiety. I don't know what I expected, maybe an entire coven of Goth-looking kids with piercings all over their faces and enough black eyeliner to permanently blind them if they blinked wrong. But Pamela was so . . . *normal*. The only "witchy" thing about her was a pewter pendant of a raven clutching a pentacle in its talon that she wore around her neck.

She couldn't have been older than twenty-five, with long

honey-blond hair that reached her shoulder blades and almond-shaped, dark brown eyes. Tiny freckles dotted her nose and when she smiled in greeting, her face lit up with a girl-next-door expression. I bet she and Levi looked like the prom king and queen when they'd been together.

"You must be Darian." Her voice was the only thing that didn't fit her cute coed persona. It was deeper than I expected and hinted at wisdom she was too young to possess. "I'm Pamela. Nice to meet you."

She held out her hand. I paused, realizing that she expected a friendly greeting, and took her hand in mine. God, I really was a freak. I was so detached that a simple handshake took a moment for me to grasp. *Fantastic. Way to display your superior people skills.* When our hands met, Pamela sucked in a breath through her teeth. "Wow, you have a super strong aura. Even for a Shaede. I'm tingling clear up my arm!"

I let go of her hand and rubbed my palm down my pant leg as if I could banish whatever tingle of power Pamela had felt. "Not to be rude or anything, Pamela, but I'm sort of rushed for time." It was already almost two in the afternoon, which gave me about ten hours before Kade went looking for Anya—and his demon bible. "How long do you think this will take?"

Pamela's mouth puckered as she seemed to be concentrating on something. "Depends," she finally said. "Magick isn't something that can be defined in hours. The effectiveness of a spell depends on the power of the caster, and your receptiveness to the magick."

I couldn't answer to my own *receptiveness*. Since I'd never dealt with human magick, I had no idea what to expect. But I had an open mind. Shit, I'd been to realms that didn't exist on this plane. What was a little witchcraft? "Well then, I guess we'd better get started. I'll try to be as receptive as possible. The rest is on you."

"No worries," Pamela said with a smirk. "I'm a powerful caster. The best in my coven." She said it as if she'd just won Miss Congeniality at a beauty pageant, which didn't bother me at all. Pride in your ability is a good thing, especially when you're trying to win over a client. And that's what I was: a paying customer.

"Levi said you usually work out your fee after a job is done?"

"Yeah, I never know how much it's going to take out of me until after the spell is cast. I'll just bill you, if that's okay?"

I wondered if she had personalized invoices printed out on pretty pink stationery. Something with a cute slogan like, WITCH FOR HIRE! HAVE BROOM, WILL TRAVEL.

"Levi told you it's not really about the money, though, right? I mean, I've got to make a living and all, but it's about so much more than that."

Levi had, in fact, mentioned it. At this point, I didn't give a shit about the nonmonetary costs. Whatever it was would be worth it if it meant I'd get to kill Kade. "I don't care about what this will cost me. I'm ready for whatever risk is involved."

Pamela led me to the center of the room where a low, rectangular table had been draped with a black cloth. Resting in what looked to be a very specific order were various items: a dagger, which looked more ceremonial than functional; a chalice; a shiny, black-surfaced mirror with a pentagram etched onto its surface; a strange-looking wand; candles of varying colors; and bottles filled with liquids and herbs. Huh. Guess I could add tonight's experience to my supernatural lexicon. File this one under: human esoteric rituals.

"Okay, before I cast and close the circle, I need you to tell me everything. If this spell is going to work, I'm going to need as many details as possible."

Pamela knelt beside the table and I followed suit, pulling out the picture Anya had given me and some notes that I had scribbled down with all of the pertinent information I'd need. She listened intently as I talked, absorbing every ounce of information like a sponge. She studied the pictures, sketches, and descriptions I'd written out and placed the visual aids on her altar while reading and rereading the notes I'd taken.

"Okay," Pamela said with a steadying sigh. "I think we're ready. You just stay put."

Pamela fetched a worn leather drawstring bag and the dagger from her altar. I studied the blade, curious, because it didn't look like it had ever been sharpened. *Huh.* She grabbed a handful of what appeared to be salt from the bag and used it to make a circle around us on the concrete floor. Once that was done, she fetched one of the colored candles from her altar, lit it, and placed it at the edge of the circle. She then held the dagger in both hands, raising it to the sky. Facing due east, she began some sort of ritual, calling on the element of water and the forces associated with it to bless her sacred circle and the workings within it. From there, she worked clockwise facing south, placed another lit candle at the circle's edge and recited similar words, entreating the spirits and elements of fire.

She continued on with another candle, this one facing west, calling on the spirits and element of earth, and closed her circle facing north, placing the last candle on the circle, calling on the air and its spirits, watchers, and whatnot. I'd never witnessed any sort of witchcraft in action before, and I have to admit the entire process was fascinating.

"Hecate," Pamela intoned as she crossed back to the altar. Instead of kneeling beside me, she went to the opposite side of the table and dropped to her knees. She lowered the dagger so that the handle hovered near her heart and the pointed tip almost pricked her chin. "Goddess of the dark moon and magick, I invoke your wisdom and your power to aid me in these magickal workings." She cracked an egg over the chalice and, from a small container, poured what looked like honey on top of it. If I hadn't known any better, I would have thought she was baking something based on the sprinkle of herbs and drops of liquid from an unlabeled bottle.

It went on like this for a few more minutes, Pamela chanting some words or asking assistance from some unseen force. At one point, she lit a small pile of herbs on fire to use the ash for her strange concoction. When that was done, she took the dagger and pricked her finger with the tip—surprising, considering the thing looked more ceremonial than functional—and added a few drops of her blood to the chalice. She leveled her gaze to mine, her countenance serious, and held out her hand. I hesitated when I realized that what she wanted was a drop of my own blood to add to hers. My blood wasn't *exactly* magical or anything, but blood was a very powerful element in Fae magic. It was ancient magic, older than the human race, and I wondered if Pamela truly realized the impact of what she was doing. And for that matter—did *I*?

I swallowed against the lump rising in my throat, pushing down my fears and worries. Big picture. Protect Anya. Save Adira. Kill Kade. That's all that mattered. I held out my hand and pulled back just before Pamela could poke my finger with the dagger. "I heal fast. You're not going to get anything with a pinprick."

Pamela rolled her bottom lip between her teeth and finally said, "The athame isn't meant for cutting. I need your blood to complete the spell."

Lucky for Pamela, my dagger was used for more than just show. I pulled it from the sheath at my thigh and dragged the blade across my left palm. A bright red ribbon of blood welled from the cut before it began to heal. I tipped my hand over the rim of the chalice and several drops spilled into the cup. I swallowed hard as the air pressure changed, almost as if something had sucked half of the oxygen out of Pamela's circle. I found it hard to draw a deep breath, and my body felt like someone had just encased it in shrink-wrap.

Pamela took the picture I'd given her, as well as all of my notes on Kade's dead girlfriend. She set them in a cast-iron bowl that looked so much like a cauldron I almost laughed. Almost. I watched as Pamela plunged her dagger—athame—into the chalice and stirred the concoction she'd made. Then she held the point over the cauldron, and a single drop landed on the picture and notes and spontaneously burst into flames. She intoned a single word in a voice that no longer sounded like her own. "Evelena."

Power slammed into me, the feeling of my skin shrinking over me intensifying to the point that I cried out in pain. I fell backward, unable to take a deep enough breath to satisfy my aching lungs. Darkness invaded the periphery of my vision, and my mind dulled as unconsciousness threatened. Pamela jumped to her feet, rubbing her hands over her arms as though chilled. And how she could feel cold was beyond me. *Holy fuck!* Heat devoured me, searing through my body as if I'd been injected with liquid fire. I screamed, unable to remain silent as I burned from the inside out. Something was wrong. It had to be. *Oh. God.* "Pamela!" I shrieked through gritted teeth. I was losing my grip on consciousness; could feel it slipping away by small degrees. I couldn't stop the pain, the darkness that descended on me. I was going to black out. "Make it stop!"

"I can't," she said as she knelt beside me. "It's too late."

Chapter 31

My thoughts cleared as the pain began to ebb. What had been the equivalent of acid racing through my veins was nothing more than a warm pulse. I still couldn't take a deep breath, though, and thought I might hyperventilate and pass out again. "Why do I feel like someone just stuffed me in a vacuum seal bag?" Without thinking, my hands flew to my throat. *Holy shit.* Was that actually my voice? "Why the hell do I not sound like me?" Panic laced my tone as I pushed myself to a sitting position. Pamela's face swam in and out of focus and I cradled my head in my hands. Except they were *not* my hands.

"Are you okay?" Pamela asked, clearly unfazed by my freak-out and subsequent blackout. "There's something seriously off about you, Darian."

"What are you talking about?" *Don't panic. Don't fucking panic. Shit!* I stretched my arms trying to banish the sensation of being encased in Saran Wrap. "Did something go wrong?"

"No," Pamela said with awe. "It worked too well. I've got power, but not enough for such a convincing spell. It's like you have some sort of magical boost or something. The illusion is *amazing.*"

Great. No matter how amazed Pamela sounded, this couldn't be good. Maybe I should have listened to Asher. Too late now. I had no choice but to finish what I'd started. "How long was I out? What time is it?"

"Almost five o'clock. You were out for a little over an hour."

"Shit!" I had only seven hours to find Kade and trick him

into breaking his bond with Adira. Otherwise, he'd be going after Anya and there wouldn't be anything any of us could do to protect her. "I've got to get out of here." I jumped to my feet, instantly regretting the sudden movement. I toppled over, sprawling out on the floor. Jesus, it was like I'd never walked before. Not a great way to start the evening.

"You can't leave the circle until I close it," Pamela said. "And before you leave, there are a few things you need to know."

Awesome. This just got better and better. "Such as?"

"This spell isn't going to be easy to break. Like I said, it's stronger than I expected. The only way to shed the glamour is to have someone recognize you."

What the hell was that supposed to mean? "Recognize me how?"

"Someone has to be able to see past the glamour and recognize you for who you *truly* are. Not the person you appear to be."

Okay. Couldn't be too tough to pull off. Sometimes I felt like Raif knew me better than I knew myself. Once Kade was dead, I'd just go to Raif and explain. Surely he'd know it was me and break Pamela's spell. "Gotcha. Anything else?"

"Just a warning," Pamela said, her words as ominous as her expression. "This is human magick, Darian, and you'll be subject to the rules of that magick. Everything you do has consequences. Levi told you that sometimes the price you pay has nothing to do with money. The effects can be immediate; other times it takes years to catch up with you. You'll pay threefold for what you do tonight. Every action, every spell has a counteraction. Whether good or bad, what you do will come back to you three times, better or worse. Do you understand?"

Well, wasn't that just a cheery disclaimer? Might have been nice to have that information *before* the spell had been cast. Again, it was too late to lament what might be one of the shittiest decisions I'd ever made. What was done was done. Time to move on. "I understand. Don't worry, Pamela. I wouldn't have come here if I wasn't ready to accept the consequences. But, seriously, I've got to *go*."

Pamela nodded, apparently satisfied that I understood the

risks inherent in dabbling in human magick. It took another twenty minutes for Pamela to close her circle and end whatever it was we'd started. I much preferred Fae magic to the human version. It was more immediate, a shitload less painful, and had a hell of a lot fewer strings attached.

It was almost six o'clock, I was down to six hours, and I'd be cutting it close. Deciding that it would be safer to stick close to home, I chose to lure Kade into Belltown. The Bell Street walkway was public enough to offer a small amount of safety, while close enough to my apartment that I could easily bring Kade there to sink Ty's dagger into his black heart without having any witnesses. Fingers shaking, I pulled my cell out of my pocket and dialed Tyler's landline. I'd made a lot of assumptions in my planning—one of them being that Ty and Adira would be at his apartment—and hoped that my plan wouldn't sink before it even got a chance to float.

After the fourth ring, Tyler answered the phone. My mouth went suddenly dry as I remembered the way I'd sent him away from Dimitri's funeral. *I'm doing this for you, Ty*, I thought as I locked down my emotions tight. *Please just don't give me any trouble.*

"Hello?" he said again.

"I need to speak with Adira." God, it was weird to not recognize my own voice. This one was higher pitched. Softer. Seemed odd that someone as evil as Kade would hook up with such a sweet-sounding woman.

"Who is this?" Ty said with suspicion. I'd blocked my cell number before I dialed. No doubt he was already on high alert.

"Please." I knew Ty would be a sucker for a sad-sounding girl, and I poured on the theatrics. "I need to speak with her. I know she's there, just please put her on the phone." I made sure to hitch my voice just right at the end so it would sound like I was close to tears. The line went silent, no doubt Tyler trying decide what he should do. The muffled sound of him putting his hand over the receiver answered me, followed by muted voices. *Come on, Ty. Just for once can you* not *be so damned stubborn.*

"Hello?"

I sighed in relief at the sound of Adira's voice. "If you want to be free of Kade once and for all you need to listen closely and do as I say."

"Who is this?" *Nice*. Like her alarmed tone was going to do anything to downplay Ty's overprotective nature.

"Jesus, Adira. How about let's not get Ty on high alert. And for god's sake, make sure he can't hear this conversation. This is Darian."

"No, it isn't."

"Yeah, it is. I just don't . . . sound like myself right now. Listen, I know that you're the Jinn who found Ty in Sudan, walking around the desert. You came to Xander's to tell me all about how happy you and Tyler were together. And"—no way to put this delicately—"I also know that you're sleeping with Kade, and whether involuntary or not, he's slowly killing you as he drains your life essence. Is that enough to convince you?"

"What do you want?" Her tone had softened, which meant she probably believed me. And if I had to guess, she'd be keeping the conversation down to a minimum so as not to clue Tyler in on what we were talking about.

"I need you to get Kade to meet me at the Bell Street walkway. Only I won't be me. Tell him whatever you can to get him there. Make something up but make it believable. Tell him . . ." This was a huge gamble. Too big, the lie would be unbelievable. Too small, the lie would be unconvincing. "Tell him he's finally circumvented *every* rule. Tell him if he goes to the walkway, he'll find Evelena there."

"What?"

"Just do it. And hurry. We don't have much time."

I hit END and stuffed my phone back into my pocket. If Kade didn't bite, I was fucked. But in the meantime, I ran through every piece of information Anya had given me, going through my mental cache so that if Kade did show, I'd be a convincing replica of his dead lover. A strand of black hair blew in front of my face, and I captured it between my thumb and finger as I inspected the dark, corkscrew curl. No way was I going to look in a mirror. It would just be too damn weird to see a foreign face staring back at me. As long as Kade bought the illusion, I didn't need to know how I looked.

Several minutes later, my skin prickled as I felt the weight of someone's stare. I turned around and leaned against the railing of the walkway to find Kade standing a hundred or so yards away, watching me. Eyes wide and wondrous, he looked even more angelic than usual.

I smiled.

Forcing the fact that Kade was nothing more than a rapist and a murdering sack of shit from my mind, I adopted a relaxed posture. In my human life, I'd had to pretend often. And if my performances weren't entirely convincing, I'd pay for it later at the hands of Henry's brutal abuse. I could do this. I'd give Kade a show worthy of an Academy Award.

Evelena was pretty much what you'd expect from Kade's mate, Darian. Anya's words echoed in my mind. *She came across as . . . innocent. But underneath that facade was a calculating mind and a cold, heartless soul. Kade loved her because she was unpredictable. She'd grace an enemy with one of her girlish, winsome smiles and then run a knife through his gut. He was absolutely obsessed with her.*

"Kade!" I called out, still startled by the voice that wasn't mine. I ran toward him, funneling contrived joy into my expression.

He started toward me, his steps hurried, but wary. You didn't get to where Kade was by running headlong into potentially dangerous situations. I'd have to earn his trust. *Evelena wasn't shy, but she never showed her feelings to others. Kade would never expect any PDA.* I slowed my pace to more of a brisk saunter and stopped short of throwing my arms around him when we finally came face-to-face. I let my expression do the talking: wide eyes, drinking him in, a blinding, seductive smile to show him just how happy I was to see him, and the icing on the cake? I focused on my own emotions until my eyes glistened with tears. Just when I felt like one tear would spill over my lid, I reined myself in, showing him instead that I refused to outwardly show him how I felt. A corner of his mouth lifted into a smirk as if he expected no less. *Academy. Fucking. Award.*

"How did you do it?" I asked, breathless. "How did you bring me back?"

"Evelena?" Kade took my face in his hands, his expres-

sion intent as he studied my face right down to the last pore.
"No. This is a trick. You're not really here."

I reached out the way Anya had shown me and brought
both of Kade's hands up between us. One by one, I touched
my fingertips to his and then pressed our palms together. His
mouth twitched, and recognition lit in his eyes. Slowly, I
laced our fingers together and lowered them between us.
"I'm here," I whispered. "And nothing will ever separate us
again."

Kade leaned his head toward mine, but I narrowed my
eyes and shied away before he could kiss me. *Uh, uh, buddy.
No PDA.* He smiled as if I'd passed his test and continued to
study my face, rapt. "I thought it was a trick," he mused, his
thumbs drawing circles on the webs between my own thumbs
and forefingers. "She said if I released her, I could keep you."

Indignation flared but I was careful to mask my reaction.
Adira. No doubt she'd seen an opportunity to be rid of both
Kade and me. She'd be free and could keep Tyler all to her-
self. Well, it shouldn't have been much of a surprise. Levi
said that Jinn are attracted to like souls. Guess Kade and
Adira were more alike than I'd thought. "The Jinn?" I asked.
"She bound herself to you, didn't she?"

"She's protected me," Kade said. Yeah, like that response
wasn't misleading as hell. He stared off in contemplation.
"But now . . ."

"Now you have me," I finished, giving his hands a little
squeeze. "I can protect you. Anya betrayed you, sent you to
your father's hellhole prison. I'll help you take your vengeance in a way the Jinn never could."

Kade's eyes darkened, and my stomach did a nervous flip
as his expression clouded over. *Shit.* It might not have been a
good idea to bring up the subject of Anya and what Kade
may or may not want from her. Not while it was so close to
his imposed deadline. "This isn't real," he murmured.

Not good. I was losing him. I wracked my brain for something, a tiny nugget of information that would help reel Kade
in. "Kade, I don't have much time. The magic that brought
me here can send me away just as easily. You have to break
the connection you have with the Jinn so she can't send me
away."

"I—I can't think," Kade stammered. He tried to pull away, but I held his hands firmly in my grip. "I need to find—"

"You need *me*," I said, infusing my tone with steely strength. "Not her. Your father imprisoned you for no reason! Kade." I looked into his eyes, willing my expression to shine with anger. "Our son is dead. If you don't break your bond with her, she'll send me away, and I will be denied my own vengeance. Is that what you want for the woman you claimed to love?"

"No," he answered. He blinked several times as if regaining some of his focus. "They'll all pay. Anya, my father, all of them."

According to Anya, Evelena's father had been human, and her mother, a powerful Fae. Her mixed parentage had somehow lent her a strange immunity to Kade's Incubus abilities. She'd told Anya once that their relationship had been fated. I wondered, could I use that information to my advantage?

"Look at me. I'm *all* you need. Let her go, Kade and stay with me. We're meant to be together. Release the Jinn."

His grip tightened around my hands. "I need her."

"You don't," I insisted. A thought took root in my mind. Something that might just push Kade over the edge. "I'll kill her. Then she *can't* send me away."

Kade's jaw clenched and he released his grip on my hand, taking a step back. I hadn't been sure to what level Adira had bound herself to him, but from his reaction, I guessed he'd gotten the platinum-level protection package. Or, at the very least, he was worried that since he'd siphoned off so much of her power, anything could happen to him if Adira died.

"You can't kill her."

I gave him a look that said, *Oh no? Watch me.*

"Evelena, listen to me. You can't kill her. We're bound. You don't understand."

I thought back, digging in my brain for more of Anya's coaching. *Evelena was fiercely jealous. I watched her rip the tongue from the mouth of a woman who came on to Kade at a bar once. She never was one for sharing.*

"Then make me understand. Do you *love* her, Kade? Did you find a way to cheat death only to tell me you need another woman more than me?" My voice escalated as I gave

Kade a dose of the sudden temper that his mate had been known for. "Maybe I should kill you both!"

Something in his expression changed. All of the anxiety, the doubt, just melted right off his angelic face. I'd struck gold with my temper tantrum. Evelena must have threatened Kade's life on a regular basis. Not much of a surprise, considering he was part Incubus. Kade needed sex to survive. It was how he drained the life essence from his victims. And since Evelena was immune to Kade's ability, his need for multiple sex partners must have been a sore subject for them. Well . . . for her.

"I found a way around her rules," he mused. "I beat death."

"You always get what you want," I said with a smile. I was totally rocking the manic mood swings. "You brought me back, and now you can let her go."

"I have more to do," Kade looked away, and I forced his face back to mine.

"And I'll help you in all things. Let her go, Kade."

This was the tricky part. I could beg and plead with him to let Adira go for the rest of my life. But unless he *truly* believed that he didn't need her anymore, the bond wouldn't break.

"You have to decide. It's me or her. I won't share you."

I could see the gears grinding in Kade's mind. He'd told me that he'd found a way to manipulate the Jinn rules. That once he'd learned how to make himself truly need everything he asked for, Adira couldn't help but grant *all* of his wishes. I had a sneaking suspicion, though, that by siphoning Adira's magic through sex, he'd inadvertently snagged her ability to grant wishes. Dollars to doughnuts he'd been granting his own wishes for a while now.

"I don't need her to be bound to me," he said as if in the midst of a great epiphany. "What I've taken from her is far more valuable than anything she's given me. You're right Evelena. I. Don't. Need. Her."

It was like Kade had uttered some set of ancient esoteric words. He truly believed it. In his heart, soul, mind, he'd decided that he no longer needed Adira's protection. I wondered, had it been the illusion of Evelena that had sealed the deal or the fact that no amount of protection could equal what he'd taken from her? A ripple of energy brushed across my skin, reminiscent of the sensation I felt whenever Tyler was near. But instead of washing against me like waves kissing the shore, the energy faded. Ebbed away until all I could sense was Kade.

Every time I'd been in his presence, the energy signature I'd recognized was Jinn. It was still there in a sort of mutated form, since he'd siphoned Adira's essence. But it felt different now. Almost sticky as it undulated against my skin. Kade's energy reminded me of the feeling you get when intuition tugs at your subconscious. The fight or flight reflex that makes your stomach clench and adrenaline pulse through your body. Kade was a sexual predator by nature. Of course, his energy would make me feel like prey.

I steeled myself against the self-preservation synapses firing in my brain. Kade's bond with Adira had been broken. She was free. Now, to finish the job Tyler had paid me to do.

"Kade," I said, my voice dripping with sexual promise. "Let's go somewhere more . . . private."

Chapter 32

I'd chosen a meeting place close to my apartment for a reason. I couldn't exactly be my usual stealthy self, bound up in Pamela's spell. My skin still felt too tight on my bones, and because of the glamour, becoming incorporeal wasn't an option.

"Where are we going?" Kade asked as we rounded the corner. My apartment building was in sight, Tyler's silver dagger tucked between my mattresses. It wouldn't take much coaxing to get Kade into bed—as it was, he was having a hard time keeping his hands off me—and when I got him right where I wanted him, well . . . his death would certainly have a poetic justice to it.

"Just a private place for us to get . . . reacquainted." I raked my gaze up Kade's body, infused my words with a husky tone. Since the real Evelena had been immune to Kade's abilities and I sure as hell wasn't, I had to play coy for as long as possible. I could flirt my ass off, though. And I figured Kade would expect nothing less from his mate. She'd make him work for it.

I climbed the steps of my building and Kade stopped short, one foot on the bottom step. "How long have you been back that you were able to find this *private space*?"

Suspicious SOB. I couldn't wait to get the bastard alone so I could kill him. "A gift." I shrugged my shoulders dismissively. "From your Jinn. Call it a going away present." Kade began to climb the stairs, and I flashed him a sexy smile. "We'll need somewhere to stay for a while. Once we kill Anya and find your father's book, we can leave Seattle and go wherever you want."

Kade paused midway up the steps, his eyes narrowed dangerously. My heart sank into my stomach as the last—and probably most important—piece of information Anya had given me played in my mind: *You can't use the book as leverage, Darian. No one knew about its existence but Kade, Dimitri, and me. He didn't trust anyone else, not even Evelena, with that information.*

Fuck. My. Life.

I'd been so careful. Goddamn it, how could I have allowed myself to slip? The illusion was too real, my words to Kade so convincing, I'd bought the lie myself. And then, I let my guard down, got comfortable in the role I'd been playing, and forgot to carefully weigh each word before I spoke. I'd freed Adira, but I'd just secured my own death.

Kade took the last three steps in a single leap. None too gently, he slammed me into the door, pinning my shoulders beneath his hands. He leaned in until our noses were almost touching. "What book?"

How to answer? A million scenarios flashed before my eyes, each of them resulting in an answer that would anger Kade and rat me out. I winced as his fingers dug into my shoulders. He took a deep breath. "What book, Evie?"

Evie. Anya had never mentioned any sort of nickname. I didn't think a girl with a nasty streak like Evelena would appreciate something as cute as *Evie*. "Don't call me that," I snapped. "It makes me sound like a fucking puppy."

Kade leaned in until his mouth brushed my ear. "Wrong," he whispered. "What's the matter, did your return trip from the hereafter affect your memory? I know it's been a while, but how could you forget what name I called out while I was pumping into you?"

Strike two. It's not like Anya would know the pet names Kade used during sex. And, *ew.* "Kade." My voice burned with a warning fire. "I've been fucking *dead.* You might want to consider cutting your fated mate a little slack."

"Fated mate?" Kade scoffed. He pulled back so he could look me in the eye. "Evelena did believe we were meant for one another, but you're *not* her. Who are you?"

When I didn't answer right away, he slammed me against the door. "Is that how you treat the woman you love?" I still wasn't willing to fold. Not yet.

"What's up there?" Kade jerked his head toward the building. "An ambush?"

If I could get into my apartment, I could get to the dagger. "Why don't you take me up there and find out for yourself?"

"Why not? I have an appointment in a few hours that I have to keep, but I could use a distraction. First, though, I want to know who you really are, because there's no way in hell you're my mate. Offer me the truth now, and I *might* be lenient with you."

I bucked my chin in the air, defiant as ever and twice as stubborn. "What's the matter, Kade? Can't believe what your eyes tell you? I'm Ev-e-lena."

He smiled, clearly amused. "Well, there's one way to tell for sure, something that can't be covered by a clever disguise."

Before I could react, he kissed me. Like the last time he'd laid his lips to mine, something pulled from my center, as if my very soul were being coaxed from my body. I tried to break away, but Kade pushed his body against mine, pinning me against the building. He reached out and cupped my face between his hands, deepening the kiss. I struggled against him, tried to force my lips tight as his tongue thrust into my mouth. Any fight I'd had in me drained out the moment he deepened the kiss. Only the pressure of his body against mine was holding me up; my legs shook, no longer able to support my weight. My body tingled with thousands of tiny pinpricks, and I grew pleasantly light-headed. Drunk. Brain-addled as though I'd chugged a pitcher of margaritas on an empty stomach and went for a ride on a Tilt-A-Whirl.

Kade broke the kiss and my stomach lurched. He pulled me against him, and his own speech was a little slurred and drunken sounding as he whispered in my ear, "Gods, how I *love* complicated women."

Strike three. *Fuck.*

My bones turned to Jell-O, and I couldn't muster the strength for a snarky comeback. Kade took a step away from me and my legs gave out. I crumpled onto the concrete entryway, bruising my tailbone in the process. A sharp pain shot up my spine and I dug in with my heels, pushing until my back was against the door. One more kiss like that and I wouldn't be able to lift my arms, let alone plunge a dagger into his heart.

With as much care as he'd show a bag of groceries, Kade hauled me up by the collar. "You're in way over your head, little girl," he admonished as he pushed open the door. One quick shove and I sailed into the elevator compartment. Something in my shoulder popped, and I clenched my jaw tight, determined not to scream. But, holy shit! It hurt like a motherfucker. Kade stepped into the elevator and slammed the gate closed. The elevator, which was nothing more than a metal cage, lurched as it started its ascent and my head swam as dizziness washed over me. "So, you want to play house, eh, Trouble?" Kade smirked as he looked down on me. "I'm more than ready to play, *wife*."

I tried like hell to think in a straight line, but whatever part of my essence Kade had taken from me kept my mind spinning in circles, and for some damn reason, all I could think about was his kiss and the fact that some crazy part of me wanted more. Pain radiated down my arm, distracting me from my thoughts. Even with my quick healing, a dislocated shoulder wasn't going to mend properly until it had been set right, and the pain made it impossible for me to raise my right arm higher than my waist. Which meant if I could get my hands on the dagger, I'd have to stab the bastard left-handed. Not ideal considering my already weakened condition.

Kade pulled the gate open before the elevator had even come to a halt. He reached for my right arm, and I recoiled, knowing if he pulled it would hurt like a son of a bitch. He sighed and rolled his eyes before dragging me up by my left arm. "This isn't going to work," he mused. Without warning, he threw me against the wall, pulling my right wrist while shoving into my shoulder with the other hand. I couldn't help the scream that burst from my lips as the joint popped back into place and another wave of nausea crashed over me. "Sorry, wife, but I like it rough. Don't want you bitching about a hurt shoulder while I'm fucking you; it'd spoil the mood."

"No *way* would you get laid without the supernatural mojo," I seethed through gritted teeth. "You might be nice to look at, Kade, but you have the personality of a rabid bad-ger."

"Such compliments from my mate," Kade purred. "You're making me hard." He grabbed my hand and pressed it against his erection, and my stomach heaved as he cupped his hand over mine, forcing the prolonged contact.

"Why don't we just drop the pretense." For once, I prayed my smart-ass mouth could buy me some time. My head still swam from the effects of Kade's kiss, but I held it together as best I could. "We both know I'm not Evelena. And besides," I added as an afterthought, "I really don't like that name."

"Oh, but you *are* my mate," Kade continued in that too-sweet voice. A heady scent floated on the air, musky and warm. Like sex. "See the truth for yourself."

He spun me around so that I could see myself in the large mirror that hung on the wall in my living room. Unnerved didn't begin to describe the way I felt as I stared at my own reflection and a stranger stared back. "Glamour."

"No," Kade murmured close to my ear. A chill raced across my skin, too pleasant and full of promise. My body rallied against my mind as it grew warm, aroused from what-ever supernatural pheromone Kade was throwing off. "You're *Evelena*. Mine."

"I'm not yours." The lazy quality returned to my voice as Kade kissed my neck once, twice, and again.

"Mine."

"No."

"We'll see about that." He turned me around, and the re-lief I felt at not having to see that alien face staring out at me from the mirror was palpable. It didn't stop Kade's assault, however. I had a feeling that defense wasn't part of the Cam-bion's battle strategy; he preferred to stay on the offense. And Kade wasn't about to let me get the upper hand. I'd just barely gotten control of my limbs and could support the weight of my own body when he kissed me again.

His kisses were a drug. Heroin. Raw, uncut, super sex heroin. The kind that rushes into your blood stream and shoots through your system with the speed of a bullet train. At least, that's how I *assumed* shooting up heroin would feel. My brain got a little fuzzy at the edges and eventually abandoned its futile attempt at rebellion, joining forces with my body to ruin me. As if my arms had a mind of their own, they wrapped around Kade's neck, drawing him closer. When he pulled away, I tried to drag him back, to feel more of that electric rush, that raw sexual energy.

"Nature favors the predator," he purred as he led me toward my bed. I followed like an obedient pet, my legs wobbling like a newborn foal. "I take what my body needs to survive. And in return, my victims get to feel unparalleled pleasure before they die."

"I-It's still r-rape," I stuttered. "Someone needs to c-castrate you, K-Kade."

"Are you the woman to do it?" he asked.

"Yes," I said, feeling anything but confident in my ability. Then I laughed. A silly, drunken giggle. "I *am* going to do it."

"Promises, promises," he muttered. Kade traced the pad of his forefinger across my cheek and another potent bloom of that musky scent enveloped me. My eyes drifted shut as a warm rush spread from my thighs outward. The tiniest sense of fright took root in my mind and that same flight or fight reflex tugged at my subconscious. "It's not rape if the victim is begging for it. And believe me, Evelena. You'll be *begging* me as well."

"Not Evelena," I said, stumbling on my own feet. My ass bounced down on the mattress of my bed as I listed to one side and back up straight. To the side and up straight. *Jesus, stop the boat, already.* I was beginning to feel seasick.

"Yes, you are," Kade replied. "You look like her. Sound like her. I wonder if you'll fuck like her."

"Go to hell."

Kisses rained down on my face, my lips, my neck. My mind reeled from the intoxicating effects of Kade's mouth, hands, and fingers on my skin. Anya had warned me that he secreted addictive venom that would seep into my pores. Somewhere, deep inside of me, I *knew* this was wrong. That the arousal I felt was contrived, forced on me by whatever ability Kade possessed to seduce his victims. This was a violation of not just my body, but my mind. I tried to focus on anything but the pulsing waves of need that swept over me, but it was damned near impossible when all I wanted was more.

He really does look like an angel. . . . I shook my head to clear my reeling thoughts. Kade smiled as he placed another lazy kiss on my mouth, and I shuddered. God, I wanted him. *Needed* him.

"Take off your shirt."

I tried not to laugh, but I couldn't help the giddy haze blanketing my mind. "No," I answered petulantly. "Better men than you have tried to get into my pants. And failed."

"Evelena," Kade whispered as his fingers feathered down my neck. "Take off your shirt."

I caught my reflection in the mirror across the room. Evelena's dark eyes stared back at me, her face framed by a torrent of black curls, and I wondered, had I lost myself completely? It looked like Pamela's threefold rule was hitting me hard and fast. I'd deceived Kade through witchcraft and trickery, using his dead mate against him. Now I was paying three times over by literally taking the place of the woman he'd lost. He brushed his palms across my breasts and my nipples hardened even as my stomach lurched. Damn it, I needed to get my head *straight*.

Every kiss, every touch sent me farther from reality. My limbs became so heavy I could barely lift them, and Kade continued his unhurried assault, taking his time and exacting his sick punishment for trying to deceive him. "I want to watch you undress, Evelena," he said, kissing my jawline. I whimpered as his fingers teased my nipples through my shirt, both wanting and repulsed by his touch all at once. Though I'd never taken any drugs before, I'd been drunk more than a few times. And right now I was absolutely shitfaced. I was past the point of rational decision making and any suggestion seemed completely logical. Kade wanted me to undress for him. *Sure! Why the hell not?*

Fumbling with my shirt, I tried to focus on the tiny pearl-shaped buttons. I had no goddamned hand-eye coordination whatsoever. And I was pretty sure I had a dagger stashed somewhere between my mattress and box spring. If I couldn't undo a fucking button, how in the *hell* was I going to get to the dagger? Kade seemed fascinated with the show I was giving him, watching with a satisfied smirk as I finally made it down to the last button. My hands got tangled up in the sleeves, and I fought with the damn shirt for another couple of minutes until I'd finally shucked it completely. *Whew*. That *was a chore*.

"The pants," Kade said, his voice dark and sensual. *Damn, he was a sexy bastard*. Sexual energy wafted off of him, buffeting the sobriety my mind sought.

I scooted up farther on the bed and slithered out of my pants until I was clad in nothing but my bra and underwear. Stretching out on the bed, I sighed, my body wound so tight that I thought I'd explode if I didn't find release. Kade worked the buttons on his own shirt, making a show of undressing himself. My eyes drifted from the hard planes of his bare chest and focused on a blinking red light on my wall next to the elevator. I blinked. The red light blinked back. I blinked again.

I'd forgotten all about Raif's security system. The light blinked green when it was set, red when it had been tripped. I couldn't remember disarming it when Kade had brought me up, which meant we'd tripped the silent alarm. By the time my gaze had wandered back to Kade, he'd popped the button and opened the fly on his pants.

Oh fuck. What the hell was I doing? Kade had drained a fair share of my energy, essence, whatever with his kisses and wandering hands. I couldn't fight him if I wanted to and when he got too close or made physical contact, I didn't *want* to fight him. His energy signature brushed against my skin, that flight or fight reflex surging within me. But something was off . . . mutated. Something else fluttered across my senses, so soft I almost couldn't feel it. Like a mist of warm rain caressing my skin. That feeling—that mutated flash of energy I felt—was my own.

Kade's gaze drank me in, a look of raw hunger plain in his expression. I stared at his light blue eyes, and noticed that the pupils had elongated slightly, slashing vertically through the iris. Holy Christ, his eyes looked . . . *reptilian*. I tried to roll away, toward the right side of the bed where I'd stashed the dagger, but I couldn't muster the energy. "I think I'll keep you a while, *Evelena*," Kade all but purred, as he kicked off his shoes. "Your life essence is even better than Adira's. She was powerful, but yours is a rush like nothing I've ever felt.

And after I take you"—those snakelike eyes narrowed menacingly— "we'll just see what tricks of yours I'll be able to borrow."

I tried to move farther up the bed, but something held my ankle. I looked down and my pulse skittered in my veins as a large, slithering tail flicked against my skin. Black scales glistened in the muted evening light as it wound up my leg and spread my thighs. My breath hitched in my chest. What the hell was that? Kade's tongue darted out to lick his lips, and I could have sworn it was forked, the ends curling before it retreated back into his mouth. I batted at the tail as it skirted the edge of my underwear, up my stomach and over one breast. Oh my god. This was really happening. This wasn't some drunken illusion or crazy trip. Kade was going to rape me, steal my life essence, and do it all over again until he'd exacted his revenge on me.

And there wasn't a goddamned thing I could do about it.

Chapter 33

"Who are you?" Kade whispered as his palms passed up my ribs and over my breasts.

"Evelena," I whispered back, arching into his touch.

"And whom do you belong to?" he asked before his tongue darted out to taste the flesh swelling just above my bra.

"You," I moaned, writhing beneath him, desperate for the rush that this touch gave me. "I belong to *you*."

Every touch, every kiss, every heady breath of Kade's scent drew me deeper into the fantasy. I'd tell him anything he wanted to hear as long as he kept his hands on me. He took great pleasure in kissing, touching, caressing, until I begged him to take me, only to have him back away and deny me. Tears streamed down my face as he traced the backs of his fingers from my chest to the edge of my underwear and back up. I couldn't help myself, even though I knew that wanting him was wrong. My body bloomed with a dark rush of sensation that shattered my self-control. And I craved it. I craved that darkness just as I craved his touch. I felt like I'd retch, revulsion welling up inside of me, but then Kade would come at me again, and the moment his mouth made contact with my skin, I found myself pleading with him not to stop.

"I can keep you like this for months," Kade snarled close to my ear. "Years. You're going to beg me to kill you before I'm done with you." That reptilian tail stroked my core over my underwear, and my stomach heaved, threatening to empty its meager contents. "But I'm not going to kill you," he said in a pleasant, hushed tone. "I'm going to play with you, slowly draining everything you've got until there's nothing left. And then"—his tongue dragged up my cheek—"I'm going to pass you around like the whore you are."

I choked on a sob, hating myself more with every passing second. Why couldn't I resist him? How could I possibly want more of his touch? My mind was beginning to fracture—it wouldn't be long before it broke apart and splintered my psyche. I wouldn't be able to recover from this, and Kade knew it.

"Open your legs for me," he commanded.

"No." I shook my head frantically and Kade grabbed my face, squeezing my cheeks.

"Don't disobey me, Evelena, or I'll have to punish you. Open. Your. Legs."

The sound of my elevator grinding its way to the entrance drew Kade's attention, and he released his grip on me, pushing himself off the bed. He fastened his pants, looked around and grabbed a short knife from a sheath at his waist and tucked it behind his back. "Behave, Evelena," he warned. "Or it'll be worse for you later."

Already I was experiencing the painful sensation of withdrawal that overcame me when Kade stopped touching or kissing me. I ached without the physical contact, my body trembling, *craving* his nearness. The sun hadn't quite set. Or had it? I tried to reach past the ache that seemed to sink right into my bones, to get a clear sense of my surroundings, anything to anchor me to reality. Raif could have come in his shadow form had the sun already set, and the whine of my elevator told me that whoever was on their way up was confined to their corporeal body, or wasn't a Shaede.

"Kade." His name burst from my lips in a keening cry as I curled my knees up to my stomach. I couldn't help myself. I wanted the pain to stop, to feel that electrifying rush that sparked every nerve ending on my body and shot through my blood like fire. My teeth began to chatter and the tremors became more violent. "P-please," I whispered. "I—I n-need . . ."

The elevator came to a halt at my entrance—empty. That serpentine tail coiled around Kade's feet, twitching the way a cat's might when it senses danger. My brain was clouded with both pain and need, and I couldn't be sure if I was imagining Kade's snakelike attributes or not. The tail flicked upward, seeming to retreat into Kade's body and disappeared entirely.

"Kade?"

"Shut up," he snapped as he padded warily toward the empty elevator.

I pushed myself up on an elbow and tried to steady my careening world. He pulled the knife from behind his back and gripped it tight in his fist as he poked his head inside the elevator's caged compartment. His gaze locked on the keypad for the alarm system and his lip curled in a snarl as he turned to me. "My mate is a devious bitch. You failed to mention the security system. What's the disarm code?"

Not that it mattered, but the silent alarm had been tripped for a while. I wasn't sure if Raif was the only one who'd be notified in the event of a break-in, but since he wasn't here already, I had to assume that no one had been alerted thus far. I wracked my brain, desperate to remember the disarm code, thinking that if I gave it to Kade, he'd reward me for cooperating and take away the pain. "Six . . ." No, not six. "Three . . . nine . . ." *Shit*. I fell back to the bed, hugging my arms around my body. God, I hurt. "Three, six . . ."

Kade's eyes flashed with anger as he stalked toward me. "Get up!" he snarled as hauled me to the edge of the bed. "We're leaving. Now."

I fell in a heap to the floor, the pain radiating through me, too unbearable for me to stand. I reached out, hoping that Kade would help me, but he simply stared down at me with disdain. Tears blurred my vision and I took a deep breath in an effort to quell my shaking form. With as much strength as I could muster, I pushed myself up until I leaned on the bed. Was this how Adira had felt when Kade had forced himself on her? Had it been this agonizing for Anya when Kade had wanted her? How had they recovered when all I wanted to do was curl up into a ball and die?

"Clothes," I said as Kade scrambled around the room, looking for something. "I need my clothes."

He smiled to himself though he appeared to not hear me. "You'll go as you are," he said as he rifled through drawers and cupboards.

"You're a bastard."

"Yes. I am. I need a better weapon than this shitty knife," he complained as he continued to ransack my apartment. "Don't you have—"

Before he could finish his sentence, an invisible force knocked him off his feet. The impact of his fall sent the knife across the room, and it skidded to a halt near the foot of my bed.

With amazing speed and dexterity, Kade jumped to his feet. I leaned forward, afraid to move without the support of the bed to hold me up, stretching my arm out as far as I could. I needed to get my hands on that knife before Kade did. He watched me from the corner of his eye, wary of whatever else in my apartment threatened him. A look of concentration flashed across his face, as if he were trying to grasp on to an idea, and in the next moment, he merged with the gray twilight becoming incorporeal just as I had done a thousand times. The shroud of gray light clung to Kade like a hazy mist, deceptive and impossible to penetrate just like the hours of twilight and dawn.

"You're certainly *not* an ordinary Shaede," Kade said triumphantly as he regained his corporeal form and scooped the knife up into his hand. "Not like Anya at all." His smile grew sinister as his gaze raked down my body. "I'm going to like having you around."

If the sun was yet to set, it couldn't be another Shaede in the apartment with us. But who or *what* in the hell was it? All I could feel was the echo of my own stolen power as Kade's mutated energy washed up against me like a mist of water blowing off the sea. Whereas my mind was getting clearer— I didn't feel quite as drunk—I still didn't think I had the strength to stand. Kade's prolonged physical contact had drained me.

Movement from the corner of my eye caught my attention, too fast and fleeting for me to focus or identify. Kade worked the knife in his palm, twirling it like a mini baton. He spun quickly around as if an attacker was at his back, and then another quarter turn to the side. "Are you a fucking coward?" he shouted at nothing. "Why not show yourself and fight me?"

Just as his physical contact affected me like a drug, the life-sustaining energy he stole from his victims obviously gave him a similar rush. And after an hour or so of unrelenting torture, he was flying high on whatever part of my essence he'd ripped from me. Eyes wide, his once elongated pupils had shrunk to tiny black pinpoints. But whereas I was physically spent and wracked with pain, he was strong, confident, and fucking *wired*.

Something shifted in the air, and through the second skin of Pamela's glamour, I perceived the faintest change in the atmosphere. Night had fallen, the dusky gray outside my window darkening to navy. The pressure in the air changed, becoming dense as if an invisible force pressed upon me. Kade backed up a step and then another, having clearly inherited my ability to sense the presence of other supernatural creatures nearby. He shoved me behind him and said through gritted teeth, "Don't utter even a single syllable, *Evelena*. If you do, I'll make sure that your pain is never ending, do you understand me?"

I nodded, afraid that simply voicing my acquiescence would prompt him to punish me. My mind was clearer, and logically, I knew that what Kade had done to me was perverse and wrong and I didn't need anything from him. Problem was, my body wasn't buying it. The withdrawal raged through me, my body fighting for control over my mind as it tried to convince me that the *only* thing I needed was more of Kade's touch. And so, I kept my fucking mouth shut.

Shadows formed at the far end of the apartment, seeming to drift from the elevator shaft to every dark corner of the vast studio space. One by one the shadows became solid as Raif, Julian, and Myles stepped from the darkness into their solid forms. Weapons at the ready, the three Shaedes spread out in the apartment forming a semicircle around me and Kade.

Raif. Jesus Christ, if there was one single soul on this earth that I could always count on it was him. And unfortunately, it was that same reliability that worried me now. What if he managed to take Kade out? My insides were on fire, my gut knotting and cramping terribly. Kade could make the pain go away, and if Raif killed him . . .

"I'll give you the opportunity to surrender," Raif said, his voice calm and ice cold. His eyes blazed with battle lust, and his expression promised violence. "But honestly, I'd prefer it if you put up a fight."

Kade's mouth curved in a charming, angelic smile. "I think I'll start collecting trophies of Shaede kills," he mused, twirling the throwing knife in his hand. "An ear or a finger. I wonder . . . what would happen to a severed ear after the sun sets? Do you have an opinion on that, Evelena?"

I tried to make my body small and unnoticeable as I shrunk behind him. My muscles cramped violently and I doubled over, biting back a sob. This was a test to see if I'd answer. I refused to speak. Couldn't risk the consequences. All I wanted was for the pain to stop.

"Who's the female?" Raif demanded.

"My mate," Kade said and turned to stroke my cheek. That musky scent filled my lungs and I swayed on my feet. The pain drifted to the back of my mind, and I leaned into his touch only to have him pull away. "Let us leave in peace, and I'll consider Anya's debt to me paid. She and her unborn child will be safe."

Raif's eyes narrowed dangerously, and Myles and Julian exchanged a dubious glance. No doubt Kade thought to buy our freedom with Anya's safety, and I half wished that Raif would take him up on his offer. No such luck. My mentor was more of a shoot-first-ask-questions-later type of guy. Well, make that stab-first. A glint of cold determination shone in his sapphire blue eyes and I knew that we weren't going to get out of this alive.

We, because if Raif managed to kill Kade, I didn't think I'd live through the effects of the withdrawal. Raif took a step forward, his sword drawn and ready. Kade gave an exaggerated sigh. "Don't be stupid, friend. You don't have a clue what you're up against."

The muscle in Raif's jaw ticked. "You killed my friend. Mind the words that leave your mouth, Cambion, or I'll cut out your tongue and feed it to you right before I disembowel you."

Kade simply laughed. He held up his hands as if in surrender, and Raif took another step forward. Shadows slithered over Kade's skin as he left his physical body behind and then regained his solid form. Raif stopped dead in his tracks, his mouth hanging slightly agape. A fleeting look of panic crossed his face and he asked Kade, "Where is Darian?"

"Darian?" Kade asked as if he hadn't a clue who Raif was talking about. Then again, I wasn't sure if he actually knew my name. He'd always just called me Trouble. And now, Evelena. "I don't think I know the name. Evelena?" Kade asked without breaking eye contact with Raif. "Do you know anyone named Darian?"

My brain screamed at me to answer, to get Raif's attention, and make him notice me. But I couldn't force myself to speak. I was still too afraid of the pain and knew that only Kade could make it stop. He shrugged his shoulders and said, "Adira lent this apartment to my mate. We haven't seen each other in a while. Sort of a honeymoon gift. Maybe she knows where this Darian is."

Bastard! He'd thrown my own lies back in my face, taunting me openly. He was clearly enjoying himself, playing with Raif just to push his buttons. It would be hard for Raif to kill him now that he could leave his corporeal body behind. He didn't have to play arrogant, Kade knew he had the upper hand. The brief physical contact we'd had was beginning to wear off, and another wave of painful cramps ripped through me. I opened my mouth to speak, to beg Raif to just let us go—

"You're a lying sack of shit, Kade." Another body joined the others in my apartment, shimmering into existence near the kitchen bar. "Adira didn't *lend* you this apartment." Tyler's expression boiled with unchecked rage as he came to stand beside Raif.

"He can join with the shadows," Raif said with obvious concern. "Tyler, she's not here."

It didn't take a conversational wizard to know that Raif feared I was already dead. Or worse. He knew that Kade could *borrow* the abilities of any supernatural creature if he stole their life essence. Shame welled up within me, squeezing all of the air from my lungs. Raif knew just how Kade went about taking that energy from his victims, too. How would I ever be able to look him in the eye again?

Ty's expression darkened as well, and the temperature in

my apartment plummeted. "You son of a bitch," he choked out. "Where is she?"

Oh, god. As if it wasn't shameful enough to have Raif realize what might have happened to me. I'd rather stay in this horrible body forever than have Tyler know what Kade had done to me—and the things I'd begged him for in return.

Kade sighed. "So. Bored. I have a codex to retrieve and a traitorous bitch to kill. By the way, thanks for leaving Anya without her guards," he said. "You've made my job tonight much easier. So if you're done trying to talk me to death, I think I'll explore the shadows for a bit before I pay that leather-loving cunt a visit."

Before Kade could react, Tyler's magic slammed into him with the force of a blizzard. My breath fogged from the cold, and though Kade's back was to me, I could sense his body stiffen. "You can't hide behind Adira anymore," Tyler said, his voice calm and even. "There's no more bond for me to acknowledge, and you're going to suffer for what you did to her."

Kade pushed me backward as he took several steps toward the bed. Tyler had managed to keep me locked in my corporeal form before. He'd done that to Kade now. I had a feeling Kade hadn't given much thought to my vulnerabilities, only my strengths. I was certainly unique, but by no means infallible. The only weapons at his disposal now were the knife in his hand and his good looks. I didn't think the latter was going to do him much good. I tripped on my own goddamned feet as Kade pushed me back, and I fell to the floor beside my bed, doubling over in pain. Every muscle in my body seemed to seize up simultaneously.

While Julian and Myles hung back, Tyler and Raif converged on Kade. He pulled back the knife in his hand and let it fly. Raif drifted into shadow as the weapon sailed right through his incorporeal form. The dark mist converged, solidifying into his physical body, and he continued forward. Kade was the one who had no clue what he was up against. "Where's Darian?" Raif asked again, leveling his sword at Kade's chest.

"If you kill me, you'll never know," Kade answered.

"We'll kill your female, then." Raif's tone couldn't have been more serious.

I gripped the side of the mattress, my breath coming in quick little pants as I attempted to breathe through the pain. "Do it," Kade said. "Kill her. She's been dead once, haven't you, *Evelena*? I doubt she'll mind a return trip to the after-life."

Tyler and Raif exchanged a look, and I knew that they'd kill me. Ty's gaze wandered from Kade, down to the spot on the floor where I cowered in pain as if this were the first time he'd truly noticed me. He studied me, his brow furrowed in an almost confused expression. My gaze locked with his. Those damn hazel eyes had always been my downfall. I couldn't look away. He sidled away from Raif, taking a step closer, and then another. I pressed my body against the side of the bed, closer to Kade and away from Ty. I just wanted the pain to stop. I felt as though my body were burning from the inside out.

Kade didn't seem too concerned with anything other than saving his own skin. "Perhaps my mate killed your friend," he suggested. "She's . . . not herself, but you're welcome to question her."

Tyler cocked his head to the side, his eyes boring a hole right through me. His lips parted, and he reached out his hand, fingers extended toward me. Raif stood wary, sword held high. "What in the hell are you doing, Tyler? Back away."

He ignored Raif as if he hadn't even spoken. Kade stepped away from me, turning slightly in a defensive stance against Tyler's approach, giving Raif a clearer view. My jaw clamped tight as another round of painful cramps seized my body, and I swallowed a scream. I hurt so badly. I wanted to wish for Tyler's help, but Kade had forbidden me to speak. And though, logically, I knew that he couldn't control me, I couldn't get my body to follow through with that belief. The addiction had been instant and crippling, and *it*, not Kade, controlled me completely.

I'd been too consumed with my own pain and anguish to realize what Kade had really been doing. He'd shifted the focus from himself, making sure that all eyes were on me. He slunk away from the bed like the snake he was, slowly put-ting distance between us. I reached out, fear coiling in my stomach. I'd die without him. The pain would eat me alive. Kade was going to let Raif kill me.

"Tyler," Raif said in a warning tone, "back *away.*"

Again, he ignored Raif, and I turned my attention away from Tyler as his hand stretched out as if toward a wary animal. I needed Kade. Needed him to take away my pain. But from the corner of my eye, I caught sight of Ty's hand coming closer, and a thought scratched at the back of my mind. A single-minded obsession that had been my mantra through all of the lonely months I'd been without him. *Only Ty could fix me. . . .*

Instead of reaching out for Kade, I turned, stretching my hand out to meet Ty. The moment our fingers touched, something sparked within me, a connection so deep and so powerful that the pain that ruled me so completely paled in comparison.

"Darian," Tyler whispered. The word rolled off his tongue with the reverence that I loved so much and I cried out, my heart beating a frantic rhythm that echoed in my ears.

Pamela's spell shattered like myriad shards of glass peppering my skin. The tightness of that second skin vanished, and though I was still feeling the effects of withdrawal, I felt as though a tremendous weight had been lifted. The air seemed to still, and my apartment grew quiet as all eyes in the room turned to me.

Kade had gotten the distraction he wanted. And the bastard wasn't going down without a fight.

Chapter 34

Kade may have been confined to corporeality, but he was anything but weak or helpless. He burst from his human facade like a football player breaking through one of those paper barriers cheerleaders hold up. If I'd thought the image of those snakelike eyes and serpentine tail were a shocker, it was nothing compared to the creature that stood before us now. At least eight feet tall and corded with sinewy muscle, the half snake, half man demon plowed into Tyler with such speed that he didn't have time to defend himself before Kade knocked him to the floor.

That tail coiled around me, constricting me in its grasp as Kade drew me to him, holding me tight against his scaled body. His forked tongue flicked out, rasping against my skin, and I shuddered, the effects of his druglike touch a hundred-fold what it was in his human form. I moaned with pleasure, unconcerned about who might hear as I went limp in his grasp.

Myles and Julian crept forward, their steps cautious. What had been a kill mission was now a hostage situation, and Kade had no qualms about using me to get out of this alive. "I've drained her." Kade's voice slithered from his throat in a gravelly rasp. "I wonder if she'll have the strength to heal if I crush her?" His tail constricted around me so tight that I felt my bones creak, and I cried out. Tyler lunged toward us. "Not a move, Jinn," Kade warned. "I won't think twice about killing your Charge." His tongue flicked out again, dipping between my breasts, and I gripped the tail wound around my body, leaning toward his mouth. That same drunken haze blanketed my mind, and all I wanted was more. "Tastes like honey," he said to Tyler. "She's a firecracker, isn't she? Before you crashed my party, I had her begging for my cock."

The sound of an enraged animal tore from Tyler's throat. A ripple shook his form, and his magic washed over my senses as he transformed into a hulking golden-furred bear. He pawed at the floor, cutting finger-wide grooves into the wood, and shook his head furiously from side to side. I hadn't seen Tyler in this form since the first time he'd saved me from an out-of-control egomaniac. I guess Kade had pushed Ty just a little too far and he'd lost whatever meager control he'd had on his temper.

Frost formed on the windows, and I shivered in Kade's grasp, as much from the high as the cold. Floating in an ocean of sensual bliss, I had a hard time focusing on my surroundings, let alone the standoff taking place in the middle of my apartment. Raif gave Tyler a wide berth as though he was just as wary of the bear as he was the demon before him. Julian and Myles closed in, their shadow forms winding stealthily to the back corner of the apartment behind Kade.

Tyler swiped out with one massive claw, catching Kade in the leg. He bared his teeth, now pointed fangs, hissing at the bear before constricting me tighter. My breath squeezed out of my lungs, and black spots swam in my vision. I tried to draw a deep breath—a rib cracked under the pressure—and a scream strangled its way up my throat despite my lack of air.

The bear threw its head back and bellowed.

Kade listed to one side as Julian came at him. He'd regained his physical form just before crashing into Kade, but the demon was so big that it did little more than nudge him. One massive arm curved in an arc as he batted Julian away, sending him sailing back across the apartment. A string of curses erupted from Julian's mouth as he rolled onto his back, massaging his chest. "Call off your pups," Kade ordered Raif. "Or I'll tear out her throat."

Raif held up a hand, and it was as good as any shouted command. Even Tyler stilled, the golden fur rippling on his massive body as he gave a worried chuff of breath. Time seemed to stand still as Kade sidestepped cautiously toward the elevator. He couldn't be bothered to navigate the furniture and just plowed over a couple of end tables. Something stirred beside us, a flash of motion that seemed more imagined than real, and Kade's head slammed to the side as if he'd been struck by an invisible fist.

"You must want her dead!" Kade shouted. "I said to call off your dogs, Shaede!"

"It's not one of ours!" Raif shouted back. From the look on his face, he was just as thrown as Kade.

No one got the chance to argue further, however. Another assault followed as something slammed into Kade, throwing us back against the wall. My head whipped back, crashing into a picture frame. Glass dug into my scalp and rained down on us, scattering like pebbles. Footsteps crunched on the shards, but aside from the sound, nothing indicated the presence of a body. I fought through the haze of my mind, past the high, the discomfort of withdrawal that was beginning to once again pulse through me. Familiarity tugged at my mind as I remembered the day I'd been working out in Xander's gym: the sensation of knowing someone was close, but seeing nothing but a fleeting shadow of movement. And then again at The Pit: sitting right across from me, and yet, unnoticed by everyone else present.

Asher.

I still had no clue how the little shit did it, and I didn't care. He was here, in my apartment and no one—not even the other Shaedes—could see or sense him, which meant something other than shadow cloaked him. The assault continued, unrelenting as Kade took blow after blow. He roared to the ceiling, thrashing his massive body, lashing out at the seemingly invisible force that attacked him. I was nothing more than a rag doll in his grasp, my body tossing like flotsam in the sea with every violent whip of the tail that held me.

How long had Ash been watching? He'd objected to my meeting with Pamela without backup; could he have tailed me? I doubt it. If he'd followed me there, he would have known about the glamour and could have broken it at any time. Right? Shit, my brain was so hazy I had no idea if my thoughts were even coherent. I had to do something. If Kade managed to get out of my apartment and take me with him, he'd continue to torture me, to keep me addicted to his touch until I died from want of it. No matter how bad I hurt, I couldn't let him take me. Not that I was strong enough—of body *or* will—to fight him.

Asher could knock him around all he wanted, but it wasn't going to put Kade down. Only one thing could do that, and I was going to give it to him. "Left side of the bed, between the mattresses!" I shouted. "Right through the heart!"

My words were just cryptic enough. But in my drugged state, the words might have come out of my mouth completely different from how I'd imagined them in my mind. I could have shouted a grocery list for all I knew. The assault on Kade stopped and my heart leapt up into my throat. Every occupant in the apartment seemed to hold their breath in anticipation of what would happen next. Furious, Kade spun and bolted for the elevator. Tyler took after him, no longer hanging back in fear of what the demon might do to me. If I had to guess, Ty was more worried that he'd manage to get away and take me with him. Kade kicked at the gate on the elevator with one massive, clawed foot, collapsing the metal into the car. He took one step inside the compartment and froze. The hilt of a dagger protruded from his chest as if he'd simply run into the damned thing. He clawed at his chest, desperate to remove the blade, and his grip on me slackened.

A pained snarl worked its way up his throat, and the serpentine tail unwound, dropping me to the floor in a heap. Tyler used the moment to his advantage, tackling Kade to the floor. Someone grabbed me under the arms and dragged me backward, and I watched in horror as my protector clawed at the demon and ripped his throat open with his teeth. An urge welled up inside of me, a desperation to protect Kade. It was the addiction holding me firmly in its grasp, and I knew it. But still, I fought against the arms that held me as I tried to keep the bear from ripping him to shreds.

"Darian, stop!" Asher said as he struggled to keep me still. "I've got you, you're safe."

"No!" I cried. Tears streamed down my face as I sobbed. "Don't kill him, Tyler! Please! I—I need him!" I'd be in so much pain soon; I could already feel the tremors move up my limbs as I fought Asher's grasp.

Asher pulled me into his arms and held me tight, more to

keep me from fighting than anything. He quietly shushed me, smoothing my hair away from my face. "You're going to be okay," he said. "I promise."

My mind had become clearer, but the pain had yet to subside. Over the sound of my own crying, I heard a warning growl. Kade lay in a bloodied mass of scaly skin and bone near my elevator, and Raif was on the phone with god only knew asking a frantic string of questions about Kade's effect on his victims, while Julian and Myles left the apartment at some order barked from Raif only seconds ago. The bear prowled toward us, his eyes locked on Asher, upper lip bared to show his huge canines. I liked Ash too much to see him turned into a bite-sized snack for Ty, and so, despite the fact that I could barely support myself, I pushed myself away from Asher. "L-let him c-cool down," I said between shuddering breaths as my body shook uncontrollably. "He's just t-trying to p-protect m-me."

Asher's eyes narrowed in Tyler's direction, but he didn't argue. Raif jerked his chin, effective as a stern order, and he left my side, but not before throwing a warning glance of his own in Tyler's direction.

The bear mewled nervously, his lips vibrating as he sniffed the air around me. He pawed at the floor, more like a nervous puppy than wild beast this time. He took a step forward, and then back before resting on his haunches. He let out a low whine and shook out his fur. I wiped at the tears welling in my eyes and watched him for a moment more. Tyler was afraid to approach me.

I held out a shaking hand, and he came closer, tentative, bowing his head to show that he wasn't a threat. My fingers dove into his soft fur, and I wrapped my arms around his massive neck as he sniffed at my cheek. I think he wanted to lick me, but he didn't. He'd seen Kade's tongue on my skin and what it had done to me and I was grateful that he held back, because I didn't think I'd be able to stand that sort of contact just yet.

Ty took a step closer so I could lean against his shoulder. The quaking in my limbs was getting worse and my muscles cramped. Over and over again, I ran my hands through the thick fur, hoping that the sensation would help to calm me down. What would happen to me now that Kade was dead? I closed my eyes, and the fur became more silky than coarse and Tyler's bear form melted away. He took me gently into his arms and cradled me as if he could protect me from every evil in the world.

The dam of my composure broke, and my breath hitched as I began to cry in earnest. "Oh, gods," Tyler lamented, his tone proof enough of his own sorrow. "I'm so sorry, Darian. I'm so, so sorry."

"Make it stop." I dug my fingers into his arm, gritted my teeth against the pain. "Please Tyler, I can't take the pain. Can you please just make it stop?"

He laid his lips to my temple as he rocked me in his arms. "I'll do what I can," he said. "Just say the words."

"Tyler," I said through my tears. "I wish you'd make my pain go away."

His embrace tightened, and his own voice was thick with emotion when he said, "Your wish is *ever* my command."

My world went dark before I could chide him for the cheesy genie line.

Hellish nightmares plagued me in my sleep. My body raged with passion and pain, my mind grasping on to images of a dark serpentine tail caressing my naked body. I thrashed wildly as strong arms held me down, as comforting words were spoken in my ear. When the images in my mind would become unbearable, a dark emptiness would consume me until I swam once again just below the surface of my consciousness, only to have the cycle start again.

I floated in and out of my semiconscious state for what felt like weeks. I shivered as if cold and felt the weight of many blankets being laid on my body until I was so hot with fever that I had no choice but to kick the covers off. I had no idea where I was or who tended to me, but I didn't care. All I wanted was more of that black, oblivious sleep that spared me from the images of Kade that were burned in my memory.

"Darian, can you hear me?" I knew the voice, but it lacked the hardness I'd become used to. My eyelids fluttered as I came slowly awake, drawn to the voice urging me to consciousness. "Darian?"

Damn, had my eyelids been glued shut? It seemed that no matter how hard I tried to pry them open, they just wouldn't budge. I rolled onto my back, every muscle in my body screaming at me not to move. The stiffness wasn't something I was used to, and for the first time since my transformation from human to supernatural, I felt very much centuries old.

"Can you sit up? I brought you some water."

One eye popped open and then the other. The light in Xander's enormous suite was muted, a single lamp at the far end of the room illuminating the space. I pressed my hands into the mattress and tried to push myself up, but my arms wobbled under the weight.

"I'll help you."

Anya reached behind me and brought me forward before settling another pillow behind my back. She helped me to recline, taking care to move my body slowly. I gave my head a little shake as I looked over her loose-fitting linen pants and matching shirt, convinced I was still dreaming. "What are you wearing?" I asked, my voice weak and hoarse. I couldn't even muster any humor into my tone.

"Did you think I'd wear leather through my entire pregnancy?" If my voice had sounded weak, Anya's was downright fragile. The sharp edge of sorrow still lingered in her tone. Her violet eyes glowed softly in the darkened room, but there was a new depth to them, an unfathomable sadness that made her appear somewhat softer. She handed me a glass of water, and I took it in my shaky grasp.

"How long have I been out of it?" The last I remembered, I'd begged Tyler to take the pain away.

"A little over a week," she said. "The first few days were the worst. We had to treat it like a detox. Your Jinn kept you incapacitated through the first several days of it. You've been sleeping soundly for a while, though, and that's how we knew you were through the worst part of it."

I looked away, shame welling up inside of me. "Anya, was it the same for you?"

"He could control it," she answered. "The way he secretes

the toxin into your bloodstream. He was able to inject as little or as much as he chose."

Not anymore, though. The bastard was dead.

Anya took a deep breath and continued, "From what I could tell by the state you were in, he didn't hold back. He transferred a lethal amount of toxin into your system. Your body was deep into the addiction. It would have killed a less stalwart soul. You're very lucky to have survived, Darian."

Yay me. "Wish I felt lucky. Right now, I just feel . . ."

"Violated."

I looked into Anya's violet eyes and bit back the tears that pooled in my own. "Yes."

"I won't tell you that the memories of what happened will go away. But it will get better."

Of course it would. All scars fade with time. "I know."

"Drink the water," Anya said in a motherly tone. Maybe she was trying it out on me. "My king has been beside himself with worry, Darian. He's hardly left your side."

Funny. He didn't seem too concerned when I was on the verge of being raped. Raif had come to my rescue. Asher. Julian. Myles. And Tyler. Where had Xander been in those moments when the pain had been unbearable?

"Darian?" Anya asked, studying my expression. "He wants to see you. Can I tell him you're awake?"

"Yeah," I said with a sigh. "I'll see him."

Chapter 35

He didn't rush to my side. Not that I thought he would. Above all things, Xander was a high king, and he conducted himself as such. He waited at the door for Anya to leave. They exchanged a look, and she gave a little bob of her head before she slipped out of the room.

"I figured she would have rather killed me in my sleep," I said as Xander approached the bed. "You know, since I'm responsible for her husband's death and all."

"You really have to learn to let go of your paranoid notions," Xander said, giving me a wan smile. "She would care for you as she would care for her own king."

"Do you know what happened to me, Xander?" The bitterness I felt tainted my words. "Did anyone tell you what Kade did to me?"

Xander looked away as if uncomfortable. "I know what happened to you." His words were little more than a warm whisper in the quiet room. "And if I had my way, I'd have killed the Cambion myself."

"*Where were you, Xander?* You came with Raif to the island when Azriel and Delilah kidnapped me. You fought for me there. Why didn't you come when Kade had me practically naked and out of my mind?" A tear slipped from my eye and trailed down my cheek. "Did you even know Raif went to my apartment? Did you worry about me? Wonder where I was? Try to call me? Find me? Were you concerned for me at all, or did you just figure that Raif would sort it all out while you sat on your throne and waited for news?"

"Do you know how badly I wish I could be like Raif and

just run out to save the day?" Xander's tone was hard and full of regret. "Don't you think it *kills* me to sit here, unable to properly protect you? *Myself.* The way a male should protect his female. But instead, I protect you the only way I know how."

I cocked a brow. "Through subterfuge?"

"I gave you Asher," he said.

Gave me Asher. "What's that supposed to mean?"

"He was assigned to be your personal guard. I knew you wouldn't simply accept the assignment, and so I suggested him to Raif as an addition to your team. The boy has a fair amount of attitude and I knew you'd gravitate toward him. That you would choose him to join you was a given."

He'd planted Asher in my team as a pseudo babysitter? "You know he's not just a Shaede, then."

"Asher's father is indeed a Shaede. But his mother is Sidhe. Her magic is . . . unique. She can project thoughts into others' minds. Asher inherited her ability."

"So, what? Ash can be, oh, I don't know, standing right in front of someone and project the thought into their mind that he's not really there. Making him virtually invisible?" The High King of *High-handedness* simply nodded. Xander and his pets . . . "He was able to follow me around because he'd made me *think* he wasn't around, is that right?"

"I told him to keep an eye on you—protect you at all times—but not to always be seen."

"So all of that bullshit about you believing I could take care of myself was just a bunch of empty words you used to give my ego a boost?"

"Of course not," Xander said with disdain. "Do you really think I hold you in such low regard? I worried for your safety. I'm not afforded the luxury of being bound to you like a second skin, as that Jinn of yours is. And so I protected you in my own way. Would you forgive Tyler his protection and condemn me for mine?"

"It doesn't matter," I said, sinking down into the pillows. "Turns out I'm *not* capable. I failed Anya, I failed Dimitri, and got in way over my head with Kade. If it wasn't for Ash, I might've died."

Xander moved to sit on the bed and I moved over, putting

some distance between us. He tried to take my hand but I pulled it back, the physical contact too much for my brain to process right now. His eyes lost that mischievous spark that I found both amusing and infuriating, and instead he looked . . . sad. "I wish I could undo what has been done to you."

"You can't," I said. "No one can."

"What can I do for you?" he asked softly. "If it's within my power, it's yours."

My chest ached with emotion, the familiar urge to leap from the bed and run away making my muscles twitch. I'd let my anxiety rule me for so long, and I'd finally overcome it. I wasn't going to let it master me again. "I need some time," I said with a sigh. "I'm moving out. Anya doesn't need me here as a reminder of what she's lost. She needs an emotionally healthy environment during her pregnancy."

"Darian, don't. I've already told you, Anya will be fine."

"But I won't be. I can't be here, Xander. There's too many eyes watching, too many whispering voices. I don't want to be waited on, observed, talked about . . . I just, can't do it."

"Who would dare speak ill of you in this house? You're my—"

"Your *what*, Xander?" My throat constricted as I tried to swallow down the lump rising in my throat. "Just what, exactly, do you think I am? Your concubine? Your kept woman? Your *consort*?"

"You are my *love*," Xander said. "Mine. Let me care for you."

"I can't be yours," I simply said. "I can't belong to anyone while I still don't even feel like I belong to myself."

"You can't go back to your apartment."

He played the king so well. "No, I'm not going back there. Not yet, anyway."

"Then where will you go?"

I thought about it for a moment. Where could I go where I'd be safe? Well, at least, marginally so. Maybe what I needed right now was, well, a *girlfriend*. "I'm going to visit Brakae in *O Anel*," I said. I'd promised I'd never leave again without letting people know where I was, so there was no need to lie or sugarcoat it. "Just for a while." It would have to be a short vacation, due to the enormous time difference. But I'd take what I could get.

Xander stood and reached out as though he'd run his fingers through my hair. But when his eyes met mine, he stopped short. I wondered how much fear reflected in my face. What did my expression betray? "Give my regards to my niece," he said as he turned to leave. "And come home soon."

He closed the door behind him, and as I lay there in the dark I wondered, could Xander have broken Pamela's glamour? I'd planned on having to convince Raif of my identity in order to break the spell, but Tyler had shattered the glamour with nothing more than a touch and my name on his lips. He'd seen past the disguise Pamela had bound me in.

That had to count for something. Didn't it?

I looked around my trashed apartment as I stuffed the last few items into the large duffel bag I was taking with me to *O Anel*. I planned to give Brakae a good old-fashioned dose of culture shock, and no way was I skimping on supplies. The light on the alarm system flashed green, just as it had the last hundred or so times I'd checked it. I didn't know if I could ever feel comfortable here again, and that pissed me off. I loved this apartment and didn't want to move. That would be like giving Kade power over me, even in death.

I wasn't giving up yet, though. Reaver promised to come over while I was gone and protect the entire building with wards. That, coupled with Raif's high-tech security system should help to make me feel safer, but I wouldn't know for certain until I moved back in for good. Raif promised to keep an eye on the place, as well as clean it up while I was gone, and though I knew that my stay in *O Anel* would be short compared to the time that passed here at home, I had to hope that the time away could help start to heal me.

My buzzer echoed loud in the quiet apartment, and my heart hammered against my rib cage at the sudden burst of adrenaline. God, I hated how jumpy I was lately—another thing I hoped would clear up once a little time had passed. I hit the button on the intercom. "Who is it?" I asked before checking the alarm system one more time.

"Adira," a buttery voice answered. "Can I come up?"

"I guess." As the elevator made its way up, I disarmed the security system. Since Kade had tried to kick his way into the car, it was making some seriously nasty rattling sounds, and I wasn't even sure if it was a safe way to get up to the apartment. Just one more thing for me to fix . . .

When the car reached the entrance, she stepped out looking just as supermodel perfect as she always did. Funny, she'd never looked run-down or a psychological mess from what Kade had done to her. Maybe he'd gone easy on her. Or maybe she was simply stronger than me.

"Tyler said you're leaving for a while," she said as her gaze wandered over my trashed apartment. "I wanted to thank you before you left."

"Thank me?"

"You convinced Kade to break his bond with me," she said as if I didn't already know. "You freed me."

"Yeah, well, I did it for Tyler."

Adira gave me a sad smile. "He loves you."

I didn't say anything in response. Tyler had already told me as much and his actions with Kade had spoken louder than any words. But after all that had happened . . . could he love me despite the damage done to me?

"I'm leaving as well," Adira continued. She looked anywhere but right at me. "I've been called before the Synod."

"Synod?" I asked.

"Our rules are strict," Adira replied. "And our rulers even more so. My bond with Kade violated our laws and endangered our secrets. Now I must answer to our elders."

I had to admit, that didn't sound good. "What will they do to you?"

Adira shrugged. "I have no idea," she said, her tone somber. "I asked Tyler to come home with me, but he won't leave the city as long as you're here."

"He cares about you." It was a hard thing to admit out loud, and there was nothing I could do to erase the history between them. "I don't know everything about the rules, but I'm sure he'd be there for you if he could."

"I'm not as strong as I used to be," Adira said with a faraway look. "Kade was my third binding. Never again will I be bound to protect another soul. . . ." Her voice trailed off, tinted with sadness. "What does one do when she becomes useless? Maybe, if the Synod is lenient, I'll go home. I miss Africa. I'd like to see the desert. Going home might help to replenish what Kade has stolen from me. And perhaps I can try to forget."

An awkward silence spread out between us. Both of us knowing what had happened to the other at Kade's hands, but unwilling to talk about it. "He'll miss you," I said at last.

She smiled. "He'll always care about me. That's just how he is. But I know he'll never love me the way I want him to. The way he loves you."

Again, I wondered, could he still love me? Despite everything that had passed between us, was there a spark of what we'd had still burning? I brought my hand up and twisted the ring on my thumb. It seemed I couldn't help but touch it when I thought of Tyler. Adira's eyes wandered to my hand and she gasped, snatching my hand and running her fingers over the silver ring.

"Nys'asdar," she said under her breath. "Gods, Tyler, what have you done?"

She looked me in the eye, worry etched on her gorgeous face. "What?" I demanded. "Are you talking about my ring? What is it? What did Tyler do?"

"We're not meant to love the ones we protect, Darian. And he must love you more than you could imagine," Adira said. "Tyler has done a very foolish thing. If the Synod were to find out about that ring, Darian, his punishment will be severe."

"What in the hell are you talking about?" My heart pulsed in my ears. I didn't want Ty to be in trouble with anyone. Let alone over something he'd given me. I held my hand up to inspect the simple silver ring. "What is this thing?"

"I can't tell you that. Just . . . just promise me you'll watch out for him."

"Of course, I'll watch out for Ty. But, Adira, you've got to tell me—"

Before I could get the sentence out of my mouth, she was gone.

Well, I guess disappearing into thin air was one way to end a conversation. I pulled the ring off of my thumb and inspected it. Aside from the fact that it had been a gift from Tyler, I couldn't discern anything particularly special about it. For all intents and purposes, it looked like any other old, worn piece of silver jewelry. But in the supernatural world, looks could be deceiving. "Jesus, Ty," I said, echoing Adira's words. "What the hell *did* you do?"

I would ask him about the ring and whatever *Nys'asdar* meant when I got back from *O Anel*. Just like Xander, I'd told Ty I was leaving, though I hadn't told him in person. After everything that had happened, I still couldn't face him. He'd seen too much, had witnessed firsthand my reaction to Kade's touch, and how I'd craved more. I couldn't bear to see the expression on his face and whatever emotions it might betray. Sorrow? Pity? Disgust? I couldn't handle it if he looked at me that way. Who knows what he thought about what happened. Maybe he blamed me. I *had* gone after Kade, after all.

Another annoying shock to my system followed on the heels of my buzzer. My apartment had turned into Grand Central Station in a matter of days. I hit the intercom, but didn't feel cordial enough for a greeting the second time around. Whoever was down there would just have to deal with the silence.

"It's Raif."

I smiled at the sound of his voice. A couple of seconds later, the elevator rattled its way up to my entrance, and I disarmed the security system. Again.

When he stepped into the apartment, I reset the alarm. Checked it to make sure I'd done it right. Checked it again. "Darian, the system is fine. You needn't check it so often. And if you'd keep the surveillance cameras connected, the place will be even safer."

The last time Ty had been at my apartment, I'd disabled the cameras so Raif couldn't see us. In hindsight, that hadn't been the best idea. "I know." I sighed. "It just makes me feel better to double check."

"And triple check," Raif said. "Reaver will be here tomorrow?"

"Yeah," I answered. "I called him this afternoon to confirm."

"This apartment will be an impenetrable fortress by the time we're through with it. Only a fool would think to attack you here." I looked down, suddenly embarrassed to meet his gaze. Raif had been a witness to the effects of Kade's attack as well. "Darian," Raif said in that chiding tone of his, "*none* of this is your fault. You do realize that, don't you?"

I didn't answer him. Couldn't. I'd burst into tears if I opened my mouth, and that was the worst part of this entire situation. I no longer felt strong, self-confident, assured of my own ability to protect myself. That, more than any other thing, scared the shit out of me.

"Darian. Look at me."

"Can you imagine what they all must think?" I choked out. "Xander, Ty, Ash, and the others?"

"Believe me when I say, they see you as they always have."

"Yeah, right," I scoffed.

"You never give those who care about you enough credit," Raif said, just a little harshly. He guided my chin up so that I was forced to look at him. "You *survived*, Darian. You were strong, no matter what you think. And all of those whom you named, including me, both admire and respect that strength. A weaker soul would have *died* from what Kade did to you."

"Then why do I feel so weak?"

"Because you've been through hell," Raif said. "Go see Brakae and give my daughter my love. Take the time you need to begin to heal. And when you're ready, come home."

"That's the plan." My bag was packed, and I was ready to go. "Hold down the fort while I'm gone, okay?"

"There's one more thing before you leave." Raif hesitated, the note of concern returning to his voice. "I grabbed your mail on the way up."

I knew what was coming, but I asked anyway. "And?"

He fished the postcard from inside his coat and held it out to me. On the glossy surface was a picture of the Space Needle towering over a darkened Seattle skyline. "Put it with the rest of the mail," I said as I fished the emerald pendulum—

the key to *O Anel*—out of my shirt. "I'll look at it when I get back."

"Don't you want to know what it says?"

The emerald began to glow as I made my intentions known. *I want to go to O Anel,* I thought. "No, Raif. I don't."

If you missed the first book in
the Shaede Assassin series,
read on for a preview of

Shaedes of Gray

Available from Signet Eclipse.

I live in the gray. It's a wonderful place, free of accountability, bereft of conscience. I've lived in the black and white, but that was before, and I don't worry about how I used to be.

I hate the cold, and yet there I was, standing on the roof of the Cobb Building, looking out across the Metropolitan Tract while the dark, cloudy sky spit snow on my face. I wouldn't have been there at all if I hadn't needed the money. Okay, that's not exactly true. I didn't need the money. I *wanted* the money. I also wanted the action. That, I needed.

"Could you have picked a weirder place to meet?" a man's voice spoke from behind me.

Marcus. *Lovely.*

"Where's Tyler?" I demanded, a little on edge that Ty had sent an errand boy instead of meeting me himself.

"Had an appointment that ran late." His thin lips turned up in a twitchy smile, and I palmed the dagger at my thigh, feeling a bit twitchy myself. "He said to tell you he's sorry and he'll call you later."

Great. It was bad enough I had to wait out in the cold. Now I had to do business with this clueless idiot. Not many of Tyler's contractors enjoyed the privilege of an in-person visit from him, but since day one, I'd been the exception. I looked Marcus over, from his dirty black hair to his soft middle and right down to his worn, secondhand army boots. Where did Tyler find these guys?

"Let's get this over with," I said. "I'm freezing my ass off out here."

"Seventy-five percent," the lackey said. My eyes narrowed

and I felt again for the dagger at my side. As if it made everything okay, Marcus quickly added, "Tyler promises he'll get the rest to you after the job's done."

I jerked the envelope out of his hand. I didn't stand out in the cold for seventy-five percent. I didn't have to. "Ty knows I won't do shit until I get the rest." I tucked the money into my coat and waited.

Marcus stared at me, shifting his weight from one foot to the other. He looked like he was trying to keep from pissing his pants. I can come across scary when I want.

"Look, Darian. I'm just the messenger." I quirked a brow and he faltered. "Y-you have a problem with what's in that envelope, you take it up with the boss man. I'm out."

He turned his back on me, and I fought the urge to laugh at his carelessness. The tip of my blade pressed into his back before he could face me again. "You know what they do to the messenger—right, Marcus?" He swallowed, and the sound was like a stone dropping into a fifty-foot cavern. "I want the rest of my money," I whispered close to his ear, and he shuddered. "Tell Ty to call me when he gets it."

I disappeared before he could open his mouth again.

A gust of wind hit me full in the face as I walked, blowing back my hood and causing my hair to billow out in soft strawberry waves. I locked eyes with a man who brushed my shoulder as I passed him on the street. He studied me for a fleeting moment before averting his gaze. Perhaps he'd picked up on the faint glow of my green eyes that betrayed my lack of humanity, or maybe it was simply the solemn black clothes and deadly expression that seemed out of place on an otherwise innocent-looking girl.

Most nights I felt comfortable roaming the streets of Seattle alone, but tonight something didn't feel right. I suppose it could've been the cold or the wind that stole my breath. Or maybe the fact that Tyler sent Marcus to meet me instead of coming in person. We'd been avoiding each other lately, and not because of our business relationship. It didn't matter that Ty had shorted me money for the first time in a long time. The only reason I'd threatened Marcus at all was because I knew he'd tell Tyler about it and he'd be forced to call me up. I didn't like distance between us, despite the fact that I needed it.

I walked, my face protected by the high collar of my duster, deeper downtown and skirted two guys and a girl hailing a cab. "Dude, you're four-oh-four if you think you've got a chance with her," one guy said to the other before climbing in after the girl.

"Four-oh-four," I whispered under my breath, committing the phrase to memory. I wanted to find out what it meant, add it to my mental dictionary. I was always careful to use the vernacular of the times.

As the cab pulled away, I thought of the many instances I'd watched from beneath lowered lashes, listening in on conversations. I have perfected the art of imitation. Mannerisms, slang, modes of dress change every day, let alone every year. I don't miss a single trend. My looks are enough to make me stand out; I don't need another excuse to draw unwanted attention.

The sleet began to accumulate, and I shuffled my boots through the muck, making narrow paths behind me. I tucked my fists into my pockets and picked up my pace, no longer patient with the weather. Hustling along, I tried not to dwell on the fact that I was alone in this world. I hadn't encountered another of my kind in nearly a century, and when I had known one, I'd been too green to ask the right questions.

Azriel. As shrewd as he'd been secretive. Answers didn't come easy. He'd kept me right where he wanted me, under the guise of love and devotion. Even as I forced the memories down, they resurfaced.

"I don't want your kisses." I looked into his handsome, ageless face. A face that would never change, despite the passing of years. "I want answers."

"As long as you're with me, there's nothing you need to know."

"Why do you seem like a mirage once the sun sets, and I seem more solid?"

"I am born, and you are made." He tried to stop the questions with another kiss.

"But you can look more solid if you choose," I said.

"Glamour for human benefit. It's nothing for you to worry about."

"You don't need glamour during the day," I pressed, eager for information.

"Neither do you," he said in an offhand way.

"What about the others? Are there others like us wandering the earth?"

Azriel let out an exasperated sigh. "No. We are the last. The only ones of our kind."

"Tell me something else," I begged. "Anything."

"Really, Darian, you are like a whining babe." His dark eyes turned cold, but he softened the cruel edge by taking my hand in his. " 'Why, why, why?' It drones in my ears. Why don't I ask you some questions?"

"Such as?"

"Are you deadly?" he asked.

"If I want to be."

"Are you strong and quick as the wind?"

"As strong as you and just as fast," I replied.

"Can you pass as shadow during the night, and are you confined to corporeal form during the day?"

"I can, and I am," I said, almost pouting.

"Then do not worry about what you do not know. We are immortal. The only weapon that can kill us is a blade forged with magic, and even I don't know where one might be. We are alone in this world, and you have nothing to fear." His mouth hovered close to mine. "Ask me no more."

I broke free from the unpleasant memories and cursed myself for thinking about him. He was long gone. Though I'd never been able to prove it, I figured he'd wound up on the pointed end of a magic blade. Dead. It was the only explanation; he'd never have left me otherwise. But that part of my life was best forgotten. My focus needed to be on the money I was owed and Tyler's absence tonight. Not a long-lost lover who'd disappeared ages ago.

Thoroughly annoyed with my nostalgic moment and chilled to the bone, I arrived at my studio apartment near the center of Belltown, the northern district of downtown Seattle. The densely populated area suited me—too many people paying too much attention to themselves to worry about me or what I might be.

I stepped from the lift that opened to the apartment and was greeted by a gust of warm air. Every muscle in my body relaxed. I kept the thermostat at a toasty seventy-five degrees, sometimes warmer.

Falling onto a chair, I drummed my hands on the armrest. I hated having my time wasted, and Marcus was a *huge* waste of my time. My cell phone rang, breaking the silence. Since I didn't have any besties calling to gab about their hair appointments and desk jobs, I knew it was Tyler.

"Speak," I said into the receiver.

"Darian?"

"Were you expecting someone else to answer my phone?" I smiled, enjoying the way my name sounded like a soft caress when he said it. "Do you have the rest of my money?"

"Yeah. I had to guarantee it, though." His tone sounded put out, but I knew the truth: Tyler could afford to guarantee my work. "What did you do to Marcus tonight anyway? He said he'd quit if I ever sent him on an errand that involved you again." The laughter in his voice put me at ease. He knew I'd been messing with Marcus, and he didn't entirely disapprove. That guy needed to grow a pair if he was going to play with the big boys.

"You should have come yourself," I said. "I don't like meeting with your errand boys."

A long silence stretched between us, and I couldn't help but wonder what Tyler was thinking. "Snow's coming down pretty hard out there." His words were stilted—definitely not what he'd planned on saying, as if the weather were a safer topic than what was really on his mind. "I'll bring the rest of your money over myself. Be there in ten minutes."

I snapped the phone shut. He knew me down to the smallest detail, and the fact that he was willing to come over so I didn't have to go back out in the cold warmed me from the pit of my stomach outward. Avoidance wasn't going to work. Not when we both made excuses to continue to see each other.

I twisted the ring on my left thumb—wide, worn silver with an antiquated carving. I'd never been able to identify the animal; it looked sort of like a bull or maybe a buffalo. Too much like a cave drawing for me to tell for sure. Tyler had given it to me after I'd completed my first job for him—said all of his people wore one. In the event a job went south, the ring would identify the wearer even if dental records couldn't. And if anyone happened to cross me? Well, according to Tyler, the ring would guarantee my protection. Apparently, one look at that bull . . . buffalo . . . whatever would set stone-cold killers to shaking in their boots. It hadn't mattered to him that I wasn't so hard to dispatch. He'd insisted I wear it, and who was I to turn down free jewelry?

I met Tyler five years ago. He's like a temp agency for the underbelly of society—a problem solver in the basest sense of the word. Tyler makes them—*poof!*—disappear. He's known in a lot of circles, and he gets paid a nice chunk of change for his services. Working for him had been a no-brainer. I'd needed a new benefactor, as my previous contact had met an untimely end at the hands of the Russian mob. Tyler needed someone apathetic and discreet. He knew I was a killer the first time he laid eyes on me, and I knew he was the type of guy with connections.

Tyler was known for his hard edge, but when his eyes met mine, they held a depth of emotion that caught me off guard. It sparked something in me I'd thought long buried. "You're not just a good-looking daddy's girl, are you?" he'd asked.

I laughed. I'd *never* been a daddy's girl. "Nope. But I've got skills, and from what I hear, they're the kind you need. The kind of skills that could earn us both a lot of money."

"What do you know about my business?" he asked, a smile in his voice.

"I know people pay you to solve their problems."

"And how do *you* solve problems?"

I pulled a dagger from the sheath at my thigh and drove the point into the bar's thick wooden tabletop. "I take them away. Permanently."

And with that, I was hired.

As promised, the elevator whirred to life ten minutes after his call.

Tyler never disappoints. He's never late.

I didn't greet him at the door. Cordiality wasn't one of my strong suits. Instead, I stood at my kitchen counter, pretending to be anything but preoccupied by who had just stepped into my apartment. It's hard to ignore that level of gorgeous, and Tyler had it in spades. My heart raced at the sight of him, and it suddenly felt like my mouth was too dry to speak. *Damn.* I hadn't seen him in a couple of weeks, and just watching him walk toward me was enough to make my stomach do a back-flip. And that was a huge fucking problem. I couldn't afford to feel anything for him. I'd learned the hard way that love is nothing more than the sharpest blade, and it can easily be turned against you. I refused to let anyone have that kind of power over me ever again.

"Is there anything in your wardrobe that isn't black?" he teased as he walked toward the kitchen.

I resisted the urge to smile, unwilling to let him see the trace of warmth his nearness caused. "I like black." I almost always wear black or white, depending on the job and the circumstances. Tyler only saw me in black. The work I did for him wasn't exactly on the sunny side.

"Don't get me wrong," he said, coming closer. "You look great."

So do you, I thought as he shrugged off his heavy wool peacoat. Ty never overdid it in the clothing department. He was a jeans and T-shirt guy all the way, but he knew how to make the simple garments complement his lean, muscular body. Tyler's not even a notch below Calvin Klein underwear-model physique, and has a tousled mop of gold-and-bronze-streaked hair and strange hazel eyes—green with a brownish star surrounding the pupil. A garbage bag would've looked like an Armani suit on him. He reached around to his back pocket and produced an envelope containing the rest of my money, and a slip of paper. "Is that for me?" I asked, reaching out.

"Yeah, the information's on the paper."

I leaned over the bar and he pressed the envelope and paper into my hand, grazing my fingers as he pulled away. Though his skin was cooler than mine, Tyler's touch left me warm. And wanting more. My skin all but burned where he'd touched me, a brand that reminded me I'd have been better off dealing with Marcus. Tyler must have felt it too, judging by the way his lids became hooded and his chest rose and fell in a quick rhythm. I took a tentative step back, irritated at my own stupidity for orchestrating this visit. *Shit.*

He ran his fingers through the thick tangles of his hair and dropped onto a stool at the bar. His jaw clenched, the muscle at his cheek flexing. "Look, Darian. I want you to be careful on this job. Something doesn't feel right."

Ty's instincts were usually right on. But I never gave much thought to things like caution. "I can handle it," I said. "You don't need to worry about me."

"I know you can handle it." Ty gave me a level stare. "That's not the point. Maybe I should take this one myself."

"No way." This job paid double my usual fee. I had no intention of giving up that kind of money. Or the kind of action a double fee usually indicated. "I've got this one. Period."

Ty shifted in his seat, and I knew his pensive attitude had nothing to do with the mark. "You ever think of a change in venue? Maybe a new line of work?"

"Sure, because I've always secretly wanted to pursue my dream of becoming a kindergarten teacher. Please. I'm good at what I do, and you know it."

Standing from the stool, Ty rounded the bar and leaned up against the sink beside me. I balled my hands into fists, more to keep them from shaking than anything. God, he smelled good. Comforting, like fresh-baked cinnamon bread or something equally delicious and loaded with rich spices. His unique scent swirled around in my head, and I wanted nothing more than to lean into him, feel the weight of his arms around me as I breathed him in. But then my common sense gave me a swift kick in the ass. There was a stack of reasons why I couldn't be with Tyler. He was human while I . . . well, I sure as hell wasn't. Plus, he deserved someone softer. A nice piece of womanly eye candy. Someone capable of giving and receiving love without considering it a bargaining chip. Someone who wouldn't stab another person with something sharp if he pissed her off. That someone wasn't me.

"How long are we going to keep doing this?" His tone, though dark, had a sensual edge to it. A yearning that mirrored my own. *Shit.*

"Tyler—" My gaze dropped to the floor. I couldn't look up because he'd see the emotion written all over my face. "We're not going to talk about this."

"Maybe I want to talk about it." His voice became softer still. He reached out, his fingers caressing me, shoulder to wrist. A jolt of excitement shot through my core, and I cursed my weakness and my susceptibility to his touch. I wanted him, and not just for the night.

"We work together." The excuse sounded as lame in my head as it did coming out of my mouth.

"Then you're fired," he murmured, brushing his fingers against my palm.

My cheeks flushed and it had nothing to do with the temperature in my apartment. These moments between us were becoming more frequent—and harder to resist. I put my palm against his chest, my entire hand tingling with excitement from the contact. He felt solid, rock hard, under my hand, and I wondered what his skin would feel like without his T-shirt between us. I pushed him gently away, severing our contact and allowing me enough space to take a decent breath. I couldn't focus with him so close. And we needed to talk business.

"So," I said, shaky, "I take it the mark's a real bastard?"

Tyler took an extra step back, his smile turning almost sad. "You know me," he said with a sigh, and the sound mirrored my own disappointment. "I don't take money to kill just any asshole. Only the scum of the earth will do."

That's why I worked for Tyler. He shared my disgust for the morally bankrupt, and I could count on him to flush them out of their holes for me. Be it a drug dealer, pimp, or worse, Tyler hated abusers just as much as I did. And each and every one of them abused their victims in one horrible way or another.

Talking business was like a gust of fresh air. It cleared my head, redirected my focus. This job was the only thing keeping me from violating all of my self-imposed rules in regards to Tyler. I'd spent decades polishing my armor, and now was not the time to let it tarnish.

I leaned back against the stove, but still, the distance between us could be closed by an arm's length. Even the air seemed thinner, as though there wasn't enough of it to share. Tyler sealed the gap, his eyes trained on my face, drinking in every detail. He reached out, his fingers feather light against my cheek, and tucked a stray strand of hair behind my ear. Time to take this conversation out of the kitchen. I needed some space, and the current cramped quarters weren't doing anything for my willpower. I tapped the envelope of money against my palm, paced away from Tyler, and rounded the far end of the polished concrete countertop. I flopped down on the overstuffed chair in the living room that bordered the kitchen. Unfolding the slip of paper, I read the mark's info with more interest than the situation called for. "I'll get ahold of you when it's done," I said.

Tyler stiffened, his shoulders square. "You can't keep avoiding this—*us*—Darian."

Who says? As far as I was concerned, I could keep avoiding it until the end of time. "If it's not broke, don't fix it. Right, Ty? We work well together. And I'm not going anywhere anytime soon. Why can't things stay just the way they are?"

"Change is the only constant, Darian."

He always said my name with care, as if the word were fragile. The sound of it made my chest ache. "We just can't . . . *be* together."

His eyes burned into mine. "Why not?"

Why not, indeed? "It's not a good idea. Trust me, Ty. I'm not what you need."

He threw his coat over his shoulders and headed for the elevator. "Why don't you let me worry about what I need? Be careful tomorrow. I'd hate for you to trip on your boulder-sized pride before you get the job done."

The elevator whined its way to the ground floor, leaving me alone.

Way to go, I thought. *You wanted things to cool down. Looks like you got your wish.* He'd forget about his fascination soon enough. It wasn't really me he wanted. More likely it was the idea of me. The exotic, preternatural creature. Tyler would find someone worthy of his adoration. The thought of his arms around another woman made me want to scream. I sat for a moment, absorbing the quiet and the hollow ache in my chest that only his absence caused. Fuck if I knew why, but the torture of having him near was almost better than the anguish of watching him leave.

Rather than continue to stew in my misery and obsess over emotions best left unrealized, I locked the envelopes—both the seventy-five percent and the remainder of my fee—in a safe tucked behind a false wall. Tyler wouldn't dare cheat me. I trusted him with my life; the money was a no-brainer.

I unfolded the paper once again and reread the name and address scrawled on it.

Xander Peck, 1573 East Highland Drive

His name rolled off my tongue a couple of times. Not exactly a Tom or Josh or Steve. But I guess Darian wasn't exactly a Becky, Suzie, or Jennifer either.

Poor bastard. I wondered who Xander Peck had pissed off to deserve a visit from me. Whatever he'd done, it must've been pretty bad. People paid through the nose for my services, and I wasn't exactly listed in the yellow pages. You'd have to have connections, and not the normal kind, to hire a Shaede to mete out your punishments.

Also available from

Amanda Bonilla

Lost to the Gray
A Shaede Assassin Novella
(A downloadable Penguin Special
from Signet Eclipse)

No one loves Darian like Tyler does. Not her friends.
Not her fellow Shaedes. Not the Shaede king who wants
her for himself. Behind the swagger and katana sword that
make her the most fearsome Shaede assassin in the world,
Tyler is the only one who sees her loyal heart and
vulnerability. But her evolving powers and compulsion to
finish every job—no matter the stakes—fills him with
fear, and he knows it's only a matter of time before he
loses her.

And when the moment nearly comes—and Tyler discovers
the trail of deceit that prevented him from protecting
Darian—he snaps. He breaks. And he leaves.

Now he must learn to live without her, even as they
remain bound to one another. And when Darian's friend
faces an unknown threat, he must find a way to help him
without crossing paths with his ex-Shaede.

Available wherever books are sold or at
penguin.com

facebook.com/ProjectParanormalBooks

S0455

Also available from

Amanda Bonilla

Blood Before Sunrise
A Shaede Assassin Novel

Having found the half-crazed Oracle who tried to
overthrow the Shaede Nation, Darian and Raif now face a
possibility too painful for Raif to imagine, and too
enticing for Darian to ignore.

Determined to reunite Raif and the daughter he thought
was dead, Darian is willing to risk everything—though
she could lose her lover Tyler in the bargain. Soon, Darian
finds herself caught between the man she loves like a
brother, and the man whose love she can't live without.

"A brand new series that absolutely wowed me!"
—Romance Readers Connection

Available wherever books are sold or at
penguin.com

facebook.com/ProjectParanormalBooks

S0379

Also available from

Amanda Bonilla

Shaedes of Gray
A Shaede Assassin Novel

In the shadows of the night, Darian has lived alone for almost a century. Made and abandoned by her former lover, Darian is the last of her kind—an immortal Shaede who can slip into darkness as easily as breathing. With no one else to rely on, she has taught herself how to survive, using her unique skills to become a deadly assassin.

When Darian's next mark turns out to be Xander Peck, King of the Shaede Nation, her whole worldview is thrown into question. Darian wonders if she's taken on more than her conscience will allow. But a good assassin never leaves a job unfinished...

**"Awesome action, as well as raw romance...
one of my favorite heroines of 2011."
—Heroes and Heartbreakers**

Available wherever books are sold or at
penguin.com

facebook.com/ProjectParanormalBooks

S0363

Can't get enough paranormal romance?

Looking for a place to get the latest information and connect with fellow fans?

"Like" Project Paranormal on Facebook!

- Participate in author chats
- Enter book giveaways
- Learn about the latest releases
- Get book recommendations and more!

facebook.com/ProjectParanormalBooks

Penguin Berkley Jove ACE NAL Signet Obsidian Signet Eclipse RoC W

M883G1011